Praise for Abiga

"This is a wonderful combination of myst
please fans of both genres. The murder mystery is well thought out and con-
tains many twists and red herrings. It will most definitely keep the reader guessing until the end. This is a book that is heavy on suspense and mystery in Agatha Christie style but still delivers with romance as well."

—Historical Novel Society for *Twilight at Moorington Cross*

"The mesmeric hospital is full of suspects, hidden passageways, and secret drawers, and Wilson pulls off even the most outrageous twists with aplomb. Meanwhile, though the romance stays chaste, the couple's chemistry is off the charts. This page-turner will have readers on the edge of their seats."

—*Publishers Weekly* for *Twilight at Moorington Cross*

"Shimmering with atmosphere and suspense, *Twilight at Moorington Cross* weaves classic Regency romance with threads of Gothic mystery to page-turning effect. An absolute pleasure to read."

—Mimi Matthews, *USA TODAY* bestselling author

"*Twilight at Moorington Cross* has all the atmospheric trappings of a classic Regency Gothic along with a sweet and stirring romance."

—Anna Lee Huber, *USA TODAY* bestselling author

"Murder, intrigue, and a possible marriage of convenience all in one Regency romance—it's enough to make a reader swoon! This is a well-told tale, and I can't wait to read more by its author."

—Sally Britton, author of *Her Unsuitable Match* and the Clairvoir Castle Romances

"I was drawn in from the very first page. Wilson's engaging prose and expert mystery-telling kept me turning pages and guessing until the end."

—Kasey Stockton, author of the Ladies of Devon series, for *Twilight at Moorington Cross*

"*The Vanishing at Loxby Manor* cleverly combines Regency romance with Gothic intrigue, and the result is a suspenseful, thoroughly entertaining read."

—Tasha Alexander, *New York Times* bestselling author of the Lady Emily Mysteries

"This Gothic mystery hits all the buttons: handsome brothers, invalid father, unpredictable mother, sinister butler, strange noises, abandoned ruins, jilted marriage pacts, and secret societies."

—Historical Novel Society, for *The Vanishing at Loxby Manor*

"*The Vanishing at Loxby Manor* is dense with Gothic incident."

—*Publishers Weekly*

"Wilson's tale of love lost, buried shame, and secret societies is a delicious blend of romance and intrigue."

—J'nell Ciesielski, author of *The Socialite*, for *The Vanishing at Loxby Manor*

"I was entranced, mesmerized, addlepated, and not a little bit bewildered as I wandered the halls of Middlecrest Abbey."

—Jaime Jo Wright, author of the Christy Award–winning novel *The House on Foster Hill*, for *Masquerade at Middlecrest Abbey*

"With a wonderfully suspicious cast of characters, intriguing clues, and lush backdrop . . . , *Midnight on the River Grey* is a captivating novel."

—Historical Novel Society

"Mysterious and wonderfully atmospheric, Abigail Wilson's debut novel is full of danger, intrigue, and secrets. Highly recommended!"

—Sarah E. Ladd, bestselling author of *The Governess of Penwythe Hall*, for *In the Shadow of Croft Towers*

"Artfully weaving shades of Gothic romance in Regency England, Wilson brings a fresh voice—and a bit of danger!—to the traditional English moor."

—Kristy Cambron, bestselling author of *The Paris Dressmaker*, for *In the Shadow of Croft Towers*

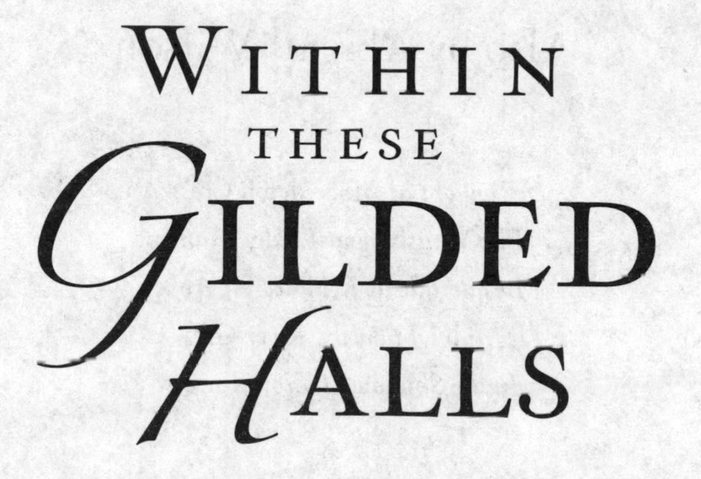
Within
these
Gilded
Halls

Also by Abigail Wilson

Twilight at Moorington Cross
The Vanishing at Loxby Manor
Masquerade at Middlecrest Abbey
Midnight on the River Grey
In the Shadow of Croft Towers

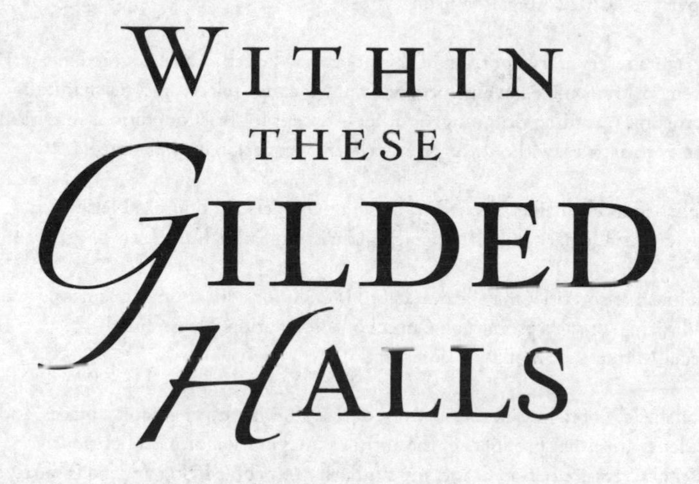

ABIGAIL WILSON

THOMAS NELSON
Since 1798

Within These Gilded Halls

Published in Nashville, Tennessee, by Thomas Nelson. Thomas Nelson is a registered trademark of HarperCollins Christian Publishing, Inc.

Thomas Nelson titles may be purchased in bulk for educational, business, fundraising, or sales promotional use. For information, please email SpecialMarkets@ThomasNelson.com.

Library of Congress Cataloging-in-Publication Data

Names: Wilson, Abigail, author.
Title: Within these gilded halls / Abigail Wilson.
Description: Nashville, Tennessee : Thomas Nelson, [2022] | Summary: "When a treasure hunt turns deadly, Miss Phoebe Radcliff realizes she's caught in a den of liars, but she can't leave the mysterious Avonthorpe Hall. Not yet at least. Not without confronting the demons from her past"-- Provided by publisher.
Identifiers: LCCN 2022014553 (print) | LCCN 2022014554 (ebook) | ISBN 9780785253303 (paperback) | ISBN 9780785253310 (epub) | ISBN 9780785253327
Subjects: LCGFT: Mystery fiction.
Classification: LCC PS3623.I57778 W58 2022 (print) | LCC PS3623.I57778 (ebook) | DDC 813/.6--dc23
LC record available at https://lccn.loc.gov/2022014553
LC ebook record available at https://lccn.loc.gov/2022014554

Printed in the United States of America

22 23 24 25 26 LSC 5 4 3 2 1

For Allison Moore
For our lifelong friendship, for always
understanding, for always encouraging
I'm so incredibly thankful that God
brought us into each other's lives

One

Southern England, 1819

"HUNTING THE TREASURE WITHOUT ME?"

I slammed the cellar door shut, sparing only a cursory glance at my friend and fellow artist as I pushed past him into the kitchens. "Please, Daniel, not all that again."

A step forward and I halted, brandishing the paintbrush in my hand like a weapon as I whirled to face him. "You know we haven't a moment to spare for your insidious quest. 'Pon my word, ever since I told you about those rumors in town there's been no living with you."

He wiggled his eyebrows. "You have to admit the villagers have compelling evidence. And there's all those caves down at the shoreline. You know . . . you're down there hunting shells all the time."

"Perhaps I am and there are caves." My lips twitched as I fought a smile. "But such fantasies will have to wait for another time. We've a ballroom to finish and we're woefully behind schedule."

I sighed as I deposited the brush into my apron pocket. "And don't look at me like that. This is not some misguided opportunity for an escape from our responsibilities like we did all too often as children. I only stepped out just now to fetch a smaller applicator. The top section of the frieze is proving to be a bit more delicate than I anticipated. So if you'll cease your half-hearted attempts at evasion and return to work with me, we might just stand a chance of finishing the section beside the column like we promised last week."

"Yes . . . well . . . you wouldn't be so eager to return if you'd been present a moment ago. Miss Drake's probably still in there barking at the walls." He sidled past me in that boyish way of his en route to the copper sink, where he refilled his glass. "Oh yes, she caught a nice long look at the section we finished this morning."

My face went cold. "Oh dear."

"Stormed right over after you left. Had a slew of harsh words at the ready for me." He crossed his arms. "In fact, she lashed out at everyone present, even her precious Arnold."

"Arnold too? Heavens." A furrow crossed my brow. "Sounds as if this mood of hers was sparked by more than your little error in the trim work."

"Indeed." Daniel rested his back against the counter, the sparkle of his youthful enthusiasm waning. "Full of mumbles about that great-nephew of hers." He flicked his fingers in the air. "Did you know the dandy arrived at the house unannounced and quite unexpected this morning?"

"Lt. Burke?" I glanced at the kitchen door. Miss Drake's nephew had only visited the house one time over a year ago and stayed but a short while. Goodness, I hadn't thought of him in some time. "Still has that dark cropped hair and—"

"The attractive countenance?" Daniel laughed beneath his breath. "At least that's what I overheard one of the scullery maids babbling about to Cook this morning." He stilled a moment, his eyes narrowing. "Now *stately* or *dignified*—I suppose I could give the swell that. But handsome? I'm afraid that's doing it a bit too brown. Granted, I'm not a young scullery maid."

"And a good thing too. With your pitiful work ethic we'd all starve." I smiled. "And that is not what I was going to say in regard to Lt. Burke."

"Wasn't it? And here I thought you one of those romantic sorts." Daniel gave me a wry shrug. "Arnold and I caught a glimpse of him on his way up the grand staircase. Good old Arnold seemed to find Lt. Burke terribly boorish the last time he was here, handsome or not."

I laughed. "From what I experienced, I would have to agree."

Daniel thrust his shoulders back and strutted across the kitchen floor as if marching into battle. "Did he prance around like this?"

"Lt. Burke sold out of the military not so long ago. Perhaps—"

"So did my cousin, but he doesn't swagger about like that. Reminded me of a deuced statue with legs."

"A statue . . . with *legs*." I touched the base of my neck. "Don't statues generally have legs?" I threw up my hands and angled for the door. "Never mind. You've had your fun, and like I said, it's past time we returned to work. We've a great deal to complete before supper."

Despite his protestations, Daniel fell in step behind me, his voice a bit playful at my back. "You know, when I first heard that I'd managed the good fortune of getting to train under one of the best artistic minds in Britain, I never imagined my days quite like this."

"No?" I led us down Avonthorpe Hall's back corridor before casting a hard look over my shoulder at my friend. "You do know you're free to leave anytime."

His steps faltered. "I didn't mean . . . well, you know . . . confound it, that's just what you'd want, isn't it? All the attention from Miss Drake once again."

"Don't be ridiculous. You know very well it was at my insistence that she even took you on in the first place." I nudged his arm. "And keep in mind, Sir Galahad, I've never considered our positions with Miss Drake competitive." I ticked my pointer finger between the two of us. "I daresay we both have a great deal to learn."

"I suppose so." He ran his hand down his face, then shot me a sideways glance. "Dashitall, Phoebe, it would be far easier to concede to the wisdom of your words if you didn't always remind me of an annoying elder sister. I swear it's something about that groove between your eyebrows, and when you get that look in your eyes"—he laughed—"right there, that's the one. If our mothers weren't the best of friends and I'd be sure to hear about it, I might just box your ears."

"Box my ears, indeed." My hand found my hip. "If you can manage to stop acting like you just left the schoolroom, I might be able to find my way to treating you more as an equal."

"The schoolroom!" He gripped the lapel of his jacket in a tight fist. "I'll have you know I was eighteen last month—a far cry from the child you enjoyed commandeering in your youth."

"Yes, but you will always be my junior by two years, and I daresay that gives me the right to impart a touch of wisdom from time to time."

He stepped ahead of me to open the ballroom door, a pert little grin on his face. "Then I'm afraid I have little recourse than to bow to your superior intellect, Miss Radcliff."

I stopped short. "Don't you *Miss Radcliff* me. Not when one of the first words out of your mouth as a baby was *Phoebe*."

He tipped his head back. "No, it wasn't."

My laugh hovered in the stagnant air as we crossed the ballroom's massive dance floor and advanced to the work area, a newfound lightness to my steps. "Well, it may as well have been. Whenever my family visited yours, it was Phoebe this and Phoebe that, Phoebe look what I've made, Phoebe take me down the hill with you." A pace ahead of Daniel, I reached the edge of the scaffolding and spun back. "You were always one step behind Juliana and me."

He reached my side. "I was, wasn't I? Pity you and your sister never stopped and allowed me to catch up."

The sudden *clip-clop* of shoes drowned out any possibility of an answer as we both angled to face the far door. Miss Drake possessed a rather uneven gait, but her stride today was a quick one, filled uncomfortably with purpose.

Daniel had not been exaggerating about her foul mood. Her pale green eyes looked pinched in the morning light, her face a bright cherry red, her sagging arms thrusting back and forth on approach. "Oh, Phoebe. It is the absolute worst timing in the world."

I cleared my throat, a quick glance at Daniel. "You mean your nephew? I just heard—"

Her hands were wild in the air, her speech clipped. "I directed Arnold to show Graham to his room, of course. What other choice did I have? He barreled in this morning as if Avonthorpe were already his."

Daniel shook his head. "If the lout's as bad as all that, why don't you just send him packing?"

Her eyes flashed. "You've the tact of a gutter rat, Mr. Hill, and a great deal too much impertinence for a man your age. Don't speak of things you know nothing about. Better yet, don't speak at all." She propped her arm against the wall as if she might swoon. "And he's not come alone this time. No, that would be far too easy. He's brought a friend as well. We'll have no choice but to entertain now."

The room fell still, the air thickening into questions in my throat. "Doesn't he realize we are in the middle of repairs? That we have few servants in residence and we shall have no time for dinner parties and the like?"

"I don't know what he thinks or why he's here. All I know is the two of them shall be sorely in the way."

I paused. "In the way? I seriously doubt—"

Her focus landed on the lower trim work that Daniel had been working on, and I braced myself. She took a sharp breath. "I hope you don't mean to quibble with me as Mr. Hill did earlier and call this monstrosity an acceptable effort."

She turned like a dragon on Daniel. "This child has only been here a month and he's already getting sloppy." Her next word was a three-syllable enjoyment. "Dis-grace-ful."

Daniel straightened. "I beg your—"

"Pardon? As well you should. Even with poor eyesight I can ascertain the inadequacies in your presentation."

Though Daniel's strokes were somewhat less refined, he was a beautiful, thought-provoking painter and deserved Miss Drake's investment in his future as much as I did. I edged between them. "Please, Miss Drake, you mustn't worry. I had already planned to go over this section a second time. I was simply allowing Daniel time to practice."

Her eyes widened. "Well, he can just as well practice on something other than my ballroom walls." Her fingers curled into fists as she stared at each completed section. "I told you from the start I expect your work to match perfectly the original distemper." There was a strange shake to her voice. "No changes, regardless of how subtle you deem them, not in color or glue. Everything must appear as it did when I first inherited this room. No Drake has altered the slightest detail at Avonthorpe over the years, and I shan't be the first to do so." She thrust out her finger. "Do you understand me, boy? Not one single line or curve out of place."

One look from me silenced Daniel again, and I took her arm. "We do, perfectly. And as I said from the beginning, you won't be disappointed in my work. I never would have taken on this project if I wasn't certain I could do just as you wish."

She grimaced as she stared down, then lifted her gaze to rake it across the room. "I just wish I knew who this friend of my nephew's was."

"You've never met the gentleman before?"

"Some new partner in that antiquities business of Graham's. He's got shifty eyes. A rogue if I ever saw one."

Daniel laughed to himself. "Then that means you haven't seen one . . . a rogue, I mean?"

The lines in her cheeks deepened as she turned back to me. "Why on earth did I allow you to talk me into bringing this insolent pup into my house? In fact, I've a mind to ship him home to his father this afternoon."

I pulled her close. "I've known Daniel Hill most of my life. Not only is he a brilliant young artist who needs your expertise, but he will learn his place soon enough."

A sheepish smile preceded Daniel's rather dramatic shrug. "Allow me to apologize for my loose tongue, Miss Drake. Goodness knows, it's got me in sticky situations before. Believe me when I tell you I consider myself fully chastised, and I have no intention of continuing on in such a way."

Miss Drake leaned in closer. "Should I credit such poppycock?"

Footsteps resounded in the corridor, echoing off the ballroom's gilded walls. Murmurs of conversation drifted through the open double doors and into the great space before two gentlemen crested the threshold and stood a moment to assess the room.

Miss Drake's great-nephew, Lt. Graham Burke, looked much as I remembered him. An angular face—but as one of the scullery maids had so deftly pointed out, a handsome one not of the usual fare—a military man as Daniel had insinuated, broad shoulders and tight arms, which he'd covered masterfully with a slender jacket of the palest blue, no doubt colored to match his haunting eyes. I found myself fielding a twinge of insecurities.

He sauntered across the wooden dance floor, the sound of his boots resonating off the white columns and floor-length windows. "Ah, there you are, Aunt Sally. I have another question to put to you."

He came to a halt at the foot of the scaffolding we'd erected for the restoration, his attention floating dangerously about the room. That is, until it landed on my face and everything about him stilled, driven by what I could only assume was a spark of memory.

Miss Drake ambled forward. "You remember my protégé, Miss Phoebe Radcliff."

"A little. It's been some time, has it not?"

My eyes widened at the hitch in his voice, and I found myself nodding in that insipid way I detested in other women. Of course, I'd been caught off guard. Strange that he sounded as uncomfortable as I was. Was something buried within such a hasty response? Irritation perhaps? Or worse, patent disinterest?

He took a step back and motioned to the wall. "It seems you've made some progress on the ballroom, though not as much as I would have thought."

"Yes." I had to clear an irksome lump from my throat. "The work we've undertaken is quite delicate. I daresay it will take some time to complete."

"As I see." He urged his companion from the doorway, where he'd been silently watching us, his shoulder propped against a nearby column. "My friend has been kind enough to accompany me to Avonthorpe to assist in my business affairs." He waited for the gentleman to reach the group, then raised his voice. "Mr. Montague, allow me to present Miss Phoebe Radcliff, my aunt's art pupil, who has agreed to help her update the house."

I gave the man a small curtsy. "Not the whole house, mind you, just the ballroom."

Mr. Montague certainly possessed that polished town look, dark hair, not overly tall. I thought him a touch handsome as well, if a bit unremarkable at first. That is, until he tossed a grin my direction and bowed. Heavens. My stomach turned. No wonder Miss Drake was at sixes and sevens at the gentlemen's arrival.

Rogue indeed. *Mr. Montague*.

I rolled his name around in my mind. Now why did the surname sound so familiar? Was he one of the Carlton House set? He was well known by the ton, that I was sure of. I pursed my lips, my focus drifting to Miss Drake's nephew at his side. So how had the uptight, reserved, inconsequential Lt. Burke made such an advantageous acquaintance, and what were the pair of them doing out here, miles from anywhere fashionable?

The thought burned my tongue, but did I have the nerve to ask? Apparently I did. "Business acquaintances? I understand Lt. Burke is an antiquarian. How did the two of you meet?"

Mr. Montague eyed me a moment. "In London, actually, quite by chance at a coffee house. It was a bit of a humorous situation. You see, Lt. Burke was—"

"Enjoying a rather fine afternoon." Lt. Burke cleared his throat. "Turns out Montague and I had interests in common." A shrewd look passed between the gentlemen.

Lt. Burke turned immediately to address Miss Drake. "Which brings me to why I was searching for you in the first place. I have a carriage full of artifacts set to arrive this afternoon at Avonthorpe. Would it be convenient if I store them with the others at the old church? They won't be there overly long. Mr. Montague plans to set up a meeting with your illustrious friend and neighbor, Mr. Haskett, to arrange a possible sale."

Miss Drake raised her eyebrows.

"I know. I was a little surprised myself that Mr. Haskett was willing to do business with us considering the, uh, Drake reputation." He waved off the thought. "Regardless, we hope to seal a deal in the next few weeks."

"Weeks?" Miss Drake's gaze danced from one corner of the room to the next. "You'll be staying that long then?"

"Mr. Haskett has expressed an interest in a sarcophagus I acquired in Egypt, although I hope he might consider one or two other items."

"Unlikely, as I've heard rumors the Hasketts are decidedly in the basket. In fact, I'm surprised he's considering purchasing any items at all."

"I couldn't say." Lt. Burke rocked back on his heels. "He extended an offer for the two of us to stay with him at his estate; however, I thought we might be more comfortable here." He glared at the scaffolding. "We shan't delay the renovations if that's what worries you."

"Not at all." Miss Drake's fingers raced along the lace trim at her waist, twisting and tugging the fragile fabric. "You may make use of the building at the old church, of course. It stands relatively empty besides the other antiquities you've stored there."

"Thank you, Aunt." A sideways glance at me. "You've been most accommodating."

The gentlemen begged their leave at once and could not have taken more than a step from the door when Miss Drake grasped my hand, her other one flopping onto her bosom. "Why now, Phoebe? Why has he come at such a time?"

My brows drew in. "I cannot say. But he did promise to stay out of the way. Sounds like it's only a bit of business that brought him all the way to the coast. Really, I cannot imagine the two of them shall be much trouble. At any rate, I'll do my best to assist with any hosting that might be required. Daniel can help as well."

Her breaths came short and rapid, her face a ghostly white. "Yes . . . hosting. I'll speak to Mr. Arnold at once. As butler, he'll know what to do, how to manage this atrocity." A fleeting glance at the trim work I'd been working on all morning. "How terribly, terribly unfortunate."

Two

I HAD JUST SETTLED MY HORSE'S BRIDLE ON THE WALL OF the harness room when a round of men's voices broke the comfortable silence of the stables. My hand stilled, their tenor mixing with the sweet scent of hay and the glittering dust particles suspended in the air.

I'd not found any grooms present in the stables upon return from my afternoon ride, and at first I assumed the voices belonged to them, but all too quickly I realized I was mistaken.

"It's not as simple as all that."

It was Lt. Burke's crisp timbre emanating from the adjoining coach house.

A curious prickle spanned the length of my spine, urging me forward, step by step, across the open courtyard and beneath the overhang of the connected shed. I halted just out of sight.

Of course, the sobering question of whether I should declare myself was buried all too quickly beneath a mountain of overwhelming interest. After all, Lt. Burke's sudden arrival had affected Miss Drake in a most peculiar way, and I was determined to uncover the cause.

Lt. Burke went on. "Officially, no one knows what happened to it."

"Not even King John's advisers?"

The added voice sent my pulse racing, and I couldn't help but peek around the corner a split second before jerking back into the shadows. I'd been right at the first. The other gentleman in the coach house was none other than Mr. Montague.

A metallic jingle breached the door, obscuring some of Lt. Burke's authoritative voice. ". . . and it was 1216, for goodness' sake. King John had a cursed rebellion on his hands."

King John . . . of course. I tipped my head back against the cold coach house wall as I connected their words. The lost treasure of Avonthorpe—I might have known. Did anyone speak of anything else around here?

"What I don't understand is"—Mr. Montague sounded both incredulous and giddy—"why old John thought it prudent to cross the boggy Fens in such a havey-cavey way? Only a fool would do such a thing."

A small laugh from Lt. Burke. "Apparently he was." Then a pause. "Granted, keep in mind he was ill at the time and in a rush to traverse the Wash. The whole carriage could have been caught up in the tidal area or the brooks."

"Or the quicksand."

"Possibly, but I daresay the landscape west of here looked quite different back then. Either way, the baggage carts were reported to have sunk into the silt, and the king died a few days later. The crown jewels were simply never recovered." I could hear the touch of awe in Lt. Burke's voice. "Which is where my rascal of an ancestor joins the story."

"I was under the impression you didn't believe he really found the jewels?"

"Our family's legend made a wonderful bedtime story for a boy in leading strings or a juicy bit of gossip for the ladies of Crossridge, but no. I don't buy into the salacious rumors that only seem to grow each year. Particularly when my great-aunt has been forced to sell off so much of the estate to make ends meet. If there were a treasure here, she certainly hasn't found it."

I edged another look around the doorframe just in time to see Mr. Montague rake his hand through his hair, a perceptive smile on his face. "But if your ancestor did indeed recover the lot from the bog and hide it for safekeeping? That treasure, my friend, would be worth a fortune that rivals the Prince Regent's."

"Which is why every Drake who has entered this house for the past hundred years has wasted every second of his paltry life looking for it. Fools, all of them, just like King John. Mark my words, when my turn at the helm comes, I don't expect to throw away my time in such a fashion."

"You never have spoken like a Drake, have you? Not in the months I've known you—too practical for that, too Burke I'd say."

"True. We lowly Burkes have never sought notoriety—military men, hardworking people, nothing of your class, I'm afraid." He propped his arm on the edge of the carriage. "If only my grandfather were still alive. He'd have thought it quite ironic that I'm to inherit Avonthorpe, considering my grandmother's family all but disowned us."

"It is strange how things turn out sometimes."

"Indeed. Who would have guessed that Aunt Sally would not marry or mother a child, and this grand structure would somehow fall into my undeserving hands."

Mr. Montague lowered his voice. "Inheritance is not always fair or just."

"True, but not for you, as you rightly stand to inherit Whitefall."

"Yes . . . Whitefall . . ." Mr. Montague cast a glance about the room as if nervous. "Enough about me. I'd rather talk about something more pleasant. Tell me about this Miss Radcliff of yours while we wait for Arnold and the others."

My muscles froze at the mention of my name.

"Let me be perfectly clear. She is not *my* Miss Radcliff." A beat of silence. "I only met her briefly a year ago. I don't even know all that much about her. What is it that has piqued your interest?"

I bit my lip, my chest burning. Yes, what indeed?

"Everything. Nothing." Mr. Montague chuckled. "I'm not entirely certain. I suppose I just wasn't expecting to find such a vibrant young lady in residence here. Interesting that you didn't mention her even once during our many discussions regarding our stay at Avonthorpe."

"I didn't think it relevant information."

Mr. Montague coughed out a laugh. "Beautiful ladies will always be relevant to me, Graham. And don't you forget it."

"Beautiful, huh? Something tells me you've been sequestered in the country for far too long if you mean to jump at the first passable lady to cross your path, particularly one with what I can only guess must be a paltry dowry since she's been reduced to studying here with my aunt."

My mouth fell open. Paltry dowry! How little he knew of my situation or his remarkable aunt. The sudden seizure that had gripped my heart vanished all too quickly as it pounded its way back to life. Passable!

Lt. Burke wasn't through, however. "You'd better take care, Montague. I will admit Miss Radcliff is somewhat intriguing, but not any more attractive than hundreds of other well-bred females with a little ingenuity and slight talent. Keep in mind, you'll need more than that *and* a sizable fortune to satisfy your father. Besides, you told me you'd sworn off women after . . . what was that chit's name?"

Mr. Montague's voice fell flat. "Mrs. Amelia Pembroke."

I stifled a gasp as I dared another look around the doorway. *Amelia Pembroke*? My elder brother's wife? That was where I'd heard Mr. Montague's name. He'd been one of her suitors.

Mr. Montague turned rather suddenly, his gaze sweeping my side of the room. I jerked away, my pulse shooting up my neck, but it was too late. I'd been seen.

The coach house and accompanying courtyard fell sickly silent until all I could perceive was the cursed *thump* in my chest. That is, until the footsteps began again, the achingly slow approach of a man on a hunt.

Escape would be impossible now. I had but a second or two to smooth out my skirt, my hands a bit shaky. I had every right to be in the stables. There was no way to know I'd been listening to a private conversation.

One last check that my coiffure held and I meandered into the open doorway, hoping I'd appear as if I'd just arrived. "Good afternoon, gentlemen. I thought I heard voices."

They both stopped cold, Lt. Burke bridling stiff as a poker, his shoulders thrust back like a general. As well he should. Discussing me indeed. I returned a cold stare.

He in turn cast a shrewd glance at the door. "Miss Radcliff, good afternoon."

I swallowed my indignation and stepped forward. "I've just returned from a rather pleasant ride. I was situating my harness just now when I heard the two of you."

It took several seconds for Lt. Burke's mouth to close and his eyes to narrow. "Interesting that we didn't hear anyone ride in. A harness, you say?"

A twinge of guilt threatened my cheeks, but I fought it back. Lt. Burke deserved every bit of awkwardness I could muster. "I arrived and saw to my horse, which I tend to do from time to time, and then . . . Well, I am glad my presence in the stables didn't disturb the two of you. I would be the last person to wish to get in the way of your . . . uh . . . business affairs."

The merest bend of Lt. Burke's eyebrow. "I'm sure you would. As it is, Montague and I are waiting for Arnold. As I intimated earlier, my Egyptian antiquities need to be removed from this carriage and taken to the church for temporary storage and safekeeping." He tapped his riding crop against his leg, a question playing with his lips. "Tell me, Miss Radcliff, do you normally see to your own horses? My aunt has grooms, does she not?"

"Don't be absurd. Certainly she does."

"Yet . . . ?"

"Egads." Mr. Montague took my hand. "Leave the lady be, Graham." A smile for me. "Allow me to apologize. My friend here can be a cursed boor at times."

A sideways glance at Lt. Burke. "So I've witnessed."

"These pettish business affairs always put him in a vulgar mood. The artifacts, you see, they are . . . well, like his own children in a way."

Lt. Burke's jaw flexed. "I wouldn't go that far, but I've spent a great deal of time recovering and restoring these pieces. They're irreplaceable."

Mr. Montague squeezed my fingers. "You see, the footmen who met us earlier saw fit to drop the first crate they picked up." A lift of his eyebrows. "To everyone's mutual satisfaction they've gone off for Arnold."

My muscles relaxed as I caught a glimpse of the broken crate at the rear of the coach. "I see what you mean and can perfectly understand your anger, Lt. Burke. I would feel the same about my artwork."

I idled over to the open crate. "I do hope nothing's ruined." Then leaned closer. "I have to admit, I'm a bit intrigued as to what you've brought with you. I've never actually seen an Egyptian antiquity before. Would it be much trouble to show me a sample of something you mean to sell?"

Lt. Burke's face softened, a touch of youthful enthusiasm moderating his movements as he drew up beside me and reached gingerly into the crate. A thrust of hay here and rustle there and he secured a palm-sized wrapped package. Carefully, he unfolded what looked to be a small, bluish stone.

He skimmed his fingertips across his jawline with his free hand before awkwardly extending the item for me to inspect. "This here is a scarab likeness, a beetle, which, as you can see, an Egyptian artist designed into an amulet."

Everything about Lt. Burke quieted as if in anticipation, then he gave a light shrug. "I believe this particular one might have been used for marriage jewelry or something of great significance. It probably dates somewhere within the early years of the Middle Kingdom."

"May I?"

He was slow to nod but did so with a wan smile.

I carefully took the amulet into my hands, the smooth blue surface of the hard clay shimmering in the bright spring light streaming through the window. It was in impeccable shape, the ancient artist's work still perfectly intact—tiny carved legs, intricate patterns on the scarab's back, so many delicately grooved indentations.

"It's beautiful." I glanced back at the cart. "Then you mean to sell everything you recovered? To Miss Drake's neighbor?"

Lt. Burke ran his hand through his hair, weaving slightly. "I've arranged to sell one very fine piece to the gentleman. A sarcophagus as I said earlier. It's in that large crate there."

"A sarcophagus?"

"A stone coffin." He cracked the lid for me to peer in through the edge. "This particular one is small, probably once used for a child. It's fairly simple with few carved decorations, but historically significant. Thankfully Montague's come to barter for a good price." A deep breath and he released the lid. "He means to secure me what I need. The rest, well . . ." He looked almost sheepishly at the adjoining crate. "It's complicated. I—"

Something creaked behind us near the door and we turned to see Mr. Arnold waltz into the coach house with a footman behind him. He had a tight look of concern about his face. "What's all this now?"

Lt. Burke's prior anger bubbled to the surface, his pointed military manner returning in full force. "As you see before you." He closed his eyes a second and measured his tone. "These artifacts need to be transferred to the church with great care. No more accidents."

Arnold bent his lanky frame over the broken crate, his slender nose wrinkling at the top. "Nothing destroyed I hope."

Lt. Burke spoke between his teeth. "Not that I am aware of. However, I'll need to catalog everything over the next few days to be sure."

"The church, you say?" Phillips here will see your crates safely to where you mean to store them." Arnold then spun to me. "As for you, Miss Radcliff, Miss Drake has been asking for you."

"Has she?"

"Something about the ballroom trim, I understand." A gentle smile. "You're the only one she will allow to touch it at this point."

"Don't tell me Daniel has been at it again?"

"I couldn't say." He extended his arm and I smiled.

Mr. Arnold had been the heartbeat of the house since I came to Avonthorpe, steady, calming, driven. As far as any butler could, he'd handled me quite kindly with kid gloves since the moment I arrived, assisting me through those lonely days when I needed it.

I fell in step beside him, relishing the comfortable escape he presented. And as we made our way from the coach house, the shuffle of crates christened our exit. I couldn't help but take a quick glance back. Lt. Burke had been somewhat cryptic regarding his antiquities . . . and protective. What on earth had he meant to say? What did he have planned for the lot of them if they weren't all to be sold? The merest shiver wriggled across my shoulder and I edged in closer to Arnold. More importantly, what exactly would complicate such an arrangement?

Three

Over the course of my short lifetime, I'd learned one unfortunate truth about many grand estates: each housed at least one nonsensical relative the family was unsure how to handle.

Mr. Fagean and his wife were Avonthorpe's.

Peculiar, easygoing, and some would say an asset to Miss Drake's famous parties, Avonthorpe's misfits had been a fixture on the estate for as long as I'd been there. I'd never, however, been able to fully understand their connection to Miss Drake. Fobbed off every time I dug into the particulars, I was left with the impression Mr. Fagean was some sort of distant cousin.

Daniel, upon his arrival, had labeled the pair nothing more than loafers and worked to avoid them at all costs. My curiosity, though, had already grown too great. I decided one way or another to learn what I could about the Fageans and why they saw fit to remain at Avonthorpe.

My investigations thus far had proved a conundrum. One minute I'd find the couple demanding the attention of valued guests, then the next, irritated to be thus situated, darting in and out of the house at all hours, absent for months at a time. Not to mention the outlandish behavior that generally accompanied such sudden trips.

Yes, I had many questions where the Fageans were concerned, yet with Mr. Fagean's judicious attention to Miss Drake, which bordered on the ridiculous at times, my instructor seemed to have been taken in as easily as any lonely, older woman in her situation would be. Thus, I found no cause to disparage Mr. Fagean or his clingy wife.

I want to say it was only a touch of morbid curiosity that drove me that evening to observe Lt. Burke's reaction when introduced to the pair before supper, but I couldn't help but relish the level of his discomfiture—the tightened muscles in his jaw, the bend to his brow. He didn't savor their presence in the house any more than I did. In fact, he intimated as much to me later in the evening.

The gentlemen had just entered the drawing room following their port, and Lt. Burke delayed me beside the pianoforte with a small smile and a motion with his chin. "I can't say I was expecting all that."

I slanted a glance at the two popinjays on the sofa. "You mean the Fageans?"

The rigidity of Lt. Burke's posture felt strangely at odds with the teasing tone of his voice. "Who else could I be referring to?"

I bit back a smile. "Who else indeed."

We observed the busy room a moment in silence as Mr. Fagean dramatically knelt at Miss Drake's side and offered her a drink. His tasseled boot caught a flicker of candlelight as his bright yellow jacket remained the focal point of the room.

A partner in my observations, Lt. Burke slid in a bit closer, his attention still across the carpet. "Have they been in residence long? They weren't here when I last visited."

His arm was warm at my side and I was a bit startled by the nearness of it, particularly after all he'd said in the stables. "As long as I've been studying here. Granted, I've only been here two years."

"My aunt has written little to me about the pair of them, although I am aware that Mr. Fagean assists her with the estate from time to time."

"I'm told he acts like a land agent here."

He drew his lips together. "Something like that."

A second of thoughtful silence settled between us before a rueful look crossed his face. He edged to the side, a newfound restlessness to his movements, then plunged his hand into his jacket pocket. "I, uh, had hoped I might manage a moment alone with you this evening. I . . . well, I brought this to show you."

"Oh?"

A nervous smile lifted his tight expression. "Mr. Montague and I spent the whole of the afternoon unloading all the crates, and I happened to come across another scarab I thought you might be interested in." A hopeful pause. "You did seem fascinated earlier. I . . ." Slowly he extended his fist and passed the small object into my own.

"Another beetle?" Beautiful in design, blue like the first I'd seen, but a little bigger. I took it to a nearby candelabra to get a better view.

Lt. Burke followed me, his eyes never leaving my face. "This one here is glazed steatite, but the most interesting part is on the underside. Turn it over."

I did as instructed, surprised to see rows of etchings separated by straight lines, which covered the whole of one side of the scarab.

He moved in quite close. "They're hieroglyphics. My friend Thomas Young is doing some vastly interesting work on understanding the ancient script. He's identified several of the phonetic signs in demotic. He's a master with patterns and such."

My gaze shot up. There was a rather likable undertone to Lt. Burke's voice when he chose to be civil, one I'd not quite heard from him before.

He gestured to the amulet. "This particular scarab is known as a seal."

I ran my finger over the symbols. "What do the signs represent? Do you know what it says?"

"We're not entirely certain, but I do hope we find out one day. If I was to guess—from my own experience, mind you—these scarabs are usually thought to be a good omen. Perhaps that's what's written on them."

A quick smile and I pushed the amulet back into his hands, feigning concern. "Or it's a curse."

He chuckled. "Hardly. The scarab was an incredibly important symbol in Egypt. It was connected with the god Khepri, whom the Egyptians believed to be responsible for rolling the disk of the morning sun over the eastern horizon at daybreak."

I glanced down at his hand. "That's rather poetic in a way . . . and I daresay you're right, likely not a curse."

"Scarabs were slid into the bandages of mummies, as they represented the heart of the dead."

"Their heart? A *beetle?*"

"It does sound a bit odd to us today, but the Egyptians had a very different culture. The heart, however"—he gave me a small smile—"I daresay, the symbol of love is universal." A deep quiet crept into his eyes as he looked down at the artifact.

I too had fallen under its spell. "Thank you, Lt. Burke, for bringing the amulet to show me. It is a beautiful piece of artwork, really lovely."

He deposited the scarab back into his jacket pocket and looked up. "You've an artistic project of your own at present." He hesitated a moment, then glanced away. "I've been doing a bit of thinking this afternoon and though I caught a brief look at the ballroom earlier, I would like to see exactly what you and my aunt have been occupied with these past few months. I'd like an explanation of what all you have planned. Would you mind showing it to me?"

"Now? The ballroom?"

He turned his open hands upward. "Why not?"

The scarab, no doubt, had been brought in as a peace offering to put me in the right mood. I swallowed hard. Goodness, the wretch had probably planned to quiz me about the project from the beginning, possibly even challenge my position in the house. Well, I had nothing to hide.

I motioned to the drawing room door. "If you'll follow me."

I paused to secure a candle as well as my companion, Miss Chant, for the impromptu excursion. Lt. Burke might think nothing of wandering Avonthorpe Hall late at night alone with a female, but my father, Lord Torrington, would certainly think otherwise. He'd hired Miss Chant to watch over me as a sort of chaperone while I studied with Miss Drake.

Miss Chant had been quite strict at first, hovering over me like a cursed governess, much to my irritation. But as the months passed, we'd come to regard each other more as friends than anything else. On the whole, I'd gained her trust and she gave me the space I craved.

Today was no different as she walked a comfortable distance behind Lt. Burke and me, glancing up at us beneath those hooded brows from time to time, clasping the bag of needlepoint she'd brought with her just in case things took longer than expected, which I had no intention of allowing.

Our destination was not all that far from the drawing room, yet everything at Avonthorpe had been designed in an ostentatious way to encourage an admiring pace—an excess of Greek-styled columns, hall after hall of painted ceilings, and then the lustrous ballroom, the true epicenter of the house—a gilded wonderland.

To call the room large would certainly be an understatement—it was massive. Exquisite tapestries hung from one wall with floor-length windows lining the two adjacent to it, each trimmed with crimson draperies and golden accents. The immense circular gallery that housed the musicians at balls jutted from the far end of the room as chandelier after chandelier dripped beautifully from the painted ceiling.

An artist's dream.

However, with nothing but a sliver of moonlight, the three of us could see little beyond the solitary candlelight in my hand. And much to my annoyance, I was forced to take Lt. Burke up the makeshift scaffolding where Daniel and I had been working so he could assess the frieze.

The wooden structure complained as Lt. Burke leaned against the railing, his arms neatly folded across his chest. "My aunt has been quite coy about these renovations. I've been wondering what drove her to the decision to renovate the ballroom in the first place, as I was under the impression money is tight at present."

So that's why he'd brought me in here without his aunt. Did he think I meant to fleece her? "You needn't worry, Lt. Burke. I consider this project a part of my tutelage. I require no compensation for my time."

He eyed the trim. "But you do consider yourself qualified to complete, well . . . all of it?" His voice fell flat. "I mean, since you're only a student."

My chest constricted. "Of course I do. And remember, we're not touching the ceiling."

He turned to face the faint lines and faded designs sprawled across the curved dome and lifted the candle. "I didn't even realize there was so much detail throughout this room. I can see why you've decided to leave that be."

I couldn't hide the flame to my tone. "I—"

He held up his hand. "As far as I can tell, you do excellent work." Then his gaze snagged on the section Daniel had completed rather poorly earlier in the day. "I just hope my aunt is aware that I stand ready to assist her with any funds required."

"You mean you're giving me the opportunity to step aside?"

An elusive grin. "That is not what I implied."

"Isn't it? I daresay you know of several gentlemen painters in London who could take over this work and do a phenomenal job with the space."

"Of course I do, but I've suggested no such thing."

I gritted my teeth. "Then what exactly are you suggesting, sir?"

"Honesty . . . nothing more."

My jaw fell slack. "And?"

He folded his arms at his chest, his eyes on the trim work. "Tell me . . . why did my aunt encourage you to take this on? Nothing in this house has been touched in years. In fact, I was under the impression it has something to do with the entail."

My gaze went distant. "You'll have to ask your aunt about that. I can only speak to the fact that she instructed me to ensure the walls will look and feel exactly as when they were first painted. She indicated that she was tired of the dingy look to it all. We both know she finds great enjoyment in hosting parties. Once, she informed me I was to ensure that her guests would be able to see every last detail of the frieze from the center of the ballroom, as they could a hundred years ago. The ceiling, however, will stay just as it is. Restoring that will take far more expertise."

He narrowed his eyes. "And how *exactly* are you restoring the trim?"

"I'm simply repainting it. As instructed by your aunt, mind you, I use a traditional recipe of chalk and pigment mixed with water, bound together with animal glue to distemper the plaster. The entire project has been quite straightforward up until this point." I lifted the candle. "However, this work here is taking a great deal longer than expected. It is extremely delicate. I never should have allowed Daniel to practice on it."

Lt. Burke leaned in close to where I'd left off. "I can see why."

"Your aunt is quite fond of this room. She demands perfection at every step. I daresay she would do the whole project herself if her eyesight were better."

He chuckled. "I'm sure she would."

A voice boomed from below. "She would what?"

The two of us jerked around to see Miss Drake crouching beside Miss Chant near the door. I sidestepped him to the railing. "I was just showing your nephew our project."

She wrinkled her nose. "Hmm."

Lt. Burke assisted me down the scaffold stairwell. "It is quite an ambitious project, Aunt."

"Yes, well . . ." Her voice was gruff. "All that's left is the far wall, and we shall finally see the room as Josiah Drake designed it." She took my hand into hers as I approached. "Mrs. Fagean is demanding your return. She's found a few more tapestries for that wretched drizzling of hers. I daresay she intends to tell you all about them."

I huffed out a sigh. "I'm sure she does."

Lt. Burke took his aunt's arm as her escort, and I fell back to accompany Miss Chant.

The two of us allowed a comfortable space to form before she whispered into my ear. "Lt. Burke is still rather affecting, is he not?"

"Shh." I squeezed her arm tight. Whatever schoolgirl notions Miss Chant had in regard to finding a husband for me in every gentleman we came across would not be tolerated. Not in regard to Lt. Burke anyway, not after what he'd said in the stables. He had no interest where I was concerned. Besides, even a romantic soul like her would understand what a poor match the two of us would make—he with his excessive formality and me with my artistic nature. Besides, I had every intention of setting up my own establishment—alone.

Miss Drake dragged Lt. Burke to a halt. "Is that it?"

She pointed into the alcove, where her favorite Sèvres vase was displayed on a delicate rococo table.

Lt. Burke cast a quick glance at me, then spoke with authority. "What do you think of it, Aunt?"

She handled the vase, examining it one way then the next, before edging it closer to the candlelight. "I suppose it will do."

My eyes were wide as I drew up at her side, finally processing the scene before me. "Do you mean this vase is—?"

"A fake. It is now." She scrunched up her lips, regret in her voice. "Graham has taken the original into his possession and plans to sell it so we can live for the next few months."

My heart sank. "Sell it?"

No wonder Lt. Burke had questioned me about the renovations. Was Miss Drake's situation as bad as all that? Had she been in fact reduced to selling off pieces of his inheritance?

Lt. Burke arranged the false vase back on the table. "I will say, as unfortunate as our situation is, I thought my man did an excellent job. Few could distinguish this one from the original."

She urged us to a slow walk. "I will need the money in my hands as soon as it can be arranged. The stonework behind the old chapel is in serious need of repair." She sighed. "I've put that off long enough. Mr. Fagean twisted his ankle there a few weeks back."

Of course Mr. Fagean would somehow be involved with the selling of the vase. I glanced ahead of me to the drawing room door. I knew Miss Drake's finances were tight, but destitute? How could I have been so completely unaware of the situation? I narrowed my eyes. Moreover, what else was going on at Avonthorpe Hall that I was unaware of?

Four

Mrs. Fagean secured my company as soon as I entered the drawing room, urging me to take a turn about the room. She was far more animated than her usual placid self—and in a strange way—her free hand batting the air, her voice clipped.

"I have in my possession two of the most beautiful tapestries I've seen of late. You'll be in rapture over them, I'm sure. And I have in mind just what I shall do with the pin money the drizzling will fetch. The spring equinox celebration is this Saturday, after all. And I shall have the first one drizzled in a trice."

I cast her a cool glance. "You mean to attend?"

"Why not? My friend Mary plans to be there. She seems to think her ancestors were druids at one time." She giggled a bit. "And it's not like the festival is evil or anything. They only spread some seeds around to bless the harvest and dance a bit. You could come . . . or maybe not." Her cheeks turned red. "Mr. Fagean encourages such interactions for me. He says he only wants me to be happy. At any rate, I must begin the tapestries at once." She tugged me in close. "They really are gorgeous pieces."

I shook my head, a sigh on my breath. "But I cannot understand. If you find the tapestries so beautiful, why drizzle them at all? As an artist I find the practice difficult to—"

"Oh, Phoebe." Her chest heaved with a pert laugh. "You've always been so archaic in your thinking. Drizzling is everywhere now. La, my friends and I could sit for hours stripping those precious little gold and silver threads from whatever textiles we can get our hands on—gowns, military uniforms, tapestries—it's a sort of art form in a way. You better than anyone should understand that." Her voice was steady enough, but her attention felt oddly turbulent as she glanced between me and Mr. Fagean on the sofa.

I'd heard that drizzling, or *parfilage* as they called it in France, had become quite popular in London; however, I'd never met a lady in the country so taken with the hobby. My steps turned sluggish. And why was that?

I worried the edge of my lip.

For the first time since I'd observed Mrs. Fagean's drizzling, a gloomier thought took hold. No doubt, Mrs. Fagean would need a new gown for the festival. Were the Fageans perhaps in reduced circumstances like Miss Drake? Could they not afford one? Drizzling was fashionable, yes, but surely there was more to her incessant practice.

Another laugh. "What do you think of that devil Mr. Montague over there? I bet *he* would enjoy the festival."

I glanced up to catch the gentleman watching us. "I couldn't say. I only met him yesterday."

"They call him the cad of Kent, you know. And if I understand the rumors correctly, he was thrown over by a young lady not too long ago." She squinted. "Although I can't remember the lady's name at present."

I lifted an eyebrow. "Mrs. Amelia Cluett perhaps?"

Her eyes widened with pleasure. "That's the one! Of course, she was Mrs. Pembroke at the time, and nobody knew anything about her. The ton was shocked of course—the cad of Kent rejected and all that. Believe me, he was quite the Corinthian last season." She patted my arm. "You wouldn't know because you weren't there. The rumors are the chit left him devastated."

I stole another peek across the room. "Shocked, more like."

Mrs. Fagean hooked her arm through mine. "Really, Phoebe, you would be remiss not to try for him. Can't you stand up any straighter? I daresay your father would be pleased by such a connection. Montague's the heir to Whitefall, after all."

I stopped us cold. "And you mean to parade me in front of him?"

"Whyever not?" Her lips curved into a smile. "You're not getting any younger, and believe me, the world is a scary place for a woman alone. Even if that stepmother of yours doesn't care a fig about your future, I certainly do."

"Doesn't care . . . your future." Her words echoed in my whisper.

Mrs. Fagean jerked back. "No need to look at me like that, my dear. I only speak what I see. If Lady Torrington had any thoughts where you were concerned, she wouldn't have hidden you away here miles from any eligible men." A pop of her eyebrow. "Well, that is, until now." Mrs. Fagean couldn't tear her gaze from Mr. Montague's dashing figure. "You've been presented with a great opportunity. If only you won't waste it."

My face tightened. "I assure you the decision to train here was mine and mine alone."

She shrugged, but my heart rate only intensified, pounding wildly in my chest. How dare she?

No matter how much I knew Mrs. Fagean's accusations regarding my stepmother, Lady Torrington, to be completely inaccurate, they still stung. I withdrew from her eager hands. "If you'll excuse me. It appears Miss Chant is in need of me." I trudged across the room before Mrs. Fagean had a chance to object, and I tugged my friend into the corner by the fire.

"I do not think I can stomach any more of Mrs. Know-It-All tonight."

Miss Chant gave me a knowing look. "That bad, huh?"

Arnold must have seen my retreat, because he drew up at our side. He seemed hesitant to speak, his lips parting and then closing.

Finally, "Are you perhaps in need of . . . refreshment, Miss Radcliff? Miss Chant?"

I let out a long breath. "Thank you, Arnold. I would love a glass of water. I daresay I need a moment to cool my nerves."

He nodded, consoling, then moved to bow but halted, offering a mischievous smile instead. "It's not my place, Miss Radcliff, but allow me this once to quip on Mrs. Fagean's remarkable ability to get under one's skin."

"You too?" I returned his grin. "I daresay she's got her clutches into us all." I turned to Miss Chant. "But we shan't regard it, shall we?"

"Quite right." Arnold nodded as he departed to fetch the glass of water.

Miss Chant leaned in close. "What was it this time?"

I would have laughed if my current situation wasn't so disheartening. "Apparently she's decided I'm to make a match with Mr. Montague."

"No." Miss Chant's eyes grew round as she covered her mouth. "That won't do. Not at all."

"I tried to tell her, but—"

"Lt. Burke." Miss Chant motioned with her chin across the room. "Now that gentleman I could more readily agree with."

Not again. I bit the inside of my cheek. "Don't be absurd. Don't you remember when he last visited here how he barked at you when you were three minutes late for dinner?"

She laughed to herself. "Yes, but he'd had a long day on the road—"

"And then he stared at me through all three courses, chewing each bite ten times as opposed to offering me any conversation."

"You actually counted?"

"How could I not? It was maddening. At the time all I could do was watch his jaw flex. And you saw him with me just now in the ballroom. We're completely at cross-purposes. In fact, in the stables he practically accused me of lying to him." I caught her nearly imperceptible surprise. "Oh yes. He's far too stuffy . . . and meticulous . . . and exacting for me."

A slight smile. "And handsome. You can't forget that."

"Believe me, I'd be out of my mind in less than a week."

"Perhaps." She nudged my arm. "Or terribly in love, which can cure a great many evils. Don't allow such brief interactions to sway your final opinion on a person."

"Unless that person proves you right. Or worse, they steal your heart and attempt to flee Britain."

She shook her head slowly. "I thought we were speaking of Lt. Burke?"

"As did I, but the more I think about it, Miss Drake's nephew is proving to have a great deal in common with my little French friend—the sort of man who puts duty above all else."

Miss Chant thought a moment. "Perhaps he does in looks and bearing, but certainly not in temperament. Lt. Burke served our country with honor. He deserves our respect."

"Did Jean Cloutier not serve France just as faithfully? He simply chose his country over me . . . and others."

"What you mean to say is he used you and tossed you aside."

"I suppose he did in a way, but he was desperate and I don't like to remember him that way. There's a part of me that will always want to believe he cared for me." I shook my head. "I'm just glad no one in my family knew about our sordid romance, particularly my father. Thankfully, you and Daniel are the only ones aware that he broke my heart."

"And I shan't ever forgive him for doing so. In fact, I blame him entirely for spawning the ridiculous notion of setting up your own household. Oh, Phoebe, it will never do. Your heart will fully heal . . . and then . . . if I ever were to see that man—"

"No. It was my fault. I never should have fallen for his grandiose promises. I was young and foolish, and he was the first person outside of my family to take an interest in my artistry. I was flattered and now he is in prison. And my father will probably never forgive me for helping him."

"You've always had a good heart, Phoebe. Don't let his actions rob you of your joy or"—a quick glance up at Lt. Burke—"your future."

My shoulders felt heavy. "You know I still dream of Jean from time to time. And those dreams seem so real. In my mind's eye he's standing before me like he used to do, watching me, waiting for the right moment to finally address me, but that moment never comes. If I didn't know he was locked away, I'd be half worried he might come looking for me, and then what would I do?"

"Send him to Jericho, of course. Monsieur Cloutier is not to be thought of. Do you hear me, Phoebe?"

I nodded once. After all, Miss Chant was perfectly right. I'd spent the last two years moving on from my childish mistake.

"That fiend presented himself in your father's household under false pretenses and exploited your affection for him to stage his escape from capture. It is a wonder your father didn't kill him when he first apprehended the man. I know the whole affair was difficult to move past—"

"Have I really though?" All of a sudden I felt tired, and Miss Chant took my hand.

"You will, my dear. You have. Time is a great healer." She tugged me to fully face her. "Believe me, honest men do exist in this confusing world."

I gave her fingers a squeeze. "You remind me daily that the perfectly wonderful love a girl only dreams of does exist. It gives me hope . . . If only they were all like Vincent," I said of her fiancé. I pressed my lips together, my attention lifting to the men standing near the fireplace. "From what I can gather from Miss Drake, I'm afraid Lt. Burke has more in common with Jean than we'd like to think. He . . ." I caught her inquisitive glare and my chest felt cold. Did I really believe what I was saying? Hadn't I just caught a glimpse of the opposite, a man terribly excited to show me a stone beetle? "It doesn't matter. Just permit me to put this idea to bed once and for all. I have no interest in either of those men over there."

"I do understand your hesitation, Phoebe, but I cannot help but wish you could experience what I have, and Mrs. Fagean has no idea of your past. She only means to help you."

"To embarrass me, more like. It's all a game with her—gentlemen, marriage."

Arnold returned with a tray of water glasses and paused only for my selection before speaking. "I'm glad to see the color in your cheeks has returned." He paused and cast a shrewd glance over his shoulder at the group that had left the fireplace to gather around the pianoforte. Then he withdrew a step, but I stalled his retreat.

"Tell me, Arnold. What do you know of Miss Drake's nephew?"

Another cool glare at our uninvited visitors. "Not overly much, I'm afraid. He's the heir presumptive of Avonthorpe, of course."

Arnold and Miss Drake had always had a special relationship, one that defied convention. If anyone was aware of the financial difficulties at Avonthorpe, it would have been Arnold. But he'd never given me any cause for concern. "I only ask because"—I narrowed my eyes—"were you aware Miss Drake arranged for Lt. Burke to sell her Sèvres vase, the one she loves so dearly? The hall already houses the replica. The original is to be sold as soon as possible."

Arnold stiffened, his eyes darting about the room. "I hadn't the least notion. I-I didn't realize the finances were at such a pass to warrant . . ." He ran his hand down his face. "She cares a great deal for that vase. She wouldn't part with it lightly."

He looked so terribly lost that I touched his arm.

"It's the only sale I know of at present. She might simply have needed a bit of extra money this month. Do not allow her decision to worry you."

"Perhaps."

I watched Avonthorpe's longstanding butler and friend pace away confused, a far more uncomfortable thought taking root. Did more than Miss Drake's impulsive act of selling her favorite vase have me off stride? No. Something felt eerily off about the current inhabitants of the house—an unnatural discord among us. And whatever had wrought such friction had most certainly originated with Lt. Burke's unexpected and unwanted arrival.

As I made my way to my bedchamber that evening, I keenly felt the springtime plunge in temperature. The shadows felt deeper, the air thinner, the insidious silence terribly alive in my ears. How I wished I hadn't tarried so long in the drawing room. The small hours at Avonthorpe had never been for the weak of heart.

I rubbed the chill from my arms and tugged my shawl tighter about my shoulders. After all, I had no one to blame but myself that I was left to wander the corridors alone. I took a furtive glance behind me. My imagination would not be stopped, nor would the cry of the ancient stones buried within the walls. Though they had been covered with plaster and wood over the years, the heart of the original structure always found its voice at night, brought to life by the coastal wind.

Increasingly anxious to reach my room, I thrust my guttering candle into the gloom and picked up my pace. And by the time I reached the corner by the family wing, I was at full speed. An eerie whisper, however, brought me all too quickly to a dead halt.

My skin prickled. My eyes rounded.

Had I actually heard something, or was it simply the moan of time?

For a throbbing second I stood there listening, watching, trying to make sense of who or what had alerted me. Then the corridor took a deep breath—not a gentle one, mind you. It was as if the surging nighttime wind had broken into the house. A shiver plunged down my spine and I fumbled to lay my newly extinguished candle on a nearby hall table.

I took a step forward, groping the shadows for the merest sign of movement, my muscles tight, my pulse wild. I'd been right to stop. Something had disturbed the hallway. A presence perhaps? An open window?

I lunged against the wall preparing to bolt for the servants' wing, intent on warning Arnold, but then I heard the ghostly sound again—a gasping sob hidden in the folds of the wind gusts. Someone was in pain, and the voice came from the direction of Miss Drake's room. My stomach lurched, my mind awash as to how to proceed, but I mustered up the courage to creep down the long hall. I could not leave Miss Drake if she was in trouble.

I found Miss Drake's door slightly ajar, her bedchamber thick with darkness. I knew very well my instructor had retired from the drawing room long before me.

Every last muscle in my legs coiled as I inched to the door. "Miss Drake?"

The metal latch felt cold on my fingers, the ominous emptiness of the room urging me forward. I called out again as I edged the door open. "Miss Drake?"

There was an obstacle on the far side, and it wasn't until I forced the door fully open that I recognized what lay at my feet. Shades of moonlight followed me into the bedchamber from the hall window, their muted glow highlighting Miss Drake's twisted form sprawled on the carpet. I covered my mouth. She had only made it one step into the room and was still dressed in her evening attire.

"Oh no!" I fell to my knees. "What has happened? Are you injured?" All I could think was that she'd fallen somehow.

Her breathing sounded strangled, strange and uneven, then I felt something wet on my knees—something on the carpet had soaked through my gown. I took a feral glance at the shadowy rug, but I couldn't seem to process what lay before me, not fast enough at least. Cautiously I rolled Miss Drake onto her back, and my heart seized, the image of what I'd discovered blurring the truth.

Darkness closed in around me, my focus painfully fixed on the arrow protruding from my beloved teacher's chest. She'd been shot, but how? Why? The scene before me couldn't be real. I wadded up part of my gown to staunch the wound as I screamed for help.

Miss Drake's cold, weakened hand found my arm. "There's nothing to be done now." A ragged breath. "I haven't much time." A cough shook her battered body and she winced.

"Don't say that." I pushed off the floor and raced to the bell pull. "You can't give up yet."

She motioned me back with a frail flick of her wrist, panic settling into her kind eyes. "There's something I absolutely must tell you and . . . if only there was more time . . ." She licked her lips. "I'm forced to . . . be brief."

I dropped onto the floor beside her, and she wrenched me close to her mouth, her voice a choked whisper. "In my jewelry box . . . beneath the panel that holds my . . . topaz broach, there's a . . . small piece of paper. Take it." Her eyes rolled to the ceiling, death crushing her voice by the second. "You're the only one who should have it. You've been like a daughter to me. I want it for you, not him."

Tears poured down my cheeks as I supported her frail head. "What are you talking about?"

Her eyes shot wide open. "The treasure, of course."

My lips parted, my mind forging through waves of shock and dread. "You can't be serious."

Her fingers tightened on my arm, like claws. "The paper. If only . . . There are . . . clues, nonsense clues, but . . ." Her face looked ashen, ghostly in the blackened room. I struggled not only to hear but to understand everything she was mumbling. "Trust Arnold. Promise me you'll follow the clues. That you'll find it for me. If you don't, *he* most certainly . . ."

Coughs erupted again, this time far deeper and more ominous as her hand wandered mindlessly to the wound on her chest. A second of motionless silence ticked away as her eyes slid shut, her final two breaths so terribly long and slow.

I cradled her in my arms until her lady's maid finally arrived and sounded another alarm. The next few moments passed like a hazy dream. I remember servants dashing in and out of her bedchamber before I was finally coaxed away from her lifeless body, and I crawled into a ball against a nearby dresser. I sat there alone for some time, stunned into the silence of tortured thoughts and wild speculation. Who would have done such an appalling thing to Miss Drake? Who was evil enough to commit murder?

My thoughts kept me pinned to the cold, hard wood of the dresser drawers as I watched the incomprehensible flurry of movement within the room, the startled screams of each new arrival, the utter disbelief so evident in everyone's eyes.

Lt. Burke was the first person to finally squat down beside me. His voice was kind, his hand warm on my arm. "Miss Radcliff?"

My nod was a slow one, a heavy one.

"I was told you were the first to find my aunt in such a state." His voice shook, but he managed to get it under control.

I forced myself to focus on his face, comforted in a way to see a glossy sheen to those pale eyes, the mirror of a man as deeply affected by her loss as I was. "I heard Miss Drake on my way to my room. She must have called out. I . . . I discovered her near death . . . just there."

"*Near* death?" His eyes snapped back to mine. "She was still alive when you found her?"

"Yes, she was."

The muscles in his cheeks twitched. "Did she say anything to you . . . before the end?"

My heart tumbled. The treasure! And here I'd fallen prey to such a sincere look of devastation. Lt. Burke was as mercenary as they came, already probing for information.

Miss Drake's cryptic instructions lay like an unsolved puzzle on the table of my mind. I had no intention of sharing her words at present, certainly not with him, not when I'd held his aunt in my arms just a few moments ago. A touch of anger coated my answer. "Why do you ask?"

He stared at me dumbfounded, his lips moving, then stopping. "Because I mean to bring her murderer to justice. What other reason could I have?" There was an uncomfortable pause before he raked his hand through his hair.

I swallowed hard. "You could have no other reason." Terribly chastised, I closed my eyes for a long second. "I'm so sorry, but your aunt had nothing to say in regard to who could have taken her life."

He was looking at me as if I'd grown two heads, then abruptly extended his arm. "I daresay you'll be more comfortable in your own bedchamber. Allow me to take you there now." He tugged me to my feet, but he didn't lead me out. "Thank you for being there with her . . . at the end. You've endured a great deal more than any person should. I've sent a groom for the parish constable, and Arnold is fetching Miss Chant to set up a trundle in your room for tonight. I don't think it a good idea for you to be alone."

He rubbed his eyes with his thumb and first finger. "Granted, the next few days will only be more difficult."

My chest tightened. "I believe you are in the right of it. I should prefer to be in my room at present."

Lt. Burke tucked my arm close to his side. The gesture felt protective . . . warm even, a blessed moment of calm in the storm. But as we made our way to the door, I finally took in the whole of Miss

Drake's bedchamber. The entire household had found their way into the room.

Mr. Fagean stood in the shadows, petting his hysterical wife. Mr. Montague, a mournful expression on his face, had propped himself against the poster bed, a slight nod for me. And Daniel—oh, Daniel, how strange he looked. Scared, edgy, as if the weight of the room might crush him at any moment.

I had little reserves for comforting anyone at this point. It was all I could do to stay on my feet with Lt. Burke's assistance. The whole experience still felt so unreal. In fact, I stopped Lt. Burke once we reached the hallway.

"It was a bolt. I saw the housekeeper remove it."

He stared down at me. "What do you mean?"

"The arrow in your aunt's chest. It was from a crossbow."

"Are you certain?"

My heart quivered. "I believe so."

His voice sounded strained as he dipped his head. "I don't understand. Why would anyone . . ." He collapsed against the wall, his hand at his head. "It seems our murderer planned every step of this."

My initial shock swept painfully into confusion, my heart thrumming in my chest. "But why?"

"I haven't the least idea. All I know is my aunt was a pillar of this community. Her death will cause ripples throughout the area." Then, almost as an afterthought, "She will be greatly missed."

My heart constricted. "By some . . ."

His face fell, his voice far away. "I loved her dearly."

I started to reach out for him but thought better of it. I'd been misled in the past, played like a fiddle, so when I searched Lt. Burke's pensive stance, I couldn't help but question whether he was indeed telling the truth. All the pieces for trust were there before me, but complete belief would take time.

I glanced back up, startled to see a peculiar look about his face.

No, not a look exactly, more like a feeling, that invisible energy of a man deep in thought but equally riddled with emotion. I'd felt it before with my father when he had much to hide and even more to lose. As a spy for the British government who worked to apprehend traitors, his life had been a constant lie to me, but he was also the best man I knew, my protector.

Wariness of duplicity settled into my core and took root as we reached my bedchamber door and Lt. Burke took his leave of me. Miss Drake's nephew was certainly mulling over a great deal. I stopped short of closing my door, watching his heavy departure clearly weighted down by such a terrible loss.

I grabbed onto a nearby table, suddenly a bit dizzy. Or was I completely mistaken? Was it not equally possible that Lt. Burke was not as devastated as he'd led me to believe, but instead burdened by the need to cover up and profit from his aunt's murder?

Five

I WAS ON MY WAY TO THE PARLOR IN SEARCH OF BREAKFAST the following morning when I came upon Lt. Burke and Mr. Montague alone. They were standing below me in the entryway at the bottom of the grand staircase, and I had yet to leave the landing.

Though I did nothing to conceal my presence, I did tarry a moment at the top of the stairs, startled in some part by the intensity of their discussion. I slid over to the railing and peered down at the pair. I'd never heard Lt. Burke's voice so anxious and deep. It didn't take me long to realize he was wearing the same clothes he'd had on since yesterday, his cravat a rumpled mess, his hair limp, no doubt from the shaky fingers that had been pressed through it time and again. He was as rigid as a statue facing the massive fireplace.

Mr. Montague, however, proved an entirely different animal, pacing in front of the hearth, a wild urgency about his movements. "Take another sip of coffee, my good man—you'll not make it through the day lest."

Lt. Burke seemed to warm his gloved fingers a moment on the cup in his hands before he took a long drink. "Constable Humphries will be back within the hour and I've the funeral arrangements to see to."

Mr. Montague edged in close. "You can't keep on at this infernal pace, Graham. You'll break. Trust me this once and take my advice. Leave the details to that stiff, Arnold. He strikes me as more than capable of handling whatever is required."

"Maybe you're right." Lt. Burke deposited his cup on a side table and turned to the fire, the wavering light lapping his stern expression. "But that shall make my next course of action even harder to implement. The whole place will have to be boarded up for now, you know, perhaps leased, or worse, sold. I'll know more tomorrow when my solicitor arrives."

Mr. Montague gasped. "You mean the whole estate?"

I clutched the balustrade as my waist dipped against the hard wood. He couldn't be serious. Not Avonthorpe! I waited for the shake of Lt. Burke's head or the one word I expected from his lips.

But he didn't deny Mr. Montague's assertions, pivoting instead to slam his arm against the mantel. "I'd hoped to raise the necessary funds to maintain this place over time, but as it stands now, I'll have little choice. My aunt was in far too deep."

Mr. Montague's voice came out breathy. "I cannot believe that."

"Oh, I speak the truth, and every day the mound of debt only gets worse. This cursed house is bleeding money from every angle."

"And the sale of our antiquities?"

"Will do little to help, I'm afraid. The proceeds, if we can sell a few pieces beyond the sarcophagus, could buy me a few months at the very least, and then what? You know I've Brooksheed Manor to maintain. Though the place is smaller and farther from London, I've staff to consider there too." He hung his head. "Under no circumstances will I turn away my late father's servants and friends who have been with my family for years."

Mr. Montague stretched his jaw. "Arnold's been at Avonthorpe a long while as well. He's pretty far into his dotage, Graham. I—"

"I shall give him a letter of recommendation, of course, but I simply cannot keep even a few servants on. It'll ruin me." He ran his hand down his face. "It's a deuced uncomfortable position to be in—for everyone."

Footsteps sounded at my back, and I whirled to see Miss Chant approaching from the far hall. One last glance at the gentlemen below, and I dragged her quietly into a nearby sitting room before sealing the door behind us.

"He's going to turn Arnold off!"

Her nose scrunched up at the bridge. "Who is?"

I pressed my lips together. "Lt. Burke. Avonthorpe is apparently not sustainable in its current state."

She gave me a peculiar look. "This bloated estate has been living on borrowed time for as long as I can remember. Surely Lt. Burke is only startled by his first dip into the finances. Miss Drake said he was a planner, a man of means."

My shoulders slumped. "She did say that, didn't she?"

We both lapsed into a thoughtful silence, the casement clock filling the void in conversation. "I daresay it's none of our business what Lt. Burke does with this place. It's just . . . I still cannot believe she's actually gone. I expect to see her walk around that corner at any moment. Every last inch of this house was so very much hers."

"It doesn't seem possible, does it?" Miss Chant lowered her gaze to the carpet. "I'm actually on my way to sit with her body now."

I nodded, tears filling my eyes. I secured a handkerchief and blotted them away, my thoughts scattering with each dab. "I suppose I should be making plans for what happens next, but it's almost too painful to think of." All at once my arms felt heavy, and I allowed them to drop at my sides. "I'll have no choice but to return to Middlecrest Abbey, and . . ."

A startling flash of concern crossed Miss Chant's eyes and my muscles stilled. And . . . what? Had I been so affected by the nature of Miss Drake's death and the subsequent fallout that I hadn't even considered what this would all mean for my confidante and friend? Moreover, what it would mean for her dreams? "We both know I won't have need of a chaperone in my father's household." I swallowed hard. "What will you do? Where will you go?"

She shrugged. "I'll have to find another position and straightaway, of course." She gathered her hands at her waist, her fingers twisting and turning. "Although it will be difficult to find something similar that pays so well."

"And Vincent Tulk? What about your future together?"

Her lips quivered and she turned away. "Oh, Phoebe, we shall have no choice but to part for the time being. Even though Mr. Haskett is a reasonable employer, Vincent . . . he told me he might not be able to wait for me . . . to travel to America. I . . . I had hoped we could sail together at some point, but we don't have the money to do so now. And yet how can I ask him to stay in Britain any longer? He's desperate to leave. His family sent a letter just last week begging him to make the journey as soon as possible. They need him to run the farm."

I spun her to face me, then grasped her hands. "He loves you. He'll wait even longer. After all, he already agreed to ten months."

"And if he cannot?" She shook her head. "I don't know if I have the courage to board that ship alone, to go all that way by myself."

"I have a little pin money left. Perhaps I can make up some of the difference. I could also write to my father—"

"No, please don't do that." She tugged away. "He's been far too generous already. He's overpaid me every month for the past two years. I dare not ask for any more. I'll find another way." She tried a small smile, but her expression grew cloudy. "If nothing else, I know how to be resourceful." She motioned to the door. "I'd best go. I'm afraid I'm late already. Miss Brooks was expecting me nigh over five minutes ago."

I followed her out the sitting room door with a heavy heart and watched her descend the grand staircase, my focus drifting painfully to the empty entryway where the gentlemen had been standing and discussing the estate just a few short minutes ago. How much money would be needed to change our current situation for my friend, for Lt. Burke—if he was indeed in need of it?

Money.

I whipped around and pressed my back to the railing, my hand cupping my mouth. Things would be moving quickly over the next few days—the funeral, an investigation into the murder, my departure from the house. I could not put off pursuing Miss Drake's dying request any longer. She'd tasked me with finding a secret paper. I couldn't leave until I'd done so.

My eyes rounded as Miss Drake's horrific and untimely death chilled my thoughts. If there was indeed a treasure like Miss Drake said and an actual clue to find it, I had best get started.

Miss Drake's lonely bedchamber had been thoroughly cleaned and straightened, yet her familiar jasmine scent had found a way back into the injured space. I paused on the threshold, my heart squeezing in my chest, my attention a prisoner to the space at my feet.

The stained carpet had been removed, but in my mind's eye I could still see her lying there, grappling for help, wrenching me close to impart her last words. I'd delayed revisiting the room, afraid of what I would be forced to confront within myself. But though sadness darkened every step forward, an equally compelling emotion fought for balance in my chest—Miss Drake's urgency. She'd made me promise to recover the paper and follow its clues. She used her last bit of energy to demand it.

With that thought to guide me, my steps lightened and my purpose felt clear. I could not neglect my dearest teacher's last request. All too soon the whole estate would be gone over by the servants, Miss Drake's personal effects would be inventoried for her nephew, and I would have no choice but to leave.

I hastened to the curved dressing table in the corner of the room and slid onto her velvet-covered seat, my fingers shaking. I knew she kept her jewelry box in the right first drawer. A wriggle of nerves capered across my shoulders, almost as if her presence had joined me, urging me forward.

Carefully, I clutched the latch and slid the wooden drawer open. There in the shadows lay the familiar carved walnut box inlaid so beautifully with sandalwood.

I lifted it into the dust-strewn light, which streamed through the leaded panes of the adjacent window, and laid the box on the dresser's smooth surface. I ran my fingers over the small plated painting at the center before lifting the lid.

There were three wooden, sectioned layers within that I lifted out one by one and arranged across the dresser. I recognized the stunning pieces of jewelry at once—the navette ring she wore to dinner parties, her onyx necklace that matched her favorite gown, the carnelian cameo that she'd been wearing the night of her death . . .

I closed my eyes for a moment, remembering her words. *"Beneath the panel that holds my topaz broach."* I knew that broach well. I'd admired it often enough, but it wasn't in the first section, nor the second.

My fingers feathered over the pieces, lifting and prodding the various items.

The sound of footsteps beyond the bedchamber door sent my heart racing, but the person wasn't close. A good reminder: I needed to be quick. The last thing I wanted was to be caught rifling through Miss Drake's jewelry. I felt around the outside of the box, tugging and pulling the carved wood, then turned my attention back to the thin section that housed the partitions. Each small compartment held a trinket. The third panel, however, had two covered partitions. I lifted the first one and found it empty, but when I opened the second, there lay the topaz broach.

At first I found nothing underneath it, but I had no intention of giving up. I felt about the section, the bottom, the side. At once, a small flat drawer popped open.

My breath stilled, memories so dangerously near the surface. I had cradled Miss Drake to my chest, agreed to all she said, but had I ever really believed her? Had she actually found a clue to the treasure? And if I followed the clues, would my fate be similar to Miss Drake's?

I held out the folded piece of paper and gently pulled back each pliable side. The note was well worn, and the parchment felt limp in my eager fingers. I had to lean close to make out the terribly faded words penned long ago:

> *Precisely at daybreak when twelve little men from the dark fight twelve little men from the light and it is declared a draw, cultivate deep the blackened tip of the First Duke of Marlborough's favorite sword.*

It was a riddle and a strange one at that. I stared at my reflection in the looking glass and repeated the words. What did I know about the legend of the treasure? Why hadn't I paid more attention to the ramblings in town?

I bit my lip. I remembered something about an ancestor of the Drakes, who had claimed to have hidden the treasure in the final days of his life, to secure it for his son who was at sea. The son, however, had never returned. He'd sadly perished abroad.

Had Miss Drake stumbled upon a clue?

I rolled the riddle around in my mind. It would take some time to decipher the meaning, *if* it could even be done.

The slow tread of someone in the hall sparked my nerves to life once again, and I rushed to reinsert the panels into the jewelry box, fumbling the entire process. Apparently the partitions fit only one way, and I'd mixed the order. Blast. My hands shook as I stumbled upon the correct arrangement and closed the lid.

Whoever advanced down the hall was almost upon me. I shoved the box back into the drawer and slammed it shut. Throbbing with muscles wound a bit too tight, I sprang to my feet and whirled to face the door, my chest heaving.

"Why, Miss Radcliff"—Arnold came to a full stop, curiosity written across his elderly face—"what brings you in here?"

A slew of excuses danced through my mind, but each one was more ridiculous than the last. Finally, my shoulders sagged. "I wanted to look over Miss Drake's things."

He eyed me a moment before swinging the door closed behind him. "I, uh, have been hoping to get a moment alone to speak with you."

He motioned for me to take a seat once again at the dresser, then lugged a slat-backed chair from across the room to join me.

We watched each other a quiet moment, each searching the other's face for a clue as to what had caused this new awkwardness between us. We'd always been easy with one another. Did he perhaps know the real reason I'd entered her bedchamber? Miss Drake had told me to trust him.

He tapped his fingers across his knee in succession, a bend to his wrinkled brow. "I saw you slam the drawer, Miss Radcliff."

I tried a dramatic huff, but it sounded guilty even to me. "What do you mean?"

"Lt. Burke told me you spoke with Miss Drake at the end."

I rested my hands in my lap, hoping to appear somewhat honorable. "I did . . . and one of her final words was to trust you."

A small but genuine smile crossed his face. "Then you have found the clue."

My fingers instinctively curled around the paper hidden in the palm of my hand. "How did you know?"

"She told me where she kept it. And I know how fond of you she was. It makes sense she would tell you all, that she would want us to work together."

Slowly, carefully, I opened my hand. "What does this gibberish even mean?"

"It's from her father's will."

I sat back. "His will?"

Mr. Arnold rubbed his forehead, his gaze lifting to the ceiling as if he wasn't certain where to begin. "I'm sure Miss Drake imparted to you that I have been assisting her in searching for that cursed treasure for the past twenty years."

"Not exactly. She didn't have time. Twenty years?"

"Which is when her father died and she inherited the clue."

I took a deep breath. "I don't understand."

"No?" He sighed. "I thought everyone around here had heard the story of Josiah Drake."

"I've heard a little."

He lifted his eyebrows. "Well, it's not a story. It's a fact. The lost crown jewels of King John were recovered just like the rumors say by a poor farmer who came upon them by accident east of the boggy Fens. Apparently a small, imperceptible brook drifted the entire contents of the official carriage yards from where it initially fell and deposited the whole of the treasure into a larger, far better concealed river.

"Walter Drake, a lowly farmer, was able to collect the entire horde of gold coins and precious artifacts from that very river. It is believed the family utilized the money slowly and carefully over the years. How else do you suppose this beautiful house was built and the land purchased?"

"I didn't know." I looked around. "But—"

"Why is the treasure hidden now? What happened to it, you ask?" He angled forward. "Josiah Drake happened to it."

"If I understand, he was a pirate."

"No, he had other interests. His son, Christopher, was the pirate . . . or rather the adventurer."

"The one who died at sea?"

"Precisely. When old Josiah Drake realized he had but a few months left to live and his son was still abroad, he hid the treasure and left a clue in his will only his son might be able to solve. It never dawned on the old bat that his son might never return to claim it."

I held up the paper. "Then how did Miss Drake come upon this? That was generations ago."

"That clue has been written into every will since that day. Josiah Drake had it included into an entail."

"And none of the Drakes found the treasure over the years?"

"None that we know of."

"Wait." My muscles pulled tight. "If the clue is in the will . . ."

"Lt. Burke will be receiving it tomorrow from his solicitor when he arrives to go over the specifics of his inheritance."

"But that would give him"—my stomach turned—"a possible motive for murder." I stared down at the riddle in my hand. "Did Miss Drake have any ideas about the clue? Did the two of you uncover anything?"

"She never got a chance to say."

My eyes widened. "What do you mean?"

"Last night in the drawing room, hours before her death, she told me she'd figured something out. We planned to meet this morning, first thing, but she never made it, did she?"

"No . . ."

Arnold covered my hand with his and squeezed gently. "Be careful, Miss Radcliff. The information you now possess is terribly valuable—information someone has already killed for."

Six

Constable Humphries vowed to meet with every last resident of Avonthorpe Hall that very afternoon and went to work turning the house upside down. In fact, the haste with which he attacked the house did nothing but frighten me. Cabinets were searched, furniture moved, servants questioned. Miss Drake had been murdered, and it seemed we were all to be suspects.

Thus I was ordered into the sitting room on the first floor at the start of his pointed examinations, a lump in my throat, the clue to the treasure still tucked in my pocket. After all, I had been the one to find Miss Drake dying on the floor—the last to see her alive.

Though I'd observed our parish constable from afar on more than one occasion, he proved up close to be a pudgy, unsettled sort of man, his boorish looks made worse by a bulbous nose and a pair of pinched eyes. He'd donned brown trousers that looked a tad tight and a shabby jacket that he adjusted the second I walked into the room.

A curt nod and he whipped his truncheon at the sofa before once more utilizing the wooden rod as a cane. "Please have a seat, Miss Radcliff."

I did as instructed, perching on the edge of the cushion as Constable Humphries paced the carpet. "Terrible business this is, I'm afraid."

"Yes." My voice came out weak, and I cleared my throat. "A tragedy."

"My one hope is to put this behind us as soon as possible. Not good for the village . . . or me." The skin on his nose tightened as he spoke, sending his reddened wrinkles jumping about. His pudgy fingers remained busy on the end of his truncheon, tightening and releasing. "The whole thing reminds me of the press-driven panic that gripped London in 1751. My grandfather used to tell me all about that time. You know, several homicides happened that year just like the one here. It was the reason he packed up and took my family to the country in the first place. How that evil has followed me from London I cannot guess. There have been reports of an alarming nature about thefts all around these parts." A nervous swipe of his forehead preceded an even quicker glance at the door.

Made uncomfortable by his jerky movements, I found myself following his line of sight, but there was no one but us in the room. The distress persisted, however, and I adjusted my position on the sofa.

Most parish officers were volunteers chosen by the local magistrate, but none ever expected to be called in to investigate murder. And the man was right. There had been reports of thefts farther up the coast but no details regarding who had committed those crimes.

Constable Humphries was already held in particularly low regard in the area due to his refusal to arrest poachers earlier in the year. Murder was something else entirely. I watched his erratic pacing. Did he know something?

He halted before shuffling back a step or two. "I understand you found, uh, Miss Drake . . . the, uh, victim."

"Yes." I tried to keep my voice even. "She was on the floor in her bedchamber. She'd a bolt through her chest." As prompted, I recalled every last detail I'd experienced as best as I could remember, stopping short of the words Miss Drake and I had exchanged in regard to the treasure. Arnold had been right to encourage me to keep the clue secret. By the looks of the constable's sweaty forehead and shaky truncheon, he was not ready to hear the whole.

The interview continued with a number of questions about the scene before he finally lifted his eyebrows. "What do you remember about the other members of the household? What did you all do earlier in the evening?"

"Well . . ." I tethered my lower lip between my teeth. "We all gathered in the drawing room following dinner, the ladies straightaway, then the gentlemen after their port."

"Everyone was there?"

"Yes. Lt. Burke, Mr. Montague, Mr. Hill, Mr. and Mrs. Fagean, and Miss Chant . . . as well as a few servants from time to time."

"Did Miss Drake seem in distress at any time, or when she left the room?"

"Not particularly, but she had been a bit concerned about the unexpected arrival of her nephew earlier."

His eyebrows shot up. "Unexpected?"

"Well, yes, it seems he has business in the area. He did not write ahead to inform her of his plans."

Constable Humphries nodded slowly. "Is this a habit with him?"

"No, he rarely visits."

"Did you observe anything else over the course of the day that might have had a bearing on what happened last night? Anything I should be made aware of?"

"No . . . I don't believe so, only I have found the atmosphere in the house rather strange of late."

"What do you mean *strange*?"

"It almost feels as if everyone is on edge. Of course, Miss Drake was terribly focused on our improvements in the ballroom. We are woefully behind schedule and she'd planned to utilize the space as soon as possible."

"For a ball?"

I shrugged. "I assume so. She didn't really say, but what else would you use a ballroom for?"

"Who remained in the drawing room when you retired for the night?"

"No one. I was the last to leave by several minutes, as I was stowing Miss Drake's knitting away."

He dipped his chin. "I would like an account of when everyone left the room."

I had to think hard on that one. "Lt. Burke and Mr. Montague were the first to leave, then Miss Chant a few minutes afterward. The Fageans retired shortly after that, around the same time as Miss Drake, in fact. I remember now. Mrs. Fagean was rather vocal about a pounding headache that took both of the Fageans to their respective rooms."

"I see."

Did he? Really, any one of us could have waited in Miss Drake's bedchamber with the intent to kill.

"Anything else you wish to include about that night?"

I shook my head, the clue to the treasure still burning in my pocket. This murder was a great deal more complicated than Constable Humphries could imagine, and I certainly had proof of that, but could I trust him? Dare I trust him?

My pulse throbbed as I turned to the door. Not yet. Not that man. Miss Drake never would have wanted him to know. He was everything she despised in a person—no backbone, rather stubborn. I didn't stop for a breath until I'd reached the empty corridor beyond the landing where I was sure to be alone.

I plunged my hand into my pocket. Was I some sort of an accomplice now? I'd withheld evidence from the authorities. I shook my head. Everything in me told me I had to keep the treasure a secret. Miss Drake would have commanded me to, but there could be no justice for her at this rate. I had to find a way to stay at Avonthorpe to uncover the treasure and expose the fiend who had ruthlessly taken her life.

"What are you doing?"

The brush froze in my hand midstroke as an inadvertent blot formed at the cross of an elegant *X* in the trim work. I jerked away, mortified at my mistake, and sought a rag with which to wipe the paint before it dried. Thankfully the error left no lasting damage.

I let out a long breath and removed the spectacles I wore while painting before whirling to face the angry voice that could only belong to Lt. Burke. "You startled me, sir."

His eyes looked pinched as he ran his gloved fingers over his face. "I do apologize for upsetting you, but I'm at a loss as to why you are in here . . . working."

I made my way down the scaffolding to get a better view of his sour expression. "The frieze still needs to be completed. I thought doing this portion here would take my mind off of things."

He took a moment to inspect the walls, then just as long to look me over. "I can understand your need of a distraction, Miss Radcliff; however, there is no point in continuing with your work."

I'd never been the fidgety type, but I found myself rolling the brush back and forth in my fingers before thrusting it down at my side. "Surely you intend to have the room completed. I thought perhaps since I was here—"

"That I would hire you on to do so?"

"Not hire exactly. I'm not asking for any money, and I would need to speak with Daniel to see if he would be willing to stay and assist me."

He cocked an eyebrow. "A bit unconventional, don't you think?"

I straightened my back, well aware of what I was suggesting, and lifted my chin. "How so?"

I thought he meant to laugh, but the amusement was short-lived.

"My solicitor arrives this afternoon, and I plan to inform him I mean to lease the estate or even sell it."

I already knew his intentions, so I was forced into a display of mock surprise before returning to my original argument. Whatever happened, I had to find a way to stay at Avonthorpe for the time being if I was to decipher the clue to the treasure. I thought the trim the perfect excuse.

I softened my voice. "I've been told by your aunt there are very few artists in Britain who can so deftly recreate the intricate strokes of the original painter. I had to work with her for some time to achieve the perfection you see before you. And the completion of the renovation will only increase the value of the house."

"True, but . . . pardon my frankness, you would be an unmarried lady living in a bachelor's establishment." He flexed his jaw. "It would never do."

Luckily, I'd thought this through. "I'm already aware of the difficulty there. You see, my father pays Miss Chant's wages. He would certainly continue doing so if I was to stay in residence and complete the job I started."

"Your father"—he let out a wry laugh—"would have my head for such an arrangement."

I gave him a convincing smile. "You underestimate my powers of persuasion."

"Do I?"

"And Daniel will be here. We're childhood friends, you know. My father would feel secure with him and Miss Chant here to, uh, protect me."

Lt. Burke stood there a moment, mirroring my smile while staring at me in that calculated way of his. "How long will it take you to finish?"

My heart fluttered with hope. "Only a few weeks."

"Weeks." He spoke under his breath, then stared up. "I daresay that will stretch your father's patience . . . and mine."

"Then I shall double my efforts."

A haze of confusion entered his eyes before they narrowed in turn. "Why is this so important to you?"

"Please, your aunt and I began this renovation over a year ago. I want to do this for her, as a sort of tribute. Since the very beginning I've felt that I was simply acting as her eyes and her hands. I promised her I would do my best. I cannot leave our artwork unfinished. It meant far too much to her."

"It did."

"And if you mean to sell the place, the ballroom would need to be complete."

His shoulders relaxed a bit, his jaw slack. "If I decide to accept the arrangement, you must write to your father at once. If he commands you home, then we will have no choice but to comply. Understand?"

"I—"

"Two weeks. I haven't the resources for any longer. Convincing Daniel to stay, as well as completing this project, lands on your shoulders alone. Mr. Montague and I must see to our business as soon as possible. I want the two of you out of the way."

I nodded. "You won't be disappointed."

He continued to hold up his hand for a brief moment, lost, it seemed, as to what to say or do next, before managing a trite, "Well, I'll leave you to it then," and retreating from the ballroom.

I whirled to the scaffolding, a mix of dread and hope churning in my stomach. I'd been given exactly what I'd hoped for—a reprieve. Yet how on earth could I finish the trim and find the treasure in the time allotted? My legs felt heavy as I climbed the wooden ladder to return to work. After all, Miss Drake had been hunting for the jewels for twenty years, and I was only just starting.

Seven

"MAYBE IF WE CONSIDER EACH LINE ONE AT A TIME, WE MIGHT discover something we can use." Miss Chant rested her head on her hands as she poured over the clue one more time. "Twelve little men."

I leaned forward on the drawing room sofa and pressed my shoulder tight against hers, all my thoughts trained on the clue in her hand. "Twelve. What on earth could that signify?"

It had taken me all of five minutes to decide to include Miss Chant in the treasure hunt. I had little chance of escaping her presence over the next two weeks, and there was no one else I trusted with my life. Besides, if we did indeed find the jewels, her problems would be over. My first transaction would be to finance her trip to America.

She tapped her cheek. "Could the number twelve refer to the months of the year? Or maybe the twelve days of Christmas?"

"See here." I pointed to the line on the paper. "It says twelve men from the *dark* and twelve men from the *light*. That doesn't sound very much like Christmas to me."

"No. Indeed it does not." She glanced away in thought. "I suppose the twelve men from the light could represent the twelve disciples of Jesus."

I scrunched up my nose, digesting her words. "But the disciples wouldn't be at war with anyone else."

"And I don't see how warring disciples would have anything to do with where Josiah Drake hid the treasure." She covered her mouth with her hand. "Let's skip down to the part about the First Duke of

Marlborough. He was a famous general from the late 1600s, right? Do you know anything more about him?"

"A little. It's been several years since I last had a governess, and I daresay my history is a bit rusty." I thought back through my studies. "If I remember correctly, the Duke of Marlborough fought and won some significant battles against King Louis XIV of France, who was the most powerful man in Europe during that time." I froze a moment, then sat up straight. "In fact, I believe there's a statue of the duke in the town square."

Miss Chant's eyes widened. "A starting point perhaps."

"Indeed, I—"

A door slammed in the distance, then a cluster of footsteps echoed in the hall. Miss Chant and I stared at the closed door in anticipation, but the walkers passed by.

I nudged her, my voice at a whisper. "If I had to guess, that would be Lt. Burke's solicitor on his way out of the house."

"If you're right, then that would mean they've been meeting for hours."

A sinking feeling weighted my stomach. "And Lt. Burke is in full possession of not only the house but also the clue to the treasure as well. I daresay they've had time to cover the will in its entirety."

Miss Chant picked at her fingernails, her eyes flitting back and forth to the door. "Do you still think it unwise to trust him? After all, it is part of his inheritance."

My posture slumped. "I have considered Lt. Burke's unfortunate place in all this from every angle." My toes curled in my shoes. "And I've thought over what we are about to attempt a thousand times, yet how can we take any other path? Miss Drake implored me not to involve anyone besides Arnold, and Graham Burke only stands to inherit Avonthorpe because of the entail. He means to lease it as soon as possible."

Miss Chant pursed her lips. "He made that declaration before he had possession of the clue. Everything may have changed now."

"Possibly, but we can hardly take the chance." I frowned. "And you cannot deny there's still one terribly important question we cannot dismiss entirely. What if he was involved in her murder? Miss Drake told me she didn't want him to have the treasure."

Miss Chant drifted sideways against the sofa cushion, her hands clasped. "You don't think?"

"I don't know what to think." I joined her against the cushion. "Someone committed an unthinkable act just two days ago. Why not Lt. Burke? He has the most to gain."

"But his own aunt?"

"Who was oddly upset at his sudden arrival. Why was that?"

Footsteps resounded again, louder this time, and Miss Chant and I jerked away from each other, the two of us perching on the sofa's edge and smoothing our skirts, ready to take on whoever meant to join us.

Lt. Burke pushed through the drawing room door before jerking to a halt. Just as quickly and self-consciously, he straightened his shoulders. "Good afternoon, ladies."

I returned something of a smile, shirking off the prickle of nerves tightening my muscles. "Good afternoon, Lieutenant." I dipped my chin. "We've not seen you these past few hours or more. A long meeting with your solicitor?"

"Indeed," he said as he wandered across the carpet, eventually collapsing into an opposing chair. "There was a great deal to discuss in regard to the entail. I've planned another meeting with him tomorrow."

"Have you reconsidered letting the place?"

"I'm afraid not." He drummed his fingers on the armrest, a palpable urgency to the movement. "You do understand that I have little choice in the matter?"

Miss Chant took a sip of tea, carefully meeting my gaze over the rim of her cup. "It was a difficult decision, I'm sure."

"Terribly difficult. I . . ." His gaze snagged on something across the room for the merest second, but he quickly pretended otherwise. "I . . ." He rubbed his forehead before stealing another shrewd glance in the direction of the fireplace. A light chuckle. "You know, I don't even remember what I was going to say."

Miss Chant adjusted her position on the sofa. "I can well understand your difficulty. Anyone would be exceedingly distracted with what you have had to bear."

He nodded slowly but with little conviction, as if all his energy were expended resisting one more glance across the room.

I narrowed my eyes. This sudden distraction of his had little to do with his aunt's murder. No. He'd made a discovery, one that had his full attention. I was certain of it. Something to do with the clue perhaps? Yes. I knew that wide-eyed wonder well enough. After all, I'd been looking at the house differently all day, but he could do little with the two of us watching him.

He casually pushed to his feet, but there was intention to his movements. It seemed he meant to try. He mumbled over his shoulder, "I daresay I should stoke the fire. It's nearly died out."

I squeezed Miss Chant's hand as I watched Lt. Burke saunter over to the fireplace. What did he know? Breathless seconds of anticipation ticked away in my chest until I too popped to my feet and trailed him to the fire.

I moved in quite close, following his line of sight. It had something to do with the fireplace surround.

He rested his arm on the mantel before absently poking at the fire.

Certain he'd give away little else, I cleared my throat. "Thank you. My hands were getting quite cold."

Even through the thick fabric of his superfine jacket, I could feel the sudden bristling of his arms a split second before he whipped to face me, a bit of a flush about his cheeks.

He stared a moment before he managed a droll smile. "It certainly has been unseasonably cold this year."

"Yes. It has."

I heard an amused sort of sigh beneath his words, and I waited for him to add something more, assuming he'd toss out some trite, meaningless attempt at conversation, but I was wrong. The air was silent yet electric between us, and I struggled to make sense of my erratic heartbeat. Was it simply the idea of a challenge, driven in part by my secret knowledge he now held the clue? Or was it something else entirely?

We stood just so, scrutinizing each other like two tigers waiting to pounce.

Which is precisely when I saw it. A plaster figure of a soldier carved into the base of the surround. The man had a long sword that ran the length of the scrolled line and pointed to the ground.

My eyes snapped up.

Cultivate deep the blackened tip of the First Duke of Marlborough's favorite sword . . .

There was no doubt in my mind any longer. Lt. Burke most certainly had the clue. He must have marched directly into the drawing room to check his first thought—the sword on the fireplace.

But this coy figure was not the Duke of Marlborough. Miss Chant and I were already ahead of him. He hadn't thought of the statue in town as of yet.

I believe I might have smiled as I turned to face Miss Chant. "It's actually getting quite late and we've yet to dress for supper."

She opened her mouth to protest when she caught the dangerous look in my eye and swayed to her feet. "You're perfectly right. Good day, Lt. Burke."

He held up his hand, stalling us. "One more thing. Mr. Haskett has agreed to join us for dinner to discuss the upcoming sale of my antiques."

I lifted my eyebrows. "A visitor? Before the funeral?"

He sighed. "It cannot be helped."

"I understand." I rose and joined Miss Chant on her way to the door.

He bowed as I passed, an inaudible salutation for me, but his thoughts were a million miles away, his gaze retreating once more to the fireplace. Not "wasting every second of his paltry life looking for the treasure" indeed. He was as bewitched as every other Drake before him, determined to solve the mystery. Miss Chant and I would have little chance to stay ahead of a man of his intelligence if we did not do the same.

Graham Burke was clever, but so was I. The race was most decidedly on.

Much to my chagrin, Miss Chant convinced me to postpone the excursion to Lord Marlborough's statue till the morrow as there was not enough time before Mr. Haskett's arrival and we most assuredly needed to be present.

Consequently supper proved a dull affair, the inhabitants of Avonthorpe Hall still mummified with grief over Miss Drake's death, and Mr. Haskett a strange addition, his appearance and behavior at odds with my expectations.

I'd been told he was a landed gentleman and neighbor, a notable resident of the village of Crossridge, but his clothes, though somewhat fashionable, were most certainly out of date. His pockets betrayed patches of loosened thread at the corners and his wide collar housed a discolored line that dipped beneath his dark hair. He spoke readily enough, yet his responses held a practiced quality as if he focused a bit too hard on his words. And worse, over bites of mutton a large silver pocket watch with a fleur-de-lis engraved on the outside emerged from his jacket pocket. His eyes slid to Mrs. Fagean with an odd intensity.

My fork froze in my hand. How well did the two of them know one another?

Miss Drake's funeral was planned for later that night, and the enormity of what lay ahead for the gentlemen descended on the group at the tail of the meal, particularly Daniel, who picked at his dessert.

He'd agreed to stay on at the house for a few weeks to assist me in finishing the trim work, but reluctantly. And later as I watched him enter the drawing room with the other gentlemen following their port, I began to question if I should have asked him to remain at all. There was a morose quality to his bearing, a fatalistic edge to his countenance.

I motioned him to join me at the bow-window seat and settled in beside him, feeling even more keenly the distance between us. I waited a moment for some spark of life, but nothing came. "I'm worried about you."

A wan look of incredulity settled in his eyes as he lifted his chin. "Me? Why?"

I had to work to keep my voice steady. "You don't look yourself at all."

I waited a silent pause as his lips toyed with his thoughts. "I've never . . ." He let out a long sigh. "The world is a far more confusing place than I once thought."

I stole a glance at Mr. Haskett and Mrs. Fagean, who had settled on the sofa. "I can certainly agree with that sentiment."

Daniel tucked his hands beneath the sides of his legs as if he were a small boy. "A part of me longs to leave this house, to escape the realities of Miss Drake's loss, but I have a feeling this wretched emptiness will only follow me home." He touched my hand. "And I know you need me here."

"Please . . . You needn't stay if you feel it best to depart. I shall get on well enough with Miss Chant. And with a little hard work, I daresay I can finish the frieze soon enough."

He let out a small laugh. "No, you can't. It's a beast of a project and you know it."

"True, but I don't like what I see in you right now."

He nodded slowly. "I won't deny Miss Drake's murder has shaken me to the core. Just like that, all my hopes for the future are gone. I daresay my father will not allow me to take another position like this one. He never approved of my being an artist. Miss Drake was a special arrangement." Then he gave his head a little shake. "Moreover, I've always believed people are inherently good, that the world, in general, is a safe place, but I suppose it's time I grew up."

"Tragedy is unfortunately a part of life, but I do understand what you're getting at. This death, this sudden change, feels different."

He motioned across the room. "Mrs. Fagean seems to be handling our teacher's passing a great deal better than the two of us. Can you believe she mentioned to me at supper that she means to attend the Equinox Festival in the town square? I cannot fathom doing so, not after we put Miss Drake to rest tonight."

"People cope in different ways. Perhaps she's in need of a distraction."

"Or she's as coldhearted as I always imagined."

I nudged his arm. "Don't concern yourself with the Fageans. I'm afraid doing so will only disappoint you."

"Quite right." He stood. "Care for a drink? That, *I* am in need of."

"No, thank you . . . and, Daniel." I rose beside him. "If you ever need to talk, I'm always here. We shall have several hours just the two of us as we work on the ballroom."

He gave me a tight-lipped smile—"I know that"—and walked away.

Disturbed by the uncomfortable nature of our conversation, I wandered about the room before making my way to the pianoforte, intent on a moment of solitude. Mrs. Fagean, having left Mr. Haskett to her husband, however, slid onto the bench beside me.

As the only other lady residing in the house, she'd been rather clingy of late. I suppose she felt it her duty to check in with me from time to time. Unfortunate that she always chose the worst moments.

She gave a diminutive sigh as she ran her fingers through the music on the stand, her eyes ticking in my direction. "Care for a duet? We've not played together in months."

I was slow to agree but did so with a tight nod, and she situated a Sonata in D Major at the front of the music stand and made quite a show of settling her fingers on the keys. However, she didn't strike the first note. "That boy is too young for you, Phoebe. You mustn't encourage him."

My hands unwittingly flexed into the opening chord. "By *boy*, I presume you mean Daniel. And I wholeheartedly agree I should not encourage him. There has never been anything romantic between us. He and I have always been like brother and sister."

The song she'd selected was familiar and thankfully did not require a great deal of focus. Clearly Mrs. Fagean only wished to talk as she joined the duet at a snail's pace. "Good, because I find him terribly straitlaced and a bit asinine."

"Daniel?"

She pursed her lips, her focus fixed on the music. "He gave me his opinion about my attending the festival tonight, and it wasn't very kind."

On edge, I finished the musical bar before answering. "Have you considered he might be right this time?"

She shot me a pert little frown. "Don't be absurd. I shall wear my blacks like a good girl and I don't mean to dance. But the equinox comes only once a year, and—"

"Twice a year."

"The festival I mean, my little bluestocking. And I promised my friend Mary I would accompany her and her brother. The celebration is designed to bless the spring after all. It's a renewal so to speak.

Twelve hours of daylight and twelve hours of night. There's such a beautiful precision to that balance. I've always felt it in my soul."

My heart took a wild turn, and I was forced to gloss over a wrong note. Twelve hours of night and day—the equinox!

I steadied my attention on the notes, trying desperately not to expose my racing thoughts. Could the solution to the clue be that simple? Could the twelve soldiers at war be referring to a specific moment in time? The only hour twice a year that the location of the treasure could be deciphered? My fingers tingled. The clue had also mentioned sunrise—it had to be the first part.

I disengaged from Mrs. Fagean the instant our duet was complete and made my way to Miss Chant, where she sat knitting in the corner.

She sensed the excitement in my manner at once, tugging me in close. "What is it?"

I took a mad glance about the drawing room, afraid to say too much in company. "Meet me at five o'clock in my room tomorrow morning. I believe it is the perfect time to take a walk."

A knot formed on her brow. "So early? And before sunrise?"

I couldn't help but smile as I met her startled gaze. "I daresay such an early walk shall prove to be quite rewarding."

She angled her chin, her slow smile stretching out to match my own. "Shall I bring a shovel?"

In that moment of excitement I felt a presence at my back and turned to find Mr. Haskett quite close, scrutinizing a painting.

He gave me a crooked smile, wrinkling the lines of a scar I hadn't noticed on his cheek. "Mr. Fagean tells me you are an artist."

Miss Chant returned to her knitting and I took a step closer to the man. "Yes, I was training under Miss Drake."

He motioned to a small painting beside the window of two gentlemen I didn't recognize. "You know, I've never stepped foot inside Avonthorpe before now."

"I-I wasn't aware." That would explain his nervousness at dinner.

"The Drakes have always been rather haughty isolationists." A glance across the room. "I do hope Lt. Burke will improve this place."

Isolationists? My shoulders tightened as I thought back over the two years I'd been in residence. Though Miss Drake had spoken often of entertaining, she never really had. "I didn't realize."

He pointed to the shorter gentleman in the painting. "Take Christopher Drake here—"

I jerked forward. "This is Josiah's son's likeness?"

"And the partner he took on all his adventures, a Mr. Ruteledge—the man on the left there. See the ear trumpet in his hand with the engraved *R*? He lost nearly all his hearing in one ear after he and Christopher had their first shipwreck."

Mr. Haskett shook his head. "It may be legend or simply rumor, but my family has always said the Drakes blamed Ruteledge for the second shipwreck that took Christopher's life. It created quite a rift between the families. Words were exchanged—threats."

"They thought this Mr. Ruteledge should be held accountable?"

"And he thought he was due his portion of the business."

I studied the man in the painting a bit closer, his narrow face and dimpled chin. "What ended up happening?"

"Ruteledge left in disgrace with little more than the clothes on his back." Mr. Haskett shrugged. "It's said that people in the village didn't take too kindly to the way he was treated by the Drakes. Bad blood can last for centuries, you know. Just think about what happened in Scotland with the clans."

"Then why would the family keep this painting?"

He huffed. "Probably due to that blasted entail. Josiah Drake made it impossible for anything in the house to be changed." Mr. Haskett eyed the painting a second longer. "That's Christopher Drake all right . . . and Mr. Ruteledge. I know because our families were quite cordial at one time. In fact, we've a similar painting at my estate, one with my own ancestor included of course. Both of the paintings were done by Jean-Marc Nattier. Have you heard of—"

"A Frenchman?"

A gentle smile. "That's right. My great-grandmother's side of the family were all French. She asked Nattier to Crossridge for a visit long ago and quite graciously he came. Did several paintings at the time."

"Extraordinary."

Mrs. Fagean made a sweeping move across the room and Mr. Haskett's eyes flicked away from mine, his words little more than a mumble. "Strange what people will do for family. Excuse me, Miss Radcliff." And he stalked away.

Eight

The Equinox Festival took place every year at midnight in the town square and involved a great deal of poetry, the tossing of seeds, and a country dance, which rarely drew any respectable members of the village of Crossridge. I'd not been allowed to attend the vulgar celebration any of the years I'd been in residence. Thus I was shocked to hear a cackle of laughter as Miss Chant and I neared the square so early the following morning.

We tied off our horses near the dressmaker's shop, and I motioned Miss Chant into the shadows of the building. "You don't think the villagers could still be celebrating at this hour, do you?"

Miss Chant shrugged. "Surely not."

The crisp morning air splashed my face as I crept along the shop's stone wall and peered around the corner. The square had been transformed. Clusters of flowers surrounded every available space and seeds blanketed the ground. The sight was beautiful really, a remnant of hope for the planting season ahead.

But a chill wriggled up my back—the streets were deserted. So who had I heard just a few moments ago?

Miss Chant spoke in a whisper. "It's almost six thirty. We need to hurry."

I inched forward and saw a flash of black. I thrust Miss Chant to a halt and pressed my finger to my lips. A quick gesture with my head. "Mr. Haskett . . . and Mrs. Fagean?"

There in the shadows of the jewelry store stood Mrs. Fagean

shoulder to shoulder with our illustrious neighbor. Their hands were quite close, but I couldn't exactly tell if they were indeed touching. My muscles tightened as I squinted into the dim light. Mr. Haskett shifted and I caught sight of the familiar scar running down his left temple.

My arm ached from the icy cold of the stone wall and I could feel Miss Chant's hesitation behind me, but I wouldn't dare move an inch, not until I knew what the pair was up to. If only I could make out what they were saying.

Then I saw it—a coy flex of Mrs. Fagean's hand, then a rakish smile. She was openly flirting with a man who was not her husband.

The Equinox Festival indeed. She'd left home on the night of Miss Drake's funeral for one reason alone—to meet Mr. Haskett. The question was—why?

Miss Chant grew even more restless at my back as the first ray of sunlight peeked over a nearby roof. "We're running out of time."

As if Mrs. Fagean were somehow privy to our growing anxiety, she thrust her cloak over her golden hair and stalked out of the shadows. With her head bowed, she stomped diagonally across the square away from us toward Avonthorpe, disappearing from view at the terminus of the lane. Mr. Haskett, however, was not so keen to depart, resting against the wall like a statue as the sound of Mrs. Fagean's light tread vanished into the quiet of the morning. Lord Marlborough's stone form presided over the entire affair.

But for the folds of his greatcoat fluttering in the breeze, I might not have been able to see the man withdraw into the kiss of sunlight illuminating the edge of the square. I would have preferred to remain hidden for some time, to ensure the secrecy of our mission, but the hour was ticking away.

Carefully Miss Chant and I crept forward to the base of the massive statue, and I scrounged for the clue in my pelisse pocket before holding it in a patch of light.

Precisely at daybreak when twelve little men from the dark fight twelve little men from the light and it is declared a draw . . .

We were certainly in the right place at the right time, but what now?

. . . cultivate deep the blackened tip of the First Duke of Marlborough's favorite sword.

I glanced up at Lord Marlborough's blade as it glistened in the morning light. "His sword's not black at all. What can that indicate, do you think?"

Miss Chant's lips scrunched up at the corners. "What does *cultivate* even mean?"

"Doesn't it have something to do with planting crops or gardening?"

Miss Chant laughed to herself. "I don't think his lordship was much of a gardener."

I paced around the base of the statue, nudging off a few of the festival flowers for a better look. Could something be etched into the rock?

Cultivate deep?

I stopped short. "A hole. *Cultivate* can mean 'dig.' It must mean we should dig a hole. And the black sword! Miss Chant, it's the shadow. See there."

The shade from Lord Marlborough's sword, made enormous by the angle of the sun, plunged across the square and pointed to the base of a large oak tree.

Miss Chant was steps ahead of me, the shovel stretched out in front of her. "This has to be it."

I heard the slam of a door in the distance and rushed to her side. "We'd better be quick. People will be up and about soon."

"Agreed." She slammed the shovel into the hard earth over and over again until she tired and I took up the mantle.

The earth was well compacted beneath the tree but loosed with each thrust. I swiped the sweat from my forehead before regripping the handle and plunging it once more into the hole we'd opened. The shadow of Lord Marlborough's sword had already retreated several feet from where we stood when we finally heard the *chink* of metal. The shovel had found something.

A few more wild passes and the shape of a large, smooth rock emerged, far too heavy for two small women to unearth and move. "What now?"

Miss Chant leaned forward and took a swipe at the loose dirt. "Wait, I think I see writing etched here."

I tossed the shovel to the ground and knelt at her side. She was right. Something had been carved into the stone. I brushed away the remaining damp dirt until we could see the inscription in its entirety.

An artistic beauty holds both life and death at your mother's pleasure. Hurry, my boy. It's all for you.

We sat up and stared at each other a moment as my hands fell lifeless into my lap. "It's just another clue. I-I didn't realize."

Miss Chant was a little winded. "How many clues do you think old Josiah left for his son?" She frowned. "I'm beginning to worry this hunt may take a great deal longer than we originally thought. What if it's impossible?" She brushed a stray hair off her forehead. "Honestly, we have no way of knowing whether anyone has found this clue before. There's no way to move the stone. All we can do is simply re-cover it." Her body slumped inward. "And here I thought we'd done it . . . solved all our problems. A bit of a disappointment, I must say."

I grasped her arm, fighting back my own frustration. "We have no choice. All we can do is take this one step at a time, hmm? We figured out the first clue. We can just as easily do so with the second."

She threw her hands in the air. "But this one doesn't make any sense."

I stared down at the stone. "No. Not on first read, but we shall put our minds to work on it. I—"

The sound of horses approaching rent the morning air, and a wave of tension filled my chest. Miss Chant's hands were moving before I could even process what was happening. "Make haste. They mustn't see."

We clawed at the small mound of dirt, tumbling it back into the hole time and again until every last inch was replaced. Then we hopped to our feet and stomped down the disturbed earth. My gloves were filthy, my hair wrangled.

Miss Chant thrust me a step into the square just as the first horse rounded the corner. "Hide the shovel in the bushes. We took an early morning ride, right? Nothing more. Oh dear, it's him."

Every muscle in my body twitched as an invisible vise tightened around my heart, but I managed a passable, "Good morning," as Lt. Burke dismounted and bowed his head.

Mr. Montague slid from his horse a second later and dashed a smile. "We've all had an early morning, I see."

My mind was a whir of motion, but I knew I had to answer him. "I found I couldn't sleep following the events of yesterday, and as you see, Miss Chant was kind enough to accompany me for an outing."

"I am sorry to hear you're distressed." Mr. Montague tipped his hat. "Trouble with sleep tends to run in my family. My mother, of course, swore by laudanum, but I'd not recommend such a habit."

Miss Chant dipped her head. "Certainly not."

"Like you, I prefer exercise." He nodded slowly. "It has been a difficult few days . . . all to be expected, I suppose." He turned to Lt. Burke. "Shall we escort the ladies back to the house?"

Lt. Burke's eyes widened. "I . . . yes."

"Please." I jerked up my hand with little thought. "I'm sure the two of you have business that brought you to town. Miss Chant and I are happy enough to continue on our way. Our horses are actually just over there."

Lt. Burke saw the discoloration of my glove and his eyes narrowed, his focus darting awkwardly to the stains on my gown as well. Finally he looked up with a shrewd glance of his own. "Have you met with an accident, Miss Radcliff?"

"Hardly." I puffed out a laugh. "I did take a small tumble onto the ground. I'm afraid I can be rather clumsy at times."

Mr. Montague extended his arm. "All the more reason to accept our escort back to the house. Now I won't take no for an answer. The four of us won't be at Avonthorpe long, and I don't mean to waste a moment of it. Come along, Graham."

Lt. Burke edged in beside Miss Chant, his voice a bit choppy. "Mr. Montague is correct. We've no set engagements at present and shall be happy to accompany the both of you on your morning ride."

I waited until the perfect moment to cast Miss Chant a hard look. Thankfully she returned a wink. I could only hope she'd set the clue to memory, because I hadn't the least chance of it now. I gave my escort a small smile. After all, Mr. Montague was rather handsome, and I was becoming a bit more confident we'd kept our true intentions a secret. That is, until I saw Lt. Burke take a long look over his shoulder at the tree.

He knew. My heart crumbled.

Just as quickly, he turned back to me, narrowing his eyes once again and angling his chin. My stomach lurched.

The situation was even worse—he knew I knew.

Nine

I SPENT THE REMAINDER OF THE MORNING IN THE CHAPEL for services, and a great deal of the afternoon holed up with Daniel in the ballroom, where we tackled a good section of the trim work. Conversation was nonexistent, our thoughts clearly elsewhere.

I didn't allow myself to step away until nearly suppertime, when I went to the drawing room in search of Miss Chant and instead came face-to-face with Mrs. Fagean alone as she drizzled. I was forced to hide my disappointment.

Mrs. Fagean beckoned me over at once. "Come see the progress, my dear. I shall have my pin money by the end of the week." She held up the corner of the tapestry she'd been working on for my inspection. The special spools she used to hold the silver and gold threads tumbled from her lap.

"I can see you've put in a great deal of work." I took a hesitant seat at her side. Though Mrs. Fagean's strange activities of the previous night had me vastly curious, I'd only the clue on my mind, and Miss Chant and Arnold were the only ones I could discuss it with. I didn't mean to stay long.

She nestled the loose spools back in her tortoiseshell drizzling box and gave me a wan smile. "The threads are quite fragile."

"I'm sure they are." My focus drifted to the window then back. "How was the festival?"

A tinge of pink lit her cheeks. "It was lovely. Mary recited a poem she'd written and Mr. Haskett provided all the seeds." She adjusted the tapestry off her lap. "We had a great time tossing them about . . . and then we danced in the moonlight."

My eyes widened. "I thought you only meant to watch."

"La, I only danced once. I couldn't help it, and rest assured it was at the very end of the night. Most people had gone by then. I-I've never really cared what people think, you know." Her body became very still. "Sally Drake knew what she meant to me. It's no one else's business but hers."

"No. But people do talk."

Her chin popped up. "Then let them. I don't care a fig for my reputation. Not since . . ."

I couldn't help but lean forward, waiting for the close of the sentence, but it never came. Instead she folded the tapestry and settled it next to her. "I only care about what happens to you. Where will you go when the trim is complete?"

I hadn't expected the raw emotion I saw in her eyes, and I turned away. "Back home to Middlecrest and my father. I have few options."

"I wish"—she found my hand—"well, I wish we could give you a home here, but . . ."

I squeezed her fingers. "Lt. Burke means to let the house. I've already heard."

Mrs. Fagean snapped rigid, her hand contracting like a claw. "Let the house!"

"I thought you knew."

She pushed to her feet. "Then he means to toss us all out."

I rose beside her and we made our way to the window. "Not toss, I hope. It's the money. There simply isn't enough of it to keep up the place."

Tears spilled from her eyes as her hands quivered at her waist. "If only he'll meet with Mr. Fagean. He hasn't yet, you know. Refused him left and right."

"He's been busy with his solicitor." One look and I saw what I'd not seen before—desperation. "Among other things."

She gave herself a little shake. "Yes, I'm sure it will all take some time to arrange the details and move forward with his plans. Mr. Fagean will know what to do." She seemed lost as she looked about the room. "I should get back to my drizzling."

"And I need to find Miss Chant." I took a step back, then paused. "Are you well, Mrs. Fagean?"

She plastered on a smile, but her gaze was fixed. "As well as can be expected. I should not have stayed out so late last night. The whole ordeal has given me a ghastly headache." Without warning she took a wild swipe at the tapestry and box before smashing them to her chest. "I daresay I should go lie down in my bedchamber. If you'll excuse me."

She bustled past me without even a glance back into the room, which only sent my mind racing. How could Mrs. Fagean possibly think Lt. Burke would allow her and Mr. Fagean to stay on indefinitely? And she wasn't simply upset. She was disturbed.

I folded my arms as I slowly made my way to the door. What tie did the Fageans have to Avonthorpe? Moreover, why was Mrs. Fagean terrified to leave?

"You'll leave me no choice but to turn you off at once."

I stopped cold in the entrance hall, Lt. Burke's sharp voice tightening my muscles. Though the door to the billiards room was ajar, I couldn't quite see inside. Who on earth was he dressing down?

Lt. Burke's rant continued with little time for a breath. "I've told you time and again what I expect, and you defy me at every turn. How am I to keep you on at this rate?"

My shock had morphed into anger as first Arnold came to mind, then several of the maids. I knew very well Lt. Burke would eventually be forced to make arrangements for them, but this was not the way to go about it.

I handled the door roughly as I pushed inside, but Lt. Burke didn't seem to notice or care. He was across the room, facing sideways, his riding crop in one hand, which he tapped violently against his opposing palm. Clearly he'd just returned from a ride as mud decorated his boots and a layer of dust clung to the folds of his greatcoat. He'd trapped the recipient of his outburst behind a wide column at the side of the room out of view.

The word *sneer* popped into my thoughts as I took in the haughtiness on Lt. Burke's face. I'd found the man exacting in the past, but this gross display of authority was beyond bearing. He might be master of this house on paper, but while I was in residence I would not allow him to mistreat the servants in Miss Drake's former employ.

I jerked my way around the billiards table and planted my feet, readying myself for a scathing attack, but all too quickly the room shifted. Well, it barked really, and my arms fell lifeless to my sides.

Lt. Burke had been dressing down a large, terribly muddy Great Dane—or something like that. Still caught up in the moment, he must not have noticed my company, as his scowl faded and he extended the riding crop.

"Don't even think about it, Creature." Then he laughed. "This is not a game, nor is it playtime. Mr. Arnold will not think kindly to footprints all over his clean hall."

A large pink tongue fell out of the side of the animal's mouth, and it looked far too much like the dog was smiling. He pawed the air a moment, then flopped onto the floor.

Lt. Burke relaxed. "That's better." He stepped forward and I thought he meant to grasp the animal's collar, but he ran his hands over the enormous floppy ears instead. "You've a great deal to learn if you mean to be a proper dog for a landowner. My mother would never approve."

Then he lowered his voice, pretending to speak for the dog. "*But, Papa.*" Lt. Burke straightened now, his fingers wrapping around the collar. "No excuses, Creature. You'll have to stay in the stables for now."

Then he whirled about only to find me standing but a few feet away. "Oh."

There was an awkward moment of silence and all at once I realized I'd been intruding on a private moment. I gave myself a little shake, but I couldn't contain the smile on my face. "I didn't mean to intrude. I heard yelling. I—"

"Came to rout me."

Lt. Burke was far too astute for my liking. Of course he'd know just why I'd stomped inside. "Not exactly."

He cocked an eyebrow.

"All right. That was just what I was about." I stepped forward, then back into place. Good heavens, why couldn't I stand still? Then without thinking, "But I'm also the sort of person to admit when I'm wrong."

I'd intended some sort of a setdown at first, but now everything felt off. Lt. Burke seemed to be struggling too as he avoided my eyes, running his free hand along the edge of the billiards table.

I opened my palms and shrugged. "How long have you had your dog?"

"Creature?"

I petted the fluffy shoulder. "A perfect name for this one."

Lt. Burke wrestled a lead from his pocket and fastened it to the dog's collar. "Can you believe a few years?" He laughed to himself. "I daresay he should be a bit more trained by now."

I mirrored his laugh. "And you are thinking of . . . *turning him off.*"

"I do threaten him with that from time to time"—a sheepish smile—"to keep him honest, of course."

"Hmm. And how is that working for you?"

Lt. Burke's smile widened and his skin crinkled near his eyes. "Not well, I'm afraid."

He motioned me through the billiards room door, and I found myself accompanying the pair across the square entryway. There was a fevered lightness to Lt. Burke's steps as he guided his dog beside us, a distinct softness about his tone.

"Creature here's a bit of a sneak."

I paused at the front entryway. "That humongous animal, a sneak?"

Lt. Burke popped open the door and stepped forward to demonstrate. "All I did was lean back just like this to take a look across the lawn and in he went. Didn't even see him at first. But I heard him. Oh, I heard him."

"And the footprints."

"Yes, how can I forget those?" Lt. Burke grasped the doorknob but waited for me to pass through, and we fell in step again.

"Did you always want such a large dog? For protection, I suppose?"

"Not at all. My mother had a pug she adored, and I thought I might get one of those, but Creature wandered across my path the same day I lost a dear friend of mine on the Continent. I couldn't turn him away."

"I'm so sorry."

Lt. Burke extended his arm. "My friend didn't die. I-I didn't mean to give you that impression."

I slid my fingers onto his blue superfine jacket in the crook of his elbow, the afternoon wind encouraging the warmth. "What happened then?"

He angled us onto the gravel path that led to the stables. "It was a betrayal in every way possible. I shan't go into the particulars, but it involved the French and a woman. Needless to say, it was a difficult time for me."

The French, and a woman?

My throat thickened a bit as my own French involvement crept into the space between us and I pulled away. "Well, I . . . I am very glad to have met your dog at any rate." I gave him a small smile. "But I was on my way to meet with Miss Chant just now."

I could see the confusion in his eyes, but I had no intention of allowing him to see one twinge of guilt in my own. Jean Cloutier was my own affair, one he would never hear about.

He nodded as any gentleman would, but his voice seemed far away. "I'd better return this mongrel to his pen, then get to cleaning up those footprints."

"Yes. Good day, sir."

I slid away from him, my heart still tumbling about in my chest. Maybe it was the way he'd looked at his dog or the added depth to his smile, but the unexpected spark of friendship between us had surprised me.

He'd spoken of a betrayal, however, one that had affected him greatly. My shoulders felt heavy as I climbed the front steps. Could I handle one more person in my life who thought ill of my actions during my confusing time at Middlecrest Abbey? I'd come to Avonthorpe Hall to forget my past, to move beyond my terrible mistake, to learn who I really was apart from all that.

No, the last thing I needed was a constant reminder of what I'd done. Would I ever be free of my lapse of judgment? Would I ever be able to forgive myself?

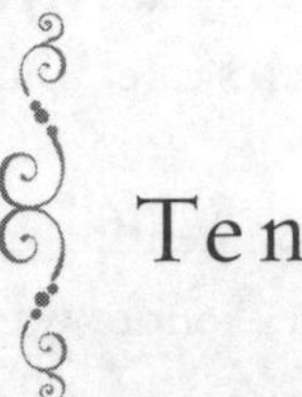

Ten

That night it rained—buckets and buckets—thankfully, as it had been unseasonably dry.

But as I sat in my window seat and stared out at a blackened night, all I could think about was the clue Miss Chant and I had found and the even greater fear that the water droplets might expose it. In all likelihood the rain would settle the disturbed earth and as soon as Miss Chant retrieved the shovel all traces of our early morning adventure would be lost to the storm. But there were others alerted to where we'd been and possibly what we'd been about.

Lt. Burke.

I ran my finger along the edge of my chintz drapes as the wry look on his face from earlier in the day popped into my mind, and a smile emerged. The fury with which he'd scolded that silly dog had not been real in the least . . . endearing more like. Clearly Creature had him wrapped around his paw. And he'd had the dog for years!

I rested against the window casing. It seemed Miss Drake's nephew had more layers to his personality than I'd first envisioned, certainly more than the military general Daniel and I had labeled him.

Suddenly restless, I fiddled with my dressing gown. Unquestionably I could not allow any more familiarity between us. After all, my path forward was clear. Miss Chant and I had little time in which to locate the treasure, and Lt. Burke was proving to be a formidable opponent.

The clock on my dresser pinged midnight, and I crossed the room to stoke the fire before settling into a nearby chair. Miss Chant would be here at any moment. I tucked my legs within my night rail and rubbed a bit of paint from the creases in my hand. Though I'd devoted most of the evening hours to the trim work, I still felt behind. Two weeks was not going to be long enough, and Daniel and I knew it.

The subtle *click* of the door latch drew my attention across the room, and I watched as Miss Chant slipped silently into the shadows of the interior. She perused the space a moment before locating me near the fire and advanced.

She seemed pleased as she plopped down in an opposing chair. "I've penned out the clue as best as I can remember it, and I've done a little research on Josiah Drake. So much of his hand is all over this house. Did you know he even had a stone installed in his pew at the church with an inscription? Something or other about the heart."

"Really?"

"One of the maids also told me he was a good friend of John Harrison, the clockmaker. Apparently back in 1714 the English Parliament offered a prize of twenty thousand pounds to anyone who could determine longitude at sea to within half a degree. Josiah worked with Harrison for this prize under the notion time was the key to solving the puzzle. Of course, no clocks at that time could be relied on at sea, so a marine chronometer was developed between the two of them. There's one of the originals still displayed on the library shelves."

I took a quick swallow. "I had no idea he was such an interesting man."

"Granted, though Harrison only ever got half the prize money and gave very little to Josiah, it was still a great discovery."

More curious than ever, I extended my hand. "Let me see what you wrote down."

She passed me a folded slip of paper, and I opened it in the firelight.

Artistic beauty holds both life and death at your mother's pleasure.

"The mother he's referring to would have been Annabella Drake." I pressed my lips together. "I don't know much about her."

Miss Chant rested her arm on the chair and tapped her fingers. "I wish we had someone to ask within the family."

"Perhaps Arnold, but it's been so very long."

"True." She shook her head, her attention on the words of the clue. "And there's something else you should be aware of."

"What is it?"

"Vincent stumbled upon Lt. Burke in town today. That would have been shortly after he escorted us home."

I sat forward. "You mean he went right back to the village."

"To the very spot."

I collapsed against my chair, flopping my arms loosely over the armrests. "Then we've done his work for him. He probably has the second clue now."

"I'm afraid it looks that way."

I grasped the paper with a renewed vigor. "We have no time to lose."

But all my hopes were in vain. The hours slipped by as we discussed what life and death could have possibly meant for Annabella Drake and what she might consider beautiful.

I sighed. "There's so little to go on."

Miss Chant's nose wrinkled at the bridge. "This may be where all the others were stumped."

I rubbed the back of my neck. "Why did he have to make the clue so personal, so difficult?"

"He thought his son was coming home. I daresay Christopher Drake would have known exactly what his father was referring to."

"It's like a slap in the face after all we've been through. We would have to know the man intimately to find the treasure."

She gave me a conciliatory smile. "I don't think Josiah was thinking about us . . . only his son. I can understand that."

A looming silence settled between us as sleep rested on my eyelids. I blinked a few times, a hazy memory emerging of a familiar figure. "I had a dream earlier . . . when I fell asleep a moment on the scaffolding before supper."

"Oh? Tell me it was a vision of what the clue meant."

"Quite the opposite actually." I roused myself enough to gauge her reaction. "I saw *him* again." A thoughtful pause. "Why is it that dreams feel so incredibly real at times?"

Her throat bobbed as she swallowed. "You're speaking of Cloutier."

"Lt. Burke told me something earlier today—that's all I can figure must have brought the dream on." Quieter then. "Someone in Lt. Burke's past betrayed him—a friend of his."

A hard look. "And, of course, you thought of Jean Cloutier."

"How could I not? The hurt was so evident in Lt. Burke's eyes, and it reminded me so much of Juliana's."

Miss Chant leaned forward, her elbows on her knees. "Your sister endured the worst sort of loss, but not because of you."

"That is what you all keep saying, yet it doesn't feel that way." I fumbled with the tie on my dressing gown. "Betrayal in any form cuts terribly deep. Lt. Burke seemed quite affected by it all."

"And . . ." She dipped her chin. "When did you start caring about Lt. Burke's feelings?"

A hint of warmth lit my cheeks and I glanced away. "Well, there was this dog . . ." I shook my head. "What I mean to say is that I saw a different side of the gentleman. I guess he just seems like the sort of person I might cry friends with. Is that so very bad?"

Her voice took a soft turn. "*Friends* now . . . interesting."

"Miss Chant!" I held up my hand. "Believe me, *acquaintances* shall do well enough for me and him." I repositioned myself on the chair.

"We'll have no more about that. We need to focus on the clue at present. How else are we going to get you to America with Vincent?"

She gathered the paper off the table before pausing to tap the edge, a curious look on her face. "Are you indeed over your calf love, Phoebe?"

"You mean with Cloutier?"

"Who else?" She pressed her lips together. "I thought you were, but a dream now after all this time—it does concern me. A first love can be a lasting one."

"I will confess, I do think of Jean from time to time, wondering what happened to him after my father turned him over to the authorities. I was told he was a terrible man, that he had a hand in my sister's fiancé's death. But the unknown can be a difficult place to find any sort of closure." I tipped my head back against the chair. "It's strange how memories affect us. Jean appeared in my dream just as I remember him on that last day, injured, his brown eyes so alive. It was moving in a way."

"Unresolved feelings, perhaps?"

"I don't know . . . I don't think so." I glanced off into the shadows. "It just all felt so familiar, like a missing part of me had finally returned. Odd that I was so glad to see him, considering I would never feel the same in real life."

"Certainly not. He's a dangerous man—a killer and a liar. You must never ever consider such a thing." Her lips seemed to quiver in the firelight. "You wouldn't, would you?"

My gaze snapped up to meet hers. "What do you mean? Jean Cloutier is probably dead or rotting in prison, soon to be so. He shall never cross my path again."

Contentment settled onto her face, but it was slow to come. "I'm glad to hear you say that." She took a long breath. "It's getting rather late. I should probably return to my room for tonight, but I promise you I'll continue working on the clue."

I didn't move from the fireside chair as she rose and stepped away, nor even when I heard the door click shut behind her. I was exhausted, yes. Goodness knows, my bed had been calling me for some time, but somewhere in the past half hour the feel of the room had changed. I was wide awake now, and something was nagging at me.

Did Miss Chant know more about Jean Cloutier than she was letting on? Though she and I had become fast friends, I could never forget she was in my father's employ, and he would do everything in his power to keep information about Cloutier from reaching my ears. I cast a shrewd look at the closed door. Was Miss Chant harboring a secret? Moreover, had Jean actually hung for his crimes like I'd assumed? Perhaps I'd been wrong all along.

The following morning, after a few hours' work in the ballroom, I took a walk alone to clear my mind and focus once again on the clue at hand.

A thing of beauty.

I stared down the sweeping hillside to the crisscrossing hedgerows and the meadows that stretched to the sky, then back up at the house where the dark stone structure towered over the valley like a king, its gray columns and crenelated parapets almost medieval in the foggy morning. Beauty could mean anything.

Was the garden a favorite of Annabella Drake? Perhaps she adored a particular sculpture located on the grounds? The only words from the clue I could really dissect related to the ideas of life and death. Surely that had to mean something. The cemetery . . . or something lethal? I'd already checked the household swords that hung on the wall and the chainmail in the hall. Nothing.

An hour later I returned to the house no better off than when I'd left and quite frankly a bit defeated. I plucked my bonnet from my head and pressed against the door only to hear a commotion at my back. I jerked about to see Lt. Burke racing across the manicured lawn, waving his hands in front of him.

"Don't let . . . the . . . please." His voice was terribly muffled by the wind, and it all happened so fast. First I was leaning forward, straining to hear, then a shadow bolted from the side of the house. I did whirl to face it, but I was far too late. Creature crashed into my legs before flinging himself straight into the cracked door and tearing through the entryway.

Lt. Burke was there in an instant, helping me back onto my feet. "I'm so sorry. Are you hurt?"

I dusted the dirt from my gown as I found my footing. "I don't think so." I had hit my head and it took me a moment to regain my bearing. It was then I realized I was gripping Lt. Burke's arm and quite severely at that. I released him at once.

But it was too soon. His arm circled my back. "I should get you inside where you can sit down."

I gladly took his arm once again and he led me into the cool, shadowed entrance hall where I gave a sigh of relief. "I do believe I'm a bit better now, thank you. I daresay I can manage on my own. You really should see to your dog." I gave him a smile as I stepped gingerly away. "I do apologize for not closing the door when asked. I've only now realized what you meant."

He juggled the lead in his hand before tucking his arms at his sides. "I'm sorry that I let that cursed dog off his lead. Why I trusted him, I'll never know. I'm only glad you weren't injured any worse."

I touched my head. "It wasn't really that bad."

His face flushed as he met my eyes and scraped his hand through his hair. His words seemed to come at me at random. "I am glad we met, however . . . I did want to ask you something . . . about the other day—"

A loud crash echoed through the hall and we jerked our attention to the back corridor.

"Oh no." Lt. Burke held his hand up as if to encourage me to stay put before he raced off, but I followed him nonetheless.

There at the terminus of the gallery, all the way across the parquet floor, lay Miss Drake's replacement Sèvres vase and Creature nursing an injured paw.

Lt. Burke's shoulders slumped as he wandered over and grasped the dog's collar.

Only a step behind him I paused and leaned down to pick up a large piece. "At least it was a fake. Can you imagine if it hadn't . . ." I caught sight of the agony in Lt. Burke's expression. "It was a fake . . . correct?"

He shook his head achingly slow.

My attention darted between the broken vase and his anguished face. "What do you mean? You said you'd replaced it. You gave Miss Drake a great deal of money to sell the original."

"I did give her money"—a long sigh—"but I also gave her back the original vase."

My mouth fell open. "You can't be serious."

He squatted down to collect the pieces he could. "My aunt has always been so cursed proud. She wouldn't take any money from me outright." A half-hearted shrug. "I came up with the idea of selling various artifacts to provide her with the money she needed to live. Avonthorpe Hall has been at a pass for some time now."

I examined the broken piece in my hand. "So you simply gave her back the originals and told her they were reproductions." My heart came to a standstill. "That means we just broke a *real* Sèvres vase?"

"Well . . . Creature did, and he's mine . . . so . . ."

"But I should have known what you were shouting at me and shut the door."

He wrapped the end of the lead around a heavy sideboard and tied it off. "Nonsense. It was a mistake . . . mine."

"Either way, you're out a great deal of money."

"True, but I had no intention of selling this particular vase. It was an artistic beauty, a favorite of the family. I've never seen another one—" He froze in place.

An artistic beauty.

The smooth porcelain tingled against my fingers. Artistic! I hadn't really considered that part of the clue. I stared down at the broken piece in my hands. That's when I saw it—an inscription on what would have been the inside bottom of the porcelain. I flipped the piece over.

Lt. Burke narrowed his eyes. "What did you see?"

"See?" I gave an unconvincing laugh, but we both knew we were on the same page.

"Life or death." He chuckled to himself. "I daresay a vase would be terribly important to a plant." He picked up one of the flowers. "Life or death, it seems." Then he tipped forward, his voice a fervent whisper. "You've been ahead of me thus far and it begs the question of how . . . and why. Whatever the reason, that stops now. What did my aunt tell you before she died?" He settled back, a strange look about his eyes. "I have a right to know."

And he did in a way. If everything he'd told me was the truth, he'd been keeping this house afloat for years, putting his aunt's needs above his own. A painful lump formed in my throat. I had no right to King John's jewels. I knew that now.

My shoulders felt heavy. "Your aunt told me where to find her copy of the same clue you received with the entail."

He stared in silence down the empty corridor behind me, obviously contemplating the depths of his aunt's choice. "Did she say anything else?"

His aunt had intimated she wanted the treasure for me, but I stilled my tongue. "Nothing of any consequence. She was quite scattered at the end."

He ran his hand down his face. "She must have thought a great deal of you to entrust you with something of such great importance."

"I-I couldn't say. All I know is I loved her dearly."

He watched me a moment. "You're like her in many ways—daring, impulsive, intelligent."

"And how could you know all that in the short time you've known me?"

He cracked a smile. "It would take all three of those character traits to send a young lady darting from the house unprotected in the wee hours of the morning, following the Equinox Festival of all things, with nothing but your companion and a wild hope of treasure." He raised his hand. "Which proved to be true, of course. But, the festival . . . have you ever been there?" A pointed blink. "It's not respectable, Miss Radcliff. Your father would call me out if he knew . . ."

Creature settled down at Lt. Burke's side, finally resigned to the truth he would not be managing another escape. Lt. Burke absently petted his head while avoiding my eyes. "I put together the statue of Lord Marlborough with the clue, but not the equinox. I'd never have uncovered that stone without you. The autumnal equinox will not come around for six months. That would have been far too late for me."

I peeked up to catch his expression, bleak at best, and it riled something inside me. "If you mean to insinuate you owe me something, rest assured, you do not. The treasure is your inheritance. I never should have presumed—"

A laugh erupted. "—to steal it from me."

I mirrored his smile. "Well, when you put it like that . . . I'm heartily ashamed."

His nose twitched. "But not entirely."

"All right. I apologize as well."

"Good." He flipped Creature's ear back and forth as he scratched his fluffy fur. "Because I should like to hire you."

"*Hire* me?"

"Just an addendum to our existing contract. The trim work still needs to be completed as well."

I stared down at the carpet, and I heard him suck in a quick breath.

"You're the only other person in the house who knows about the clues, and I cannot hunt for the treasure alone, particularly if you're hunting against me. Clearly you've a mind for riddles, which leaves me with two choices. I could simply send you away, or . . . I would rather . . . Well, would you perhaps consider"—a gentle glance up at me—"becoming my partner in this ridiculous business? Will you help me decipher these clues? I'll be nothing but honest with you. It goes against my better nature to trust anyone at this point, but if we can come to some sort of an agreement, find a way to work together to locate the jewels, the money rumored to be involved would save not only Avonthorpe but also your friend Arnold, who depends on this estate for his livelihood. I've managed arrangements for the maids and cook, but Arnold . . . He's just too old."

He relaxed his stance. "I thought myself immune to the lure of the hunt that so many of my ancestors have fallen prey to, but I find I cannot walk away from this place without trying everything in my power to provide for Arnold. Will you help me?"

The words escaped before I could even consider the ramifications. "Of course."

He reached across the broken vase to squeeze my hand, his voice a whisper. "Thank you."

"But . . ." His gaze snapped up, and I had to fight the surprising tingle of emotion his touch had brought about. "There are two things you should know before we proceed."

He returned his hand to Creature's soft head, a look of concern settling across his face. "Go on."

"I am not the only one in the house who knows about the clues. Miss Drake took Arnold into her confidence years ago. They were working together, but never advanced past the first clue. And I told Miss Chant. She's been helping me thus far."

He nodded slowly. "I had my suspicions about Miss Chant, but Arnold is a surprise."

"He's quite discreet and I'd rather not tell him I've taken you into my confidence."

"And Miss Chant?"

"She'll have to know, of course. I'm around her far more."

He dipped his chin. "Really?"

"She's my companion, you know. My father arranged for her to accompany me here."

"I'm fully aware of her position in the house. I only question her commitment to it. I've found you alone over the past week more often than I've found you with her."

I bit my lip, warmth flooding my cheeks. I suppose it would look to others like Miss Chant was neglecting her duties, but we had an understanding. He couldn't know about Vincent and her time with him. "I believe my father merely meant her presence at the house to lend a level of respectability to my training." I focused on his eyes. "He trusts me. You needn't concern yourself with the particulars."

Amusement lit his face. "I didn't mean to suggest anything to the contrary. I am certain you can manage your own affairs; however, as far as my responsibility goes as your host and as a gentleman, I am glad of her present knowledge of the clues. I wouldn't want to be . . . well . . . indiscreet."

"You mean entrapped by an unwanted marriage, perhaps."

He rubbed the back of his neck. "That is not what I said."

"Wasn't it? Because I daresay that would be like a death sentence, one I certainly would not relish partaking in." I pushed to my feet, retreat heavy on my mind, but the smooth porcelain of the vase piece drew my attention to my hand.

Lt. Burke stilled me with a touch. "I was only concerned with your reputation, Miss Radcliff, and the thanks I owe your father for allowing you to stay here. I don't want either of us to fall into a situation we might find uncomfortable."

I lifted my head. "Agreed. I shall inform Miss Chant her presence is appreciated."

He gave me a wan smile.

"And speaking of Miss Chant. If she is to be a part of this hunt . . ." I raised my eyebrows.

He nodded once again to himself. "She should be in a position to receive some of the money."

"Exactly. She requires the purchase of a ticket and enough income to start her new life in America."

"So that's the way of it. Vincent Tulk, I see."

"How did you know?"

"Mr. Tulk mentioned his plans to Mr. Haskett. He said he means to depart Britain in a few months."

My brows drew in. "I didn't realize he had a fixed date."

"Apparently his family has been pushing him to leave for some time."

"Yes, yes, I know that, but he has more than himself to think of now."

"Hence Miss Chant's neglect of you."

I crossed my arms. "It's not neglect when I give her permission."

"And your father would agree to this arrangement?"

"He's miles away from here." I pressed my lips together. "And I would not be the first young lady not to confide everything in her father."

"Nor am I the sort of gentleman to break a lady's trust . . . within reason."

"Then let me speak plainly. If I am to keep your secret, I expect you to keep mine."

His eyebrows sprang up. "That sounds almost like blackmail."

"Take it how you will, but I am twenty years old with every intention of finding a way to set up my own household. My father simply needs to get in line with that."

Lt. Burke slid the shard from my hand. "Sounds like this treasure will help all of us out of our present predicaments." He studied the engraving. "What do you think this means?"

The fifteenth, my boy!

My heart stilled. "Oh dear. I haven't a clue. A date or the number of something?"

He stared at the piece as he turned it in his hand. "It's a shame really, about the vase."

"Such a terrible waste of money."

"Yes, but"—his face went slack—"that isn't exactly what I meant."

"No?"

"You wouldn't under—" He shook his head a little. "What am I saying? Of course you would. The vase was a work of art from another time—1740 to be exact, which was not so long ago in the grand scheme of things. But even artifacts like these give us a glimpse of another world. They help us to understand what it means to be human. They strengthen the link between all civilizations. I actually work off and on with a friend of mine who manages a section of the British Museum. He was interested in Sèvres porcelain for display and I was considering donating this fine example once I came into possession of it. I can't do that now."

A light shudder fluttered through my chest as I took in the man before me. The word *mysterious* still hovered in my mind, but everything else I'd once believed about Lt. Burke had softened at the edges.

He was demanding, yes, militarylike in the extreme, but there was another part of him, an immense likability. I'd have to keep his intangible appeal in check.

I watched as he straightened his jacket and untied Creature from the side table. His movements were methodical and careful, gentle but direct. And all at once a certain person came roaring into my mind.

My eyes slid shut. No wonder I'd felt drawn to Lt. Burke and equally repulsed by him. He was just another gentleman cut from my father's cloth—proper, respectable, terribly caring, and a great demander of excellence. My relationship with Father had ended with his utter disapproval of my actions. My fault, but a disaster nonetheless. Perfect was something I could never be. No, I'd resolved to stay clear of the sorts of people who tended to be inflexible.

Oh, I'd help Lt. Burke find his treasure all right, for my own independence, for my friend's plans of marriage, but I would keep his attractive self at arm's length. A smile of confidence lifted my face. And if I played my cards right at the end of it all, the lot of us would part ways forever and I would be free to set up my own household—alone.

Eleven

FOCUSING ON THE DELICATE STROKES OF THE TRIM WORK the following morning proved disastrous. My mind was elsewhere—the treasure hunt, the murderer still on the loose, and of course, Lt. Burke—thoughts that only brought more questions.

Though I'd settled in with the best of intentions to complete a section of the wall that looked something like the letter *V*, within a few hours I made a rather large error. My back ached, my fingers shook. It was past time for a break. Daniel's mood continued to be as dismal as my performance, and I postponed work for the both of us till the afternoon.

Thus I fetched my bonnet and gloves and burst from the house, hopeful the serene combination of sea air and cloudless sky would settle my thoughts. The windy path that headed east from Avonthorpe called to me as it did quite often of late, and I set out up the incline at a steady pace. The cliff trail was a rugged one that ventured first through the grassy swell of the hillside and then across the pale bluffs, which rose and fell like waves along much of the coastline near Dover.

There was a small wooded area near the peak that hid Avonthorpe's old chapel from view, but beyond those trees the majestic church was a sight to behold. The ancient walls, still perfect, endured like an old guard peering over the cliff's edge to the rocky water. The spire on the roof glistened in the morning sun as a salty wind whipped around the corners.

Though the chapel had been well maintained and a vicar once

walked the halls, the church had been abandoned for decades. I'd been told the poor man's living had been reduced to a paltry 150 pounds per annum before it was finally eliminated by the archbishop upon the vicar's death. So the beautiful little chapel stood empty, gathering cobwebs between the pews, enduring the inevitable passage of time.

Routing my walk around the structure, I peered as I always did into the arched windows, a touch of sadness on my shoulders. The vaulted ceiling, a work of art in itself, drew my sight first, then the delicate woodwork of the three-decked pulpit and the box pews, which at one time were rented by the upper-class families of the village as they were numbered accordingly.

I'd never stepped foot inside as the door remained locked, but I enjoyed peering through the dusty windows. In fact, I spent several minutes lost in thought, my nose pressed to the cool glass. It was only when I stepped away that I felt a presence at my back.

"Good morning, Miss Radcliff." Lt. Burke gave me a flowery bow.

Where had he . . . ? "Good morning." On impulse my hands flew to my cheeks. "I must confess, I didn't hear you arrive. I—how long have you been here?"

He gave me a quick, stunned look. "Not long. But you seemed so peaceful, I didn't want to disturb you."

"Oh." I smoothed out my black mourning dress, a touch of uncertainty between us. "This is such a beautiful little chapel. I daresay the serenity captured a very willing prisoner."

He moved in closer, his shadowy figure almost looming over me. "I stopped by the ballroom earlier."

So he'd been looking for me. "Is something amiss?"

"Not at all." There was a sharp bit of silence before he propped his boot on a nearby stone wall. "I thought you might like to hear about my meeting with the constable this morning."

"Oh?" I laid my hand on the wall. "Was he awful?"

He gave a light chuckle. "More of the same, I'm afraid. He's learned nothing about the death of my aunt."

"Nothing at all?"

"Oh, he has theories, mind you, but they all border on the ridiculous." Lt. Burke folded his arms across his chest. "My present favorite is the scheme he's concocted to explain away any wrongdoing of one of the neighbors. That possibility would be far too much trouble for him. Apparently he's got word about an escaped prisoner from Gaol Lane. He surmises this man, upon his escape, went straight to Avonthorpe Hall and ended my aunt's life, all without even knowing her." He rubbed the back of his neck. "Convenient . . . and like I said before—patently ridiculous."

I hesitated, but only for an instant. "What evidence does he propose to corroborate this idea?"

"None at all. Whoever this prisoner is no doubt left the area some time ago. Constable Humphries only means to tie up my aunt's murder and the thefts along the coastline as neatly as possible. No more trouble for him."

"But no justice for Miss Drake."

He hung his head. "I'm afraid the true murderer will never be revealed. We have little to go on. I was hoping . . . well, since we've come to an understanding, if there was anything else you could tell me regarding that night . . ."

"I wish I could. The crossbow bolt is the only evidence we have."

I saw the faintest flinch about his jawline.

"Did you recognize it?"

He leveled his gaze. "It was mine."

"Yours?" I gasped.

His voice was cool, controlled. "Whoever chose the weapon meant to point a finger at me. The crossbow that fired that bolt came from one of my collections."

I narrowed my eyes. Lt. Burke had certainly looked shocked the moment I told him about the bolt. And to be so open with me now . . . surely he wasn't involved. "Do you have any idea of who could have stolen it?"

Another clench of his jaw. "None whatsoever." He absently rubbed the black mourning band on his arm. "I just keep thinking, if we were to find the treasure, it might lead us in some way to the murderer. How can the two not be linked? My aunt was a wonderful woman. There is no other reason for anyone to have taken her life."

"Indeed." I nodded slowly. "We have so little to go on, and the clues—they are not what I expected. Have you discovered anything about the number fifteen?"

He let out a heavy sigh. "I've counted windows and columns, rooms and fireplaces, paintings and halls. Nothing."

"I found myself counting nearly everything in the ballroom the whole of the morning, which is why I left the house for a walk—to clear my mind."

He gave a tight laugh. "'Tis madness."

I tried a wan smile. "We should acknowledge the very real possibility we may never get any answers at all."

"The thought is rather sobering, isn't it?" He nudged a loose rock with the toe of his boot. "But I shan't give up yet. I do, however, need to leave you just now for my work. I'm to sort the antiquities for Mr. Haskett. Mr. Montague and I have a meeting arranged with him in a few days. He's quite pleased with the sarcophagus. Things are moving a bit quicker than I anticipated."

"Are all the Egyptian artifacts here at the church?"

"In the outlying building just ahead."

"Ah, that's right. Well, I hope the sale goes well"—I widened my eyes—"for all our sakes."

He returned a tight-lipped smile and tipped his hat. "We need time to solve these clues, and the sale to Mr. Haskett will ensure that happens."

I pulled my bonnet ribbons tighter beneath my chin and settled my hand on my hip. "I hope so, Lt. Burke. I hope so."

The small stone path that led from the back of the church took a wild turn down the cliff side and, step by step, was carved intricately into the uneven gray rocks. Miss Chant had declared the long descent a treacherous one and forbade me ever to take it, but I'd no intention of giving up my hunt for seashells. I'd amassed a great collection over the two years I'd been in residence. After all, once I'd seen the grotto at Oatlands Park, I had every intention of creating one for myself someday, if not on a property of my own, then at Middlecrest. And my vision needed shells—thousands of them.

Off I wandered down the winding stone steps, my hand sliding along the cold stone wall until I reached the shoreline panting, my gown dirty at the hem. To date my collection included unique specimens of whelks and piddocks, but my favorite were limpets, which I'd have to ease off the rock surfaces with a kitchen knife.

I assumed I'd have the shoreline to myself and was surprised to make a rather curious discovery—Mr. Montague.

He seemed just as startled as I when I came upon him at the foot of the stairway. He fumbled where exactly to place his hand, finally propping it against the rocky cleft. His rakish smile, made somewhat amusing by awkwardness, brought a dimple onto his cheek. "Good morning, Miss Radcliff."

I scooted past him to find a flat place where I could stand at ease, then looked up. "It seems we had the same idea. Beautiful day for a stroll on the beach."

He motioned toward the shoreline, then offered his arm. "Indeed. I was on my way back, but you've convinced me to extend my walk."

The cliff side dipped inward a few yards in front of us and swept in a circular motion to cradle a small sandy cove. Mr. Montague directed me toward it with ease.

"No companion today?"

I hadn't even thought to engage Miss Chant, as I'd been taking my walks alone for some time. Granted, no gentlemen other than Mr. Fagean and Daniel were in residence before now, and they rarely came down to the shoreline. "Actually Miss Chant doesn't approve of my use of the stairs at all. Mr. Fagean fell down them some time ago. I, however, would not be so clumsy." I laughed as I considered my words. "Well . . . maybe."

He gave me an artful look. "So you've escaped the house alone." Then a small smile. "Cannot say I blame you. This cove does have an appeal." He glared ahead a long moment, then spoke a bit softer. "Have you ever come across anyone else down here? Villagers perhaps?"

"No, not at all. I've always thought of this as my special place, which is why you surprised me."

He nodded, but his thoughts seemed elsewhere. "Interesting."

"Why do you ask?"

"I thought I saw someone . . . a few minutes ago." He motioned behind us. "I was standing up on the cliff there, but when I got down here, no one was about. Do you know, is there another way out of this cove?"

"Not by land, at least. The stairs are the only way."

He chuckled a bit to himself, but the sound was uneasy. "Must have been a bird or some other animal. I probably put myself out for nothing. Well, not nothing. I get the very fine opportunity of your company for a stroll, and that was more than worth the effort."

"You flatter me, Mr. Montague."

He seemed to think better of his familiarity, his tone stiffening. "Don't take my compliments to heart. I'm a notorious flirt, you know." He pressed my hand. "Hopefully not one past redemption, but a bit wounded at present." His voice turned somewhat monotone. "I suppose your brother mentioned me?"

I nodded carefully.

A deep breath. "Everything has been rather strange these last few months. I'm still finding my footing."

"I do know a little of what you've gone through and can well understand the feeling of the rug being pulled out from beneath you. I too was forced to leave an unfortunate relationship behind. It's one of the reasons I came to Avonthorpe."

He stole a sideways glance. "You surprise me, Miss Radcliff."

My heart sank. Had I revealed too much? What did Mr. Montague know of my situation at Middlecrest Abbey? "Please, let me assure you my reputation remains intact. I simply needed some time away from my family and all they think of me. I'm determined to start anew."

"Ah, familial expectations. Now that can be a tricky thing. I should know. And though space can give one perspective, if I may be so bold . . ." He slowed our walk. "Don't try to simply dispose of the person you were before—it's not really possible, nor advisable. That person will always be a part of you, whether you want her to be or not. Take me for example. I've never met my father's expectations. I used to delude myself into thinking an advantageous marriage would change my father's opinion in some way. But through hope and rejection, I've come to learn I have no control over my father's thoughts or feelings, and I'm finding a way to be comfortable with that fact."

I didn't know what to say. Mr. Montague possessed a depth I'd not realized on first meeting. No wonder Lt. Burke had taken him as a confidant.

He went on. "I would urge you to embrace yourself, faults and all. It's the only way to really move on." He released my arm to pick up a rock and toss it into the sea. "But who am I to give advice? Lt. Burke would be a much better listener than I."

I too picked up a stone but stopped before releasing it. "Why do you say that?"

He gave me a knowing look. "Graham's been a good friend to me, the best."

"Oh." I tossed the rock—hard.

Mr. Montague raised his eyebrows. "Impressive." He smiled, then his gaze drifted across the sea to the other side of the cove. "I daresay he only brought me along on this business transaction to save me from myself. I don't care a fig about Egyptian artifacts at all. Oh, he told me I could help barter for price, but I know he could handle that. He is determined only to sell a few items."

"Only a few?"

"He means to give the rest to the British Museum."

"You mean like a donation." I stopped cold. "Why would he do so when he is so short on money?"

Mr. Montague's attention shot up, and I lifted my hand. "He told me the house is to be leased."

"Did he?" A wry glance at the sky. "Graham is rather particular about his convictions. You'll have to ask him why he does what he does regarding his antiquities. I simply follow orders when it comes to that. I have no wish to get entangled in his outlandish politics."

"Oh . . . look." I pointed to the waterline. "It's just a common cockle, but a pretty one."

Mr. Montague crossed the wet sand to retrieve the shell twinkling in the sun and handed it to me. "Are you a collector then?"

"I am." As I moved to secure the shell in my pocket, a flash of movement caught my attention. Mr. Montague darted a look up at the cliff as well.

I shielded my eyes from the sun as I squinted to get a better look.

Mr. Montague drew up at my side. "Perhaps we've found my figure."

"I doubt it." I shook my head. "That's only Daniel. He's not one to venture down here."

I watched Daniel a long moment, curious about the decided lurch to his steps and the uncomfortable rushed nature of his pace.

Mr. Montague sighed. "Wonder what's got the lad all ruffled up."

I glanced around as if the rocky hillside might provide the answer. "I'm not certain. He's been sulking all day. I-I hope he's not looking for me."

"At the chapel?"

"I like to walk there from time to time." I turned and headed for the stairs. "Daniel's taken Miss Drake's death quite hard. I'd better go and find him."

Mr. Montague jogged to catch me. "Allow me to help you up the stairwell."

"No . . . thank you."

He withdrew, his eyebrows squished together.

"Please, I don't mean to be rude. I'd prefer to approach Daniel alone. He can be a bit temperamental at times. We grew up together, as our families are quite close. He's like a younger brother to me."

Mr. Montague's face relaxed and he motioned up the stairs with his hand. "Then by all means. I'll head to the house."

Though I felt his presence the entirety of the way up the criss-crossing stairway, Mr. Montague hung back at the cliff's edge. As promised he tipped his hat, nodded, and took himself off.

A slew of errant clouds had amassed during my excursion down to the shore, and the sun had escaped into hiding, starving the landscape of its bright hues. The playful breeze that had accompanied my earlier walk felt heavier, more persistent, as a slight chill slithered across my shoulders. Miss Chant would have taken the cue and demanded we turn back for the house at once, but after a quick survey of the sky, I didn't anticipate rain . . . And Daniel needed me.

A short walk brought me back to the chapel, and I climbed the stile over the stone wall. How altered the old building appeared in the bleak light, how lonely in a way, the twisting creepers scaling every corner of the walls, the shadowy windows like rows of vacant eyes. It wasn't the first moment I wished I'd brought my shawl with me, but the day seemed so warm when I set out.

"Daniel," I called into the gloom, but there was no answer.

Carefully, I circled the structure before making my way between the tuft of forest on the far side of the chapel and the little gated cemetery. I ran my hand along the iron railing, absently reading the tombstones of the dead. There were quite a few Drakes laid to rest on the estate, but none I recognized.

A *crack* sounded at my back, like a person had inadvertently stepped on a twig.

Every muscle in my body turned rigid. And though it made perfect sense to call Daniel's name once again, somehow I knew it wasn't him. Silence prevailed in that terribly insidious way it does, exposing nothing yet revealing everything at the same time. I was not alone, and whoever watched me from the folds of the forest did not wish to declare himself.

My breathing turned ragged, my eyes unable to blink. I clawed at the cold rough metal of the cemetery gate, preparing to dash away. Should I run or hide? The world around me blurred as my heartbeat thrashed in my ears. That is, until an all-too-familiar figure took shape within the shadows of the trees, and my focus narrowed in on the man's face.

My vision blurred as my mouth fell open, my muscles frozen. How could this be possible?

Jean Cloutier, the Frenchman who had betrayed both me and my family, clutched a nearby tree for support, his eyes hauntingly direct on mine. His hair ragged, he looked terribly lost, spent in a way, dirty. Nothing like my recent dreams.

The past crept into my chest on a weighted breath. Memories I'd repressed rose dangerously near the surface. Why had I been told Jean was to be hanged for his crimes? By the look of him, he was near death.

I blinked, my eyes wide with a hint of anticipation. Here he stood, so close I could walk forward and touch him, and yet . . . my hands stilled.

Miss Chant had been right. Jean Cloutier was my enemy in every way, an accomplice to murder. He'd been involved in the death of my sister's fiancé, and he'd used me along with all the rest of my family. I had given him up years ago, so what wrought the tug on my heart?

I looked over my shoulder, searching the churchyard for an escape from the danger he posed and the dreadful confusion charging my heart. Tears welled. I'd come to Avonthorpe to escape the biggest mistake of my life, a sore that would never really heal. And here it was staring me in the face once again.

"Don't go." His voice breached the subtle wind so soft and pleading . . . exceedingly memorable in every way.

I closed my eyes a brief second, hoping I'd conjured Jean from the depths of my imagination, only to open them and find him creeping nearer. He held his hands out as he approached, much like a horse trainer confronted with a filly poised to bolt.

How little he knew.

"Donne-moi une chance d'expliquer."

Dare I listen? Dare I stay? My fingers found the gate at my back, my voice a whisper. "What are you doing here?"

"Please." A part of him looked older, windswept and frail. "How much I have been missing that beautiful face these past two years."

My entire body felt numb with shock, and I stood completely motionless, my throat thickening, as he made his way across the courtyard. "I ask again, how is it possible you are here?"

"Escape, *ma cherie* . . ." He plunged his hand through his tangled hair. "I'm on my way home to France." He looked down at the ground. "I-I need money. If you would be so—"

"Don't." My hand shot up. "Don't you dare ask for my help, not after what happened at Middlecrest."

His face contorted in the gray light as an array of emotions swept across his features. Clearly he had endured much during the years he'd spent in prison. A shell of his former self. "I have no one else to ask, and"—his voice sounded hollow—"I thought perhaps . . ."

My voice came out a bit weak. "I have nothing for you. Nothing."

His gaze wandered. "I did not know you were in residence at Avonthorpe, not at first, then I heard your name." He pressed his lips together. "I did not realize how much you could still affect me. If you have no money to spare, all I can do is ask for your silence. Surely you would be willing to give it to an old, dear"—a hard swallow—"friend."

A turbulent mixture of fear and hurt slipped unbidden into my words. "Why should I do that . . . for *you*?"

"Why should you indeed?" He stepped forward. "Look at me, Phoebe." A long pause. "What you see before you is nothing but the remains of a Frenchman who loved his country . . . and loves you still." His chin jutted out as his eyes filled with tears. "Believe me when I tell you I did not know who that poison was for. I was ordered to take it to Middlecrest. I never would have—"

"Stop." My heart was pounding now, my hand unsteady.

"Do not fret, please. It hurts me to see you like this. I mean you no harm. I could never . . . I plan to leave these shores as soon as can be arranged." His lips curved up at one side of his mouth as they used to do seconds before he'd kiss me. "You would not send me back to hell, would you?" Another tentative step forward. "I'm only in need of money to make the journey, and then you'll never see me again. Again, if you have any to spare—"

"I've none on me."

"Then later maybe. Perhaps you can acquire some."

I wish he hadn't absently rubbed his ear in that boyish way of his—a patent reminder of the intimacy we'd shared, how well I thought I knew him. Then the meaning behind his words hit me. "*Later*? Where are you staying?"

"Never mind that." A panicky glance over his shoulder, then his hands were soft on my arms. "I have to go now, but oh, how much I wish to stay." A reckless squeeze and release. "Promise me you'll keep our little secret."

"I don't know."

He winced. "I trust you, at any rate, what we shared, what we meant to one another. I cannot believe you will be the cause of my death." He dipped his chin. "Because that is just what they will do if they catch me once again."

All of a sudden I couldn't breathe. I whirled away from him and pushed through the gate, torn all the way to my core. The cause of his death? What was best to be done? Should I sound the alarm? Should I risk everything—to what end?

Jean only wanted to go home—that's all he'd ever wanted. Perhaps Lt. Burke could help him do so in some way. My shoulders tightened. No, Lt. Burke would turn Jean over to the authorities without a thought and Jean's and my relationship would be exposed. No one but Miss Chant and Daniel knew of our ill-fated romance. If I told a soul, I would be ruined and Jean sentenced to death. I shook my head. He was right. Silence was the only choice to save us both.

I stared a long while at the church before angling back to face the man I'd loved with all my heart, confident I had some control over my emotions at last.

But the forest was completely empty.

Twelve

Once I decided to remain quiet about Jean's visit, I had little confidence in my ability to hide my utter shock and confusion from Miss Chant, and if she knew of his presence, she would certainly sound the alarm. Thus, I was forced to fob her off with concerns about the timeline for the ballroom restorations. Granted, I wasn't sure she believed my rushed explanation.

Strangely enough though, her matter-of-fact tone and calming words proved the best medicine for a scattered mind, and something she said on parting did help me manage my way through supper. She delayed me outside the dining room door, stared me straight in the eye, and whispered rather tersely, "We do the best we can with what we're given. No more, no less."

My heart was a throbbing mess. I *had* done the best I could, but what now? Should I leave Avonthorpe at once? Was I even safe presently? Shouldn't my father be told?

My head felt dizzy, my legs weak. Again, if I revealed any details regarding Jean's whereabouts to him, I would be forced to expose the whole truth about our prior relationship, or Jean certainly would. The very idea sent my insides folding inward, twisting and turning, until I thought I might be sick. Moreover, how could I bear my father's censure?

Clearly Jean was the escaped prisoner Constable Humphries suggested committed the thefts along the coast. He had to eat after all. Considering he was on foot, the locations of the robberies would put him miles from Avonthorpe Hall the night Miss Drake was killed. I bit my lip, somewhat comforted by the thought. At any rate, I'd never really considered him a cold-blooded murderer. I'd staked my reputation on that fact two years ago.

Though he had admitted to a hand in my sister's fiancé's death, I also took relief in the fact he'd only procured the poison—if his story was true. Some could even argue his actions at the time were those of a man who had sworn his duty to his country, not of a fiend, as my father had labeled him. But what did I think? My head hurt.

I stumbled into the drawing room following supper more confused than when I'd entered, crossing the large drawing room carpet to the bow window. I propped my hands on the sill, utilizing the woodwork to stay upright. How perfectly tight-lipped I'd been after Jean escaped from Middlecrest, a consummate actress. I'd fooled them all—my stepmother, my sister, and my father. Why did I find it so difficult to remain silent now? I closed my eyes, drifting back to a world I'd run away from, to another time, another place, another me.

The feel of Jean's lips on mine was as fresh today as it had been two years ago, his hands so strong at my back. I thought I loved him then. I'd had to be so careful. No one at Middlecrest knew about the many times I stole down to see him, how I'd paid my father's servants to turn a blind eye, how I'd been ready to leave him untied if he'd only asked.

Of course, I never had the chance to prove my love. I was nothing but a pawn in Jean's plan. Though he'd professed his intentions for us to make a life together in France, he didn't even say good-bye the day he left. I was abandoned to an empty house and an empty heart.

I wiped away a stray tear. Surely I had moved past all that . . . at least I thought I had. I'd delved into painting and plans for my future. So why now? Why here?

"Why are you loafing about over here with no gentleman to entertain you?" Mrs. Fagean flopped down onto the window seat. She didn't even bother waiting for an answer. "My husband's with Lt. Burke in his office right now. They will be joining us following their port."

"Oh?"

She flicked her fingers in the air. "None of my business, he says. Well, he'd be shocked to learn I know every little thing he does around here." She swirled the contents of her glass. "You think we don't all know where our drink comes from . . . at such a fantastic price."

My eyes rounded. *Smuggling?* Were the Fageans . . . ?

She hiccupped. "Miss Drake was not so coy with me. She included me in every little conversation."

Undoubtedly Mrs. Fagean's loose tongue had everything to do with how much liquor she'd consumed over the evening. Mr. Fagean usually kept her on a tight lead. I smiled at her and settled back against the windowpane. Perhaps I would have a chat. "So you mean Mr. Fagean wants Lt. Burke to . . . what exactly? Buy his goods from the Continent?"

She cast me an incredulous look. "Certainly not. He simply wants to continue his use of the cove for off-loading his merchandise on his return trips from France. It's perfectly situated to avoid the excise ships, and he and Miss Drake have run a tidy little business for some time."

A knot formed on my brow. "You mean Miss Drake not only knew about the smuggling but condoned it?"

A neat little shrug. "Of course. She needed the money, and Mr. Fagean provided heaps of that. How do you think she kept up this house with such little income?"

As a stickler for rules and regulations, Lt. Burke would never agree to a scheme with the Fageans. I pressed my forehead. It all made sense now. The odd hours the Fageans kept, no talk of when they would be in and out of the house. A legitimate shipping business by day and a corrupt one by night.

With money tight, Miss Drake must have had no other choice

but to trust the pair. I tethered my lip between my teeth. What a tangled web of lies Miss Drake had taken on. No wonder she was at cross-purposes when Lt. Burke suddenly arrived. They were probably expecting a shipment.

I caught Mr. Arnold's concerned gaze from across the room and felt reassured by the lift of his brow. Was the staff aware of all the treachery? I excused myself as soon as I could manage a retreat and made my way into the hall. Arnold joined me at once.

I drew in close. "Where can we talk?"

A thoughtful pause and he motioned me into the billiards room, slamming the door shut behind us. "Is something amiss?"

"It's Mrs. Fagean."

He rested back against the door. "I might have known."

"She had a bit too much to drink tonight and happened to reveal the fact that both she and Mr. Fagean are *smugglers*."

He went stone cold. "I've had my suspicions, of course, but I had hoped otherwise."

Mr. Arnold had always been a quiet support about the house, but his manner this evening felt more like a father's than a servant's. A smile emerged. I hadn't realized how much I'd been missing a connection like that.

He hung his head. "Miss Drake was no doubt just like the rest of the Drakes, mercenary to the core."

"Mercenary?"

"Oh yes, Miss Drake's father used to pinch every farthing he came across. He never cared who got hurt in the process. And Miss Drake was not exactly the saint she presented to you and Daniel, not with the tenants anyway. If it weren't for Mr. Fagean acting as a land agent these last few years . . . well . . . few roofs would have been repaired or fences mended."

I felt sick. "I feel like every time I turn around, someone else is lying to me. And I fall for their smooth words over and over again."

"The world is a complicated place. I suppose we must simply do the best we can."

I stepped back. "Miss Chant said something similar earlier." I picked up one of the billiard balls and rolled it around in my hand. "I'm glad we had a second to ourselves. I have quite a bit to tell you regarding the treasure hunt."

His hand retreated to the lapel of his jacket. "You've solved the clue."

I nodded fervently. "Then was presented with another and another."

His focus darted about the dim space. "Tell me everything."

And I did, careful to keep the confidences I'd agreed to, but Arnold and I had begun this adventure together.

He seemed a bit stunned, his words slow to come. "I cannot believe you've learned so much so quickly. What is our next step?"

"I have no idea. Fifteen! What can the number mean?"

He sauntered over to the billiards table and drummed his fingers on the edge, his eyes alive with thought. "Fifteen is a triangular number." Carefully he rearranged the balls on the table. "See?" He counted the rows aloud. "1+2+3+4+5=15."

"Extraordinary. You did all that in your head?"

"Yes . . ." He rubbed his chin. "Or perhaps it's something quite different. The Magna Carta was signed on July 15, 1215, you know. I was just reading about it earlier today."

I pressed my hand to my mouth. "Why stop there? Queen Elizabeth was crowned on January 15, 1559, but I don't believe those dates mean anything." I glanced back at the triangular balls.

"Wasn't the first Jacobite Rising known as 'the Fifteen' because it occurred in 1715?"

"I think you're right."

He nodded slowly. "All things to ponder."

"Indeed," I whispered. "But I'd better return to the drawing room. Mrs. Fagean will no doubt come looking for me if I'm gone too long."

He smiled. "We wouldn't want that."

I returned to the drawing room to find Mrs. Fagean more out of control than when I'd left. She'd cornered Daniel at the pianoforte and I could see clear as day he needed rescue. Her hands were flapping in the air as she spoke, an uncomfortable lean to her stance.

I hastened to join them, straight into a heated discussion that lifted the hair on the back of my neck.

"This isn't a game, you know," Mrs. Fagean was saying.

Daniel pressed his palm onto the pianoforte. "I never said it was."

"Then stop acting like a child." Mrs. Fagean's voice was cold and direct.

Only then did Daniel catch sight of me standing there, gaping. He jerked his arm in front of him to fiddle with his jacket sleeves, his face red. "Phoebe here, no doubt, would agree with your sentiment about me."

Mrs. Fagean's movements were lazy, her speech slurred. "I have no intention of airing my dirty laundry in company." She pushed past him and slunk onto the bench, only to strike a dissonant chord on the pianoforte. "I'm a lady, remember."

Daniel gave her a cold stare. "How could I have forgotten?"

A charged silence froze the three of us until Daniel stepped back. "Good evening, Phoebe, *Mrs.* Fagean." And walked out the drawing room door.

Mrs. Fagean stared at the music in front of her with disgust. "How old is that child, anyhow?"

"Eighteen." My voice came out as a whisper, my attention still heavy on the door. "Has something happened?"

She laughed. "With him . . . not at all." A well-managed pause. "I was simply lamenting Mr. Fagean's and my plight."

I settled onto the bench next to her. "Your plight?"

"The will, of course." Her fingers retreated, then extended back onto the keys, but she didn't play anything. "Miss Drake left us nothing, you know."

I stilled a moment. "Miss Drake had nothing to leave you. Avonthorpe is entailed and there was no money. You know that already."

She huffed. "She promised my husband the cottage."

I sat up straight. "The vicar's cottage."

She started the opening bar of the song. "That's the one."

"But why . . ." The lines of music blurred before my eyes. "The two of you wanted easy access to the cove—to continue your nightly dealings, I presume."

"Shh!" She abruptly halted the song to press her finger to her lips. "Mr. Fagean will take me to task if he finds out I've been talking." Then she motioned across the room.

I'd not even noticed the gentlemen were returned from their impromptu meeting. Lt. Burke had left Mr. Fagean and retreated to the sideboard for a drink. I watched as he returned the stopper to the decanter, then paused to pinch the bridge of his nose.

Heavens, whatever they discussed had not gone well.

Mrs. Fagean went on quietly. "It is beyond comprehension—after my husband doted on her all these years."

I touched the base of my neck. "Miss Drake specifically told you she meant to leave the cottage to the two of you?"

"Not in so many words, no. But she informed Mr. Fagean at one time, and the cottage is not part of the entail. We assumed she meant—"

"I see." Though Miss Drake had always been uncomfortably close with the Fageans, I never would have presumed she'd leave a cottage to them, not with so many other deserving people to receive it. My heart did a little turn. "Who *did* she will the cottage to?"

She grasped her cross necklace and ran the pendant through her fingers. "Lt. Burke. Can you believe it? After all she said about him over the years."

"That is . . . odd." Why had she given the cottage to her nephew? Mr. Arnold seemed a better choice, especially with the state of affairs at Avonthorpe. But as I was learning, she was a Drake—proud to a fault. She would have rather passed the entire estate to her son, her blood. Lt. Burke was the next best thing. But the treasure? She'd given the clue to me. Granted, I was the only one to stumble upon her there at the end.

The memory of her dying in my arms proved too great and I stood to shake it off.

Tears came to me quick and easy of late and I wasn't in the mood to share them with anyone. I made my way back to the bow window, hoping to wait out the remaining evening hours in solitude, but I was foolish to think that possible.

Lt. Burke was at my side within minutes. He was slow to sit and even slower to address me. He wrestled his handkerchief from his pocket and held it out.

I thought I'd managed some level of control, but he'd seen through my weak smile. "Thank you." I dabbed my eyes, then clutched the cloth in my lap. "I don't know what to say. I'm rather emotional this evening."

He rested his arms on his knees, his voice low but soft. "We needn't say anything at all if you'd prefer. I recognize the look of loss. I've seen it in my looking glass often enough. It comes on so unexpectedly." He allowed a comfortable moment of silence. "I wouldn't have dreamed of disturbing you just now, but I happened to overhear Mr. Fagean say something about asking you a question. He was moving this way. I-I thought that might not be welcome at present."

I glanced up. "You mean you came over here to save me."

"From the likes of Mr. Fagean—anytime."

I couldn't stop a genuine smile. "Then I am in your debt."

He returned a grin as he nodded. "I'll keep that in mind."

Mr. Montague's words from early in the day trickled into my mind. He'd called Lt. Burke a good listener. "How do you deal with the difficult memories?"

He propped his hands on the window seat on each side of his legs. "I wish I had a good answer. For me, it involves a great deal of prayer and time. Though terribly difficult, some things just have to be felt."

Mr. Fagean had joined his wife at the pianoforte and chose the moment to belt out a song.

Lt. Burke and I shared a knowing glance, a lingering one. I hadn't even noticed how blue his eyes were, how delightfully they curved at the corners when he smiled. He lacked the overt handsomeness of Mr. Montague, but he had a presence I couldn't ignore. If only we'd met at a different time and place. If only I could tell him about my encounter with Jean Cloutier earlier in the day. Why did I suddenly think he would be the only one to understand my decision to remain quiet? Because I knew that wasn't true . . .

I swallowed the thought at once. "Mrs. Fagean told me her husband approached you this evening about smuggling."

"Smuggling?" His eyes widened. "He assured me his shipping business in the cove would remain aboveboard."

"Well, as far as I know he does do some legitimate trips across the channel." My shoulders felt heavy and I let my hands slide onto the cushion at my sides. I knew Lt. Burke wouldn't have considered such a thing, and I wouldn't have wanted him to.

A prickle of warmth met the outside of my hand and all at once I realized the error of my movement. My head swam, but I didn't pull away. It was a simple mistake really, just a slight contact, nothing more. I hadn't even realized his hand was so close. If just one of us adjusted, our fingers wouldn't even be touching.

Surely he would be the one to do so.

Mr. Fagean's song intensified, washing over the throbbing in my ears, and I glanced up. But there it was again—a wave of tingles. Had Lt. Burke actually moved closer? I couldn't even look at him. We just sat there like two cursed statues. Did he even realize we were touching one another? Perhaps it was all in my head.

Thus, I should be the one to move.

The thought only grew as it swirled in my mind, yet I couldn't seem to pull away. Had I gone mad . . . or was I simply enjoying myself?

The Fageans' musical display ended rather abruptly and only then could I fully comprehend the buzzing in my ears, the sudden force of my heartbeat. I shoved to my feet, every muscle in my body wound a bit too tight.

"Good evening, Lt. Burke." I struggled to meet his eyes as I took a step away from him. "Thank you." I was quick to add, "For rescuing me from Mr. Fagean, that is." I wouldn't want him to get the wrong idea.

He seemed to be smiling at nothing, then his eyes tilted up to mine. "Would you be free for a walk in the morning?"

"I—"

"The work in the ballroom can wait."

The air in the room felt strangely thin. "Can it?"

He gave a little shrug. "After looking over my antiquities and running a few numbers, I believe we should have a few months at least."

I scrunched up my lips in the corners. "I don't know if my father will allow me to stay that long."

He stood. "Then I shall have to be persuasive in my next letter to him." His smile widened. "We have a treasure to locate, you know."

I gave him an incredulous look. "You've figured something out, haven't you?"

"Not entirely, but I have a few ideas."

Suddenly I was giddy. "I have some of my own as well."

"Then this shall be an interesting walk, I daresay."

My heart did an uncomfortable flip I wasn't prepared for. "Yes, yes, it will."

Thirteen

Lt. Burke was waiting for me in the entry hall the following morning, his shiny black boots glistening in the flame of the morning fire. His black jacket and cravat were perfection, his dark hair combed back, not a lock out of place.

I was relieved to see a slow smile build, his expression entirely friendly as I approached. Perhaps the confusing emotions that had sparked the previous evening were all on my side. And true to form my toes caught the edge of the Aubusson rug, causing a near stumble, but thankfully I recovered myself unassisted only to stare up, mortified.

He gave me a slight chuckle and extended his arm. "Shall we?"

I gripped the reticule I'd brought with me, certain my cheeks were cherry red, and made my way to the door. "Have you a destination for our walk today?"

A brief shrug. "Perhaps just a turn in the garden?"

I held up the purse. "Well, I have other plans."

"Do you?"

I gave him a hopeful smile. "I've a mind to take the stone stairs on the back side of the church down to the shoreline to look for shells."

He swiped a quick glance at the hall behind me, then leaned forward. "We'll likely miss Mrs. Fagean's daily luncheon."

I hesitated, laughing. "You say that like it's a bad thing."

He looked at me seriously. "You'll not be hungry then?"

"Possibly, or not. I really couldn't say, but in general my day is not really all that scheduled. I eat when I have a mind to." I hesitated as I watched his thoughtful expression. "We'll not starve, you know."

"No, I suppose not." He gave me a curious look. "But such havey-cavey comings and goings—doesn't that make it a bit difficult on the servants?"

"I'm always prompt to supper, I assure you, and if I miss a scheduled luncheon, well, I do know my way around the kitchens."

He nodded, allowed a shy smile I found a bit charming, and extended his arm. "A shell hunt it is then."

Thus we crossed the front lawns with the sunlight pouring over us, warming my back and exposed arms as the breeze urged us toward another adventure.

The days had been long of late, the nights heavy, but today, for the first time since Miss Drake's tragic death, the world felt different. I felt different. Lt. Burke and I had a morning to ourselves, shells to uncover . . . and what? My chest felt deliciously tight, but I wouldn't allow my thoughts to wander, not too far at least. I needed a day off—in every way.

We said little as we climbed the hill, a look here, a smile there as the spring grass tickled the hem of my gown and glistened in the light. It seemed we both needed the breath of space. In fact, it wasn't until the chapel took form on the cliff's edge that Lt. Burke finally cleared his throat.

"Shells, huh?"

I gave a little laugh. "Another art project of mine."

We followed the curve of the land, skirting around the chapel's manicured lawn and the cemetery. He released my arm to allow me to step in front as the path narrowed. "And what do you mean to do with the shells that we find?"

"I've actually been collecting them since I came to Avonthorpe."

His voice sounded curious. "You come down here often . . . alone?"

"Nearly every week. I hope to create a grotto someday, if I have the space to do so. Or if not, I shall create it at my father's estate." I glanced over my shoulder. "Have you ever seen a grotto?"

Having reached the edge of the stairs, he hesitated to answer until he drew up at my side. "Not in person, no. Though I've heard of them." He edged forward a bit, then crept back, seemingly unsure whether he should go first or allow me to lead the way down the steep, uneven stairs.

He finally smiled over at me. "I suppose you don't need my assistance if you come here often." Another harried look down the cliff. "Although this entire setup seems quite treacherous."

"Afraid, Lt. Burke?"

He coughed out a laugh. "No . . . just careful. I prefer to think things through. The stone could be slippery after all. Mr. Montague told me Mr. Fagean took quite a fall here."

I slid past him. "The route is safe enough. Mr. Fagean . . . well, everyone knows he's rather clumsy."

He stilled my arm. "I shall be right behind you nonetheless."

Something twisted in my heart at his fervent touch, and I turned away, unwilling to allow him to see how he'd affected me.

I could hear the *whoosh* of his fingers as they slid along the rock, the careful placement of his boots, and I took a long, slow breath. "We'll be down soon enough."

He laughed. "Just not too soon. I'd rather not take the short way down."

I followed the zigzagging steps around the sharp bend, which gave me a chance to pause and glance back at my escort, relieved to see his arms at ease, his steps assured. So his concern had been all for me.

He smiled down. "Tell me more about this grotto of yours."

I took the next row of steps. "I shall need a small cave, but one I can easily stand in. I would love to decorate the walls, the ceiling, and the floor in different patterns. I've been collecting various colored shells to do so."

"Sounds like you have it all worked out. Have you been to many grottos?"

"I have. Lord Shaftsbury has one at Wimborne St. Giles in Dorset. His was made of imported shells and cost over ten thousand pounds. I, of course, will have to make do with the specimens I find on the beach here. I'm just so lucky to be situated so close to the coast." I reached the bottom of the stairway and turned to wait for Lt. Burke to join me on the sand. "There are several grottos I've yet to see. The pope has one in Twickenham, you know."

"Really? I had no idea."

"I've heard it's quite lovely."

We started forward along the shoreline, the gusty wind at our backs. But a few lazy steps and Lt. Burke's hat tumbled from his head, leaving his hair to flap loose in the wind. I couldn't help but notice how the sudden change gave him a rugged, natural appearance.

He caught my glance and smiled. "What is it?"

"Your hair."

His fingers found his wayward locks. "It's pretty windy today." There was a rueful hesitation to his movements, but he didn't look away. "That bad, huh?"

"No. It's just that you usually keep your hair so neat and tidy." Another gust and I had to resecure my own bonnet ribbons. "I think I like it."

Silence settled between us as Lt. Burke averted his attention to the horizon. His face was serious when he turned back. "What have you learned about the number fifteen? You said you had some notion of what the clue meant."

I recounted all the ideas Arnold and I had tossed about in the billiards room. "But I haven't seen any triangles."

"An interesting idea. I was thinking quite differently." Something captured his attention and he leaned over to pick up a shell. "Ah, what about this one?"

It was a common periwinkle. "Pretty, but not the type I'm looking for to affix on a wall."

He eyed me a moment. "What exactly are you hoping to find?"

I toured the shoreline with my gaze. "Cockles or gapers . . . but what I'd really like more of are pure white limpets. I have so few of those. And I have a mind to create what looks like a starry night on a part of the ceiling."

"Limpets, huh? Remind me exactly what they look like."

"They are triangular with ridges, or sometimes they can be smooth. On the inside, they always have a horseshoe shaped impression—from the animal that lived there. They tend to stick tightly to the rocks and can be brown, gray, or black. I found several pure white ones with no markings my first month here and then . . . very few more."

I walked along the water's edge before stopping to pick up an oyster. "What are *your* thoughts regarding the number fifteen?"

He rotated his hat in his hands, his face cooling in the breeze. "I was reading the Bible the other day and came across that very number, which got me to thinking. There are scriptures written in different parts of the house."

"There are. Matthew 6:21 is painted over the gallery in the ballroom. But that has nothing to do with the number fifteen."

"No, nor Acts 2:46, which is in the dining hall. But considering the first clue led to the equinox, I was thinking about the Jewish Feast of the Tabernacles. It begins on the fifteenth day of the seventh month."

I rubbed my arms. "Yet there is nothing else in Josiah's clue. How could that possibly lead anywhere?"

"I thought the same. Thus, I made my way to Crossridge and stopped in at the vicarage. The only thing Rev. Gibbons could remember on hand about the number fifteen occurred in Hosea. Apparently Hosea paid fifteen pieces of silver for his wife's deliverance. Gibbons seemed to think the number fifteen could symbolize deliverance or restoration.

"Considering Josiah Drake's only son was away at sea, he could have been looking forward to the day his son would be restored to him."

"But when he left the clues, he knew he was dying. So heaven would be the only place for a reunion."

Lt. Burke stared up the cliff at the shadowy silhouette of the old church. "I'd like to look around the chapel a bit more thoroughly. I haven't had a chance to count anything there. The idea of restoration certainly makes me think of a church."

"I wonder why Christopher Drake kept away from his father for so long."

"As far as I know he was an adventurer, some would say a pirate."

"Yes, but sometimes there are other reasons."

Lt. Burke skimmed his fingertips along his jawline, casting a subtle look at me. "Like an art project perhaps."

"Yes, well." I walked away. "Among other things." In my swift retreat I caught sight of movement on the stone stairs and came to a halt. It was Daniel, carrying a box. I checked. Why on earth would he be coming down to the shore? I called his name into the wind.

He went motionless, staring down at us, then completed his descent.

I hastened to meet him at the bottom and was nearly gasping when I spoke. "What are you doing here?"

He struggled to answer at first. "Needed a walk, I suppose."

"With a box?"

His fingers curled around the corners of the crate. "Just a chore for Mrs. Fagean actually."

"Down here?" I didn't mean to sound so incredulous, so I softened my tone. "I thought you were going to touch up the edging on the trim."

He dashed a smile. "Already done."

"But . . ."

Lt. Burke wandered up. "Good morning, Mr. Hill."

Daniel edged back a step. "Beautiful day, but I haven't time to linger." He tapped the crate. "I've a few things to leave by the vicar's cottage when I'm done here."

I couldn't help but stare. "That box looks heavy."

"Not at all." He shifted his way around us. "And I'd better hurry if I'm to be back at the house to help you this afternoon."

"But where are you—"

"Oysters!" The word popped out of his mouth like a firework.

My lips parted. "Mrs. Fagean wants you to collect *oysters?*"

"For Cook, I believe, and I did make a promise. Well, it was a bet really, and I lost."

I stole a glance at Lt. Burke, then turned my focus back on Daniel. "Since when are you on speaking terms with Mrs. Fagean?"

"I-I felt bad about what I said to her in regard to the Equinox Festival. Anyhow, I'd better be off. And don't worry. I'll be available for anything you need later today."

Lt. Burke and I watched as he skirted the coastline and was lost to view around a rock outcropping.

I moved in quite close. "What do you think all that was about?"

"I haven't the least idea, but it had nothing to do with oysters. That I'm certain of. Should we follow him?"

"No, he'll be watching for us now. And at the end of the day, I know I can trust Daniel. I'd rather approach him later in private for a full account. What do you think?"

"Agreed, but did you smell that?"

"What?"

He wrinkled his nose. "Coming from the box. Smelled like ham to me."

I laughed. "I suppose Daniel was a bit more prepared than the two of us. He brought his own luncheon for his adventure today." I took one last look at the rock outcropping, then shifted back to face the stairs. "Shall we make our way up? I will concede to a bit of hunger myself, and we've got something of a walk back."

Lt. Burke stared over my shoulder for one full second, then smiled down at me. "I'm afraid we weren't too prosperous with our shell hunting today."

I gave him a lazy shrug. "Then we shall have to come again another day. I'm absolutely determined to find a pure white limpet."

Fourteen

Yet we didn't return to the seaside. Not for the whole of the week. Lt. Burke spent the majority of his time walled up with his antiquities or counting random items at the chapel. He simply couldn't turn his thoughts away from the idea of restoration.

I, however, was convinced that the answer to the clue might be triangular or simply fifteen of something since the riddle was so incredibly short. Miss Chant and I divided up the house searching every last nook and cranny in our spare time, but to no avail. It seemed Mr. Josiah Drake might just have taken the secret meaning of his clue to his grave. What we needed was a little luck.

But none came our way and by Saturday afternoon, when Lt. Burke suggested a drive to town, I was heartily glad to leave the house and my painting behind and think of anything other than the number fifteen.

Crossridge was a small village built around a town square, with the Duke of Marlborough guarding the heart of it. I gave the stone-faced peer a sideways glare as I took Lt. Burke's hand and departed the carriage. "Back where it all began. It feels like a lifetime ago."

He chuckled. "Indeed it does." And settled my hand on his arm. "Where to first? Finch's?"

"I have need of some new gloves, as you are all too aware of what happened to the last pair, then I've brought Mrs. Fagean's gold and silver threads to sell from her drizzling."

"I'd like to swing past the post office. I've been awaiting information from my solicitor."

I stalled for a second. "You mean so you can eventually let the house."

"Unfortunately, yes. I have nightmares about the number fifteen, you know. Even with months at our disposal, we may never get past this one."

"I didn't want to say it aloud, but I've had similar thoughts. I don't know where we go from here."

He gave me a tight-lipped smile. "Then let us have a few hours away from it."

The afternoon was a cool one, the village alive. From every direction came the pleasant sound of chatter and the rattle of people going about their day. A peddler had set up his wagon across the square and called out to the people passing by to consider his eight-page chapbooks. A badger had brought in grain to sell, and another butter and cheese. The bakery was the busiest at the moment as the baker had assembled a tray of quarter loaves at the window, the sweet scent peppering the breeze.

We stopped in at the post office—no letters for Lt. Burke—then the dress shop where I stumbled upon a pair of kid gloves for five shillings. I had taken them out to admire them once more when we approached the bank, where I tugged Lt. Burke to a halt. "Don't forget Mrs. Fagean's drizzling."

A quick nod and Lt. Burke steered us inside.

Creassey's Bank had been in Crossridge since 1796 and had ties to Hammond & Co. in Canterbury. This particular establishment dealt mostly with wealthy landowners and the gentry. The Savings and Friendly Society had a location across the square and served the working poor. I had been in Creassey's but one time and only to accompany Miss Drake.

The entry room was narrow and dark and it took a moment for my eyes to adjust. Lt. Burke led me over to a tall desk, where a clerk had to lean forward and poke his head over the edge to see us. His hair was scanty, gray and wispy, his face wrinkled into a frown. It took me a moment to gather my thoughts and present the threads. He took the bag of drizzling and escaped the room to examine it.

The bank was abuzz with a layer of silence, and Lt. Burke leaned down to my ear. "I'm surprised Mrs. Fagean has had time to drizzle with everything else going on."

"I agree."

He rubbed his chin. "Bit of a strange hobby—drizzling."

"She assures me it's quite fashionable in London."

He coughed to cover a laugh. "And she would know, I suppose."

My gaze fixed in place as I considered Lt. Burke's words. "Since I learned of the state of Miss Drake's affairs, I have been rather curious about the Fageans."

He edged closer. "You think they might be in reduced circumstances as well?"

"I'm beginning to wonder."

"*Mr.* Fagean certainly doesn't give off that air. He promptly pays his debts of honor, and regardless of how insidious he's seemed at Avonthorpe, he's highly regarded in town."

"Due to his"—I dropped to a whisper—"smuggling, do you think?"

"Perhaps, but he also seems like a good businessman, a compassionate one. Nor one to play deep."

I pulled my arms in close. "Could it be Mrs. Fagean then who's in need of the money . . . and straightaway? She practically begged me to take her drizzling with us today."

"It could simply be for a new gown or some such nonsense. I wouldn't put it past her."

"Yes, but—" I caught sight of a lady beyond the window, and I stormed over to the bank's large glass panel. "I don't believe it."

Lt. Burke drew up beside me. "What is it?"

"Mrs. Fagean!" I motioned across the square. "And she's with her husband."

Lt. Burke and I stared at each other a long moment, but we hadn't a second to voice our confusion as the clerk returned to his desk.

I secured the bank notes in my reticule as quickly as possible and hastened from the bank, but Mrs. Fagean had already disappeared.

My arms flopped down at my sides. "So we've missed her then."

Lt. Burke gave my arm a nudge. "I daresay we know where she lives."

We settled into a comfortable walk. "Why on earth did she act so desperate for me to handle this transaction if she already had plans to come to town?"

"Those plans were with her husband." His focus dropped to my reticule. "Reasonable to presume whatever she intends for this money, she doesn't want Mr. Fagean to know about."

My stomach lurched. Lt. Burke was right of course. Mrs. Fagean was always one to pounce on an opportunity. "Well . . ." I let out a sigh. "I shall simply ask her about it later. She can't deny being here now."

Lt. Burke called for the curricle, then assisted me onto the cushioned seat. My gaze darted around the busy square one last time, but Mrs. Fagean and her husband had vanished.

Lt. Burke settled in beside me and took the ribbons. "A prosperous day, I'd say. A pair of gloves and a bit more information about our houseguests."

"A very little."

He tried a smile. "But you shall remedy that soon enough." And slapped the ribbons.

The horses tugged forward, the scent of animals and dust sliding through the wind until it faded to the rugged green fields of the countryside.

I settled my hands in my lap. "Have you everything ready for Mr. Haskett's tour of your antiquities?"

"Yes . . . and no. It's a bit complicated."

"You keep saying that . . . How?"

A sideways glance. "Mr. Montague and I have a longstanding disagreement on how much should be sold."

"All of it, surely. You're in need of the money after all."

He stared down at the reins. "That is true, but I've been saving some very valuable pieces for the British Museum."

I sat up straight. "Ah, I remember. Mr. Montague mentioned something about a donation . . . but I don't understand."

"I suppose it's a matter of conscience." He sat for a moment rather silent and somber, the wind playing with the edges of his hair. "I'm afraid these antiquities of mine, these moments of history, will be lost once I allow them to be sold. The whole idea of private collections goes against my better nature. Everyone should have access to extraordinary pieces of history, to understand where they came from and the people who used them. How else are we to learn from the world?" His voice deepened. "Why else are we bringing anything back here? Why did I rescue these specific items from what I can only guess were thieves if they are not to be shared?"

So this was what Mr. Montague was referring to when he made the remark about Lt. Burke's political ideas. "It must be terribly difficult to decide what's best . . . when money is involved."

He nodded slowly. "I oversaw a project one time where a farmer had uncovered a trove of Roman antiquities. I ended up buying the lot with the intention of donating most of it. So much of my available income is tied up in curiosities right now. It has left me with the few options you see before me."

"Which is why you've not been able to invest in Avonthorpe."

He grimaced, his eyes trained to the road. "It's a daily struggle."

"And the Egyptian antiquities?"

"I've selected a few pieces, the sarcophagus for one, but I'll need to part with more than that to give us ample time for our treasure hunt. I only hope our pursuit of the truth can lead us to both the treasure and the person responsible for my aunt's murder. It is my one driving force."

I picked at the edge of my glove. "Have you finished all your inquiries at the house?"

"I've spoken to every last person."

"And there's no new information?"

"None till today."

I lifted my eyebrows. "Today—then you suspect Mrs. Fagean?"

He huffed a laugh. "I suspect both of the Fageans. They're hiding something, and I believe it's more than his smuggling operation." He directed the horses right down the main road to Avonthorpe. "Have you had a chance to speak with Mr. Hill about his presence at the beach?"

"Daniel?" His name came out a breathy question. "Not exactly. We have been working together daily . . . only, he's not himself. When I questioned him, he stuck with his story about oysters. You don't suspect him, do you?"

"I cannot discount anyone in the house that night. He was a bit glib about what he was doing when it happened, you know. Do you realize he was one of the last to come to my aunt's room? A full half hour had passed before he arrived."

Unwittingly my hand settled on Lt. Burke's arm. "Give me a bit more time with Daniel. I've known him all my life. He would never commit a murder—he couldn't. He's always been so kindhearted, a true artist."

Lt. Burke took a long look down at my fingers curled around his jacket sleeve, and I carefully slipped my hand away. "Daniel's young. He has the world before him. Believe me, he was terribly pleased to get the chance to train with your aunt."

"I'll give you the fact he seems affected by her death."

"Like I said, he feels things deeply. And we all grieve in different ways."

Avonthorpe appeared at the crest of the hill, and Lt. Burke slanted me a wan look. "All I know is that I plan to pay a bit more attention to the Fageans. I've refused any illegal business dealings with Mr. Fagean for now, but I also left the door open for legitimate ones. I've offered them hospitality for the time being, which will keep the pair in residence and under our noses. I fear the truth of what happened the night my aunt was killed lies somewhere between the two of them, and I mean to root it out."

I headed to my room, intending to rest before supper, but instead encountered Miss Chant in the hall a few steps from my bedchamber. She wore a weary expression I'd not noticed earlier in the day, and when she sidestepped away from me, I stalled her at once. "Is something amiss?"

She looked up a bit sheepishly. "Certainly not." Then a hesitant smile. "Did you enjoy your outing to the village? Lt. Burke good company?" She carefully leaned against the wall.

"I did. I found a pair of gloves I particularly like. And Lt. Burke was"—a slow smile—"a perfect companion for the afternoon."

She brightened a bit and folded her hands at her waist. "I am particularly glad to hear you say that, Phoebe. Marriage is really the only option for you. Your father will be pleased to hear—"

"My father!" I hunched forward, my chest tight. "You misunderstand me entirely. Please, you must say nothing of this to him." Then a huff to myself. "I haven't altered any of my plans. Lt. Burke and I are simply friends."

Her jaw flexed, her lips pressed tight. "Friends indeed. I don't know where you acquired this passion for independence, but it'll never do. Don't you see, this could be the perfect answer to all your problems. Lt. Burke is a fine match for you, a respectable one at any rate. *He* would never be involved in a scandal."

"You mean like me?" My discomfort turned all too quickly to

anger. "You think Lt. Burke will finally make me respectable? Or is that my father talking?"

She stiffened. "That is not who I was referring—"

"Jean, of course." I gritted my teeth. She was right in a way, but I could only imagine what Lt. Burke's face would look like when he discovered I'd aided and abetted a French spy to escape from Middlecrest. He'd never speak to me again. There would be no romance between us. And Miss Chant was not being fair. "Have you forgotten all I've shared with you? The proceeds of the treasure will afford us to . . ."

She shook her head slowly. "Don't be a fool, Phoebe. We may never even uncover it."

Suddenly I felt tired. "I should like to lie down a bit before supper. Good day, Miss Chant."

I dragged myself away from my friend in heavy silence, her words like ice in my heart. How dare she insinuate marriage was my only choice? I had talent—hope. She'd been so cold, so exacting with her demands. I took a quick glance behind me. Had she ever really spoken to me that way before? Moreover, what had caused the confrontation in the first place?

I was not entirely myself when I pushed through my bedchamber door and closed it behind me. Yet I stopped cold a few steps in nonetheless as a fresh wave of anxiety washed over me. Was something off in the room? A quick scan revealed nothing untoward as I took myself across the rug.

Surely it was just the intensity of my argument with Miss Chant or a spark of an overactive imagination.

Then a chill wriggled its way across my shoulders. The unnerving silence thrummed in my ears. I turned first right and then left, still certain something was not as it seemed.

A heart-pounding second of indecision, and then I saw it. My jewelry box had been moved to the center of my dresser.

I padded forward without a sound, my heartbeat intensifying with each step. Someone *had* been in my room, and they'd been looking through my things.

The clues!

I raced to my dresser and slung open the lid to the jewelry box. Empty. They were all gone. I pressed my hand to my face as I shook my head. How could this have happened? Who would have been in my private room? Who would have known?

Immediately I thought of Miss Chant. No, she had no reason to take them, nor Mr. Arnold for that matter. I had been completely open with them. Yet we'd had that strange conversation in the hallway . . . No, she wouldn't have done it.

I felt a bit shaky as I slumped into my dressing chair, my gaze on the empty box. Lt. Burke and I must not have been discreet enough. Someone was on to our hunt. Daniel? Mr. Montague? The Fageans? Or a person I'd not even considered.

I went straight to the ground floor and summoned Arnold to the privacy of the library. If any of the servants were involved, he would be the best person to ferret it out.

I ceased my pacing in the center of the room and held up my hands. "All my clues have been stolen."

His eyes rounded. "What do you mean?"

"Someone has taken them out of my jewelry box."

"Lt. Burke?"

I shook my head hard. "No. He is working in concert with us. It is someone else."

The wrinkles on Arnold's face deepened. "Is there any way you could have misplaced them? Forgotten where you left them?"

"Not a chance. Besides, I have them all memorized. I haven't even bothered to look at them in days."

He stopped short. "Then this theft could have happened at any time."

"Oh dear. You don't think whoever it was is already hunting for the treasure?"

He began to pace. "I most certainly do. But who could have known about any of this? Miss Chant—"

"Would never betray my trust."

He dipped his chin. "Then it has to be someone else."

"Perhaps a person has been watching us—like the Fageans."

His jaw flexed. "I wouldn't put it past either of them."

"It's all so strange. I saw them in town today, rushing through the square."

"Oh? You don't say, because I was informed they were making a call on Mr. Haskett earlier."

"Liars." I met Arnold's pinched eyes. "From now on, you must keep a watch on those two and report back to me everything you learn. Somehow we have got to stay ahead of them."

"Why not simply have Lt. Burke turn them out of the house? Surely he has the authority to do that."

I let out a sigh. "Lt. Burke doesn't want them to leave as of yet. He believes they might be responsible for his aunt's death. He needs more time to prove his suspicions."

Arnold gasped. "Be careful, Miss Radcliff. Lt. Burke may think himself a consummate military general, but as far as I'm concerned, the man is playing with fire."

Fifteen

THE NEXT DAY ALL INDICATIONS OF SPRING HAD VANISHED. A cloudy gloom moved in over our little corner of Britain during the night, blotting out the morning sun and ushering in a cold wind. The perfect sort of day to stay indoors, but Mrs. Fagean had other plans.

I caught sight of her out the window at the bottom of the stairs, heading west from the manor house, her cloak clutched tight about her neck, her pace rapid. Most of the house remained asleep in their beds. Thus, I was forced to throw on my pelisse and race from the house without the luxury of an escort if I meant to see what she had planned.

Thankfully I was quick enough to keep her in my sights. She took the path that led to the church but turned away from the coastline at a small intersection at the edge of the woods. I lingered a moment at the turn, having never trod this way before.

The path was dark, the trees so thick, clumps of mist circled the great trunks like flowing robes. Moss carpeted every available space, kept damp by a lack of sun. I could hear the subtle pitter-patter of Mrs. Fagean's progress and I followed it for some time, weaving gradually down the hillside until I crossed an oozing stretch of water, shallow enough for me to hop across the rocks.

The forest was quieter here, the air still and wet, the gray light of day playing tricks with the shadows and colors as it crept between the thick tree branches. That's when I came to a wide section in the path, which curiously disappeared into the trees and the overgrowth of the forest floor.

I stopped cold. Which way had Mrs. Fagean gone? I turned first one direction, then the next, but I couldn't make out a location where any sort of path resumed. She had simply vanished. I held my breath, straining to hear footsteps, but the shuffle I'd been following had completely disappeared.

There was a possibility she'd turned once again at the subtle brook, using the smooth stones that littered the shallow water, but such a move would be far more difficult than simply continuing along the brook's edge. Strange that I hadn't seen any footprints for some time.

A surge of wind rolled through the trees, whipping the leaves into a shimmering fury and my nerves into chaos. The thickness of the forest almost seemed alive in my mind, able to draw in closer and closer, each individual tree stretching taller, darker, more ominous. I hastened back to the brook, pausing from one huge tree to the next, my fingers groping the rough bark.

With every passing second I became less and less certain I was alone, my imagination producing a presence that watched me from the folds of the shadows around me. I knew that couldn't be the case. And if anyone was near, it had to be Mrs. Fagean . . . or . . .

My muscles contracted. Was it Jean again? He had told me he wanted money, that he might return, but why would he linger in the area only to be caught? Such a notion didn't make any sense.

Then I heard a twig snap.

My body went still, all but my heart, which pounded like a hammer in my chest.

I remained like a scared doe for a painful second before darting off into the trees, away from the sound, running as fast as I could, anything to escape.

The forest blurred around me, the brush clawing at my pelisse as I threaded the space between the trees, but I didn't slow, not for some time, not until my sides ached and I gasped for breath. Only then did I stare back at the woods.

There was no shuffle of pursuit, no shadow emerging from the trees. I pressed my hand to my chest as I leaned forward, the muscles in my stomach cramping. My sudden flight had managed to create some space between me and whoever had been watching me.

Then quietly, carefully, I sneaked farther into the dense forest, making certain whoever had been near would be equally unable to track where I'd gone.

I wandered watchfully for several minutes until I was fairly certain I was out of danger before crouching down beside a large tree trunk, my knees at my chest. The ground felt cool, the moss damp. I tilted my head against the hard bark and allowed my breathing to return to normal.

I perched my chin on my knees, my eyes trained to the forest, which is when I made a rather interesting discovery. Emerging from the mist, several yards away, stood a two-story building, somewhat overgrown with ivy and hidden by the trees. I pushed to my feet and crept forward to get a better look. Dark wooden beams framed red-brick walls, the windows and door trimmed an attractive white.

My mouth fell open—the vicar's cottage.

I was standing at the rear of it. The remains of a garden wall darted through the trees. Was this the building Mrs. Fagean had thought she would inherit? Had she come here for some reason this morning?

I stepped over the remains of the stone wall and pushed my way through the weeds to a large back window. After cupping my hands to the glass, I pressed forward and squinted to see inside.

A smallish room emerged in the dim light, a layer of dust coating the stone floor. Most of the space looked empty, deserted, but for a few crates lining one of the walls. The house hadn't been lived in for some time.

I skirted the building to the front and emerged onto what must have been at one time a manicured lawn. The front of the house had a nice view of the cliffs, and if I looked hard I could make out the outline of the church perched at the top.

There was a slow movement on the horizon near the chapel and I smiled. It was Lt. Burke riding up on his horse to continue his work. I shrugged off the unnatural feeling I'd endured in the woods and the loneliness of the abandoned house. Could it have been Mrs. Fagean who'd chilled my nerves to the core? Either way she'd eluded me, and the world felt terribly distant at the moment.

As I stared up at the hillside my shoulders slowly relaxed, a warm tug wrapping my chest. Whatever concerns I had regarding Lt. Burke, I enjoyed his company—moreover, his protection—and that was all I had the space to think about at present. Everything else would simply have to wait.

I found Lt. Burke in the back of the chapel's adjoining building sorting through his curiosities.

"Good morning."

His head popped up over a crate and stilled a moment. I expect he was a bit surprised to see me, but he ran his hands through his hair and smiled. "Good morning yourself. What brings you up the hill so early?"

Only after he rounded the boxes and pressed his hand to the back of his neck did I realize he'd removed his jacket and cravat as well as rolled his sleeves to his elbows. And why not? It was warm in the room and he'd not been expecting company.

I hid my blush by taking a circuitous route about the room. "A useless mission, I'm afraid."

He rested against the nearby wall. "Do tell. I could use a distraction from all this."

"I followed Mrs. Fagean into the woods."

"The woods? What took her that way?"

"I have no idea. I lost her almost at once . . . and"—I rubbed a chill from my arms—"I became patently aware how alone I was. I imagined someone had come upon me." I pushed a stray hair from my face before worrying my fingers at my waist. "And then I heard a twig pop."

He stood up straight. "You mean someone was actually there with you?"

"I don't know." I frowned as my stomach tensed. "I took off running at full speed. I was terrified."

Lt. Burke stepped forward, absently taking my hands into his. He opened his mouth to speak, then his gaze plunged down. "You're freezing."

I gave a little laugh, but it was wholly unconvincing. "I ran a good bit, and the wind is cold this morning."

"No, it's more than that. You're still scared."

I glanced behind me. "I suppose I am."

He slid his hand around my back. "I wish I had something warm to offer you to drink. Come with me into the sunlight at once." He led me over to a small square window and motioned for me to sit on a nearby crate before fetching his jacket and wrapping it around my shoulders. He settled down close at my side. "Tell me again exactly what happened."

I recounted every detail, but I had little information to offer in regard to the person in the woods. Granted, none that I could share with Lt. Burke.

He must have sensed my dark thoughts. "I recommend not venturing out of the house alone in the future. Or at the very least take Creature. No one could get by him."

"I left in a hurry, anxious to learn what Mrs. Fagean was up to. Clearly I made a mull of it. Well, in part."

He lifted his eyebrows, a hint of amusement about his face. "What do you mean?"

"My flight led me straight to the vicar's cottage."

He nodded slowly. "That old place. My aunt used to store some things there."

"Did you know Mrs. Fagean was under the impression Miss Drake might leave that very cottage to her and her husband?"

His eyes widened and then he laughed. "Why on earth would she do that?"

"I have no idea."

He grinned to himself. "A Drake would never break up the estate for nothing—a stingier group of people you'll never meet. Charles Drake, the cousin who ultimately inherited everything when Josiah died, cut off part of his own family entirely as he saw them as a liability."

"Goodness. A happy man indeed."

Lt. Burke splayed his palms against the crate behind him and rested back against his arms. "One of the many reasons my mother distanced herself from her cousins. We Burkes are more honesty-and-integrity-type people."

"I can see that."

He nudged my arm. "And what are the Radcliffs like?"

"I can't speak for my entire family, but I've been told on more than one occasion that I'm an impulsive, independent, and maddeningly adventurous type of woman." And now I could add Miss Chant to that list.

He mirrored my wry smile. "Hence the sudden jaunt into the woods and the unpredictable eating schedule."

"Exactly."

He ran his hand down his face, peeking over his fingers as they passed. "I suppose any urging of caution on my part will fall on deaf ears."

I shot him a sideways glance. "Not entirely. After today, I find myself a bit warier than before."

"Then I will only say this—trust your instincts. From what you described, you knew there was someone following you, watching you, long before you heard a sound." He leaned forward, his attention wandering the dusty ground. "I only wish I'd trusted my intuition when I was in France fighting the war." He sighed. "I suppose I can claim there was love involved."

My heart threw a wayward beat. "Oh?"

"Well, not mine. I told you earlier I was betrayed, but there's more to the story. You see, over the course of our travels, my friend was introduced to a lady—a Frenchwoman. She was helping the coalition in their fight against Napoleon. She was presented to us with such a glowing recommendation I never questioned her words or actions, not at first at least. She made my friend happy and that was all I cared about.

"Soon enough though, little inconsistencies in her behavior emerged, but I disregarded them. After all, my friend was deep in love and I wanted the best for him, so I kept my mouth shut. Within the month, however, she'd stolen an important dispatch in my possession from General Wellington, and when I went to confront my friend with what had happened, he was gone, deserted. All I can guess is that they left together. Complete and utter betrayal by both of them. I still cannot fathom how my friend had such a weak character that he would run away from his responsibilities and the military. Moreover, how could he do such a thing to the men, his own comrades, who had given their lives to protect his?"

Throughout the afternoon I could think of only one thing. Was I any better than Lt. Burke's friend? Had I, too, betrayed all the brave men who'd died on the Continent by my continued interactions with Jean? Where did my loyalties lie?

Moreover, at this point, what could I even tell the authorities? *"I . . . uh, I came face-to-face with a Frenchman from my past, a man I had a deep relationship with, but I decided to keep his whereabouts a secret because . . . well . . . it's complicated. I have no idea where he is now."* That would go over quite well.

Lt. Burke would know just why I'd kept the truth to myself. And after what he'd revealed about his military friend . . . How could we even move past such a thing?

And my father. As soon as he learned Jean Cloutier was in the area, I'd be whisked back to Middlecrest Abbey, where I'd be in no position to help Miss Chant, Lt. Burke, Arnold, or even Daniel. Besides, I'd made a promise to Miss Drake. Everything I'd endured thus far would be for nothing. There was really no choice but to keep quiet.

I was in this perverse state of mind when I came upon Mr. Fagean standing in the hall admiring one of Avonthorpe's many paintings. He was deep in thought, studying a large rectangular canvas that displayed a ship in the throes of a storm, its narrow bow thrusting upward upon a wave, its sails at full mast. I'd always admired the beautiful artistry of the moment of crisis and the intricate workmanship.

I paused beside him, curious as to what had caught his eye.

Mr. Fagean was not a tall man nor the least bit attractive in any way, but I'd always found him a bit mysterious with his auburn hair and fluffy sideburns peppered with gray. His eyes were set rather close together and tended toward beady at times.

He released his chin and gave me a questioning look. "I've always appreciated this painting."

"It is a glorious work," I said in awe. "An early William Hogarth, is it not?"

His voice took on an acidity I'd not expected. "Not because of the artist—the ship, the voyage. I've heard so many tales of Christopher Drake. Pity the man didn't make it back alive."

I studied the artwork anew. "I didn't realize the ship depicted here belonged to Christopher Drake."

"He was an adventurer. A pirate. A businessman. Everyone in the family still has much of the same blood running through our veins."

I nodded carefully, curiously.

"This piece was commissioned by Josiah Drake following his son's first voyage. This particular ship of his was lost at sea after being fired upon by none other than the British government. Christopher amazingly stayed alive by gathering up driftwood from the wreckage. When he returned to Avonthorpe, he told the harrowing story of how he floated for two days before being found by an East Indiaman en route home. Romantic, is it not?"

Mr. Fagean pursed his lips as if to hide a smile. "I think Josiah Drake wished he could have joined his son when he set out on that second trip. He was a well-respected cartographer after all. There are maps and maps of his in the library, but age catches up with us all. Christopher was instead forced to take on another business partner."

He hedged a moment. There was an unnatural silence, then an abrupt, "Good day, Miss Radcliff."

Stunned by what I'd uncovered, I stood and listened to Mr. Fagean humming to himself as he pranced away, then I turned my attention back to the painting, fishing my spectacles from my pocket and moving in a bit closer.

In the painting Christopher was depicted manning the helm, a dashing figure commanding the ship. He looked to be about nineteen or twenty at the time, a young man in every way. So the painting depicted his first voyage. There were several men accompanying him at the moment of crisis, grabbing ropes and masts, trying to keep the ship afloat. Mr. Fagean had said the ship was eventually lost, and the men—

I lurched forward, my gaze captured by two small ordinals etched into the main mast.

Fifteen!

My heart nearly leaped out of my chest. Christopher Drake's ship was engraved with the number fifteen. What did it mean? How could this relate to the clue? It was the connection Lt. Burke and I had been looking for.

I had to find him and straightaway!

Sixteen

Arnold directed me to the library so I might locate Lt. Burke as soon as possible, but he didn't prepare me for what I'd find.

Lt. Burke's back was to me at the fireplace, one of his arms pressed to the mantel, the other outstretched in front of him, a letter pinned between his fingers. He stood very still, his eyes tight on the folded paper.

As I crossed the room silently, Lt. Burke crushed the missive into a ball and launched it into the flames. Startled, I stopped but a few yards away. He grasped the iron poker from its holder and pushed the paper into the heart of the fire, then tossed the poker against the fender with a loud *clang*.

The sound made me jump, and for a tricky second I thought I might be able to retreat without being discovered, but in his haste to quit the room Lt. Burke whirled about, nearly crashing into me.

"Miss Radcliff." He drew up short, extending his hand to steady me, then plunging it through his hair. The black centers of his eyes looked enormous, his skin flushed.

I took a hasty step back as the air felt strangely thin between us. "Pardon me." Had I stumbled upon something I shouldn't have? I drew in a sharp breath. "Arnold informed me you'd be in here. I never meant to intrude."

My focus shifted painfully to the fireplace as a distressing thought crept into my mind. The clues to the treasure had been stolen from my room. Was Lt. Burke involved somehow in their disappearance? Was he disposing of them?

We stood for a long moment cautiously appraising one another until he gave a definitive shrug. "I see your mind at work. Have you a question for me?"

Flustered, I shook my head. "I'd never be so bold." But I couldn't take my eyes off the flames.

He lowered his head. "It was a group of letters of mine."

"Letters?" Could I believe him?

He paced the available space between the sitting area and the casement of books. "They were from my friend, the one I told you about."

My shoulders relaxed. "You mean your friend wrote to you after his betrayal."

A slow nod. "I've kept them far too long already."

I pressed my hands against my stomach as my chest tightened. Lt. Burke had finally decided to move on from his friend. How could he feel confident enough to end any chance for a reconciliation? Loyalty to his country obviously ranked above all else. My heart beat erratically as I considered what this meant for me and my secret. There was no question now. Lt. Burke would never understand about Jean. Our relationship or whatever it was would be over forever.

I grasped the back of the winged chair, somewhat winded. Why did I care what he thought of me anyway? I'd always prided myself on my plans for complete self-reliance. I had dreams.

"You said"—Lt. Burke's voice was softer now, vulnerable as he stepped closer—"you came here to see me?"

I lifted my gaze to meet his kind eyes. The imperceptible pull I'd felt the first day I'd met him intensified, narrowing my mind into one forceful thought. I was attracted to him. But it was more than that. Physically, emotionally, somewhere along the way our time together had grown strangely comfortable.

As if he'd read my thoughts, he gave me a gentle nod. "Care to sit for a bit?"

I managed to settle into one of the chairs, equal parts numb and elated. Was there a way to keep my past behind me and focus instead on the future?

I caught an errant smile and the delightful intensity to his familiar gaze. Did Lt. Burke want to be a part of it? The thought brought a grin surging to my lips. Could I even stop him from being a part of it?

Over the next half hour I disclosed everything I'd experienced over the last few days—the stolen clues, the discovery I'd made about the painting in the hall—stopping short of revealing my encounter with Jean Cloutier, of course.

I couldn't hide the delight in my voice when I took Lt. Burke to the painting and pointed out the small fifteen on the mast.

He seemed giddy as well, his hand so utterly comfortable and reassuring at the small of my back. "This has to be the connection we've been looking for. But how can a number on a ship have anything to do with the hidden treasure here at Avonthorpe? Especially if the ship was lost at sea? Unless . . ."

"What?"

"I received a letter from my solicitor, and he answered a few questions I asked about the infamous Christopher Drake. He told me there was quite a bit of bad blood between the family and Christopher's business partner after the son died. But that could be just rumor."

A knot formed on my brow. "Mr. Haskett told me something similar. He was told the surviving Drakes thought the partner responsible for Christopher's death in some way."

"Ah, well, my solicitor has a different take. He says the business partner, Mr. Ruteledge, came to Avonthorpe demanding repayment on a rather unconventional loan. There was nothing in writing, mind you. More of a deathbed declaration. Charles Drake, the inheriting cousin, as advised, refused to honor what he believed was a lie. Thus, Mr. Ruteledge fell upon hard times. He ended up losing everything in the end."

"But surely Mr. Ruteledge was entitled to something?"

"Pirating and adventuring are not recognized by the law. My solicitor assumes the man had little recourse but to shrink away, his tail between his legs."

I flexed my jaw. "Mr. Fagean says Josiah Drake was a mapmaker. Perhaps it's time to return to the library and examine his maps. Maybe one of them points to the treasure."

Pounding footsteps halted our conversation, and we both turned to face the corner in anticipation.

Daniel flew around the bend, his arms crossed, his face scrunched up in fury. "There you are! I've been looking for an age."

My hand flew to my mouth. "Oh dear. I'm so terribly sorry. I completely forgot I'd arranged to work with you on the trim this afternoon."

He mulled a moment, staring down at the floor. "You always do whatever pops into that head of yours. Well, such inconstancy can hurt other people, you know. Just ask your sister. I stayed here for you. No one else."

My mind reeled. "You're right. You needn't remind me of my shortcomings. I did ask you to remain, and I've managed to leave you at every turn. I promise I had no other choice today. I was doing what I thought was best."

He huffed out a sigh. "I wish I could believe you."

My vision blurred. Never before had Daniel taken me to task so painfully . . . and after my tiff with Miss Chant, it cut deep. "You needn't stay in residence any longer if you wish to return home. Lt. Burke has graciously given me more time to complete the trim. I don't think—"

He threw his hands in the air. "It's too late now. What's done is done. I'm here and I mean to see this through."

What was the source of the venom in his voice? Surely this anger ran deeper than me forgetting to work with him in the ballroom. "Is there something else—"

"Forget it. Shall we start again tomorrow morning?"

"I'd like that." I sounded wounded and it irked me.

Lt. Burke stepped closer, but I waved him off. The last thing I needed was for this to come to fisticuffs between Lt. Burke and Daniel.

Daniel trudged off, his steps less pronounced but no less painful to my ears.

I shook my head. "I cannot believe I completely forgot him."

"It's understandable." Lt. Burke crossed his arms. "Regardless, a gentleman should never speak to a lady in such a way."

"I might have said something, but he caught me off guard. It's not like him to behave so recklessly."

"I daresay he's nothing but a child who needs to grow up."

"He is a bit immature for his age." I stared down the hall. "I thought bringing him here would do a great deal of good for his disposition. His mother coddles him so. But then the murder happened . . . and I've been so distracted."

I don't know why that confession sent my attention darting to Lt. Burke's face, but there it was, his ready smile waiting for me. Was he thinking the same thing?

Apparently not. His eyebrows drew in. "What's all this about your sister?"

My heart stopped. Under no circumstances could I tell him the truth behind Daniel's accusation. His offhand remark had everything to do with my inadvertent betrayal of my sister and the lie I'd told to conceal my relationship with Jean Cloutier. Daniel knew it all.

I swallowed hard. "Our family has had our fair share of tragedies."

His smile faded.

I rambled on. "My sister's fiancé was killed just days before her wedding. Juliana still has not recovered. I doubt she ever will."

His mouth fell open. "Mr. Giles Harris? He was to be your brother-in-law?"

Warmth flooded my cheeks. "Then you've heard of our situation."

"The news was widespread."

I should have anticipated Lt. Burke's knowledge of current events. Granted, most of the details remained hidden.

"Really, I should have made the connection when you told me your father was Lord Torrington."

My chest burned as my emotions boiled over. "He's not really my father, you know."

His eyes widened. "Come again."

What was I saying? I reached out for the wall to steady me. "I don't know why I just came out with all that."

He leaned in close. "Is it true then?"

"Yes, and a rather large family secret. Miss Chant knows, of course. I don't keep anything from her. I only meant Lord Torrington is not my natural father. He has stood in for the man my whole life. I love him dearly." We'd always had a special relationship . . . that is, until my mistake.

"I understand." Lt. Burke's hand wrapped mine. "And I'm glad you felt comfortable enough to share something so personal with me."

Comfort? Was that what I'd felt? No. Evasion, more like. I'd meant to shock him out of asking any more questions about my sister. I glanced up, guilt pounding in my chest, and all but melted under his tender gaze. Though I'd revealed a family secret for the wrong reasons, I was glad somehow that he knew the truth about my parentage. "Then you'll keep my secret?"

He seemed almost taken aback. "That goes without saying. I feel like the two of us have an understanding—nothing but trust."

I didn't deserve the butterflies that whipped around my stomach, nor the tingling warmth of his fingers, but for two years I'd been longing for something. Was this it? Was it real connection that I'd been missing all along? Perhaps that's why I'd brought Daniel to Avonthorpe—for equal companionship. Miss Chant was a dear friend, but she was also employed by my father.

I gave Lt. Burke a tentative smile. Friendship, attraction, whatever was blossoming between us—now that I'd felt it, I had no intention of letting it go, not without a fight. If only my past would remain there.

By morning I felt as light as a bird, swinging my arms, humming to myself as I coasted onto the landing. Lt. Burke and I had split up a large pile of maps that we'd located in the library the previous day, and I'd stayed up quite late examining them. Though I had little to go on at present, I had high hopes the number fifteen had something to do with Josiah Drake's cartography skills.

That is, until I stumbled upon two upstairs maids near the alcove at the top of the grand staircase, clearly embarrassed to be seen by me. They lowered their conversation, but I could still hear them, the intensity to their interaction dampening my mood.

I tarried a moment near the balustrade. It seemed one of the maids had not completed her duties up to standard. The other was angry, her voice sharp. "I meant for you to clean all the stairwells in the house, particularly these steps." The duster flipped back and forth in her hands.

"I'm sorry, mum. I'll get on it at once."

The head maid tipped up her chin. "All fifteen of them, mind you. Fifteen!"

I gripped the wooden railing. Fifteen stairs! Avonthorpe had fifteen stairs? Why had I not thought to count the steps? I took a wild glance around me, but there was nothing obvious about the stairwell.

I gritted my teeth, irritated I couldn't search more thoroughly at this very moment, not with the maid at work, so I journeyed down to the ground floor, darting a furtive glance back up the curving banister. Did the top step look a little darker than the rest? Or was it my imagination?

The maid descended the stairs with her head bowed.

"Excuse me." I ran my fingers down the corner of the wall, hoping to sound casual. "Lt. Burke has tasked me with assessing the artistic value of the house, concerning the upcoming lease, of course. I happened to notice that the wood color on the grand staircase does not match all the way to the top."

"Oh that." She flicked her hand in the air. "You have Josiah Drake to thank for that."

My skin prickled.

"I'm told that after his son's miraculous escape from death, he used the driftwood from the wreck in various locations in the house." She motioned forward. "The fireplace mantel in the drawing room has a piece of it. I believe there's a chair somewhere in the house as well, but I can't really remember which one. He was sentimental, I suppose."

"And the stairs?"

"If I understand correctly, that came later, near the end of his life. Josiah Drake had the top step replaced with the last of the wood. I think it had something to do with his journey to heaven or some such nonsense. Who knows? I'm told the man was a bit mad at the end, but there are so many rumors. No one knows what to believe."

My pulse raced. The fifteenth stair was made with a piece of the mast that saved Christopher Drake's life—the very mast that had the number displayed in the painting! I'd figured it out. It had nothing to do with the maps. My heart did somersaults in my chest.

But I left the maid to finish her cleaning. Now was not the time to investigate.

Hoping to find Lt. Burke in the breakfast room, I hastened into the salon. But I was met first by Miss Chant in the hall.

I tugged her into an alcove, our petty argument dissolving beneath my excitement. "I believe I've just figured out the clue about the number fifteen."

She blew out a sigh of relief, but it was a tight one. "You mean to tell me we can stop counting everything?"

I hadn't realized she was still doing so, not since our disagreement at any rate. I motioned over my shoulder with my chin, things still not wholly settled between us. "It's the top step on the grand staircase. There are fifteen stairs! We cannot search it at present, however, as the maids are cleaning there."

I heard the distant *squeak* of a wooden chair emanating from the breakfast room and I pulled away. I'd much rather share the news with Graham. I gave her arm a friendly squeeze. "I'll be sure to tell you more about it all later, but I need to speak with Gr—Lt. Burke as soon as possible."

She nodded slowly, her lips pressed tight.

But I had little time to consider her cold reaction as I hurried down the hall and into the breakfast room where I was met with nothing but disappointment—only Mrs. Fagean.

She gave me a wafting look, then returned to her newspaper. Drat, Lt. Burke would have to wait. I'd been meaning to speak with her alone.

"Good morning, Mrs. Fagean."

A forced smile. "Good morning."

I procured a plate, a few slices of ham, and a muffin and took a seat opposite her. "I saw you rushing from the house yesterday morning."

"Oh?" A shrewd glance up.

I forked my ham. "Where were you off to so early? It's not like you."

She rolled a bite of food in her mouth. "Just a walk."

"Into the woods?"

Several hard blinks. "Yes. Why do you ask?"

I fiddled with the napkin in my lap. "Just curious. Also, I have the money you requested I obtain for you at the bank, for your drizzling, or have you forgotten all about that?"

Her eyes snapped up. "And did you get what I asked for?"

"Oh yes."

"Thank goodness. Where is it?"

"In my room. I'll be happy to get it for you, but first, may I ask a question?"

She adjusted her position in the chair. "Certainly. We've always been close, you and I. Is it about Lt. Burke? I saw the way he was looking at you last night."

My heart did a little flip. Had she really seen something? Though I'd felt a great deal on my end, he was so much more difficult to read.

I straightened in my chair. "I do have a question . . . about the day I took your drizzling to town."

Her chin popped up.

"I saw you with . . ." A flash of movement caught my eye out the drawing room door and I lost my train of thought for a moment. It was Daniel and Mr. Fagean rushing by on their way out of the house. Strange that they should be going somewhere together.

I turned back to Mrs. Fagean. "Interesting the very person I saw you with yesterday should pass by just now."

Mrs. Fagean went ghostly white, her lips quivering around her breath. "He told you, then?"

"No, I saw the two of you."

She hunched forward and lowered her head. "I can only guess what you are thinking."

"Lt. Burke and I—"

"He was there too?" She thrust to her feet and retreated to the window. "How is this even possible?"

I opened my mouth, but nothing came forth. What on earth did she mean? I stood and crossed the room to her side before peeking around her stoic profile. "Lt. Burke had things to do in town. I told you he was to be my escort. You seemed pleased with the arrangement at the time."

She stared at me and then the room as if searching for answers, then all at once her shoulders relaxed and her mouth turned up at the corners. "You're speaking of my sudden trip to the village with Mr. Fagean."

I nodded easily enough, but now *I* was off stride. What did she think I was speaking of?

Relaxed now, she gave me a small trill of a laugh. "My foolish husband thought to whisk me away to the jewelry store to make a sort of peace offering. I wasn't expecting to leave the house at all, as you well know. I had plans, but I was forced to cancel them. He had been a trifle rude to me the previous night, but when he came to me with those puppy eyes, how could I say no? I must add, I had no idea he could be so romantic." She extended her hand to reveal a new emerald ring. "What do you think? Isn't it delightful?"

I found it difficult to form the right words. Weren't the Fageans short on money? "It's lovely and probably cost a great deal."

She wiggled her fingers as she turned her hand to appraise the ring herself. "Mr. Fagean has always been extremely generous with me." A sharp glance at the doorway. "And speaking of my delightful husband, while he's out, I should like to pop into your room and get my money. Where did you say you left it?"

"I'll come with—"

"No need to bother, my dear. I can certainly find my way."

Still distracted by our conversation, I motioned to the door without much thought. "It's on my escritoire in my—"

Her smile widened as she moved to the door. "Thank you, dear," she said over her shoulder before floating from the room.

I stood there a long moment, replaying every second of our conversation in my mind. Why had Mrs. Fagean blanched as white as a sheet? What had I said that set her off? It had been right after Daniel and Mr. Fagean passed the drawing room door.

I swallowed hard. I'd not used Mr. Fagean's name in my questioning at first. Had she thought . . . ? Oh dear. I had to grasp the side of the sofa, as my legs felt weak.

She'd presumed I was talking about Daniel.

Seventeen

I WENT STRAIGHT TO LT. BURKE'S BEDCHAMBER AND pounded on the door. Valet or no valet, this couldn't wait.

Miss Chant would be appalled by my actions if she'd been around, but since our argument, we'd been avoiding one another. She claimed she was far too busy with Vincent even to stop by my room at night; however, I knew the real reason—we both needed some space. Besides, Lt. Burke was proving a far better hunting partner.

I pounded on Lt. Burke's door a second time. This time harder than the last.

Where was he at this critical moment? I might very well have found the—

His bedchamber door flew open to reveal him in nothing but a night robe. "What the devil?" He closed the door to a crack. "Miss Radcliff, I do hope something as serious as a house fire has brought you to my bedchamber alone."

I grimaced. How had I forgotten what a stickler for rules Lt. Burke could be? "Hurry and get dressed, then meet me in the entryway room."

His door didn't shut. He simply leaned his head against the door.

I splayed open my hands.

He chuckled. "You do realize there are servants you could have sent to fetch me."

"I guess I didn't think my actions all the way through, but I assumed a person like you would be up and dressed at the crack of dawn, being a military man and all that."

He sighed. "I had a long night . . . a lot on my mind."

I folded my hands across my chest. "Well, I'm sorry to say, but you're about to have more."

He tugged the door open another inch, probably to see me better. "Am I?"

An appealing wave of nerves carried me backward into the shadows of the hall, my hand retreating to my throat. "I said the entryway, sir, and *dressed*. Now hurry."

Upward of twenty minutes later Lt. Burke sauntered into the front room, dressed smartly in a dark blue jacket, brocade waistcoat, and black band; however, the memory of him jerking open his bedroom door, his hair a beautiful mess, his chest mildly exposed flashed violently into my mind.

"What part of *hurry* did you not comprehend?"

He smiled. "This"—he motioned to his morning attire—"takes a certain amount of time."

I tugged him over to the grand staircase. "I suppose treasure hunters should keep a level of respectability."

"So it is about the clue."

"I believe I have decoded it."

His mouth fell open. "Tell me at once."

I recounted all I'd learned from the maid. At the close of my speech, his attention darted up the steps with an eager tilt. "You don't think it's just right up there?"

My heart ticked to life. "I don't know."

Carefully, we ascended the stairs, and once we were certain we were alone, we knelt down beside the darker wood. "I cannot believe

Josiah Drake kept the driftwood from that notorious accident. You say Christopher brought it home with him?"

"It did save his life."

Lt. Burke ran his fingers all over the sanded surface of the step, feeling for a release of some kind. I did the same, brushing over the smooth top until I couldn't quite reach anymore. I ducked down to extend my reach, inadvertently pressing my shoulder against Lt. Burke's as our arms crossed. The jolt of anticipation was instantaneous. Something had certainly changed between us.

And before I knew quite what we were about, our fervent searching went motionless, our arms entwined. I could hardly breathe as I lifted my head to meet his eyes. We didn't speak.

I felt the muscles in his arm tighten. "You need to meet me after dark." Then he sat back against the railing. "I'm afraid we're going to have to rip this stair apart."

"Yes . . . the stair." Why was my voice so scratchy?

"We cannot risk anything in the daylight."

"No. We've tarried here far too long already."

He helped me to my feet and we descended the stairs. A gentle touch on my arm and he leaned in close to my ear. "Midnight. On the landing."

My heart was a mess. "I'll be there."

"Perhaps we're at the end of all this."

"Maybe." I took a mad look back at the grand staircase, a knot forming in my stomach.

For the first time since I'd left home, I felt a part of something.

It was a night bereft of moonlight, the gloom saturating the hall. I had to grope along the wainscoting to find my way to the landing without a candle. I'd been forced to dress for bed, as Miss Chant had stopped by my room to chat about her day with Vincent, leaving only a few minutes before midnight.

Thus I had no opportunity to redress. I covered my nightgown as best I could in a heavy robe.

On edge, I waited for Lt. Burke at the corner of the landing, imagining all sorts of people lurking about. Daniel was first, still angry with me about forgetting him, though I had kept my promise to work with him today. Followed by Jean Cloutier, who simply stared at me in the dreariness like he'd done that day in the forest, a specter from my past always hovering about my mind. I blinked and his imaginary form disappeared. Then my father's voice filled my head—recounting his disapproval for my previous mistakes, adding a new one about my present course. Finally there was Lt. Burke, glowering at me from across the landing as if he'd learned my secret.

No. Wait. That one was real. I stepped forward and he met me in the center of the landing, taking my arm.

His voice was a whisper. "You've been standing completely still for over a minute."

I pressed my forehead. "I guess I was lost in thought. I was thinking about my father actually."

A long pause, his face concealed by darkness. "You miss him?"

"Every day."

"I can understand that." He was still holding my arm as if he might lose me in the blackened night. "I've a brother I'm quite close to. When I left to fight in France, it was terribly challenging being away, particularly knowing I wouldn't return for some time."

"How long were you gone?"

"Two years." His tone was a mix of sadness and grit.

"Were you there for the end of it all—when Napoleon was finally defeated?"

"Not at Waterloo, but in France, yes . . . chasing down those stolen dispatches."

"Oh." I pulled away and angled to the stairwell. "How are we going to disassemble the top step?"

He held up an iron rod that took shape in the dim light.

"A crowbar, good, but we'll have to be quiet."

"Indeed." Lt. Burke tiptoed down a few stairs, and I followed his lead, settling on the far end of the step.

He silently slid the bent angle of the bar beneath the overhang of the step, then glanced up for a long look at me before thrusting it down. A relatively loud *creak* ripped through the night air and we both froze.

Lt. Burke felt around in the blackened space. "Can you see anything?"

"Not in this darkness."

"Blast. We need a candle."

I scurried down to the bottom floor and secured a tinderbox and solitary candle from the fireplace mantel before returning to his side. "You don't think anyone will see us, do you?"

"We'll have to take the chance."

I passed the small metal box into his hand and listened as he arranged the striker, the flint, the spunks, and the candle atop the lid. A pause, then a few sparks burst forth, illuminating his face for seconds at a time, then the tinder flamed. I'd not noticed his hair on arrival, but it was inescapable now—no pomade or perfect brush strokes, just a tangle of dark locks. I wondered if he remembered what I'd said that day on the beach or if it was simply late and he was distracted.

I couldn't help but smile. Of everyone I knew, Lt. Burke was the one man who thought through every step.

He handed the lit candle to me as he returned the contents to the tinderbox and secured the lid. "We'd better hurry."

I crept down a few more steps until I was eye level with the small opening he had created. I moved the candle in close. It was difficult to see into the interior of the step, but it appeared to be nothing but empty space.

"I can jar the wood open a bit farther." I felt the cold metal of the crowbar as it grazed my arm.

"Wait! There's something written on the overhang of the step . . . underneath." I turned my head. "It's upside down. I'll have to . . ." Without really thinking I twisted onto my back as Lt. Burke took control of the candle. "I can read it like this. Lower the light a bit."

Lt. Burke was forced to move down the steps until he was next to me to get the light quite right.

I squinted to make out the words.

Chiseled into iron, discernable only by the
fish or an adventurous little boy.

I propped myself onto my elbows. "The fish? Sounds like another clue, another ridiculous one."

"Seems like Josiah Drake made every clue personal to him and his son."

"Do we know anything about their fishing habits?"

He ran his hand down his face. "Lost to time, I'm afraid."

"Regardless, I do think this clue is leading us out of doors."

"Agreed." A muscle twitched in Lt. Burke's jaw. He reached out as if to grab something, only to clench his fist and return it to his side. Then suddenly, like a ball from a cannon, he was back on his feet. "There's nothing else we can accomplish tonight."

"No." As I sat up I realized the ribbons on my robe had loosened and the edges had slid open to the stairs below me. Though I was hardly exposed, I couldn't stop the heat from filling my cheeks or my fingers flying to right the folds of my gown.

At first I thought I might address my embarrassment, but then I swallowed hard. I couldn't have said a thing if I tried.

Lt. Burke just stood there, leaning against the banister, a look of confused determination across his face. "Good night, Miss Radcliff."

"Good night . . . Lt. Burke." And we fled the stairs.

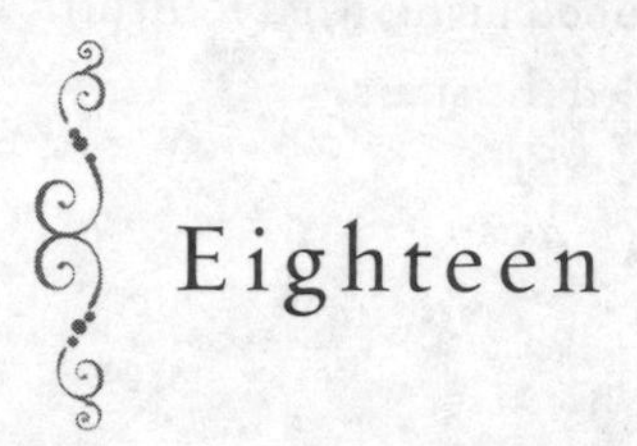

Eighteen

I ROUSED MISS CHANT AT THE BREAK OF DAWN FOLLOWING a fitful night of little sleep. No matter which way I turned or what my mind settled on, I couldn't get the look on Lt. Burke's face out of my mind. Moreover, the depths I'd perceived in those piercing blue eyes haunted me.

What was happening to me?

My heart matched my frantic energy as I tugged a rather tight-lipped Miss Chant through the front door and into the misty morning. I had decided my plans for treasure hunting in the night, and I had every intention of making progress first thing . . . if only I could shake the intimate encounter with Lt. Burke. I skipped down the stone steps before whirling about at the bottom.

Miss Chant seemed to follow my thoughts as she descended behind me, her eyes narrowing in turn. "You're in an awfully good mood this morning."

I gave her a shrug, unable to hide my smile. "Well, of course I am. We've found another clue, which only brings us one step closer to the treasure."

She gave me a wan smile. "What are your thoughts this morning? I know you mustn't have slept a wink."

"The Drakes have always been sailors, have they not?"

Miss Chant dipped her chin. "Some would call them pirates."

"Well, I would call them adventurers—my sort of people, you know."

She chuckled as she settled into a walk beside me, but the ghosts of our prior disagreement joined us as well. "I suppose you would want to be one of those people—to leave Britain on a whim to chase down glory. I must admit, even the thought of taking that boat for America terrifies me."

I kept my voice even. "I will admit to being a little impulsive, but to leave my homeland . . ."

A sideways glance. "Impetuous, passionate, reckless. You know that's how your father described you. He told me to watch you at all times."

She'd mumbled the comment in jest, but the truth behind her words sliced straight into my heart. My father was terribly disappointed in me, but I'd never heard those words from his lips. Knowing what he'd actually said when he allowed me to leave Middlecrest brought all the feelings of that difficult time rushing back tenfold.

It felt like yesterday—the despair, the self-hate.

I'd been sitting in my room at the worst of it, my eyes dry and painful from hours of crying. I'd resolved to finally reveal the whole of it to him—the kisses I'd shared with Jean Cloutier, how empty I felt at his leaving—but there was no time. My father had departed at once to save us all from my reckless mistake. The cold look on his face told me everything I needed to know. My father was disillusioned by what I'd done, and he'd never think of me in the same way again.

And when an opportunity presented itself to leave Middlecrest, I jumped at the chance. It was easier for everyone that way.

My legs felt stiff as I pushed forward, my enthusiasm a million miles away. Jean was free again, which meant all my father's efforts had been in vain. How could I ever go home now?

Miss Chant crossed the manicured lawns to the trail that led to the church and the ocean.

She shook her head as I pivoted her to the right. "You're not going to make me go down those steps again, are you?"

"Please. I don't want to go there alone."

She stopped us cold. "*You* don't want to go alone? I'm astonished."

I'd always shared everything with Miss Chant, but I couldn't tell her about Jean or what I'd seen and felt that day in the woods when I'd followed Mrs. Fagean. Such a revelation would go straight to my father and only confirm her argument that I should marry and straightaway. I motioned us forward. "Ever since Miss Drake's death I've not felt at ease. And Lt. Burke cannot always be by my side. He offered his dog, but—"

"Always by your side?" She blinked. "And he offered that brute?"

"He's simply being cautious. He . . . I . . . we share more in common than I once thought. I agree with his concern, and I find I like his company at times."

Miss Chant's stride lengthened. "Oh, Phoebe. When I told you to secure him, I didn't mean like this. I'm supposed to be your chaperone. My dear girl, I've been far too distracted of late. I'm afraid I've done you a terrible disservice." She held up her first finger like a mother would scold a child. "Tell me you've not . . . you know . . . been indiscreet. If your father hears of anything, I'm through."

The candlelit image of my night robe lying open flashed before my eyes, but the accident had been entirely innocent and no one had seen. Lt. Burke was always the perfect gentleman, maddeningly so at times. The thought of him leaning on that banister, gaping at me like a schoolboy, came to mind. I fought a smile. All right, not exactly a schoolboy. Either way, he'd never do anything untoward, and neither would I.

I cleared my throat. "I'm not the same young lady who was taken in and used by Jean Cloutier."

"I didn't mean . . ." She sighed. "We seem to be at cross-purposes of late. Lt. Burke is nothing like that Frenchman. It makes me wonder why you keep comparing them."

The observation settled like a rock in my stomach, and it took me a moment to respond. "I don't know."

"That ridiculous puppy love you felt for that . . . that horrid charmer is nothing like the real thing. Believe me, I can tell the difference." She took my arm and drew me in close. "You'll know it is love that will last the moment you stop thinking about yourself and instead find yourself thinking about him—what makes him happy, what makes him sad, what dreams he has. And when it's right, he will do the same for you."

Everything had been wrong with my first experience of love. The problem was, I might never escape its clutches. Lt. Burke had said he judged people by their actions. If only I could go back in time and change mine. Juliana had been right when she'd spoken to me in anger. What respectable person could trust me now?

We arrived at the hillside stairs in due course, and I helped Miss Chant to descend ahead of me. She paused midway to speak over her shoulder. "What are you hoping to find down here?"

"Like I said earlier, the Drakes have always been obsessed with the sea."

"Yes. But what does that have to do with metal or fish?"

"Not much, I grant you. However, there are several interesting cave formations along the seashore. Daniel has often spoken of them. He explored them all early on. He mentioned finding a lantern in one."

"Then you think Josiah Drake might have had a similar notion to explore the caves?"

"He and his son likely would have utilized this remote shore as the Fageans have done. It makes sense he might include it in a clue."

We searched every crevice of the rocky hillside for hours without finding a thing. Well, not entirely. Miss Chant found a brown limpet and I tucked it into my pocket. One step closer to my grotto. I patted the outside of my pelisse. How long ago those days seemed when I would stroll the seashore and dream about my future as an artist. Those hopes were lost now, replaced by a treasure hunt and a murder investigation and a man with a rather affecting grin.

The cackle of seabirds resounded from the cliffs. They nested away from foxes and rats beneath the puffy clusters of roseroot full of yellow star-shaped blooms. I watched as a large black-and-white gannet took flight, soaring over my head before it dove headfirst into the sea. The scent of fish hung heavy on the air.

Miss Chant turned around and gave me a shrug. "Guess we're at the end of it then."

"The tide's just too high. I know there's an inlet around that bend, but it must be up ten feet from the last time I was here." I stepped onto one of the rocks and crawled out as far as I could to peer around the outcropping.

Miss Chant sounded far away. "Oh, Phoebe, you'll ruin your gown."

I lifted my muddied palm. "Too late for that."

I was forced to stretch almost beyond bearing to get a glimpse of the quiet cove around the bend. It appeared much like the one we'd just searched with grooves and folds in the rocky cliff. At the far side there was a small, dark indention, but I couldn't fully see what it was. A cave perhaps, or simply a small overlap. Either way, I intended to come back, preferably with Lt. Burke. I glanced back at my companion. Miss Chant was little help.

As I maneuvered to make my way down the rock, I saw it—carefully slid into a furrow—a curved wooden item. The narrow hollow was several feet off the ground, and if I hadn't climbed up on that rock to see, I'd never have discovered it.

My pulse quickened and my hand shook as I guided the item out of its perfect little resting spot.

Miss Chant's voice took flight on the wind. "What have you got there? Is it a clue?"

"No." A surge of breathlessness overtook me as I held the T-shaped item into the sunlight. "It's a crossbow, the very weapon used to end Miss Drake's life."

Agonizingly, I had to wait until the next day to show Lt. Burke what I'd found. He had spent the whole of the afternoon with Mr. Montague and our neighbor, Mr. Haskett, showing him the artifacts Lt. Burke had selected to sell.

When I learned Lt. Burke and Mr. Montague would be dining at Mr. Haskett's estate, it was almost too much and made for a particularly nerve-racking evening of whispering with Arnold or bickering with Miss Chant when I had the opportunity. Neither could imagine who could have possibly killed our dear friend and stowed the weapon on the cliff side.

I, however, had an idea, one I didn't mean to share. Daniel. He'd been right by that spot days earlier, and he was so different of late. Could he actually have been involved somehow? And I'd told Lt. Burke otherwise. Another foolish mistake on my part. I could no longer ignore Daniel's odd behavior.

The following morning, I perked up the moment I saw Lt. Burke enter the breakfast room. If only we had been alone, I would have blabbed the whole thing at once, but he caught my look easily enough and followed me into the hall.

There was an ease to his movements, a ready smile that transformed his face. He tugged me behind one of the pillars and didn't even bother to release my arm.

"We only sold the sarcophagus and two small pieces, something about Mr. Haskett's dwindling funds. I know Avonthorpe needs the money, but in a way I'm glad. It will do for now and the rest can go to the museum." There was an amusing pause. He finally realized he was still holding my arm and released me.

"That's good, I guess." But my smile fell.

"What is it?" He glanced behind us into the empty hall. "Did something happen while I was away?"

"Miss Chant and I took a walk along the beach yesterday." I'd been aching to show him what I'd found, but as I stared into that thoughtful gaze, a part of me shrank back. This would only bring back the clouds that had been hanging over him since Miss Drake's death.

"And?" He was anxious now, his jaw clenched tight.

"I stumbled upon a small hiding spot along the shoreline. It was high up on the cliff. I was climbing a rock when I found it."

A wan little half smile peeked from the corner of his mouth, but it was short-lived.

"It was the crossbow. I can only imagine it matches the bolt used in your aunt's murder. You're the antiquarian. You'd be the best person to say."

His face went slack. "Where is it now?"

"Up in my room. Follow me."

I led him up the stairs and down the long hall to my bedchamber, but it wasn't until I shut my door that I realized the impropriety of our situation. We were alone, and we were not indifferent to each other.

But none of that mattered, not with Lt. Burke's grief so evident. I went straight to my wardrobe and wrestled the medieval weapon from behind my gowns. It was a trifle heavy and I had to sling it onto the bed for inspection. Lt. Burke stared down for several seconds before moving in closer.

He took the bow carefully into his hands. "This would fire the bolt we found in my aunt's chest. I'm well acquainted with this particular weapon."

I craned forward. "You're certain?"

"Years ago my aunt had me catalog the antiquities of Avonthorpe, so she might know what pieces of value were in the house. Most were part of the entail, but some items came from her personal inheritance from her mother. She moved those to the vicar's cottage."

I stepped back. "You don't think?"

"Mrs. Fagean." His focus dropped to the bed. "It is possible since she was walking that way that day in the woods. It shows she's familiar with the place, but I'm not certain she could wield such a device to commit murder."

Daniel could. My shoulders fell, but I straightened them just as quickly. Daniel and Mrs. Fagean? Why was I not convinced either was responsible? "I think it prudent we go to the cottage, look through what's there."

He nodded slowly. "I was thinking the same. If our murderer has been rifling through Miss Drake's private things, he just might have left us the evidence we seek."

The vicar's cottage appeared out of the grim little forest just as I remembered it, lonely and forgotten, a sad relic of a happier time and place. However, with the sun full out and Lt. Burke close at my side, I felt none of the apprehension I'd experienced during my first encounter.

The building was actually quite lovely, red-bricked with a gabled roof. Lt. Burke jostled a set of keys from his pocket and let us in the front door. A musty odor met us in the entryway, but it wasn't entirely unpleasant. Lt. Burke explained how the furniture had been sold, leaving empty rooms inhabited by dust and spiders.

"I saw some crates through the window in the back room." An echo played with my voice.

Lt. Burke led the way beneath a curved doorway and down a short hall. "The sitting room is through here. I believe that's where my aunt stored her personal things."

The walls were covered in white paneling, the room cheery and bright, made only more so by the floor-length windows that opened the house to the sun. Dust filled the slanting rays as they poured through the leaded glass and reached for the floor. Silence pressed against my ears as I saw the stacked boxes in the corner. That is, all but one, which had been separated and opened.

Lt. Burke was at the crates in an instant, digging through his aunt's personal effects. "This is certainly where the murderer acquired the weapon."

I thought of Daniel and my heart lightened. "Whoever took the crossbow must have already known it was here. They only opened the one box."

"Or heard someone mention where it was kept."

"Seems they knew exactly where to find it."

Lt. Burke crossed his arms. "That would suggest the Fageans . . . or someone working with them."

Working with them . . . Daniel's interaction with Mrs. Fagean came to mind. I couldn't entirely dismiss my friend, no matter how much I wanted to.

Lt. Burke stood. "These other boxes are sealed tight, but I shall find my catalog from years ago and return to take a thorough inventory."

I looked around us. "It would be prudent to check the other rooms before we depart."

"Agreed."

We meandered through the empty kitchens and the servants' rooms, then perused what would have been used as a library. Not until we breached the dining room did we slow to linger.

I ran my fingers along the edge of the long, rectangular table protected by a Holland cover. "I thought you said all the furniture had been sold."

A line crossed Lt. Burke forehead. "It was. This wasn't here before."

We stood there a moment staring at the long white ghost hovering in front of us before Lt. Burke lifted the sheet. His eyes rounded. "What the deuce?"

In one swift jerk the sheet was flopped onto the floor at the side, and the surface of the table was entirely exposed. My mouth fell open.

Newspaper clippings, handwritten notes, and various sketches were pinned to a large board. I leaned close to one intricate drawing. My hand flew to my lips. "It's your Sèvres vase."

Lt. Burke began pacing, his sharp eyes on the table. "And look here—a rendition of the clue we found on the bottom."

I sidled over, my gaze flashing over the multiple slips of paper. "It seems someone else has been on a treasure hunt."

"For quite a while." The grit to Lt. Burke's voice was unmistakable. "Look. This newspaper clipping is dated January 1817, shortly after you arrived at Avonthorpe."

"Why would someone keep this?"

"See the second paragraph here." He pointed to where he had been reading. "It's all about the Equinox Festival."

"What is this?" I turned over a large metal funnel-shaped device. "Oh, it's an ear trumpet."

"Wonder what that's here for?"

"Possibly another dead end." I leaned in close. "It has a letter on it. Looks like a *P* or a *B*, but it's rather old."

Lt. Burke shrugged. "I have no idea." Then he ran his hand down his face. "All I know is someone's been ahead of us at every step."

"Until now." I met his stunned glare. "There's nothing on this table about the clue we found on the underside of the stair."

He nodded slowly. "I think you're right. Here's William Shakespeare's Sonnet 15. And a list of the fifteen mysteries of the rosary. Whoever gathered all this information was as stumped as we were about that one."

A shiver ran down my spine, chilling my muscles in place. "This confirms our suspicions. As the crossbow was stolen from this very cottage, it stands to reason whoever collected this information about the treasure is most likely the same person who ended your aunt's life."

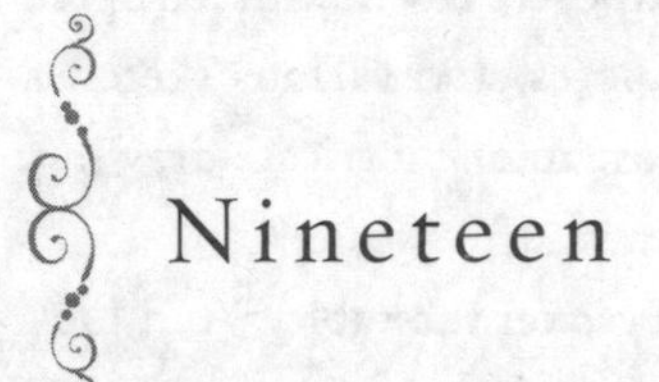

Nineteen

By afternoon I found myself yearning to escape the confines of the house to not only think but plan. The list of people who could have committed Miss Drake's murder was shrinking and rather fast. Miss Chant had made prior arrangements with Vincent, which was just to my liking. I needed to be alone.

Dusk lurked beyond the trees and gathered along the hillside, ready to spill over into the valley with its cool gray air. I'd time enough to take Creature with me for a walk if I made it a brisk one. And Lt. Burke was right, I did feel safer with the humongous mongrel beside me. Thus, I gripped the end of his lead, tucked my hands into my muff, and plowed forward.

Each and every person residing at Avonthorpe flitted through my mind. Though I'd never really considered Mr. Montague a likely perpetrator, thanks to the date on the newspaper, he was now probably off my list, if he hadn't clipped it and brought it with him. But why would he? Daniel, for that matter, had only arrived a few months ago. So why couldn't I dismiss him as well?

My difficult morning came to mind. He'd spent a good portion of the early hours dutifully assisting me with the trim work he'd promised to do, but his conversation remained terribly clipped, his demeanor a morose collection of scowls and placid disinterest—nothing like the Daniel I knew when we were children or the one who'd enthusiastically come to Avonthorpe.

Could my dear friend actually be involved in Miss Drake's

murder in some way? And if so, another person had to be pulling the strings. If only I could get at who. I had to be careful where Daniel was concerned—watchful and patient—or he would certainly bolt for home. The image of him walking away from me through the ballroom door came to mind: the fluidity of his jacket, the shadows dithering in and out of his cheekbones. There was no question—he'd lost some weight.

"Creature, wait!" I tugged on his lead, reminding the enormous dog of his duty to me.

His master, Lt. Burke, was busy at the chapel for the afternoon preparing Mr. Haskett's antiquities with Mr. Montague. Afterward, he would return to the cottage to finish the inventory there, so there was no chance of his joining our adventure today.

A hint of hesitation swept through my chest as I glanced down the lonely path. With Avonthorpe's lake high on my list of possible locations for the latest clue, it seemed a natural destination for my much-needed escape.

Though I kept Creature close by my side, he was happy enough to trot along a few feet away, delightfully oblivious to the fact he could break free from my grasp with the least bit of effort. He was huge after all.

It wasn't long at all before the lake appeared like a blanket lying across the ground, brilliantly blue-green and utterly calm. I slowed our approach to take in the scene, memorizing every delicate hue of the vibrant color palette before padding down to the shoreline. The lake's depths appeared fairly shallow, and I'd been told by Arnold that this particular lake had been formed by the installation of a simple sluice gate hundreds of years ago at the far end, which the steward manipulated from time to time to control floodwaters and aid the farmers downhill.

A gust of wind set me searching at once for the answer to the clue as sunset was hard on my heels, and I led Creature around the small gate and up the far bank. I had a feeling whatever I was looking for might be located beneath the water somewhere, but the green of the lake permitted little visibility, as the frogbits and other floating plants crept straight up to the grassy shore.

Creature had a grand time sniffing every rock and wading into the edge of the lake. The water forget-me-nots were in full bloom, decorating the various inlets in vivid blue.

An adventurous little boy.

I couldn't help but think of Creature as he splashed one direction, then the next. He'd probably jump right in if I let him off his lead; however, I had no intention of taking a swim, not for treasure or anything else.

As the season had been unnaturally dry, the lake was low, permitting the remains of an old fountain in the center to crest the surface of the water. I stared at it a long moment, uncertain whether the square structure had anything to do with the clue. Unfortunately it was too far away to make any real observations. Really, I would have to be in a boat to fully investigate, and that would require Lt. Burke.

I finished searching the far shore, then corralled Creature across the Baroque-style bridge, which traversed the small brook that fed the lake. I resigned myself to simply getting an overview of the location, then laid out a blanket to sit on.

Creature seemed happy enough to join me, his eyes never leaving the basket of food I'd brought.

"All right. It's time."

His large pink tongue flopped out of the side of his mouth, his furry eyebrows adding a distinct flair of their own. Really . . . how could anyone refuse such a darling? I ripped off a bite of cold ham and launched it onto the blanket. He scarfed the meat down within seconds, then lifted his head to beg for more.

I rubbed his ears. "One moment, sir. While you've been busy lapping up all the lake water, I've had nothing to quench my own thirst.

Cook was kind enough to include some lemonade, and I am in great need of it."

I uncorked the bottle and lifted it to my lips to drink, but something in the woods beyond the lake drew my attention from the glassy rim. What sounded like a whisper took flight on the wind. A small growl and Creature leaped to his feet, his fur standing on end. He didn't bark, however, which reassured me in part.

Had someone followed me from the safety of the house once again? Jean Cloutier ripped into my mind.

A gentle breeze stirred the water plants and brought the scent of fish to my nose. A bird fluttered overhead. Creature turned back to the basket at my side, nosing in quite close.

"No you don't."

I gave his collar a tug and he jerked his head rather violently to lick my face. The sudden onslaught of dog tongue and heavy paws threw me off balance and I was forced to use my arm to stay upright. Unfortunately, it was the hand still gripping the lemonade bottle, which tumbled into the mud, spilling every bit of its contents.

I thrust the dog away and whirled to appraise the accident.

"No, no, look what you've done!"

As if the dog perfectly understood my frustration, he bounded over to the uncorked bottle. He gave me one quite pitiful look before lapping up whatever he could of the spilled lemonade, although the majority of the liquid had already soaked into the dry ground.

I crossed my arms. "I told you how terribly thirsty I was. You . . . you Creature."

His ears turned down as he crept back over to his side of the blanket, but his paltry remorse did little to quash my irritation. "I believe I have some stewed fruit in here somewhere. I suppose that shall have to do for now."

I tossed the remaining ham at Creature before lifting my gaze once again to the far side of the lake, my concerns still raw.

That's when I saw them—three men emerging from the trees, yards away, heading in the direction of the house. I couldn't quite make out who they were. They were dressed in breeches and wide-cut shirts. Working class, no doubt. One of the roads that led into the estate was not all that far from where they walked, and the men seemed friendly enough as they talked with one another, oblivious to my eyes following them. They'd probably come to meet with Mr. Fagean as he ran some of the estate business. I felt nothing amiss as I watched them trudge up the hill.

That is, until one of them turned around and I got a good look at his face. It was Mr. Tulk, Miss Chant's fiancé. I'd know him anywhere. I glared at him with disbelief until he eventually disappeared from view. If Miss Chant was not spending the day with her fiancé, then where was she?

On return to the house, Creature collapsed onto the ground the minute I led him into his pen. At first glance I thought him only tired. He could be quite dramatic at times, but the pained look on his face told me otherwise.

My heart quivered. What was wrong?

I sent a groom rushing for Lt. Burke as I cradled Creature's head in my lap. Surely Lt. Burke would have returned from the church by now. The dog was panting, his gaze ethereal as it remained fixed in place. Then the salivation began. I stroked his head over and over again as I watched in agony for Lt. Burke to come running through the gate. Surely he would know what to do. Had Creature eaten something that had made him sick?

I could feel the large dog's heart racing in his chest, and he snapped a low growl as my hand neared his stomach. Something was terribly wrong. A resulting yelp and he tugged away from me only to empty his stomach in the tall grass. I pressed my hands to my face.

"What happened?" Lt. Burke's voice was at my back and I whirled about. He fastened the gate behind him and sprinted inside before kneeling next to the two of us.

"I don't know." The intense comfort of Lt. Burke's presence struck me afresh. He was the kind of man who proved capable of anything he set his mind to—perhaps even saving his poor dog's life. "He simply fell to the ground when we returned from our walk."

He looked over Creature's bedraggled form. "Has he had other symptoms?"

"Not many, not until moments ago. His heart is beating terribly fast and he's been drooling . . . and more." I motioned to the area beneath the tree.

Lt. Burke's brows plunged inward. "Did he stop to eat a mushroom or something else that might have caused all this?"

"No, I . . ." My hand flew to my mouth, a cold sensation filling my throat. "He only ate what I brought with me from the house, and that was over an hour ago."

"What?" A moment of confusion and then Lt. Burke was on his feet, his hand raking through his hair. "Did you share anything he ate, even one bite?" His hands shot out and he cradled my chin as he stared into my eyes, a desperate quality to his look. "Have you felt ill in any way?"

"No, I'm quite well." I shook my head. "We only shared a bit of ham. You see, my lemonade spilled before I could eat or drink anything more." My lips parted and I turned back to stare down at Creature. "He lapped up what he could when it spilled." My eyes widened. "You don't think . . ."

"There was something in your drink?" His hands were wild now, rubbing my shoulders, clenching. "I don't know what to believe." He slowly shook his head. "Do you still have the bottle with you?"

"Yes, but there are only drops of liquid left."

"Give it to me at once."

I wrestled the empty bottle from the basket and passed it to Lt. Burke. "But what are we to do about Creature?"

His shoulders slumped. "I'll have my groom watch over him, give him plenty of fresh water. I'm afraid there's no other way to help him at this point but wait and pray."

I pulled away, somewhat numb, but the whisper of my name stopped me cold.

Lt. Burke's face held a troubled expression. "If there was indeed something added to the lemonade as we suspect—" He took a long whiff of the remaining contents in the bottle. "You know, there's definitely a malty smell to it . . . like milk that has spoiled." He sniffed again. "The kind of rancid concoction that could make a person sick."

I stared down at Creature. "But hopefully not dead . . ."

"Probably not." He pressed his lips together. "However, I do think it prudent to be careful, at least until I can speak with Cook and get to the bottom of what happened today."

I stilled once again. "Why would someone do such a thing?"

He closed his eyes for a brief second. "This incident may have nothing to do with you or the lemonade." A grim line crossed his forehead. "Or maybe someone at Avonthorpe would like to cease your treasure hunting for a few days. Either way I mean to keep you safe." As an afterthought: "Your father entrusted me with your care."

His whole body seemed to slump forward an inch. He opened his mouth to speak, then hesitated. "We'll talk more later . . . when I've had a chance to think, and . . ." He looked back at his dog.

Lt. Burke had complained endlessly about Creature's ridiculous behavior, but he loved that mongrel. I slid my fingers around his loose hand. "He'll make it through. If tainted milk was indeed the culprit, I'm fairly certain Creature ingested very little of it. He stands an excellent chance at recovery."

Lt. Burke nodded to himself, his sigh possessing that halting quality I recognized in my father when his back was against a wall. And when he looked up at me, pain marred his face. "I'm worried about Creature, of course . . . but believe me, the whole of my concern lies with you."

"*Me?*"

"Miss Radcliff, how can I possibly put words to the fear pulsing in my veins at this very moment? Someone in this house may have struck out again, and I have no idea who that person is, why they wish to harm you, or, most importantly, what the devil they mean to do next."

Lt. Burke would miss dinner that evening, as he intended to remain with Creature in his pen as much as possible. A note arrived shortly before I'd finished dressing for the meal. At first I was terrified to open the missive, but when I saw Lt. Burke's handwriting, my concerns dissolved.

He'd met with Cook, and apparently the supplies for my impromptu picnic had been left unattended in the dining room for several minutes. Anyone could have tampered with the lemonade.

My hands shook as I refolded the letter. Someone wanted me out of the way for at least a few days. Did that mean they were close to uncovering the treasure?

Dinner, in turn, proved challenging in different ways. I found myself staring at every new dish brought in from the kitchen, wondering how easy it would be for someone to try again to make me sick. Cook had drawn me aside in the hall and promised to preside over everything that was served. Granted, the footmen still brought each course into the room alone.

I decided I had little choice but to act as if nothing was wrong. I picked apart the duck on my plate, swallowing each piece with a rather dry gulp, and continued in such a way for the length of the meal, pushing my suspicions aside. After dinner, however, they roared back to mind when Mrs. Fagean flopped on the sofa in the drawing room, eager to offer me some tea.

She turned up her nose at my curt refusal. "Not interested, I see."

I slid the cup and saucer onto a nearby table. "Not at present, no."

"I can understand such sentiment. I vow, I couldn't eat a thing at dinner just now."

I checked. "What do you mean?"

She gave me a dramatic sigh as if such an affectation was explanation enough before draping her hand over her breast and leaning in close. "It's Mr. Fagean. He has decided to delay our next shipment across the channel."

I thought a moment. "Perhaps he senses now is not a good time to leave you here alone."

Her eyes narrowed. "Whyever not?"

Whyever not, indeed. "Or there's something else . . . he is, uh, waiting on." I paused to assess the layers of her countenance. "And this delay upsets you?"

She drummed her fingers on the arm of the sofa. "Certainly it does. After we were so callously left out of Miss Drake's will, we are rather short on money."

My gaze snapped to the emerald ring on her finger, and she caught my sudden interest.

"Since you have never had to manage your own affairs, my dear, you would have no idea what I suffer." A terse nod. "Good evening, Phoebe." Then she shoved to her feet and stormed over to Mr. Montague across the room.

If she was looking for sympathy, she'd not find it with me. Moreover, what was all that concern about a shipment? Clearly the Fageans were not seeing eye-to-eye of late. She seemed to be going from one melodramatic argument to the next, placated only by the acquisition of jewelry—jewelry they couldn't even afford.

Mr. Montague welcomed her, seemingly pleased by her sudden attention. I could hear them laughing from clear across the room, but the fawning all but stopped the second Lt. Burke sauntered into the drawing room. Mr. Montague was on his feet in an instant, and the two gentlemen skirted to the side of the room where they could have a private conversation.

Lt. Burke had chosen a perfectly elegant black jacket and brocade waistcoat, well put together at every angle, but his face told a far different story. Gone were his tight smile and affective eyes, replaced by a scowl. Whatever he had to impart to Mr. Montague was done quickly, his hands engaged in the conversation. Mr. Montague eventually nodded and departed the drawing room without another word, leaving Mrs. Fagean to join her husband at the fireplace.

My stomach turned as Lt. Burke crossed the room to meet me on the sofa. By the look on his face I wasn't certain I was fully prepared to hear about Creature, but I gathered what strength I could muster.

Lt. Burke was slow to speak at first, resting his elbows on his knees and intertwining his fingers. There was a defeated quality to his movements, and my heart ached. "Is Creature . . . ?"

His eyes brightened. "Doing much better actually. I believe he shall pull through. Tonight will be the test."

My shoulders relaxed. "That's wonderful news." Then my brow tugged inward. "Then what was all that with Mr. Montague?"

He glanced at the door. "Business."

"Nothing with the upcoming sale to Mr. Haskett I hope."

"No." He gave me a wan smile as if he thought it would reassure me. "I've given Cook strict instructions regarding the preparation of your food from now on."

I clasped my hands in my lap. "Thank you, but—"

"I'm at a crossroads. I know you shouldn't even stay in residence, yet . . ."

I blinked, then swallowed hard. "Please, it was only spoiled milk. It could have nothing to do with the treasure, and then—"

"But what if it does?"

I didn't mean to raise my voice, but it escalated unbidden. "Then I shall be safe enough here under your watchful eye."

The room fell silent as every eye shifted our direction. After a long pause Mr. Fagean's voice rang out. "Did she say *safe*?"

Lt. Burke waved them off as if they might have misheard.

Quieter now. "And I appreciate the concern. I share it on every level." I slowly shook my head. "But you know very well I cannot leave Avonthorpe, not now."

It was no more than a look, but he caught my gaze and held it fast. "The treasure is not more valuable than your health."

Something twisted inside me. "It's not that." I closed my eyes. That is, till I felt his hand on mine.

He contracted slightly. "There's something you aren't telling me. You bristle every time I mention Middlecrest Abbey. Why don't you want to go home?"

I couldn't help but wince. "It's complicated."

His voice dipped. "Has someone there been unkind toward you?"

"No! No. You don't understand. It's not that at all. I-I came here with such dreams. I honestly thought I could make my own way in the world, perhaps never return. To go back there now would seem a failure. It's . . . it's just a lot to take in."

He said nothing as his thumb grazed my skin. "I fear there's a great deal more hidden behind your words, but I won't press you." He tightened his hand for a moment. "You have a place here at Avonthorpe for as long as you wish, or as long as I believe I can keep you safe."

I don't know what I expected to feel as I digested his words, but not the intense mixture of longing and security that filled my heart.

Lt. Burke was risking a great deal housing a young lady at his estate after everything that had happened. Granted, I had a chaperone. So why did I feel like that was the crux of what we were actually talking about? Had my father written to him, disclosed something about my past?

No. He promised me he would keep my role in Jean's escape a secret. He would never betray my trust. I thought about how he'd kept quiet about my true parentage, burying the truth until I pressed him for answers. My father was good at keeping secrets—even difficult ones.

Carefully I disengaged from Lt. Burke and stood. "I'm so glad to hear Creature is doing better. I was so worried."

His lips parted. "Phoebe, I . . ." His eyes widened and he gave his head a little shake. "Miss Radcliff, pardon me. I didn't mean to presume."

Silence overcame me for a full minute. What had prompted the use of my Christian name? Moreover, how long had Lt. Burke inwardly regarded me in such a way? We'd grown close over the past week. "Please, don't apologize. I've always felt more like a Phoebe than a Miss Radcliff anyhow. To me, Miss Radcliff is the sort of person who does everything right. She's proper and careful, performs anything asked of her and straightaway. She practices her pianoforte and writes all her letters. She's rather droll, I daresay." I smiled. "I'm afraid I shall never be Miss Radcliff—that's my sister—no matter how hard I try."

Lt. Burke mirrored my smile, a curious expression lightening his face. "I'm not certain I would have had the same answer just a few weeks ago, but from where I stand as of now, I'd rather hunt for my family's treasure with Phoebe." His lips twitched. "She's smart and unpredictable and—"

"And what about you? Am I to hunt with Lt. Burke or . . . ?" I tilted my chin.

"Graham." His answer was soft, childlike. "But I have to be honest with you, I'm not certain I can separate Lt. Burke from Graham. We are one and the same, I daresay."

"It's not about separating them. It's about finding out who the real Graham is and accepting it."

He pressed his lips into a grin.

I mirrored his smile. "Then we are agreed. We shall row out to the remains of the fountain tomorrow"—I dipped my chin—"as Phoebe and Graham."

He drew back. "The fountain?"

Twenty

After I explained my ideas about the fountain, Graham led me across the carpet to bid me good night. We never made it to the door, however, because one of the paintings on the adjoining wall, a portrait of Josiah Drake, caught his eye. He stopped short, his arm tethering me back. "What the devil?"

I followed him behind the pianoforte, where he leaned in close to the small canvas perched neatly above the wainscoting. "Phoebe . . ." A sly smile peeked from the corner of his mouth as he said my name, which took us both by surprise. "Look closely. This is supposed to be a Hoppner."

"*Supposed* to be?"

His whole face scrunched as he scrutinized every inch of the portrait of Josiah Drake's likeness. He sounded incredulous. "It's a forgery."

I neared the canvas and had to admit at once that the work did appear terribly sloppy, a poor recreation of the original.

Graham could read my thoughts as he crushed his fingers into a fist, then whirled to face the couple seated across the room. His voice came out like thunder. "Tell me, Mr. Fagean. Have you perhaps seen the original version of this painting on your ship?"

"This painting? My ship?" Mr. Fagean lurched to his feet, all while fumbling with his quizzing glass. "What do you mean to imply, Burke? Is this an accusation?"

Graham stood deathly still. "Only if it's true."

"Egad, my boy. I've never seen that artwork out of this very drawing room." He walked over, his eyes wide like a scared doe. "I may avoid a bit of excise tax from time to time, but I'm no thief."

Graham blinked hard. "Any person who avoids his fair share of tax steals from us all."

"Really, Lt. Burke." Mrs. Fagean was on her feet now, ready to perform. "How do you even know you're looking at a fake and not the original?"

"There are very few items in this house that were not part of the entail. This so happens to be one of them. I had the original evaluated for a possible sale for my aunt."

She gave a breathy laugh. "Then you've got your answer. Your aunt sold the painting and replaced it with whatever that is."

"She would not do so without approaching me first."

Mrs. Fagean took a willowy stroll to meet her husband. "You're awfully confident when you are so seldom here, Lt. Burke. Allow me to say, I may know your aunt as well as you."

Mr. Fagean gave his wife a hard look. "You may be in the right of it, Burke. Miss Drake always refused any offer I made to sell anything. She trusted you and you alone." He took the last few steps remaining between him and the painting, staring at the canvas with fresh eyes. "Do you think it could have been switched by a servant or someone outside the household? The Drakes have made quite a few enemies over the years. Christopher Drake was certainly a character."

Graham appraised Mr. Fagean with a newfound curiosity. "It is possible someone else could be involved in the theft of the original."

A cold wave of nerves washed over me. What did he mean someone else could be involved? Had Graham told me everything he knew about the state of affairs at Avonthorpe?

Mr. Arnold's voice sounded from the far side of the room. "Might there be any other items tampered with? Should we have the servants make an inventory?"

Graham ran his hand down his face. "I'd rather sort through the pieces myself."

Arnold nodded his approval. "You would be the best situated to do so, of course."

"I'll begin first thing in the morning." A side glance at me. "Well, not first thing. I promised Miss Radcliff a walk."

Still a bit numb, I cleared my voice. "If you'd rather postpone?"

"No. The house will be waiting for me when I return." His gaze ticked around the room. "When I give my word, I mean it."

Graham was waiting for me in the entrance hall just as he said he would be, dressed in a perfectly pressed olive frock coat and velvet collar. He glanced up over his newspaper as I descended the stairs, and there was a moment of comfortable hesitation before he stood to greet me.

"Good morning." He ran his fingers over his cravat to ensure it was properly situated.

"And how is Creature?"

"Still a bit sluggish, but recovering nicely. The staff promises to keep an eye on him while we're gone." Graham opened the front door and we crossed the threshold.

The wind ruffled a few stray hairs above Graham's ears and he tucked them into his hat. "It was touch and go yesterday, but I can finally say I feel confident we're out of the woods."

I settled my hand on his offered arm as we descended the front steps, a budding spirit of hope between us, as if the emotional storms of the previous night had all but dispersed, leaving warmth and sunlight behind.

Conversation flowed easily as we walked. I learned more about his love of history, how he worked for a time at the British Museum after he'd sold out of the military, and how his months in Africa sparked his interest in antiquities. He spoke of his father, who was a general, and the strict upbringing he reveled in. I was coming to see all the different brushstrokes that had created the artwork that was Graham Burke.

A natural break in conversation brought the inevitable question to Graham's lips. "What about you? I'd like to know more about your family."

I fumbled with a ball of lint in my pelisse pocket. "There's not all that much to tell really. My sister and I grew up without a mother, and my father was gone a great deal. I suppose that's how I found my way into art—on canvas I could create whatever I wanted."

"And what did you paint?"

"I began with the countryside, then the estate, but before long I began drawing people, and places I've never been, things I've never done."

He grinned and it almost felt as if he tugged me a bit closer. "I see you're a dreamer like myself."

I took a feral glance at the perfectly shined metal buttons on his jacket, then down at his shiny hussar boots. Could Graham Burke really be a dreamer?

He gave a small laugh. "Wouldn't think it to look at me, but I spend a great deal of time in other worlds—ancient Egypt and the Roman Empire. My collection has become something of a passion for me."

"Was it difficult to part with the pieces you were forced to sell?"

He frowned. "Not entirely. I just hope I can protect some of what I discover and eventually find a way to share the world's antiquities with others. As I've said before, I don't see how private collections can do that, but I must make a living. The earth is such a vast, beautiful place, and many have seen so little of it. Can you imagine how much people might evolve if they could exchange ideas and a look at something outside of themselves?"

"It is a sobering thought indeed. And a much-needed one." I stared off across the green grass. "If only we could all see the world through curiosity and hope." I smiled. "You are a dreamer, Graham Burke. Don't ever stop."

An osprey took a low dip over our heads and drew our attention to our first view of the lake. Graham had arranged for the rowboat to be set up for our use, and he led me straight to it. A wry look at me and he crouched over to push the boat from the shore and into the shallow water.

The angle afforded me a glimpse of something metal in his inside pocket and I stepped closer. "What is that?"

He jerked his head up, his eyes scanning the far shore. "What?"

"No. In your jacket pocket."

Slowly he turned to face me. "Security, of course."

My eyes widened. "You brought a pistol with us?"

He straightened. "I'll take no more chances with your life, thank you."

"Well, I hope it hasn't a hair trigger."

He laughed. "Me too."

"You mean you don't know?"

His laugh deepened. "Certainly I do. Now get in the boat."

I thrust my shoulders back. "Yes, sir . . . Captain, sir."

Graham assisted me into place on the bench across from him before pushing off the bank with his foot. He took his seat, then secured the oars. A few strokes and he offered, "You should have brought a parasol."

I grinned at him. "I have no use for such things."

"No?"

"My bonnet will protect my face well enough, and I'm not one to burn easily."

The oars sloshed through the water as Graham rowed. "Did

you believe Mr. Fagean last night when he denied selling the original painting?"

"I actually did."

"As did I." His attention drifted across the lake. "Have you any idea who might have taken the artwork, then profited from the sale?"

"Mr. Fagean offered the most logical notion—one of the servants."

He eyed me a moment. "What about your friend Daniel?"

"Daniel?" My voice lost tone. "I will admit he's surprised me of late. And he's always been rather boyish. I suppose he could have got in deep, a lark or a debt of honor he couldn't pay."

"Possibly, but I cannot help but wonder if his strange behavior has some connection to my aunt's murder."

"I will admit to concerns there." The nose of the boat bumped into something hard and I twisted in my seat.

Graham crouched forward. "See if you can grab onto the corner there."

There was little left of the stone fountain, but I found a decent enough handhold.

Suddenly the boat shifted. "Graham!"

He eased in next to me. "Sorry, but how are we to search the thing without moving?"

"How are we to do so at all? Most of the structure is under the water. I'm afraid we've come out here for nothing . . . unless . . ." I gestured to the water with my fingers.

Graham froze where he knelt, his jaw jutting to the side as he stared over at me. "You're not serious."

"Clearly there's nothing written on the exposed surface. The clue referenced fish and an adventurous little boy. What if Christopher Drake liked to swim here?"

Graham's hand was against his chin, his fingers flexing and releasing. "You do have a point."

"Well, I can't get in there." I looked deep beneath the water's surface. "Or maybe I could. I do know how to swim and I'm not so stuffy as to be unwilling to try."

"Stop!" Graham plied his jacket button open, his eyes darting a look at the sky. "I'll do it."

I smiled. "Just be sure to hand me your cravat. I wouldn't want it to get dirty."

His fingers stilled. "You had no intention of jumping in there, did you?"

I lifted my eyebrows. "Is it a challenge then? Because—"

"No. I shan't risk your impulsivity or your gown drowning you, but I will task you with holding all my clothes as I don't want a single item ruined." He thrust his jacket from his shoulders. "That is, except my breeches . . . and my shirt."

Carefully he unwound his neckcloth and placed it into my hands, followed by his waistcoat. Then he thrust out his boot. "I'm afraid I'll need your help with these." He settled back on the opposing seat, and I tugged his hussars off one at a time before watching him remove his stockings.

In that charged second, when his bare feet emerged from his boots, the startling intimacy of the moment fully registered in my mind. Here we were alone and I was holding his clothes for goodness' sake—and the entire plan had been my idea!

"What is it?"

Had he caught me staring? I swallowed hard. How to explain myself? "I suppose I've just never seen a man's feet before, at least not this close."

He wiggled his toes. "Are they everything you expected?"

I couldn't help but laugh as I unwittingly peered closer. "I had no idea you had dark hair"—I pointed at his toes—"there."

Graham stood and the boat rocked. "Sorry, but really, Phoebe, what will you say next?"

"I suppose you can see why my father employed a chaperone."

He laughed, but a bit of an awkward silence crept in. I would have none of that ruining my day. I motioned to the water. "So are you just going to jump in?"

"I was thinking more along the lines of easing over the side."

"Just be careful you don't tip us."

"Believe me, that is my chief concern. I might be able to explain away my wet clothes, but I don't relish finding a reason for yours."

I smiled. "We would simply tell the truth—that you knocked me into the water."

"I am not that poor of a rowman."

"So it's your pride you cannot swallow."

One hard look and he thrust himself over the side of the boat. I was forced to grasp the edge to steady myself, but I was never in any real danger of tipping over.

Graham's head popped out of the water and I splayed my hand across my chest. "Thank goodness you can swim."

He looked a bit bewildered. "And you're asking me that now?"

"I only just now realized that I could not lift you back into the boat if I needed to."

"Thank you for your confidence." He meandered along the edge of the boat until he was closer to the fountain. "Wish me luck." Then he dove into the depths.

I watched as he toured the square, stone remains beneath the water, splashing at times before coming up for breath. He took a long look at the back section, then continued on, working his way back around to the boat.

Finally his head emerged and he jerked his wet hair to the side. "Nothing."

"Really?" I straightened my back to see a bit better. "Did you feel in all the crevices for loose rocks, anything that might dislodge?"

"I'm not certain we're in the right location."

Without warning, he held up his hand to silence me, then pointed at the far side of the lake. "Get down." His voice was a sharp whisper and I dropped into the bottom of the boat. I knew as well as he did we didn't want to be seen searching the area.

After several minutes I stole a peek over the side and was rewarded with a view of the same three men I'd seen the day before. This time I could see all their faces, particularly one who had a scar—Mr. Haskett.

The boat rocked, a gentle reminder of Graham's concerns as well as his awkward situation. I ducked back down. There was more than one reason not to be seen.

It felt like forever before Graham finally deemed it safe enough to drape his arm over the side of the boat. I shifted back into my seat.

He had a hard look about his eyes. "Did you get a good look at anyone?"

"Mr. Haskett was one of the group. And Vincent Tulk. He's the gardener at—"

"Ah, I thought I recognized him." He squinted into the bright sunlight. "Wonder what brought the two of them to Avonthorpe."

"Mr. Haskett has been a busy man. I never told you he was at the festival with Mrs. Fagean, and yesterday I saw that same group walking here at the lake as well."

His eyebrows shot up. "Were they?"

"They crossed ahead just as they did now."

I looked up to catch Graham staring at me. He couldn't help but smile. "How exactly do you propose I get back in the boat?"

"You could swim alongside and walk out on the shoreline."

"In that mud? No, thank you." He glared about him. "And we both know you can't pull me in."

"As I said." I laughed to myself. "Maybe if you use the stone wall as leverage."

"Good idea." He propped his foot on the exposed base and launched himself upward and over. For a second I thought he might not make it, so I grasped his arm and pulled. He rolled up into the bottom of the boat, rather indelicately, I might add, which caused the balance to shift.

The boat tipped so far to one side, I was forced to lean the opposite way to right it. Of course, Graham had the same idea, the both of us causing an even greater imbalance. Water poured over the side for a second or two, and Graham swung back the other way to save us.

The movement jerked me forward, right off the seat, and at first I thought I'd managed to balance, but I was terribly mistaken. The planks were not entirely flat and the toe of my half boot snagged.

One final wave sent me reeling straight onto Graham. The sudden shift proved too much even for his agility, and we were both slung onto the waterlogged floor of the boat.

I gasped as the chilly water made its way through the folds of my gown, and I pushed myself into a sitting position. "Ah!" I could barely breathe. "Why didn't you tell me it was ice cold? Oh, Graham, and I made you swim in that and you were forced to stay in so long. You must think me the worst person in the world."

"Not the worst." He assisted me back onto the bench where he knelt, our laughs drifting slowly away until we simply sat there staring at each other, his natural confidence charging the space between us. His thin shirt clung to the curves of his chest, the dip in the cold water bringing out the brilliance of his smile. My pulse raced as it sought to warm my body.

He angled his chin. "You know I had little choice about my swimming. After all, we'd come for the clue, hadn't we? And with you threatening to jump over the side of the boat—"

"Not exactly jump." I pressed my forehead. "You poor thing . . . and I managed to get wet anyway."

"Not soaked through thankfully." He laughed as he shook his head, water droplets flinging all directions. "We are nothing short of a mess, but I think we shall make a passable go of it. The walk shall help dry us off at any rate." He reached out and felt my arm. "You're not too cold, are you?"

"No." And I wasn't, far from it. His sudden touch had brought my skin to life in a rush, followed by a curious mix of longing and dread. My muscles tensed, then relaxed as heat flooded my cheeks.

His hand slipped down to my elbow, but he didn't move away, his eyes focused on my hands tucked in my lap, as if what? Did he want to hold them?

I closed my eyes a long second, trying desperately to center my emotions. But I realized then and there I had little control over my own heart. He fell motionless before me as if caught up in the same spell, the air so perfectly still, his hand so soft on my arm. How had everything shifted in a matter of seconds?

The water droplets in Graham's hair caught the sunlight as a smile emerged. He blinked as if he hesitated to say something. Goodness knows I'd come to appreciate his slow, calculated way, always considering his words before speaking, but in that moment I needed to hear his thoughts.

A fish jumped in the water beside the boat, breaking his concentration, and when he looked back at me he seemed different somehow, more in control. He settled back on the opposing bench and secured the oars. "We'd better start back. We've already stayed out too long."

My chest hurt. My feet smarted from the cold. But most importantly, Graham had chosen to stop anything from happening between us. If only I knew why.

Twenty-One

I LAY AWAKE THAT NIGHT QUESTIONING EVERYTHING.

First and foremost the connection I'd felt with Graham. We were certainly more than friends, but what did that matter really? We were so terribly different, and he could have said anything in that moment, anything at all, yet he'd pulled away.

Perhaps I should return to Middlecrest to gain a better perspective. I flopped my arm over my forehead, tears close to the surface of my eyes, but they wouldn't come. I'd made a mull of everything—my journey of self-discovery and independence, the treasure hunt, the investigation into my teacher's murder. Maybe it was time I face the full effects of my choices, revisit the version of myself I wasn't even certain I would recognize any longer.

I'd been nothing but a child when I left, naïve, hopeful . . . devastated.

Jean Cloutier drifted into my mind like he always did with his black hair, full mouth, and beautiful French words.

I recognized at this point why my schoolgirl affection for him had only struck so deep. He'd awakened a part of me I'd not known existed, but the resulting surge of my heart had never been lasting love. His smooth words and even smoother compliments had been shared with me for one purpose and one purpose alone: to get me under his power.

I thrust my coverlet off me and swung my legs over the side of the bed before pausing to take in a breath of the cool night air. Juliana and I used to seek out the kitchens on such a night, warm milk and a pastry or two the only balm for such feelings. How I missed her. If only Jean hadn't stolen everything.

A slight chill swept over me as I sought out my slippers and robe, then lit a candle with the embers of my fire. I tied the robe's ribbon tight around my waist before edging open my bedchamber door. I stood there a moment, staring out into the blackened loneliness of the house at night before crossing into the hall.

The corridor was even chillier, the silent shadows absolute. For a second I considered making my way to Miss Chant's bedchamber to ask her to join me, but ever since our argument, nothing had been the same between us. Thank goodness she'd felt it too and mostly stayed away.

The angles and curves of the landing's balustrade took shape in the candlelight as I made my way to the grand staircase. One step down and I hesitated. Graham and I had been so happy when we discovered the clue beneath my feet. How different everything felt now. The treasure hunt had proved to be far more difficult than we had imagined. It was meant to be a personal one for Josiah Drake's son. Graham and I were fighting the intimate bonds of family and of time . . . and I was growing weary of the hunt.

Footsteps echoed below, then a diminutive light emerged from the gloom bobbing in the hall toward the front entryway. A moment of indecision passed before I blew out my candle and shrank against the wall.

Closer the light swayed until a face took shape in the darkness.

The tension vanished from my shoulders. "Graham."

He darted a hard look up the stairs. "Phoebe." Then a sigh of relief. "What are you doing up at this hour?"

I descended to meet him at the bottom of the stairs. "I couldn't sleep. I needed a walk."

His eyes looked like dark pools in the shifting light, the flame from the candle mirrored in the center. Time seemed lost for a second as he appraised me, but then he could hardly hold still, jerking into a hard pace back and forth across the carpet. "I sent Mr. Montague to look into a matter I've not discussed with you."

I edged down onto the sofa. "Oh?"

His hands gestured one way, then the next. "There was a man the other day at the beach. I-I was alone and I thought nothing of it at first."

"You went back down the stairs . . . to the ocean."

He stopped, his chest heaving. "I heard this man speaking French."

My heart went dead cold, my nerves ticking to life like tiny spiders on my back. "So that's why you've been on edge. And?"

"I didn't give it much thought at first, but then I remembered what Constable Humphries told me . . . about the escaped prisoner from Gaol Lane. Questions only grew in my mind, all the dreaded what-ifs, until I finally decided to send a missive to a friend of mine to ask for more information regarding this prisoner." His fingers wriggled into his pocket and he pulled out a letter. "I received word from him tonight." A well-placed pause. "The man who escaped was French, Phoebe—a Napoleon loyalist.

"And there's more." He lowered his gaze to read from the paper. "The prisoner's name is Jean Cloutier, the same Jean Cloutier who was involved in the murder of Giles Harris two years ago."

"No . . ." My voice was little more than a whisper.

Graham flexed his jaw. "You know as well as I if Cloutier's in the area, you aren't safe. He knows who you are. Your father must be told."

"No! Wait . . . please don't say a word to my father." I must have made some small movement, or perhaps it was my eyes that gave me away, but I noted the shift between us, a subtle look by Graham that lasted a second longer than it should have, the sort only a person well acquainted with the other could possibly recognize.

I denied the feeling with everything I could, pretending not to notice the question in his voice. "You think I should keep quiet about this?"

"There was never any real proof he assisted Giles's murderer, just a Frenchman trying to get home."

Graham smashed the note in his fist. "Killer or not, what if the constable was right?" He narrowed his eyes. "What if Cloutier was involved in my aunt's death?"

My fingers shook as I ran them down the edge of my robe, and I wished I'd kept my hand at my side. I had every reason to believe Jean was not involved, and his life absolutely hung in the balance now. I took a deep breath. I had to be very careful what I said. "What possible motive could Cloutier have for your aunt's murder? And the crossbow—how would he even know where to find it?"

He raked his hand through his hair. "I don't know, but he is on the estate now . . ."

"And the thefts down the coast. If he committed those, that would put him miles from here the day your aunt was killed."

There was no perceptible change in Graham's face, but my heart told me something lay beneath his words. I stood and sought the window for comfort.

Graham's eyes remained steady on me, then he shoved the letter into his pocket. "I must confess . . . I find the ease with which you've taken this information a bit surprising. Were you perhaps aware of this before now?"

My stomach lurched. Withholding information had been silently eating me alive, but to outright lie . . . I looked up, unable to hide the strain in my voice. "Not that I recall."

"Not that you *recall*?"

I avoided his eyes. The undercurrent of his suspicion was swelling. Graham Burke had always been far too observant, too methodical in his thinking. He was a student of antiquities . . . of people. I tugged at the collar of my robe, unable to pretend any longer that a chasm hadn't opened up between us, but I was caught in a terrible quandary. If I revealed the fact Jean had asked me for money, I would be putting his life at risk. Graham would most certainly use such knowledge to apprehend Jean. "You do know I would never stand in the way of justice for your aunt, don't you?"

His shoulders slumped. "Not exactly."

I cringed beneath his terse answer, but it wasn't Graham's accusation that brought tears springing to my eyes. It was the truth behind his words. I was holding back and it felt awful. I rubbed my upper arms for comfort.

He guided me to face him, and just like that, the flame to his tone vanished, like a candle doused in water. He jerked back a step, his eyes wide like an owl's, his voice a pained whisper. "It's been a long night. I'm not accusing you of anything." Clearly thoughts were running wild in his mind, his breath anxious to evolve into words.

I peered carefully into his eyes, weighing the intimate parts of my heart against secrets I'd buried too deep to expose. "I believe it's past time I returned to my room. I-I need some space."

He drew his lips together, his body sagging ever so slightly forward, then he released my shoulders. He pressed the palms of his hands against his closed eyes, his neck bobbing with a hard swallow. "Please don't leave yet. There's something else you need to be made aware of."

Unknowingly I grasped the window for support. "What is it?"

"I've uncovered another false vase in the house."

"Another one?"

"I've only had time to inventory the ground floor. There could be many more." He sighed. "Someone has been stealing from my aunt for some time."

"Or they murdered her to do so."

His jaw went slack. "The thought has crossed my mind. The Fageans are about to make another shipment to France. I cannot help but wonder—"

"It's been delayed."

"Delayed?"

"Mrs. Fagean told me so herself earlier in the evening."

He turned to the window. "I wouldn't think they'd wish to dally with stolen goods."

"Then someone else? Someone desperate for money."

"It could be any servant, any visitor. My head is too pained to think on it any more tonight. I'm considering employing a Bow Street Runner."

"I'll speak with Arnold tomorrow to see if he has any insights on the staff. At least we can eliminate some of the servants from suspicion."

He ran his fingers across his forehead. "Agreed."

I touched his arm. "No more tonight."

He nodded slowly and I turned to leave, but I felt his hand at my back. "Oh no, you don't."

I glanced over my shoulder, a mix of elation and confusion at his fervent touch. "What?"

"If we have a thief and a murderer in this house, there's no way I'm letting you return to your room alone at night." The ghost of a grin spread across his face, easing some of the grim lines.

"I think you enjoy telling me what to do."

He laughed a bit, first to himself then somewhat louder the longer he thought about what I'd said. "Oh, Phoebe, you have no idea."

My locked bedchamber, while safe, felt particularly lonely that night. Graham had escorted me back to my room the way any proper gentleman would and waited in the hall for me to shut the door. However, I didn't hear his footsteps—his familiar military march, so even and assured—not for at least a half hour or more. I listened intently for them, but it wasn't until I'd settled into my bed and neared sleep that I finally caught the soft pounding of retreat.

I plumped my pillow for the thirteenth time and rolled to face the window. The heavy chintz curtains had effectively eclipsed the moon; only a ghostly outline remained. His watchful exit, though prudent, felt terribly personal. I traced the dull white light with my mind's eye, my thoughts running in all directions.

Did Graham actually have suspicions about my involvement with Jean? What did he really know about it?

I had no real idea what information Graham was privy to. My father had mentioned in his last letter that he retained a distant relationship with Mr. Montague. It was one of the reasons he'd allowed me to stay at all, which only concerned me. Was Mr. Montague involved in my father's business for the government? If so, he might already be aware of what happened with Jean Cloutier's escape from Middlecrest.

The urge to flee Avonthorpe surged once again into my chest, but I thrust myself upright in bed and gripped the bedsheets. Not this time.

I'd promised Miss Drake to see this through. And Graham . . . Even if I couldn't bring myself to reveal all the sordid details of my past, I owed it to him to stay and help him find the treasure and, far more importantly, expose the person responsible for his aunt's murder. My strained relationship with my father came rushing into my mind accompanied by a fresh ache in my chest. The wound there was still raw after I'd left in such a way.

I glanced over at the door to where Graham had stood watch on the other side, alone in the night. There was no way in the world I would make the same mistake as I had two years prior—not with him.

Twenty-Two

I CONFRONTED DANIEL IN THE BALLROOM THE FOLLOWING morning.

He'd just completed the lower section of the trim he'd been working on in uncomfortable silence when I leaned back to assess his work—exceptional.

I smiled down at him from my perch on the scaffolding. "That's brilliant. I knew you had it in you." Then as an afterthought, "Miss Drake would have been proud."

He eyed me a long moment before giving me something of a shrug, a half smile sneaking out the corner of his mouth. "Guess I'm feeling more myself this morning."

I hesitated to probe his statement, but too many questions surrounding my friend swirled in my mind. Carefully I descended the ladder and motioned for Daniel to join me on the lowest level of the scaffolding.

He eased down onto the uneven wood planks with a creak. "What is it this time?" I could see layers of concern in his face as he ran his hand through his hair. "Is Lt. Burke demanding more?"

"Lt. Burke?" I glanced around us at the work we'd completed, admiring the artistry of the original painter, the intricate swirls and loops of his creation, the vivid reminder of Miss Drake's vision for the restoration of the space. "Not at all."

Daniel extended his legs for a good stretch. "Then what's to do,

Phoebe? You look like my mother did when she told me I was to go to Eton for my studies."

"I-I need to ask you about the painting."

He checked. "You mean the trim work? Really, I daresay we've done our part. If Lt. Burke feels the need to criticize it, he can go jump in the lake for all I care."

His offhand comment sent my mind racing, followed by a wave of discomfort. Was he aware of our excursion to the fountain? I shook the thought away. "Not our painting . . . *the* painting—the one of Josiah Drake, which Lt. Burke identified as a fake."

He appeared a bit blank a moment before he straightened his back. "And you think I have something to do with that?"

"I don't know. You must admit, you've been acting rather strangely of late."

He stared. "How so?"

"Your short temper for one."

He dropped his hands into his lap and turned away. "I've been under quite a bit of stress."

"Even so . . ." The urge to reach out and touch him swelled, but I kept my arms pinned to my sides. "You've never treated me so coldly before. And then there's that business with Mrs. Fagean."

He jerked to his feet, his fingers wrapped tightly around the scaffolding railing, his voice a cold mixture of anger and pettishness. "What about Mrs. Fagean?"

"You've never been a friend of hers . . . and now . . . I don't know, I see you together quite often." I leaned in to better see his face. "Arnold has said the same—"

"What does Arnold know?" He jammed his hands into his trouser pockets. "And why does it matter if I cry friends with Mrs. Fagean?"

I blinked away my discomfiture. "It doesn't, not really. I just find your relationship with her odd after all you said—"

He kicked a discarded paintbrush on the floor. "Dashitall,

Phoebe . . ." Then fell all but motionless. That is, until he raked his gaze hard on me. "I went to the Equinox Festival, all right."

My mouth slipped open. Of all the ways the conversation could have gone, such a bizarre revelation was the last thing I expected. Words wouldn't even come.

He fiddled with his quizzing glass as he waited for my response. Then he became impatient, pacing in front of me as he spoke. "I was embarrassed. She . . . I . . . I didn't want you to know."

I stood, my heart all but frozen in my chest. "Embarrassed about what exactly?"

"Dancing with her in such a way . . . dishonoring the memory of Miss Drake . . . the whole dratted thing. I wish I'd never come here." Tears threatened his eyes and he turned away.

I watched him lean back as he fought for control of his emotions. "I think you'd better start from the beginning. Tell me, what took you there in the first place?"

He shook off any remaining reticence and collapsed onto his seat on the wooden scaffolding. "It was her idea, but a part of me wanted to go."

"Mrs. Fagean?"

"She found me near the stables in indecision. I was pretty upset at the time—my life unraveling and all that. I wanted to forget all about it, even if it was only for a little while."

"Your life unraveling? You mean because of losing Miss Drake and the tutelage you were to receive here?"

His chin snapped up. "Of course—what else could I mean?" He released his death grip on the lowest rung of the ladder, then huffed out a sigh. "I thought I had troubles at the time. It took me a great deal to convince my father to allow me to come here at all. I wasn't certain I could do it again, transfer my studies elsewhere. He wants me to go into the church or the law." He shook his head. "I'd been drinking that night . . ."

"And Mrs. Fagean asked you to accompany her."

Slowly he nodded as if it pained him to do so. "I went out of anger and . . . other things."

I lifted my eyebrows. "She is quite beautiful."

"I got in too deep, too quick, Phoebe. Please don't chastise me for it now. I've done it enough to myself already and I need a friend."

I took a deep breath, forcing any consternation from my voice. "What happened?"

"Like I said . . . we danced, and then we . . . well, I kissed her—"

"You what?"

He threw back his head. "I knew you wouldn't understand. This is why I hesitated in the first place."

The initial shock ebbing away, I managed a trite, "Go on. I won't say any more."

"Please, you must believe me. I wasn't myself and she cornered me. Sort of, I guess. It all happened so fast. I thought . . . never mind what I thought." He stared long and hard at the ballroom floor. "I hope you don't think different of me now. I-I've since spoken with her." A small, injured smile emerged. "She's not all that bad. I . . . we're in a much better place. We understand one another at this point."

"And is Mr. Fagean to be told?"

"Dashitall, Phoebe. No!" Softer then, "No. Do you think I'm a flat? I'd rather not meet him across the field."

He did have a point there. Mr. Fagean had already survived two duels that I knew of, and I couldn't say the same about the other gentlemen. "And there's to be no more between you and Mrs. Fagean?"

"Nothing whatsoever. I plan to leave Avonthorpe at the close of our work here and never look back."

I bit my lip, then nodded. "All right."

He dipped his chin. "All right, you'll keep my secret?"

"For now."

He touched my gloved hand. "You've always been a good friend to me. I won't forget this."

I couldn't help but revel a bit in the return of our companionship and the easing of my worries. Daniel was terribly important to me, the only person I felt close to from home, and now I knew his behavior had nothing to do with Miss Drake's murder. He'd simply been ashamed of his actions with Mrs. Fagean, a married woman, nothing more. Our friendship was still intact.

He smiled as he rose. "It's a deuced relief to get all that off my shoulders."

I mirrored his movements. "I'm sure it is."

Then he edged forward. "Particularly since we've yet to identify who murdered Miss Drake. Even through all of this, I've been doing my part, watching and questioning people in this house."

"Have you?"

"Indeed. I want to help you and Arnold uncover whoever it was."

I gave him a careful look. It was Lt. Burke I had been working with since the start, but I had no intention of apprising Daniel of that fact. Strange, though, that he'd assume Arnold was the one helping me. Granted, the butler and I were certainly in communication about the treasure hunt. "Anyone in particular you've been watching, anyone you suspect?"

"Not a person per se. Rather a building. Take that old church for instance. Why are so many people in and out of there?"

I rested my arm against the edge of the scaffolding. "Surely you've heard that Mr. Montague and Lt. Burke are selling some antiquities kept there."

"Yes, but why did I see Mr. Fagean poking his nose around there as well? Through my dealings with Mrs. Fagean I've come to understand she isn't entirely trustful of her husband." He added rather quickly, "I've not been able to stop her from pouring all her concerns into my ear."

I thought a moment. "Do you think he might have had something to do with the stolen painting from the drawing room, or even worse, Miss Drake's murder?"

Daniel ran his fingers along the seam of his trousers. "All I know is that I followed him to the lake early this morning. I fish at the sluice gate at least once a week and I stumbled upon him accidentally. What do you know, but Mr. Fagean pranced right up to my favorite spot, not fishing at all, just examining the gate itself."

"The sluice gate?" I stiffened a second before my shoulders slumped back at ease. "Mr. Fagean manages quite a few things around here. I suppose he was simply—"

"Maybe so, but the way he was looking beneath the water in that calculated way of his—well, it sure felt havey-cavey to me. And when I called out good morning to the man, devil take it, but he looked rattled. He said all that was proper and pranced out of there as fast as he could." Daniel tapped his cheek. "Makes one wonder what he was up to."

"Indeed." I swallowed hard the truth that had gathered so tight in my throat. The sluice gate! Why hadn't I checked there already? The next clue could certainly be hidden somewhere on the gate. And if that were indeed the case, Mr. Fagean was already one step ahead of us.

I feigned nonchalance as I smoothed my way to an exit, but every last muscle inside me twitched in alarm. "Thank you for all your help this morning on the trim. We've made a great deal of progress. I think we've worked enough for today. After all, I've a few engagements this afternoon that will keep me away from my work."

Daniel followed my movements with a keen eye. "And Mr. Fagean?"

How to handle this? Daniel could be an ally in the hunt, but did I trust him like Graham? A ping hit my heart. Did I trust anyone as much as I trusted Graham? The answer was assuredly no. "I-I think you're right to watch Mr. Fagean. Keep doing so, and report anything you learn to me."

He nodded, then winked. "Already in the plans, Phoebe." Then he gave me a chin pop. "Till tomorrow morning then."

I bade him good day with as much ease as I could muster, my heart on a race of its own. The sluice gate! Why had we been so stupid?

Now where had Graham told me he planned to spend the length of the morning?

The church!

I was out of the house in an instant, my fingers working to knot my bonnet ribbons beneath my chin, the folds of my dress like anchors holding me back. There were so many questions that needed answers. How on earth had Mr. Fagean learned of the clue under the stair? And how had he solved it as well as we had—better even?

I stopped cold in my tracks, the icy fingers of fear gripping my chest. Did Mr. Fagean kill Miss Drake to obtain the original clue? It was entirely possible. Was he the person who had used the vicar's cottage to make the connections he needed to find the clues he had thus far?

Gravel crunched beneath my half boots as I launched forward once again. My breaths came short and fast as I barreled across the manicured lawns and down the path that led to the church. There was a distinctive scent on the breeze, that pleasing mixture of soil and leaves, which the sun had finally released from the early dew, but I could hardly appreciate it as I broke out into a jog.

I had slammed through the first gaggle of trees when a figure appeared quite suddenly from the shadows. I only slowed a moment to decipher the man's identity. Graham was walking my direction with Creature on a long lead. Relieved and a bit giddy at my fortune, I waved with excitement.

Graham met me beneath the branches of a thick oak. "What are you about?"

I averted my gaze to Creature, absently petting his head. "I have news. I was on my way to find you just now."

"With everything that is happening at the house, I'm beginning to wonder if you should be traipsing around here alone."

I gave him a little smile. "*You're* alone."

He gave a sigh. "Yes, but no one tried to make me sick"—he rested his hand on his jacket pocket—"and I never leave the house without protection."

I nodded more to myself than to him. "Protection, hmm? I'm fairly certain Miss Chant can procure a pistol for me if you haven't a second. Although if I had to guess, that weapon in your pocket is in all likelihood one of a smart pair of dueling pistols. You are a gentleman, are you not?"

"You know very well that is not what I meant; however"—he ran his hand down his face—"you may be in the right of it. Perhaps it would be wise for you to carry something with you." He eyed me a long moment. "Tell me, can you shoot at all?"

I cocked an eyebrow as my brother had taught me to do years ago to annoy my father. "Can I shoot, sir? Lord Torrington is my father, after all. He made certain his children were well prepared for whatever came their way."

A smile curved his lips as he slid his hand into his pocket. "Why don't you just show me then?"

I gestured to the woods. "Here?"

"Certainly, that is, unless you exaggerated your prowess—"

"I never exaggerate."

He passed the heavy pistol into my hands, and I got my first good look at it. The wood ran smooth all the way down the two barrels, the metal inlays beautifully intricate. At the handle was a large scripted G embossed in silver. "Did you have this specially made?"

"I did. I first saw these double-barreled flintlocks in France and had one fashioned before I left the Continent. No twin for this one I'm afraid. I've never been much of a dueler. Most arguments can be settled without violence, you know."

"I presume you loaded it properly."

He smirked. "I was in His Majesty's dragoons, lest you forget."

"True." I glanced around us once again. "What should I aim for, Captain?"

He pointed across the small glen. "It is Lieutenant, and see that tree? Do you think you can hit the knob there?" He took a step nearer. "This isn't a pistol designed for a lady."

I extended my arm and took aim, the pistol a bit heavier than I'd anticipated, but I had no intention of allowing him to see my surprise. "I daresay I could hit whatever needed." But my confidence was flagging. I'd never leveled anything so large before.

"That's right. Keep it even." He moved in terribly close beside me, and I watched the barrel waver as a shiver stole across the exposed skin on my arm. The mounting twinge of attraction I felt only grew as his whispered words slid across my shoulders. "Something tells me you'll be a crack shot."

"As I said." I closed one eye and squeezed the trigger. An explosion sliced through the quiet woods, my arm shaking in recoil, a large puff of smoke drifting in the breeze. We stood a moment in wretched silence simply staring through the haze before moving forward.

I'd hoped to hit the knob dead on, but I had been close, just a few short inches above the target.

Graham smiled at me with a brilliance I was unprepared for. "And that, my dear, is how it's done. You shall have a pistol and straightaway."

I let the gun hang loose around my finger, reveling in the fact I'd impressed him. "You mean I don't get to keep this one?"

"Not a chance." He shot me a wink. "It'll be a lady's muff pistol for you so you can hide it in your reticule or your pelisse, and one with a lock to keep you safe. I'll have Montague obtain one immediately."

The sudden *crack* of a branch drew our attention to the far woods. I felt Graham's fingers wrap around the pistol and I released it into his hand. The crunch of footsteps grew louder, and then a man wearing a dark jacket materialized between the tree trunks.

Graham's arm relaxed and he slid the weapon into his interior jacket pocket. "Frampton," he called out, then whispered to me, "Are you acquainted with our main tenant farmer?"

I nodded seconds before the burly man was within earshot. Bronzed from the sun and sweaty with the work of the day, Mr. Frampton snatched his hat from his head and hastened to meet us. "Good afternoon, Lt. Burke, Miss Radcliff." His eyes danced between the two of us like a girl in her first season. "I'm sure glad I've come upon you, Burke. I 'twas on my way to speak with Mr. Fagean, ya see, but perhaps I'd better discuss the issue with you. If you've the time, a' course."

"Go on, my good man."

"'Tis the water, sir. It's washed out my small bridge downstream."

Graham stood a second in silence. "The water? Besides that one storm it's been terribly dry of late. What are you referring to?"

He fumbled with his hat. "The release . . . from the lake this morning."

Graham narrowed his eyes. "What release?"

The pieces clicked together in my mind as the two men spoke. Mr. Fagean. The sluice gate. The clue had to be on the gate. My muscles tingled in anticipation. "Lt. Burke?"

He shot a quick look at me.

"Perhaps Mr. Fagean was testing the sluice gate. I heard on good authority he was seen examining it."

A nearly imperceptible line crossed Graham's forehead, then vanished. He gave me a tight nod before turning back to face Mr. Frampton. "I will send my man to assess the situation at once."

Mr. Frampton seemed hesitant to leave. "Then I needn't take this up with Fagean?"

Lt. Burke stiffened. "Certainly not. As of my aunt's untimely death, Mr. Fagean is now simply a guest here at the house, nothing more. My land agent will handle any further issues that arise."

Mr. Frampton seemed to flinch. "You don't say." Then gave a whistle. "I'll be sure to spread the word." A pop of his eyebrows. "Good day, sir."

I watched him walk away before Graham tugged me over a bit forcefully. "How long have you known about the sluice gate? This could very well prove vital to the treasure hunt."

His abrupt closeness sent my heart racing. "I just learned of the information from Daniel. I was coming to tell you straightaway."

"And yet—"

"You distracted me when you questioned my ability to shoot. I forgot all about why I'd rushed into the woods. You know I can't pass up a challenge."

He laughed as he shook his head. "I'm learning, Phoebe. Goodness knows, I'm learning."

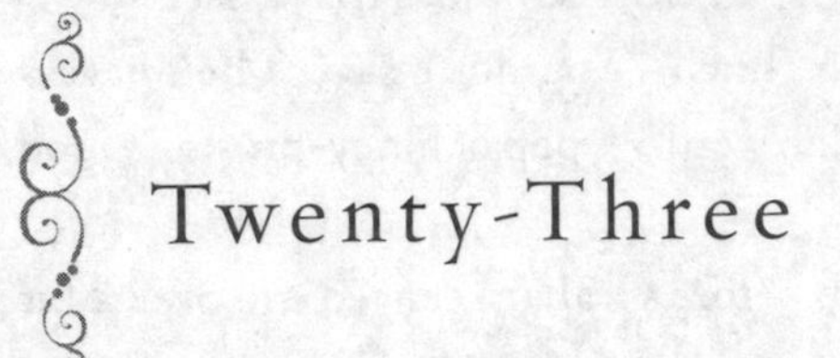

Twenty-Three

"WAIT!"

Graham jumped into the icy water of the lake, then reemerged at the surface, a bit of a youthful smile on his face. "This will have to be quick or Mr. Frampton will be livid. See the arm crank there? When I tell you, I'll need you to turn it."

"You don't think we should warn him somehow?" I teetered on the edge of the rock. "Besides, I thought we'd discuss a plan. This is madness."

Graham fought back a shiver. "We haven't time to give any warnings, and I thought you wanted me to be a bit more impulsive. I believe *stuffy* is the word you used."

"I didn't mean . . . This seems dangerous. Won't you be sucked in? And I'm not even certain I can turn the crank to lift the gate."

Graham coughed out a laugh. "If Mr. Fagean could do it . . ."

I returned a chuckle, but it was short-lived. "I don't like this."

He swam over near the stone corner. "I'll keep myself tucked nicely out of the pull of the water. I'm well aware of the force it will exert. But there's no way to read the clue . . . unless." He plunged under the water, and I was forced to wait for him to resurface. He did so with a smile. "I'm right. Thanks to the drought and Mr. Fagean's release, I've a chance. It shall take several passes, but I believe I can read the words."

"You're not too cold, are you?"

His eyes flashed. "Excited more like."

"But Mr. Fagean has already read it."

"True, but he isn't near as clever as you." He took a deep breath and dove under the murky surface of the water once again.

He was gone several seconds before thrusting up. "Where your treasure is . . ." Another submersion and splashing return. "There your heart will be also."

"The Bible verse?"

"Yes, but there's more." He took another deep breath and plunged into the icy depths. It felt even longer before he returned. And this time he pushed himself into a sitting position on the low shelf, his muscles convulsing with the cold. "It's a set of numerals. Simply the ordinals one through six and the words 'Don't forget to look up.'" He shook off some water from his hair and stood. "Come with me into the sun. I've a blanket over there."

I didn't notice he untied his shirt as we walked until we reached the blanket, where he gathered the loose ends in his hands. A quick glance at me and he stilled. "Uh . . . if you'll excuse me a moment, I brought a fresh shirt with me."

At first I didn't understand, then a rush of heat filled my cheeks and I turned away from him.

I heard a shuffle at my back, then a *whoosh* of the blanket. "If you don't mind sitting a moment, I'd like to allow my breeches to dry some."

Slowly I edged back around. "You've taken a dip twice now in that horrid lake—"

He chuckled to himself. "And I don't intend to do so again." He motioned to the seat at his side. "Join me. We've a new clue to dissect."

I eased down into the available space and crossed my feet at the ankles. "I'm getting the strangest feeling we're nearing the end of this whole thing."

"Of the hunt, you mean?"

"Precisely." I propped my arms behind me. "Where your treasure is. Josiah Drake didn't use those words lightly. They must have a deeper meaning."

"Agreed. But the verse could simply be a warning—to place your treasure in heaven."

I blinked a moment. "You don't think the treasure isn't real, do you?"

"No." He readjusted his wet legs. "The Drakes clearly came into a trove of money at some point."

"Perhaps they spent it all and Josiah Drake—"

"Was no saint, but he'd never send his beloved son on a wild-goose chase just to impart some biblical meaning. It has to be a clue to somewhere specific."

"The graveyard perhaps."

He lifted his eyebrows. "The graveyard? That would be looking down, not up."

"I was only thinking about heaven and where Josiah would be when his son went searching. In fact, we should probably hunt there as soon as possible."

Graham watched me a moment, a curious bend to his brow. "This impulsiveness . . . is this how you approach everything in your life, straight ahead without looking back?"

I thought a moment. "In some ways, yes."

"Like when you decided to train with my aunt? Many ladies your age would not have taken the opportunity, declared it foolish even."

"That decision . . . well . . . was different."

"How so?"

I bit my lip as I combed through a tangle of emotions. "Let me ask you this: Have you ever prayed for something for so long, then a door opens—maybe not the one you were expecting, but one opens nonetheless—and suddenly everything shifts into place?"

He gave me a thoughtful nod. "So you just up and left everything you knew behind."

"I can't explain the decision, not satisfactorily. I simply had this overwhelming feeling of hope. I suppose it's the dreamer in me, the believer." I sighed. "It's almost as if I could hear the voice of adventure calling for me to come here and test the unknown, to see what I was made of, to make the impossible . . . well, possible."

A slow smile. "That's beautiful." Then his gaze lowered to his lap. "I do understand what you are saying, and I felt a similar pull in my youth." His smile fell away. "Yet war changes a person in every way possible, stole a part of me I may never recover. Ever since I returned from the Continent, I've found it increasingly difficult to make decisions, to find hope in the unknown. Instead, much to my chagrin, I find myself constantly second-guessing everything and everyone. It can be paralyzing at times. I wish"—a gentle sigh—"I wish I could go back somehow. But at the same time, when I string together the threads of my life, I realize one has to be careful with reactionary plans. Running toward something, even with the best of intentions, can also mean running away from something else."

I didn't move for a full minute. My chest felt cold, my arms heavy. Graham was right. How easily he'd dissected my complicated emotions.

He seemed to detect my flailing mood and sat forward at once. "I didn't mean to get so philosophical. A weakness of mine, I'm afraid."

My voice came out at a whisper. "Wisdom should never be considered a weakness."

We sat in silence a moment before he tapped his finger on the blanket. "Perhaps we should get back to deciphering the clue." A peek over at me. "What do you think those blasted numbers mean?"

It took me a moment to shift my thoughts, to crawl my way out of my embarrassment, but I did so on a wave of optimism. "Could it be a direction of some kind?"

He flopped his head back. "Why did it have to be another

number? Turns my stomach. You know how long it took us to figure out the importance of the number fifteen."

"Heavens, yes. Don't remind me. Although Josiah's ridiculous clues do help us in a way."

"How's that?"

I gave him a wide smile. "Mr. Fagean will be just as lost as we are."

"And now that we know he's a player in all this, I can set Mr. Montague to trailing him."

"Interesting that the tenant farmers regard him as a sort of land agent. I've even heard Miss Drake refer to him in such a way."

He blew out his cheeks. "I had no idea how deeply Mr. Fagean had got his hooks into this place. As far as I can tell, he's set himself up to be indispensable. When he challenged me on the smuggling venture, he was not without grounds."

"The villagers think well of him too. He supplies quite a bit of their goods—duty-free. His departure will have an economic effect on the entire village."

Graham rubbed his forehead. "His friends run quite deep around here. We'll have to be careful, particularly you."

"Me?"

"We still don't know who put that rancid milk in the lemonade."

I held up my hands. "But what possible threat am I to Mr. Fagean?"

"Like I suggested before, he might mean to stall your hunt."

"Yes—however, you would be at just as great a risk. You were given the clue in the will and are searching as well."

"Yes, but is Mr. Fagean even aware of that fact?"

I opened my mouth to speak, then closed it a second. "I don't know. Arnold knows of the clause in the will."

"Only because my aunt trusted him implicitly."

I sat a moment in silence. "You may be right. I shall certainly steer clear of Mr. Fagean."

"And his wife."

I gasped. "You don't think—"

"I certainly do. She's as shady as he is."

My opinion of Mrs. Fagean only worsened when I came upon her by accident in the rose garden the following afternoon. Miss Chant was supposed to meet me for a little walk around the gardens, but I encouraged her to go with Vincent again. She hadn't been happy since our argument, and I was in no mood for her dramatics.

Mrs. Fagean had her back to me, her shoulders hunched, as she ran her hands along the thick ivy leaves at the rear wall. I came to a standstill almost at once as there was a nervous energy to the wild garden, a fleeting breeze that disturbed the plants and the hairs on my arms in surges. I could not shake the chill.

The sound of the gate slamming shut brought Mrs. Fagean jerking to face me as a whispered word disappeared on her lips. Her face, which at first held a mix of eagerness and anxiety, faded into placid disinterest.

She made a show of pressing her free hand against her chest in a fist. "Oh, Phoebe, it's only you." A sly glance behind me.

I followed her line of sight as I advanced nearer. "Were you expecting someone?"

She laughed and lowered her arm, but her fingers remained tight. "Don't be ridiculous. You just startled me is all."

I couldn't help but stare down at her hand, gripped tight in a ball.

She gave her head a little shake. "I was actually just leaving. If you will excuse me."

Another lie, but I swallowed it as best I could, nodding as she expected. Nothing could possibly be gained from a long conversation with Mrs. Fagean, not at this point. But I couldn't help myself. "I spoke with Daniel earlier today."

Her steps slowed. "Daniel?" But she didn't turn.

"He told me what happened at the Equinox Festival. He was ashamed."

"Oh." Like a snake, she coiled against the wall, a sly smile stretching across her face. "Boys will be boys, you know." A long pause. "What you must think of me, I cannot guess. But I assure you, what passed between me and Daniel is most assuredly at an end . . . at least on my part."

I could feel the heat of anger boiling in my chest. "Be careful, Mrs. Fagean. Daniel is a particular friend of mine. I won't allow you to toy with him."

"Toy with him?" She burst out a laugh. "*Me?* You'd best turn that finger back on yourself, young lady. I've seen the two of you together." She narrowed her eyes, obviously pleased by my sudden bewilderment. "No one toys with him more than you do."

I stepped back a pace. "We grew up together . . . It's nothing like that."

"If that is what you tell yourself so you can sleep at night, go ahead, dream on, my poor little innocent, but that boy has plans where you're concerned."

"Plans." I said the word more to myself than Mrs. Fagean, an element of truth hitting me like a brick. Was she right? Was there more to Daniel's good nature, more to his kind regard? More to his remaining at Avonthorpe? It was possible.

But he was younger than I was, still a child.

I heard the metallic squeak of the gate and looked up just in time to see Mrs. Fagean deposit something into her pelisse pocket. I would have missed the object entirely if the sun hadn't sneaked from behind a cloud and illuminated the garden. A bright flash of blue reflected the light and feathered between her fingers as she plunged her fisted hand into the depths of her pocket.

She stamped out the gate, her movements swift and accusatory, leaving me no opportunity to inquire. Granted, I was also in shock. I collapsed onto a nearby bench for a good half hour to process Mrs. Fagean's accusations about Daniel as well as the strange concealment of the blue item. If only I could have followed her—but alone, that was out of the question.

Why had she been so secretive? . . . It was almost as if . . .

A rushed set of footsteps erupted beyond the wall, then the gate swung inward as a man stole into the interior of the garden and straight into the shadows of the wall. He was gasping as if he'd been running.

I leaped to my feet and backed away.

"Phoebe?"

The familiar voice terrified me. Every last muscle in my body twisted tight as I managed to whisper, "What are you doing here? You were supposed to set sail for France."

Jean Cloutier stepped into the light, his broad shoulders straightening to his full height. "I mean to leave as soon as possible." His voice was a bit incredulous. "I-I've made arrangements, but—"

"But what?" I took a wild glance at the gate to the rose garden, frustrated Jean had positioned himself so perfectly to prevent my escape. Had he done so on purpose?

His eyes appeared even grayer than at our first meeting, his cheeks gaunter. He shook his head as if in denial. "I . . . I needed to see you one last time."

A tremor shot through my hands to my fingers as I gripped my muslin gown. See me? Suddenly the garden felt terribly small, my throat too swollen to allow a breath. Though I'd dreamed of hearing such a declaration so many times, Jean's words slithered into my mind like a venomous snake. No elation surged into my breast, no warmth, nor even a lowly sigh of relief. Indeed, I felt nothing. Here was what I'd been searching for the past two years—perspective. I could finally see Jean for who he'd always been—a desperate French spy caught in a foreign land who would do anything to survive.

I cringed at the thought.

Misreading the depth of my silence, Jean stepped closer, that familiar look of ownership transforming his face as he boldly ran his fingers down my arm. How memorable his touch felt, yet my aversion was swift and absolute. I jerked away. "What is it that you want from me?"

His hand froze. "I . . . already told you . . . money." I could see his emotions dancing across his face as he digested my rejection. I would not be so easy to manipulate this time.

I shook my head, my heartbeat thrashing its way into my ears. "We've been over this. I have none to spare."

The wind shifted, and the gusts turned colder and more persistent. I secured my arms close.

Jean lifted his brows. "Anything will help, you know." Then his eyes filled with longing. "If you ever cared for me—"

My heart contracted. "There was a time I would have done anything you asked, but all I can feel for you now is pity." I swallowed hard, his betrayal, my unrequited feelings, shifting into focus. I felt like a bird at last, free to fly away from the man who'd held such power over me. Miss Chant was right. It was time I moved on from Jean in every way.

In the charged silence I thought he might advance toward me, but a wan smile crossed his face and he gave me one last pained look.

Then he was gone.

Twenty-Four

It was unseasonably chilly when I saw Graham the following morning, gray clouds gathering en masse across a windy sky, the trees bemoaning their plight, popping and cracking in repetitive gusts. He needed to visit the smithy and I'd agreed somewhat reluctantly to join him for the quick jaunt into town.

Jean's continued presence around Avonthorpe lay like an unspoken wall between us, yet Graham hadn't the least idea of what ached in my chest. He tried a slight nudge. "You're not too cold, are you?"

"No." I turned my face into the wind. "Refreshed more like."

He watched me a long moment, then gave me a smile. "Good. Because I was a bit worried to bring you out in all this. Yet at the same time I didn't want to leave you at the house."

A tiny ping hit my heart. "You're still worried for my safety?"

"I will be until I've exposed whoever took my aunt's life. I cannot get the crossbow out of my mind. Such a choice of weapon seems personal in a way. At the least, the killer had to have known of it, and where it was kept. I'm beginning to see your perspective that Jean Cloutier had nothing to do with my aunt's death."

"Graham, I . . ." I looked up and my words were lost to the heavy breeze. Was I ready to put Jean's life at risk? I knew he wasn't involved as he had been miles down the coastline at the time, but his continued presence in the area was troubling. My heart folded inward, a shiver prickling my skin. How I wished I could go back to the beginning and disclose everything from the start. I replayed the first moment

Jean had approached me in the woods beside the church. I'd not been honest with myself regarding the complicated emotions at play in my heart. I'd been infatuated with Jean at one time, but he had no part of my future.

My future . . .

I loved Graham Burke . . . I loved him. I sat up straighter, rolling the thought through my mind over and over again. Had I ever really admitted the truth to myself outright? The whole idea of him and me had snuck up on me when I wasn't paying the least attention. But now—I glanced over at him, my heart contracting—if I could find a way to assist him in uncovering the person behind his aunt's tragic death, I wouldn't wait one more minute to do so. His needs at this point were far greater than mine.

I opened my mouth, but Graham was ahead of me. "Phoebe, I"—he slowed the horses to a walk—"I have something . . . well . . ."

All I could guess was that Graham was thinking along the same lines as me, pondering the murder and my safety . . . so why was he looking at me like that?

After passing the reins to one hand, he slid his other into his jacket pocket. "It's taken me a few days, but I finally found something I've been on the hunt for."

"Oh?"

He held out a small item wrapped in a handkerchief and passed it into my hands. I first thought it was another Egyptian antiquity, but somehow I knew that wasn't what he'd brought with him for our drive.

His gaze was piercing, so full of life. "Well, open it."

Carefully I parted the folds of fine linen until a small white shell lay exposed in my palm. I had a racing moment of breathlessness as I flipped the treasure over. There on the underside was the horseshoe-shaped impression from the animal that had lived in the shell.

Graham had to keep his eyes on the road, but I caught the quick turn of his head more than once from the corner of my eye. "It's for your grotto." He leaned in close and flipped the shell back over. "I couldn't believe my luck when I stumbled upon this pure white one." He hesitated a moment. "It is the kind of limpet you were searching for?"

My throat felt thick, and my voice was slow to come. "The very one." My heart swelled as I touched his arm. "I cannot believe you went looking for this . . . for me."

He smiled down at my hand on his arm. "I was determined to find the shell after you described it—like a small treasure hunt of my own." He stared a moment, then a furrow crossed his brow. "Don't you like it?"

"Oh, Graham." I fought tears and the waver threatening my voice. "It's the most beautiful shell I've ever seen."

He smiled again. "I'm glad you . . ." He blinked a few times, then pulled the horses to a standstill. "I can't believe it." He pushed to his feet and extended his arms before turning about. "It's snowing!"

I jerked my attention down to my lap, where little white flakes had already gathered in the folds of my gown. "It is."

I stood too and we laughed, clumps of snow settling on the brim of his hat. He caught my gaze and grasped his beaver, flipping the flakes into the air. Then his arm dropped to his side, so dangerously close to my waist. One little tug and I gladly would have fallen into his arms. But we just stood there staring at one another, the snow filling the air so thick around us that it felt like we were the only two people in the world.

The horses eased forward and I sat hard, gripping the edge of the seat. The spell was broken and Graham dusted the snow from his curricle seat. "The village is just ahead. Perhaps it's best for us to wait out the storm over coffee at the coach house. I don't think this little spring flurry shall last all that long."

He sat and flipped his coattails behind him to settle in, my heart doing a flip of its own. Goodness, I can't say he was sitting any closer, really, but he felt nearer, his arm comfortably pressed to mine. I closed my eyes for a brief moment as the snowflakes tickled my cheeks and the wind swirled around my ankles. Carefully, naturally, Graham slid his hand through the crook of my arm, feigning concern for the steady clip of the horses. I relaxed against the seatback. Everything in the world felt perfectly in place. If only we could stay there forever.

Graham arranged for a private parlor and, much to my chagrin, the innkeeper's wife for chaperone, as we settled in for our nuncheon and coffee at the posting inn. Clearly aware of my irritation at the addition, he gave me a long look before directing me to a small table by the window.

"I'd prefer to keep your reputation intact if at all possible."

I cast a quick glance at Mrs. Brisbane across the room. She already had her nose in a book and a cup of tea in her hand. "I'm sure you would."

Graham laughed as he took a seat across from me. "We won't be here long."

A large fire snapped at our backs as the steady scent of cooked meat and ale surrounded us. White cloths lay across the table, which was illuminated by a rather large candelabrum. I looked over the teal wallpaper and heavy drapes.

"I've never been in here. It's rather nice."

Graham fiddled with his napkin. "I agree."

I turned to the window as a servant brought two steaming cups of coffee. "Rather late in the year for snow."

"It probably won't last all that long."

"But beautiful all the same."

Graham took a sniff of his coffee before enjoying a long drink.

I warmed my hands on my own cup. "Do you enjoy coffee often?"

He smiled. "In London, yes. I . . ." His cheeks flushed pink. "I lecture at the Grecian Coffee House on occasion."

I angled my chin. "You lecture? Now why does that not surprise me?" I took a sip, watching him over the rim of my cup. "On antiquities, I presume."

"I have traveled quite a bit with my business affairs and confess I find the conversation stimulating at that particular coffee house. You see, people from different walks of life frequent it, and . . ." He seemed hesitant to go on.

"And?"

"Well, at any rate they seem to understand my passion for preserving the treasures of the world." He shrugged. "This desire for preservation only grows the more I deal in antiquities."

"I can understand how that would be."

"The looting that has taken place in Egypt . . . it's concerning." His fingers curled into a fist on the table. "But at the same time I cannot help but question my own role in all of it. When I remove antiquities from their homeland and sell them to whoever will pay, am I any different from a common thief?" His hand slipped to his lap. "I don't want to do so any longer. I-I won't. I hope at a bare minimum to at least work with the British Museum."

"So you lecture about preservation?"

He nodded, then grinned to himself. "The Grecian is actually where I met Montague. He stumbled upon one of my more passionate arguments. He probably kept me from a rather awkward duel. You see, the disagreement was with his father."

I sat up straight. "His father!"

"Allow me simply to say, the master of Whitefall does not share my opinions."

I tapped my cup. "I assume he has a private collection."

"A rather large one I'm afraid." Graham cleared his throat. "He didn't take kindly to being called a thief."

"And now you and Mr. Montague are friends . . . and business partners."

Graham smiled. "He can be quite persuasive."

"You trust him?"

"I do. Only this morning he came to me in regard to a missing item."

"Oh?"

"He was working with Mr. Haskett's men to transport the sarcophagus and the other antiquities to Haskett's estate when he noticed a scarab was missing. Actually it was the very scarab I showed you a while back. The one with the hieroglyphics on the underside."

My stomach turned. "The blue one?"

"Yes." He watched me a moment, his eyebrows tugging inward. "What is it? Do you know something?"

I stared down at the table. "Maybe. I crossed paths with Mrs. Fagean yesterday in the rose garden, and I happened to catch sight of something blue within her hand. She was concealing whatever it was and stormed off. You don't think . . ."

"That she stole my scarab?" His hand flew to his mouth. "It is entirely possible. Mr. Fagean no doubt has keys to every building on the estate. She could have easily got in there and . . ." His eyes widened. "If she would take the scarab, would she not do the same with a painting or a vase?"

"You mean you think she's responsible for the fake items in the house?"

"Why not?"

My gaze danced around the corners of the room, my mind wild with the added depths of her involvement. "She's so desperate for money right now. Take her drizzling habit for example."

Graham leaned forward. "Then our question is: What would Mrs. Fagean need to buy, and why the devil is it so expensive? That scarab will fetch a pretty price."

"I saw her speaking with Mr. Haskett the night of the Equinox Festival. Perhaps the sarcophagus was not all the man desired to add to his collection, but he hadn't the money to buy more. And we saw him walking back and forth between his estate and Avonthorpe—twice."

Graham sat back in his chair. "Indeed. And if Mr. Fagean is seeking the Drake treasure . . ." He pushed back from the table. "I don't believe we should tarry here for long. Time is not our friend."

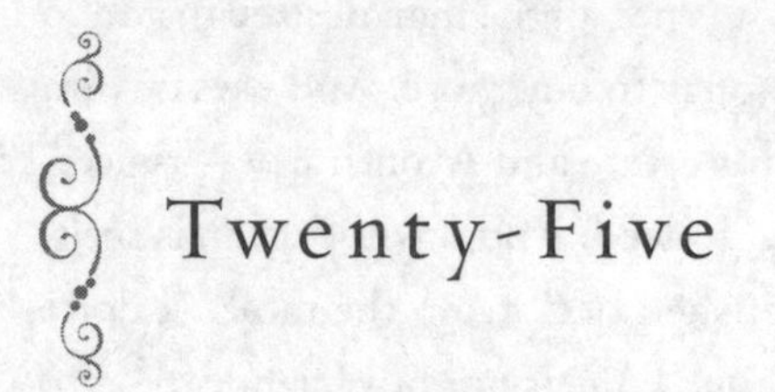

Twenty-Five

THE CURRICLE RIDE HOME PROVED CHILLY BUT NOT uncomfortable, the delicate dusting of snow lying like a white blanket across an otherwise green landscape. The fickle sun peeked in and out of a cloudy sky, commanding the tiny water crystals on the ground to sparkle.

Graham, however, had little time for the beauty. The minute we were out of earshot of the village, our conversation turned straight to the treasure hunt. He slapped the ribbons, urging the horses to a steady clip, his voice tight. "I cannot help but feel Mr. Fagean has a start on us."

"True, but honestly, how could he know any more than we do?"

Graham hunched forward, his jaw set. "I've been doing a bit of thinking, Phoebe."

I hesitated to probe further, the grim lines of his face a rather telling indication of a difficult conversation. "Yes?"

"There is no possible way Mr. Fagean could have unraveled the clue about the fifteen stairs. Solving that involved a great deal of luck."

My wayward focus followed the advancing trees as my mind circled Graham's suggestion. He'd come to the crux of it, of course. The murder, thievery, smuggling—more was afoot at Avonthorpe Hall than we wanted to admit. "You mean to suggest that one of the Fageans has been watching us?"

A hard look. "That . . . or someone else has betrayed you."

"Betrayed me?" My voice must have come out sharper than intended as Graham slowed the horses a bit.

He ran his hand down his face. "Perhaps it's best if you remind me who knows the details of our hunt."

"Well, Arnold does, of course." I swallowed hard. "He's been a part of this since the beginning, but he knows nothing regarding the latest clue at the sluice gate. I've not had time to tell him."

I closed my eyes a moment, shaken by the sudden image of Daniel that sprang into my mind. "The idea of a hidden treasure has always fascinated Daniel. He's been pondering its existence since the second he arrived . . . but I see no evidence he's privy to what we've learned so far."

"He's been with Mrs. Fagean. We cannot dismiss that fact."

"As I told you earlier, their interactions resulted from nothing but a schoolboy infatuation."

Graham stared down at his hands. "I agree with your assessment that Daniel lacks the maturity to be so devious, but let us not forget Mrs. Fagean may have used him and sworn him to secrecy. I'm not willing to put anything past her."

The curricle took a turn as the road swung wide of the church's property and the hill jutted out toward the sea. I adjusted my pelisse around my legs, fighting a growing chill. "As you know, Miss Chant is also aware of the ins and outs concerning the clues, but I feel confident she would not betray me. I've known her some time and it's not within her character to do something so risky and bold."

His voice remained poised, but I could feel the added tension lacing his breath. "What about an error in judgment—could she perhaps have mentioned something to someone early on that inadvertently tipped them off about the hunt?"

My thoughts took a violent turn and I sat up straight. "Oh dear."

Graham's eyes widened but he kept his focus on the road. "What is it?"

"Nothing . . ."

That induced a quick sideways glance, and it was certainly justified.

I struggled to explain, as I could hardly bring myself to believe anything ill of Miss Chant.

Graham's tone was far from idle. "Nothing indeed. I'll not be fobbed off, not this time. We're coming to a pass in all this. No more secrets."

My stomach hardened. "I just can't believe she would do such a thing."

Graham had to work to keep his tone level. "You think she might have told Vincent Tulk?"

I floundered a gasp. "No . . . she couldn't have."

"I've had the same suspicion for some time, especially if . . ." A moment of tight silence, then he stretched his neck. "Is everything settled between them then? A marriage offer?"

I nodded quickly, shaken a bit by Graham's understanding. "They want to journey to America to start their lives as soon as they can. You see, after the Enclosure Acts, Mr. Tulk was no longer able to provide for his aging parents or his dependent siblings. Their holdings on the farm here were too small to follow the new method of crop rotation. He sent his parents to America and took the position with Mr. Haskett only until he could secure funds to join them there."

Graham took a measured breath. "Considering the deep connection between them, I believe it is fair to assume Mr. Tulk knows everything."

I checked, my stomach turning. "But Miss Chant promised me faithfully. I told her I'd help her in her plight . . ."

A hard smile settled onto his face. "It is difficult to manage divided loyalties, particularly when it concerns a person you've pledged your life to." His tone softened. "Love is a powerful force. We both realize Vincent Tulk probably knows it all."

I stared off into the distance, a deeper chill winding its way to my core. How could I have ignored the possibility till now? Of course, Miss Chant and Vincent would want the treasure for themselves. The desperation in my voice startled even me. "Then you think she's made the conscious decision to work with the Fageans?"

He slammed his hand onto his leg. "I don't know what to think. Every last person residing in my house has to be considered."

I sat motionless, the lull of the curricle jostling my bonnet ribbons, as the specter of my mistaken trust poisoned the air around me. Graham jerked the horses to a standstill.

A large field stretched out to the right of the lonely road, sugared white with fresh snow, the howling wind our only companion. Graham lifted his eyebrows ever so slightly, the complexities of compassion clear on his face. "I understand quite well what it feels like to be deceived. Betrayal is personal; it cuts deep. Such a sudden and remarkable loss of trust can undermine every thought, every action." He took my hands in his. "Let us be perfectly certain about Miss Chant before we condemn her."

My chest tightened, making it even more difficult to take in the frigid air.

Condemn. I swallowed hard. The word felt like a knife at my throat. What would he say when he learned *my* part in all this? I slid away from him, inching to the side of the curricle. I barely even felt the hard ground as I leaped from the far side and stumbled into the undisturbed snow.

"What are you doing?" The astonishment in Graham's voice ceased my reckless retreat, but I didn't turn and face him, not yet at least. I had too much emotion to control.

A scramble sounded at my back as he no doubt rushed to follow me. "Phoebe, darling, what are you about now?" His tone was generous but strained as his footsteps slowed.

I inhaled a sharp little breath, my skin alive with confusion as I heard him stumble to a halt. Every last nerve in my body sensed how near he was—the subtle scent of his cologne on the breeze, the sight of our shadows merged into one slender line on the white ground, the unconscious feel of his presence behind me.

Yet all I could do was stand there and absorb the endearment he'd called me—something I'd dreamed of hearing for some time.

Panic swelled in my chest. My ears throbbed. I couldn't turn around, not without disclosing the entirety of my past and my part in withholding vital information. My jaw clenched. "I have something to tell you . . . but oh, Graham, I'm at a loss as to how to begin or what will happen when I do."

His hands were at my shoulders, his touch terribly gentle. "Then allow me to go first. I too have something I wish to share."

His announcement caught me wholly off guard, and I spun to face him, my eyes wet with tears.

His fingers twitched as he drew me closer, a pent-up sort of angst fixing his gaze like nothing else could. "I've been contemplating how to reveal something to you this entire day." He closed the remaining space between us. "It's why I asked you to come with me in the first place." He peered into my eyes like he was searching for something, then he shook his head. "I hope the devil you'll forgive me."

My heart had turned feral long before, but now my muscles coiled tight in anticipation. What could he be referring to?

He cast me a wry look, still watching me without moving, as a subtle shift lifted the air between us. He gave his head a little shake. "Oh, Phoebe, I knew how this was going to go from the start—the day you pranced into the stables and saw my antiquities for the first time. I remember that moment in such vivid detail." He smiled to himself. "You got the prettiest little look of bewilderment on your face, the same spark of unbridled curiosity I've seen over and over throughout our time together." His fingers contracted. "I was lost then, but not nearly as much as I am now."

My heart thundered in my chest, every last muscle in my body frozen.

He lifted his hand slowly, running his fingers down the side of my face, stopping only to feather a loose curl. "I've never met anyone in my life who would jump out of the side of my curricle without a word or plunge straight into the woods without a care. You have me jumping into the lake, leaping rocks along the shoreline, hunting a treasure. I used to loathe recklessness in all its forms." He gave a small laugh. "And do you know what? I still do, but not in the way I thought I would. Sometimes you scare me to death. I only ever want to keep you protected."

I couldn't help but hold my breath as every last hair at the nape of my neck stood to heart-pounding attention. Heavens, the way he looked at me, the way his words made me feel. Graham Burke—the man I'd come to love with all my heart—cared for me.

Tentatively I shifted into the warmth of his chest. The ache to be near him was too great. I had to satisfy the urge to touch him, to know him. My boot, however, engaged a loose leaf on the ground, which was covered quite neatly in slippery snow. All at once, I lost my footing as my leg slammed forward.

In the split second of falling I grappled for Graham, but then the world shifted too quickly. Graham responded as best as he could, his hands shooting out to steady me, but it was no use. The two of us lost balance, sliding forward. Graham moved quickly to circle my back with his arm a split second before we hit the ground hard and lay wrapped together in stunned silence.

Merely a second passed before I felt his anxious hand in my hair, searching for injuries.

"Are you hurt?"

I gently shook my head.

"You did warn me you were not all that steady on your feet." His hand drifted carefully to my arm as a daring look filled his eyes—a peculiar mix of concern and longing, care and passion, which only deepened the longer he stared down at me. My back smarted against the cold, the snow a soft but frigid mattress. Yet I couldn't move an inch, not with Graham regarding me in such a contemplative way.

He misread the resulting intensity no doubt at play on my face. He expressed a sigh. "Let me help you up. You must be freezing—"

I stilled his movement. "Not really."

A curious smile emerged as he stilled so close above me. A nearly imperceptible cock of an eyebrow and he angled back down onto his forearm, meeting my gaze with a startling one of his own. Then he chuckled, flushing a bit more boldly, his eyes so brilliantly blue. "Have you a plan for me, Miss Radcliff?"

I smiled up at him. "Not exactly." Strange that I'd never noticed the flecks of copper in his dark hair or the way those precious locks tended to curl at the ends when wet. "Just a sudden feeling . . . an impulse I find I cannot ignore."

"An impulse, huh?" His eyes glinted with anticipation. "Believe me, I am not as straitlaced as you seem to think. Nor could I possibly pull away from you now."

He moved to support my head with his hand, prompting a shiver that raced through my body, igniting every nerve across my skin.

Graham Burke was the last man on earth I thought I would have been attracted to when he marched into Avonthorpe like a military general, but every bit of me surged forward to meet his kiss.

A gusty rustling of leaves sounded, followed by a swirling splash of cool air, then it all disappeared, every last inch of the world beyond Graham's tender lips pressing closer with each second and the uncontrolled energy drawing us deeper together.

I'd been kissed before by a man well versed in passionate love, but that experience had left me wanting, confused—captured by a curious mix of anticipation and aversion, the type of experience reserved for young ladies who had no idea what real love was.

Graham's fingers ran along the small of my back, and I smiled against his lips. Strange that he had in all likelihood kissed very few women, maybe none at all, but he knew just what was needed to make me feel safe, desired, and cherished.

I suppose this was what it was like to be kissed by a gentleman, my equal in every way.

One of the horses huffed, and ever so gently Graham pulled away. He looked mystified, plunging his hand through his hair. Then he edged a glance at me. "You have no idea how long I've been waiting to do that."

I grinned up at him. "Well, I'm glad you got over whatever reservations were holding you back." Then my smile fell. He still knew nothing of my involvement with Jean.

Graham helped me to my feet. "I was trying to tell you something earlier. I must do so at once. You see, I sent a letter to your father and received a response today." His voice came out as if he were addressing a group of dragoons.

I saw a letter clutched in his hand and my eyes widened. "What do you mean you wrote to my father?"

"I asked him to come to Avonthorpe as soon as possible."

"You did what?" My mind couldn't race fast enough to keep up. "Why?"

"Propriety demands it, Phoebe. We shouldn't even be here in this field until I've had a chance to speak with him."

I pressed my hands to my forehead. "But you don't understand. My father and I . . . we are not on the best of terms. I left under strained circumstances."

Graham fell quiet a moment. "There's something you're hiding from me. You have been for some time. If it involves your father, I'm sorry for it. I had no way of knowing."

"Oh, Graham. It's so terribly complicated."

Graham paced in front of me before turning hard on his heels.

"Do you consider him a father? Does he hold that place in your life?"

My gaze fell to the snow at my feet. "Of course. I love him dearly."

"Then I shall go to him just the same."

Marriage—my breath stilled—he was speaking of marriage. Of course he was. Somehow I'd managed to stumble into the arms of the best man in Britain. I should have been giddy, but the painful lump that had taken up residence in my stomach only swelled.

"Graham, if it were only my questionable heritage that you must know and understand . . . but what I have to tell you is far, far worse."

Twenty-Six

I WATCHED THE EXCITEMENT DRAIN FROM GRAHAM'S eyes as he became unnaturally still. "Your heritage?"

I shifted away from him. "There's so much you don't know."

"I want to." His voice was thready yet hopeful.

I swallowed hard. "You know that Jean Cloutier was apprehended near my home, Middlecrest Abbey, by my father."

He narrowed his eyes. "Yes . . ."

"What you are not aware of is how well *I* knew Jean Cloutier. He spent several weeks in our conservatory under guard."

"Several weeks." He whispered the words more to himself than anyone else.

"Though I was warned away from him, I couldn't help but satisfy my curiosity about who the man was, why my father was questioning him. I-I didn't understand everything involved. My sister's fiancé had just been murdered and the house was in an uproar."

Graham took my arm and led me to a grove of trees where a large, round stump could be utilized as a small bench. "Sit down with me."

I did as instructed, everything about me numb. "Jean complimented my artistry. He was so very flattering. It wasn't long before I was visiting him in earnest. One of my father's footmen was a personal friend and was willing to turn a blind eye to our budding relationship. It was difficult at first, which only made my visits to him more attractive. I was young and naïve and I'd never experienced love before."

A muscle twitched in Graham's jaw. "You had feelings for this Frenchman?"

"Confusing ones, yes. My father had brought home a new wife. My sister was stricken by grief. I had no one to talk to, no one to advise me. I was lonely and a fool. Jean Cloutier ultimately used me to escape. He altered a painting I'd given him to notify his accomplice in the house. He left me confused and devastated."

I pulled my legs close to my chest. "I was so ashamed I made plans to leave Middlecrest as soon as possible. No one knew about our romantic involvement, only my role in his escape. Later, I uncovered the truth of my parentage from my brother, Ewan, the same week I received a letter from Miss Drake offering me a position to train here. It all just seemed to mix together in my mind. I never really told my father why I left."

Graham's arm snaked around my back and he tugged me against him. "It seems we've both fallen prey to people who exploited our trust. Yours was a mistake, same as mine, nothing more. Unfortunate that he's been so close to the estate. It must have brought up quite a bit of feelings from the past."

He grasped my unsettled fingers with his free hand. "It's been two years, Phoebe. It's time to let this difficult part of your past go, to finally forgive yourself. Broken relationships can eat you alive. I know because I have experienced one myself." He leaned forward, his tone soft, nothing like the anger I'd expected. "You've such a beautiful genial quality. It's just one of the many things about you that I love. Yet at the same time I've always detected some sort of dissonance inside of you, one I feel I finally understand. Pretending to be happy is not the same as actually being so."

My throat felt thick.

He went on. "I would never presume to direct you in regard to the relationship with your sister or your father. I'm not privy to the intricacies of your past, but I can tell you what I see. You've a thirst for life, a kind heart, and an adventurous soul. Don't allow the past to steal the joy aching to join the present, our present. It took me years to find peace through prayer and even longer to find rest from my misplaced trust during the war. People lost their lives in battles that could have been prevented. But it wasn't my fault, not really. We cannot stop looking for the good in people."

The pain growing in the back of my throat intensified as I visualized what I must say next. "Graham." I swallowed hard. "I saw Jean Cloutier here at Avonthorpe twice. I believed him when he told me he only meant to travel back to France, but he's still here."

I felt the life drain from Graham's arm as it loosened and released me. A silent beat of confusion swarmed his face before he stumbled to his feet and crept away. He hesitated a moment before pacing to a nearby tree and propping his arm against the bark. He gave a little head shake, then plunged his hand into his hair. "You chose to keep this from me."

"I did, and I'm sorry for it. I didn't know you at first, and then—"

"Then what? You wanted to spare me . . . embarrassment of some kind? For harboring feelings for a woman whose heart was elsewhere?"

"No, I—"

"I gave you so many opportunities to tell me the truth. We discussed him on more than one occasion." Graham's eyes set. "Didn't you trust me at all . . . even a little bit?" His anger was ebbing some and it only brought tears to my eyes.

"You're the one man I trust with my life." I rose and stepped forward. "I made a terrible choice just a few short weeks ago, and you have every right to loathe me."

He steadied himself against the tree once again. "I don't loathe you. I love you, which makes this a hundred times worse."

I drew up behind him and laid my head against his back. "I love you too."

I could feel his heart pounding, the swell of each tattered breath, but he didn't turn. "I need some time and space to sort this out. Perhaps it's best if we return to the house now. The horses have been standing too long already."

"I . . . understand."

We made our way back to the curricle like two mourners in a funeral procession. It must have taken a great deal of restraint for Graham to offer his hand to help me onto the seat. Especially when he caught sight of my pitiful gaze.

He gripped the edge of the carriage hard. "I suggest you get to work finishing the trim in the ballroom. Your father may wish to take you home with him when he arrives."

I did not see Graham again that evening, only Mr. Montague as he brought me my new, small silver pistol after supper. Offhandedly he mumbled something about Graham needing to spend the evening at the church cataloging his antiquities, but I knew otherwise. He wanted to be alone. Away from me.

The following morning I did just as he'd asked. I set to work on the trim.

Daniel joined me around nine o'clock and by noon we'd made considerable progress. He wiped the sweat from his forehead with his shirtsleeve. "Is this all we've got left?"

I eyed the small upper section against the corner of the balcony. "I daresay if we make a day of it, we'll be done before sunset."

"Indeed." He stepped back to appraise our morning's work. "The original artist had a brilliant design. Everything contrasts so nicely with the gilded accents and the detail . . . I only noticed the numbers this morning."

A shiver ran along my skin. "What numbers? What do you mean?"

He pointed to a swirling design. "See here right next to the Bible verse reference—it's the number fifteen. You just need to back up to the centermost spot in the room to perceive it. Brilliant, I say."

"Fifteen!" I flew down the ladder to join Daniel where he stood. "Show me."

He followed the churning details with his first finger in the air until he'd traced the calligraphic number for me. "I'm not certain, but I know a great deal about paint textures, and I suspect these lighter sections had a subtlety to the hue that has faded over the past seventy years. Our restoration has brought it all back to life."

I whirled to my left—Matthew 6:21—as a distant thought came to mind. Like many of the rooms in the house, a reference had been painted beautifully across the gallery's trim. "Do you know this verse?"

He gave me a small smile. "Of course I do. It's the one about the treasure, you goose. You know, where your treasure is, there your heart is, or something like that. I noticed that a few days after I arrived. It's one of the main reasons the villagers believe the treasure is real."

"Hmm, interesting." My heart ticked faster in my chest as my gaze toured a swirling line that led to the number one in a unique script, then on to the first section of trim we'd worked on.

Daniel shrugged, ignorant of my wild thoughts. "But I've searched all around the gallery—nothing. Wild-goose chase, I suspect."

I tried to keep my voice even. "Now what were you saying about the numbers you noticed on the trim? Have you seen any others around the room?"

"Actually, yes." His smile brightened as he pivoted me to the right. "See up above this section, on the crest of the crown molding there—it's the Roman numeral five. Each of the six sections has a similar marking. Curious, isn't it?"

My focus danced from one marked section to the next—all six of them. It had to be part of the clue; it was right in line with the Bible reference. Josiah Drake had designed this room with a purpose. But why the number fifteen? We'd already solved that one.

Daniel was watching me with eagle eyes. "Do you think the numbers mean something?"

"I haven't the faintest idea." And I didn't, not really. Careful not to cause alarm, I cast him a cool glance. "All I know is that I would love for the two of us to finish everything this afternoon. My father is due to arrive before dinner."

Daniel checked. "Lord Torrington is coming here—tonight?" A grim line settled across his forehead. "Why?"

"Lt. Burke wrote to him. I-I might be leaving soon."

Daniel fingered his watch fob, a sudden uneasiness to his movements. "I had no idea."

My voice felt weak. "It was an impulsive decision, and I'd like to have this project complete before I go."

Daniel rubbed his neck while inching closer to the door. "I do hate to leave you like this, but I have a prior engagement in town just now. I promise, however, I shall be back straightaway to assist this afternoon. I think we have a great chance of finishing it all."

The curious nature of this abrupt "engagement" of his was not lost on me; yet at the same time I needed a moment alone to decipher the clue. I bit back any questions and gave him a smile. "Don't be too late."

"I won't." And he bolted for the door.

Almost an hour passed before Graham shuffled into the ballroom, a steady look on his face. Though we'd parted under uncomfortable circumstances the previous day, I was wild to tell him what I'd learned.

"My valet said you needed me." His voice was a touch cool.

I motioned behind him. "Close the doors, please," I said.

"It's the clue, Graham." I was a bit breathless it seemed. "Daniel and I accidentally stumbled upon part of it."

His eyes widened as the strain between us ebbed away. "In here?"

"It's been here all this time. In fact, I've been unwittingly recreating it."

His gaze shot to the trim and he circled his finger in the air. "The restoration!"

"It seems your aunt had a very good reason for wanting it done. She had to have been further along in the treasure hunt than we thought. She too must have discovered the final clue was in the trim work, but her eyesight was poor. You can only make it out from the center of the room. She must have set out to have it restored in order to read it, to figure out what was hidden within the original artist's brilliant strokes."

Graham paced over to the center of the dance floor. "Tell me what you know so far."

"See the six sections around the room? Each one is marked with a Roman numeral on the molding." I pointed at each crest. "One, two, three . . . six. Just like in the clue. Well, beneath each section is another number, a hidden one, an ordinal, written in calligraphy and concealed in the intricate work of the trim. I might never have even noticed them without Daniel's keen eye."

"Daniel, hmm?"

"He knows nothing, although he raced out of here to town just after showing them to me."

"I don't like the sound of that."

"Neither do I, but we haven't time to waste." I held out a slip of paper. "This is what I've found so far in the trim—the numbers fifty-one, six, and two on the first three sections on this wall, and the numbers one and fifteen on the opposing one. The last section, you see, is yet to be finished. On closer inspection my guess is the number one again, but I cannot be certain until I restore the entire section and step back. It's like a horrid puzzle, and we're so close."

"How long till completion?"

"With Daniel's help, I could be finished this afternoon. Without him, probably longer."

Graham ran his glove down his face. "Your father is due to arrive—"

"I know. It shall be a tricky business, but I'm up for the challenge." I dipped my chin. "Are you?"

He couldn't help but smile, a genuine one that crinkled his eyes. "Torrington will have to stay one night at least."

"Then it shall be a long night indeed. I haven't the least idea what these numbers could possibly stand for . . ."

He nodded and cast a quick glance behind him. "How would you feel about a locked door this afternoon? I don't want anyone disturbing you and Daniel, no wandering eyes on the trim. Promise me you will keep this a secret; only you and I can know what you've found. We're too close to the end."

"All right."

He turned to leave.

"And, Graham, perhaps you could bring me a bite to eat."

He shot me a wink. "I'll be right back."

Twenty-Seven

THE AFTERNOON FLEW BY IN A FLURRY OF WORK. DANIEL returned to the ballroom as he said he would, but he was on edge.

"We're out of paint." He slammed his hand onto the scaffolding and a drop splattered onto the floor covering.

"Careful." I cast a quick glance at the lower corner where he'd been working, disappointed to see a small section left. "I'll head to the cellar. I need some more water at any rate." I descended the ladder and moved to the center of the room, hoping I could make out the last number, but it wasn't complete. "We're so near the end."

"We'd be done if I hadn't been so sloppy and had to redo that small part."

"Nonsense, we're making good progress." Thankfully my section was all that really mattered. I had to be sure about that last number, and the tedious nature of my painting had given me a much-needed chance to think. Could the numbers represent letters in the alphabet? Or distances of some type? Steps, feet? I'd pondered it all, and I was running out of time. What good would the final number do me if I didn't know what any of them stood for? I only hoped Graham was making more progress than I was.

I was still deep in thought when I took the back hall that led to the kitchens and nearly ran straight into Mrs. Fagean.

Her startled gasp was one for the stage at Covent Gardens.

"Pardon me."

"Really, Phoebe, you must be far more careful where you are

going. You nearly scared me to death." Her hands were wild in the air, the green emerald on her finger glistening in the heavy light from the window.

It was then I noticed she had her reticule in her free hand and her pelisse buttoned to her chin. "Where are you off to?"

"It's Mr. Fagean. 'Pon my word, he exists just to vex me." She gave her head a little shake. "Wouldn't you know, after he declared he was to delay his next shipment to France, he up and tells me we're to leave tonight."

"Tonight?"

"Now I must rush about to ensure we have everything we need. It is really the outside of enough. He treats me as if I am some sort of hired hand to order about. He plans to load and leave straightaway."

"But you were originally hoping he would do just that."

Again, that insidious half smile. "Well, yes, but he could have told me before now. I daresay he enjoys ruffling my feathers. The wretch. Granted, I always seem to come about."

A faraway voice sounded from the direction of the front entrance hall, and it was all I could do to steady myself on the edge of the wainscoting. My heart sank just as it had two years prior—when I'd told my father Jean Cloutier had used me to escape. I closed my eyes and took in a deep breath. How long ago that all seemed, and yet so recent. Would my father look different after two years away? What would I even say to him? How would I start?

Mrs. Fagean motioned behind me with her chin, her eyes narrow. "It seems we have a visitor." She blinked a few times. "And something tells me you know just who it is."

I nodded gravely. "It's my father, Lord Torrington."

She gave a neat little gasp. "Well, that makes a great deal of sense." She patted my cheek. "I'd better pop off, dear. I've quite a bit to do before Mr. Fagean sets sail. Give my best to your father."

I watched her leave with the growing trepidation we were talking at cross-purposes. *Makes a great deal of sense*, indeed. What on earth was she referring to?

Arnold's voice invaded my thoughts and I rushed toward the front of the house. The butler wore a look of surprise on his elderly face. "I'm terribly sorry, your lordship. I wasn't informed of your arrival. It will be a few moments before we can ready a room."

I traversed the long rug beside the massive fireplace and came to a halt before the two men, my hands folded at my waist. I turned to Arnold first. "Lt. Burke sent his groom with a letter only yesterday. He must not have had a chance to update you." Then a fleeting look at my father. "Good afternoon, Papa."

The past two years, the first two with his new wife, Elizabeth, must have done my father a great deal of good, as he looked years younger than when I'd left. The severity to his eyes had eased, the tight set to his jaw relaxed. He gave me one of those alarming grins. "You look well, Phoebe."

I rocked up onto my toes without thinking, my hands behind my back like I used to do as a small child. "Thank you, as do you."

We both waited for Arnold to fully depart before stepping nearer, the comradery we'd shared for years lost somewhere below the surface. He reached out as if to embrace me, then thought better of it, motioning to the drawing room instead. "Will you join me?"

I could only imagine what Graham had put in his letter, as my father seemed unusually short of words. My heart sank. Whatever it was, the conversation would not be pleasant.

I strolled behind him to the drawing room door. At any rate, if my father took me home, so be it. I'd uncovered the last clue. Graham could finish the hunt on his own.

I took a hesitant seat on the sofa across the rug from the slat-backed chair where my father sat. He'd always possessed a sort of probing look with those unnaturally pale eyes, and he turned them on me without reservation. "Avonthorpe Hall is lovelier than I imagined. Granted, Miss Drake was an exceptional artist. I should have expected it."

So we were to have pleasantries at first. I smoothed out my skirt. "Miss Drake was reclusive, yes, but not without standards."

A long pause, then he leaned forward and rested his elbows on his knees, a commanding intelligence to his movements. "I should have come for a visit long before now, but—"

"You've been busy. I know. How are Elizabeth and the baby?"

He gave me a droll smile. "Harry is maneuvering about the house making a perfect nuisance of himself."

"So he's walking already?"

"Running more like."

I picked at the edge of my glove before casting a careful glance up. "And Juliana?"

"Existing." He ran his hand down his face. "She misses you."

I bit my lip. "Then there's been little improvement?"

It was his turn to adjust the fingers of his glove. "Giles's death will always be a part of her. Her struggle is in finding a way to move on." His hands stilled. "As you have done."

I found myself unable to remain still and paced to the window, a lump forming in my throat. *Me?* Move on? Oh, I'd left home all right, but was I any less captured by the murky waters of the past than Juliana was?

The sound of my father's footsteps kept my attention glued to the window, his soft voice like a ghost from my past. "What is it, Phoebe? I'd convinced myself all this time that I was imagining a certain coldness in your letters, but now that I am here in your presence, I know for sure. Elizabeth urged me to give you space, but now . . . Where did this wall spring up between us?" I could hear the tension in his voice, the desperation. "Has it to do with your parentage, because I never—"

"No." I edged my arm against the window trim. "Please, it's not that at all." My shoulders relaxed. "You're the only father I've ever known." I swallowed hard as tears filled my eyes. "All I ever wanted was for you to be proud of me. It's—"

"Stop right there." He turned me to face him. "I've always been proud of you . . . always." A deep line crossed his forehead. "This strange distance between us. You have me concerned. Has something happened to you at Avonthorpe? Lt. Burke?"

My eyes flashed. "No! Not at all. I . . . well, I do have something to tell you . . ."

He stood in silent anticipation as waves of fear and doubt raced through my chest. I'd guarded my secret for two years. How strange it felt to give it up now. But Graham was right. I could not move forward without honesty.

My hand shook as I touched my head. "There's more to what happened after Giles's murder than you are aware of at present."

His lips parted. "What do you mean?" He looked lost. "That was so long ago. We've had no further issues."

"No, but I lied to you all then, and I don't want to go on doing so any longer." I held up my hands. "You must know it all."

His gaze darted about the room as if searching for answers.

I stilled his movement with a hard look. "Oh, Papa, Jean Cloutier and I were involved romantically."

Slowly my father enacted a knowing nod. He grimaced but did not express the shock I'd been expecting. Had he heard me correctly? I'd said *romantically*!

I squirmed. "You don't seem surprised."

He gave my hand a light squeeze. "Honestly, Phoebe, Elizabeth and I thought that quite likely at the time. We assumed you had feelings for him. How else would he have been able to use you so effectively?"

I grasped the edge of the sideboard. "You mean you already suspected that he and I . . . ?"

"We didn't know for certain, but . . ." A small, awkward laugh. "You are my daughter after all. I've always thought the two of us had quite a bit in common. You well know I made an equally foolish decision in my youth."

I could barely breathe, let alone form a response. I'd spent the past two years running away from what I thought was an irredeemable mistake and my father's ultimate censure. Was it possible he knew all along? And he understood it? Still loved me despite all I'd done?

He seemed to follow the turmoil in my mind and took my hand in his. Gently, he led me back to the sofa before taking a seat at my side. "Is this what's been eating at you?"

I nodded, my throat still thick.

He shook his head, that steady gaze of his soft on my face. "My darling girl. All I've thought about since you left is how much I miss your vibrant presence at Middlecrest Abbey. Believe me, I didn't desire you to leave home, but I knew how much you wanted to make your mark on the world. Your talent deserved a chance. Never, ever question my utter pride or love for you. What happened in the past was forgiven a long time ago by me . . . and Juliana."

I glanced up, startled by his words and even more by the sudden release of tension throughout my body. Tears ran down my cheeks as I gasped my way through a few breaths. "You have no idea how much I needed to hear you say that."

"Nor I to know that you are well and happy."

"I am—for the first time in so long—I am."

He drew me into a tight embrace and upon release he held a wide grin. "Now if it wouldn't be too much trouble, I'd love to see this project you've been working on. From what Lt. Burke says—"

I sat up quickly, wiping the tears from my face. "What does Lt. Burke say?"

"He extolled your virtues with such passion in his letter that I had to get here as soon as possible"—he laughed—"to see what wool you've pulled over his eyes! Moreover, why I hadn't received a single letter from Miss Chant warning me about this infatuation."

I chuckled to myself. "Graham couldn't possibly—"

"—care for you?" My father dipped his chin. "I know what a man sounds like who's in love."

"Oh, Papa." I pressed my hands to my face. "I've made a mull of everything."

He stared at me a moment, then added a smile. "His letter proves otherwise."

"Oh, but I have." I closed my eyes a moment, then forced myself to face the truth once again. "I saw Jean Cloutier here at Avonthorpe and told no one."

My father jerked back an inch. "What are you talking about?"

"Jean Cloutier. He's escaped from prison. I assumed Graham told you in his letter."

"No." The whisper was more for himself than for me.

"Jean's been to see me. More than once."

"How is that even possible? He should have been transported or dealt with long since. And I placed Miss Chant here to watch over you. Why—"

"Excuse me?" I blinked.

"Miss Chant—you know full well that I hired her. The woman was to keep an eye on you. And she was trained by Whitehall and everything."

I narrowed my eyes. "Whitehall? You mean she's more than simply my companion? She's a spy?"

He rubbed his chin. "I'll put it to you this way: Do you think I would let you leave my side after all the enemies I've made due to my secret work with the British government? Moreover, would I have let you stay after Miss Drake's murder? I would have allowed none of it if she hadn't been in residence working a side job for me."

My gaze fell to my lap. "I always thought you were just too busy with your work and Elizabeth to worry over me."

"Not at all." A hard look settled into the grooves of his face. "Lt. Burke gave me his word he would protect you with his life. And Miss Chant assured me Avonthorpe was safe. I planned to come weeks ago, but with Harry ill, I was forced to make other arrangements. I thought I had—"

"Papa—how to tell you?—I've hardly seen Miss Chant these past weeks. We had an argument and, well, I've been rather preoccupied myself."

"Working on the trim?"

"Yes, that—among other things."

He stood and motioned me forward. "Let us go see this ballroom of yours. Lt. Burke told me your work is nearly complete."

I rose and led him to the door, speaking over my shoulder. "The full restoration has been the most difficult project I've ever worked on." I couldn't stop the pride filling my voice. "It's right this way." We crossed the main hall and went straight through the double doors of the ballroom.

He was speechless as first, padding out into the center of the large room, before he slowly spun in a circle. "This is marvelous. What a space. However did you manage all this?"

"I was instructed only to copy what had already been painted on the walls and trim." I pointed up at the domed ceiling. "See there? It's a strain, but you can still make out the original paint across the curve overhead. We didn't touch the ceiling."

His gaze toured the old plaster designs and the sweeping beams overhead before his brows drew inward. "I can see now the original paint. If I didn't know any better, I'd say those lines there remind me of a map my grandfather used to keep in his study."

I froze in place. Had I ever really looked at the ceiling from this very spot?

My father went on. "The map once belonged to a friend of his, the Duke of Gloucester. See there?" He pointed up. "It's like a globe stretched flat. And over there—those could almost be the numerals for longitude and latitude that circle the map. In one of your letters you said Mr. Josiah Drake was a sailor, correct? I think his travels may have inspired the decorations."

"His son sailed." I felt almost faint as I studied the ceiling with a fresh pair of eyes. How had I missed the entire concept? "But Josiah Drake was a cartographer."

My father grinned down at me. "Ah, then that would make perfect sense." He couldn't know the shock racing through my veins as he rubbed his chin. "Perhaps one day you could have the ceiling and the world map restored in its entirety. It's really quite lovely."

Lovely, but not necessary—not to find the treasure. Miss Drake knew it and now I did as well. Everything I needed to know was in the detail work of the trim, because I had studied the maps from the library. This particular one, a map of the world, I too had seen before. It was in essence a part of the clue, but not the essential part—that was hidden within the numbers decorating the four sides of the map. Josiah Drake had displayed the longitude and latitude of the treasure in plain sight, and no one knew it but me.

Twenty-Eight

I THOUGHT MY FATHER WOULD NEVER RETIRE TO HIS room to dress for dinner. Even worse, Graham was nowhere to be found, not until he sat across from me in the dining hall, doing all he could to avoid my gaze. I could do nothing but widen my eyes and press my lips together, attempting to get his attention between bites of turtle soup.

Clearly he was still mulling over my earlier revelations about Jean, and my father's presence seemed only to add to the rigidity. I was forced to bite my tongue until the men entered the drawing room following their port. Privacy would be a challenge, but I offered a song on the pianoforte and Graham reluctantly agreed to turn the pages.

The wretch.

His arm grazed my gold-spotted muslin sleeve as he reached for the first sheet of music and I whispered as loud as I dared. "I've something to tell you."

His arm went motionless. "Now?"

"My father helped me make a connection in regard to the clue. We need to talk alone as soon as can be arranged."

He edged carefully around the instrument, placing his back to the room. "After everyone retires for the evening. With your father here, every eye in the room is on us tonight." He ran his finger over the curve of the pianoforte. "They must suspect why I brought him here. They mean to play audience to a misguided little performance, I suspect."

I fumbled a complicated rhythm. "What are you talking about?" Confusion puckered my brow. "Do you think they're aware of the danger we're all in?"

"That's not what I . . ." He seemed to wince at my suggestion, then glared across the room. "I wasn't referring to the attempt on your life." His gave his head a slight shake. "It doesn't matter now. I'd just as soon get this evening over and done with."

I lifted my eyebrows, unable to hide my annoyance. "As would I."

A steady hum of conversation drew my focus over the top of the music, and my skin tingled. Graham was right. There was a strange energy about the room—a sudden commotion that as far as I could tell had nothing to do with us.

Daniel had cornered Mrs. Fagean near the back terrace, his hands wild as he spoke. Mrs. Fagean, however, seemed to be enjoying herself. My father, on the other hand, sat knee deep in conversation with Miss Chant, all while remaining stoic and controlled. If her expression was any indication, it was not a pleasant talk. And then there was Mr. Montague standing alone like a Greek god at the fireplace, his attention hard on Mr. Fagean across the room.

What was he anticipating? What had set them all off?

I skipped to the final bar of the music without anyone taking the least notice.

Graham, however, was ahead of me, anticipating the conclusion. He moved in close to my ear. "We'll meet in your room as soon as I can get free."

But it was Arnold who came to my room with a note, and I stalled him while I read it quickly.

It seemed Graham had been delayed, but he would come by as soon as he could. I folded the paper and slipped it into my dresser drawer before turning to Arnold, who was loitering a bit by the door. Was he interested in some sort of an explanation about the note? And why not? It was hardly proper. I motioned to the dresser. "The letter from Lt. Burke was nothing untoward, I assure you. It's just that we're rather close to solving the next clue." I wasn't certain how much to reveal to Arnold as Graham had specifically asked me to keep the trim a secret. "You'll be the first to know when we do, of course."

Arnold nodded, his eyes narrow. "You know I'm here to assist you in any way that I can."

He was right. Arnold had been a help on so many levels. As butler he was uniquely situated to observe the members of the household without notice, and he'd given me so many ideas regarding the early clues. Perhaps he could solve the newest mystery plaguing my thoughts. "There is one thing I haven't had the chance to tell you about . . . Lt. Burke and I found some surprising items inside the vicar's cottage."

He gave me an incredulous look. "The vicar's cottage? I was under the impression that place was only used for storage. You went there?"

"We did, and we found a table with items hidden cleverly beneath a Holland cover: newspaper clippings, an ear trumpet, a—"

"Ear trumpet?" He gave me a closed-lip smile. "That is odd indeed."

"But more importantly, there was information regarding the number fifteen, notes as if the person was attempting to decode the clues."

He shook his head slowly. "You don't say." He rubbed his hands together. "And you want me to . . . what exactly?"

"This proves without a doubt someone else is searching for the treasure."

He edged back a step. "A dangerous thought."

"Which is why it needs discussing. Do you perhaps have some insight as to who might have had access to the cottage all this time?"

He watched me carefully, his answer slow to come. "My first thought would be the Fageans."

"As is mine."

"But I have no proof to condemn them."

I edged forward. "What have you learned of their shipping business?"

"Nothing other than what you already told me—that they smuggle alcohol in from France, then return with legitimate cargo."

He angled a bit to the door. "Which does make one think—tonight would be a great night for a little investigation. His ship is due into the cove."

I nodded quickly. "Yes, it would be."

He gave me a playful nod, his eyes keen to please. "I'll let you know what I learn." A droll smile and he slipped from the room.

Over the next few hours wind gusts shook the panes of my bedchamber windows like a prisoner struggling for freedom. I edged in closer to the small fire still flaming in the grate and held out my hands. In the letter Graham had promised to come as soon as he could, but evening disappeared into night while I waited.

I'd secured a few maps from the library after Arnold's visit, but I'd been unable to decipher the exact location the numbers from the ballroom represented. I'd never studied longitude and latitude. I hoped Graham would have more information.

It was quite late before I finally heard a quiet knock. I hastened to the door and slid it open an inch. The hallway lay in darkness beyond, but I heard Graham's voice at once. "I wasn't certain you'd still be up."

I held the door wide and he sauntered in, his hand at his temple. He motioned me to my window and thrust open the drapes. "I'm afraid Mr. Fagean has already left the house."

I followed the point of his finger through the glass into the turbulent night, where I saw a small light visible on the hill.

Graham's movements were a bit frantic, his eyes anxious. "There's a ship anchored just offshore."

I tilted my chin, taking in the disorder of his hair and the rumple to his cloak. "You've been out there."

He thrust his hand into his pocket. "To the cliffs, yes."

I moved in closer to the window. "Mrs. Fagean did say the ship would set sail tonight."

Graham's jaw clenched. "He promised me no more smuggling here at Avonthorpe. I forbid it! This night arrival and departure can only mean one thing."

My hand slipped down the glass to the rim of wood on the casing. "They intend to unload whatever they've brought under the cover of darkness before they set sail again."

"Your father and Montague have plans to descend the stairs to observe what Mr. Fagean is about. I shall go to meet them as soon as I can. I had to let you know first . . . since we made an arrangement."

My heart stopped in my chest. "You told my father? He'll assume we've an assignation."

A wry smile emerged. "Don't be ridiculous. I told him I had business in the house. Although an assignation would have served."

My hand found the base of my throat. "You wouldn't dare."

"No, I wouldn't." A sheepish look. "Yet here I stand in your bedroom."

I paused a moment, struck by the hope Graham had softened over the course of the day, and he seemed to follow my thoughts, his face blanching.

"Phoebe," he whispered. "I understand . . . why you did it. Why you kept Cloutier's presence at Avonthorpe a secret."

I swallowed hard, my muscles frozen. "Do you?"

"It took me the good part of a day to come to the heart of my anger, to confront feelings I'd been fighting inside myself for years." He gently took my hand in his. "Maybe you didn't want Cloutier to die, or perhaps it was simply you were ashamed about what happened at Middlecrest." He squeezed my fingers. "Either way, it doesn't really matter, not anymore. I forgive you, wholly and completely. Over the past few weeks I've come to know your heart . . . and I find no matter how much I resist, I cannot help but trust it with my life."

"Oh, Graham." My eyes slipped closed for a long second. "I never, ever meant to hurt you, nor would I make the same foolish decision again. There's so much more to you than I ever imagined."

He gave me a pleasant sigh, his fingers contracting and releasing. "People are not always what they seem or defined by one bad decision."

"Regardless, I should have told you the truth from the beginning. When we started working together to find the treasure, I knew . . . The treasure!" My eyes widened and my hand flew to my mouth. I'd nearly forgotten. "Graham, I know where it is."

He stopped midbreath. "The trim is complete? You deciphered it?"

"I believe so. The numbers are coordinates—longitude and latitude—which makes perfect sense. Josiah Drake helped solidify the use of longitude at sea for goodness' sake. Although I'm not familiar enough with the chronometer to—"

"Of course!" Graham's eyes lit up. "Fifty-one degrees, six minutes, two seconds north by one degree, fifteen minutes, *one* second east."

"You know where that is?"

"My family's cove is only one minute off that number."

"The cove!" My gaze retreated to the darkness beyond the glass. "You think the treasure is down near the Fageans' ship? In the caves perhaps?"

Slowly he shook his head. "A minute's difference. It cannot be the cave. What was the clue again? Didn't it have something to do with the Bible? About treasure and the heart?"

My chest felt numb as the answer materialized in my mind. "The meaning of the verse is to place your value in heavenly things, not things of the world. It's got to be in the church on the hill."

Graham's hand slid down his face. "And the church is on the cliff, exactly one minute inland of the cove." He grabbed my hands. "That's it. The treasure has to be hidden somewhere inside." He jerked back and headed for the door. "I'll be right back with an iron bar and shovel. I'm not certain what we shall face. Don't go anywhere."

"Shouldn't we wait until morning—for light?"

"I wish we could, but with the Fageans' men in the area, we can't leave this to chance. We don't know how much Mr. Fagean knows or what he's deciphered. Besides, your father and Montague will keep his ship under watch at the shoreline, freeing us up for a little side mission of our own."

Guttural wind gusts surged through the trees and across the path as Graham and I trudged our way up the gradual incline of the cliff and Avonthorpe disappeared into the night behind us. Devoid of the moon, an array of stars blanketed the heavens, creating a strange, ghostly darkness on the earth, as if teams of spirits shifted back and forth just beyond the light from the lantern in Graham's hand.

Our pace was a quick one and my muscles tightened under the strain of anticipation and dread. Every now and again I heard the clank of metal as Graham shifted the shovel and iron bar on his shoulder, but little else.

That is, until the fork to the stairs appeared ahead, and Graham hesitated at the clearing. "The Fageans' ship." He pointed into the gloom.

I had to squint to make out the schooner anchored in the middle of the cove. There was movement on the shoreline, shadows crawling in different directions. Graham took a step forward. "I don't believe it."

I drew up at his side, the salty air surging against me.

He gave me an incredulous look. "My sarcophagus. Look there on the beach. Bound for France? Extraordinary."

A gaggle of men slid a crate into a rowboat. It didn't take me long to agree with Graham. It was most assuredly the sarcophagus he'd brought back with him from Egypt.

Graham's gaze set. "I suppose it's Mr. Haskett's to do with as he wishes—none of my affair."

"You'd prefer to see it in a museum."

"I have no control over private collectors. I'm only surprised is all." He motioned me toward the church. "Granted, there are other far more valuable antiquities to consider at present."

I couldn't help but smile. "What if King John's jewels are actually in the church?"

He returned a sly grin. "Then I—no, we—will have made one of the most important finds in British history."

I nudged his arm. "Is that what you are looking for—notoriety?"

His face grew somber. "No, I simply wish to understand and admire the past."

I watched him a moment as the breeze played with a stray lock of his hair. He was right—Graham Burke wasn't seeking his family's treasure for money or anything else. He only wanted the treasure to be protected. "You're a rare breed, Lt. Burke."

He shot me a quick look. "I hope not." And headed down the path.

I jogged to catch him, but he didn't slow. We were so close I could actually taste it. Over the stile, across the graveyard, and around to the large front doors. Graham fiddled in his pocket to locate the key as I stepped back to appraise the structure with new eyes. "Where do you think Josiah Drake meant specifically? We could tear this place apart and still not locate the hiding place tonight."

Graham thrust the doors inward. A loud *creak* sounded, then a puff of dust rose, shimmering eerily in the wavering lantern light.

Darkness had taken over the interior of the church save the muted beams of starlight that feathered in from the side windows.

Graham gave me one last look and extended his arm, and we crept forward. Inch by inch the center aisle took shape in the lantern's light until a larger section of the room was visible. The cavernous space amplified my voice as I said to Graham, "Where should we begin?"

"Perhaps the altar?"

I bit my lip. "Possibly. Or the pulpit."

"One for each of us, I suppose." Graham rested the lantern on a central pew and we set to work.

I ran my hands along all three decks of the pulpit, pressing and twisting every piece of wood, before focusing in on the vicar's desk. Drawer after drawer—empty.

Graham shuffled by. "I'll go through every last box pew."

I turned to nod and inadvertently came in contact with something metal. I felt it fall, then cringed at the resulting clatter as it hit the ground.

Graham's head popped up over the high-sided box pew. "Are you all right?"

I fumbled with the item I'd knocked from a hook on the side of the pulpit and held it into the light. "Just an ear trumpet from what I can tell. Oh look, it's engraved with a large *D*."

Graham smiled. "Looks like one of the Drakes was hard of hearing."

I returned the triangular-shaped item to its place. "The church remains much as they left it long ago—like a museum of sorts." Then it hit me. Everything about the small church had been designed by the Drakes. Carefully my gaze toured the room to where Graham was searching. No doubt Josiah Drake would have rented a pew box or had one built specifically for the family. "Graham?"

His footsteps stilled. "Yes."

"The Drakes had their very own pew at one time, correct?"

"Yes . . . yes, they did."

"And are they numbered?"

"Yes."

In between the gallery wall and the start of the trim at Avonthorpe I'd noticed the number one separated in script. "I think you are to go to the first one! That has to be part of the clue." Why had I looked over it at the time?

There was a great deal of shuffling as Graham plodded his way down the pew boxes, then he called out, "Here it is." A quick motion with his hand indicated I should join him, and he waited to say any more until I was at his side. "This is the Drakes' pew all right. See here, the *D* for Drake. The space is quite ornate. But I've already searched it. Just a pew box, I'm afraid."

We both stared a moment at the empty area.

A sudden and faraway sound drew our attention to the windows. Graham stilled a moment, his lips pressed tight. "I just can't get the sight of my sarcophagus out of my mind. Mr. Haskett told me he meant to display the antiquity in his study." He ran his hand down his face. "Which only brings that cursed scarab to my thoughts as well."

"The scarab?"

"How many items do you think are being shipped out of Britain tonight?"

My mouth gaped open. "No wonder Mrs. Fagean was originally thrown off by the change in departure. Quite a few arrangements to be made if they included stolen goods."

He met my hard gaze. "Mr. Haskett asked me for that scarab, but at the time I-I wanted it . . . well . . . for you. And now the sarcophagus I sold him is being loaded into her husband's boat."

"With your scarab, no doubt. The little fiend. Here she's been, all this time, living off your good graces and taking items from the house right under Miss Drake's nose. Thankfully my father is in residence to haul them all straight to the constable when we tell him. I imagine he'll also have some difficult questions to put to them about where they were the night your aunt died." I blinked hard. "Mrs. Fagean probably stole the crossbow from your collection as well, hoping it would incriminate you."

"Yet can you imagine Mrs. Fagean discharging such a weapon? I cannot. She probably couldn't even aim the thing."

"True, but—"

His hand came down softly on mine and my heart gave a little jump. "I won't rest until we get all our answers, but for now we need to focus on the task at hand. Time is not on our side."

"You're right, of course."

He absently pressed the letter *D* on the front of the box, then ran his fingers through all the divots—nothing. It was just a large, open wooden pew area.

I bit my lip. "What was the second part of the clue again? The verse part—where your heart is? We know the church is probably the right location—it has to be some sort of a cipher"—my hands were riotous—"the heart, treasure, heaven. What could it mean?"

I stopped cold. The heart . . . now where had I heard something about that? Unwittingly my gaze plunged to my feet as an errant thought took root. "Miss Chant told me Josiah had a stone installed within the church—in his pew. You don't think?"

Graham dashed for the lantern and rested it shakily on the ground. A wild glance at each other and we both crouched.

Sure enough, the massive Drake pew was lined with small ancient, interlocking stones. And there hidden in the darkened corner lay an intricately carved rock, which bore the Drake name and the inscription *Love conquers all.* I moved in closer, my heart hammering in my chest, before running my fingers over the smooth surface.

"Love—heart! This has to be it. The verse stands as a warning to us all, which perhaps Josiah meant to remind his son about before the end."

Graham squatted down close at my side as I felt along the seams of the stone. "Look, it's almost loose."

He too caught the delicate edge of the stone. "I think you're right." Then his eyes shot to mine. "Almost like it was designed that way."

He grappled for the iron crowbar he'd brought with us and managed to slide the smooth end under the stone's grooved edge. A hard push and the stone popped up a bit. His voice turned breathless. "Hold this a moment."

I secured the bar in position as he added the shovel for additional leverage. The stone seemed almost immovable until a high-pitched scrape resounded and the rock shot up an inch over the adjacent smooth stones. Graham wriggled his fingers beneath the edge and wrestled it free. A cautious look passed between us, filled with exhilaration, as we leaned forward and looked down—darkness—which meant a hole in the earth.

"Dashitall." Graham was forced to reposition the lantern once again to make out what was below.

My heart was overwhelmed. As the light crested the opening, a small black crate materialized before our eyes. A split second of excited wonder charged my thoughts until I saw the broken lock on the lid. "You don't think . . . we're too late."

Graham fumbled with the rusty lock, his fingers terribly anxious as they flipped open the lid.

Then all the life left my lungs.

Empty. The treasure was gone.

Graham pushed to his feet and swung away from me to slam his palm into the high side of the pew box. "I cannot believe it . . . after all we've been through."

I could barely speak through the shock. "How could anyone possibly decipher—"

"The Fageans are sailors, remember. Once you pointed out the map on the ceiling, he probably noticed the corresponding degrees and minutes. Anyone with any maritime experience would do so."

I collapsed back onto my legs, which were tucked behind me. "Clearly they've been studying Josiah Drake for some time. Don't forget the items in the cottage. This has been a passion of theirs for years."

Graham glared over his shoulder before springing to his feet. "I daresay they're transporting more than Egyptian antiquities, and they mean to leave tonight."

"But how could they have even seen the final clue? We locked the . . . wait." My throat grew thick. "The ballroom. It was already open when I took my father to see the finished product. I didn't even question it at the time. I wasn't thinking. Anyone could have wandered inside."

"Did Daniel have a key?"

"Yes, but . . . he could have made a mistake. He saw the numbers, but he didn't know what they meant. How could he betray what he didn't understand?"

Graham ran his hand down his face. "What I don't comprehend is how the devil they plan to smuggle the jewels into France. They would be instantly recognizable."

My eyes widened. "The sarcophagus!"

He sat up straight, then slowly shook his head. "That devious little snake. Haskett had this planned since the beginning. He's using my antiquities to avoid suspicion. Of course." His rage suddenly stilled, a strange look crossing his face. "You know, it is entirely possible Mr. Fagean is unaware of what he's transporting."

"I doubt that."

"Do you really? I can't get that look on his face out of my mind, when he learned of the fake Josiah Drake portrait. He was as shocked as we were."

Mr. Fagean's clumsiness came to mind, the awkward way he walked and talked. "I will admit that I cannot imagine him arranging all this."

"And that day . . . in the drawing room, it was *Mrs.* Fagean who sprang to his defense."

"You think she could actually manage all this without her husband's knowledge?"

He clenched his fingers into a fist. "With Mr. Haskett, yes. In fact, I'd stake my life on it."

"Mr. Haskett was quite interested in the paintings in the drawing room when he came to visit. He knew an awful lot about the family as well."

Graham's eyebrows flew up. "And if we're right and Mr. Fagean isn't involved, I have a chance."

"A chance at what?"

Something caught Graham's eye and he staggered forward. "There still may be time . . . possibility . . ." He plunged his hand into his pocket and jerked out his pistol. "You must stay here."

"What are you doing?"

A curious smile lit his eyes, half eagerness, half dread. "Oh, Phoebe, I'm going to recover once and for all what is rightfully mine, rightfully Britain's." Without so much as a by-your-leave, he strolled past me for the door.

"Shouldn't we think this through? I-I don't want to lose you." My words brought him to a halt. I raced up behind him and spun him around.

His face looked flushed, his eyes wide, a newfound confidence filling his voice. "Don't you see? I can finally hear it—the voice of adventure, the one you were talking about that day at the lake. It's come calling for me." He squeezed my arm. "Stay here. Stay safe. I'll return as soon as possible. You must see that I cannot allow this opportunity to pass me by. I was complicit in France. I swore I'd never be so again. Mr. Fagean's outside of all this. I can feel it. All I need to do is expose his wife and Mr. Haskett in the right way."

He stumbled back, hesitated, then bolted through the open

chapel doors and down the steps, turning just for a moment, his smile so wide and infectious I couldn't help but mirror it.

"I've been trying to find my way back to dreaming again." He threw up his hands. "What do you know, but I was looking in all the wrong places. Turns out it was always there, within me."

His declaration, the elation on his face—it all happened so quickly that I didn't even respond, collapsing onto a nearby pew to digest all he'd said. Was it possible Graham had changed so much in just a few short weeks? Moreover, was it possible I had? A small smile curved my lips. Could it be that we'd brought out the best in each other?

With an ache in my heart I imagined Graham sneaking down the stone steps and confronting Mr. Fagean. Could he be right? Was there cause to hope?

My errant gaze settled on the ear trumpet I'd knocked from the side of the pulpit, tracing the engraved *D* in my mind. I angled my chin. The ear trumpet looked remarkably like the one I'd seen in the vicar's cottage, only that one had borne the letter *P* or *B*, but it was difficult to read. My muscles tightened, thoughts running rampant in my mind. Was I mistaken about the letter?

A knot formed across my brow. After all, why would the Fageans have brought an ear trumpet to the cottage in the first place if it wasn't . . . ?

What had they found?

I rubbed my hand across my forehead until everything went still. Ruteledge was Christopher Drake's business partner, who had lost his hearing in one of his ears during the shipwreck. Mr. Haskett had pointed the ear trumpet out to me in the painting, and the one in the portrait had a large *R* engraved on the outside.

If I was right and the trumpet at the cottage had once belonged to Christopher Drake's partner, then how had it found its way there? Mr. Ruteledge certainly would have taken his own ear trumpet with him when he was run from town—he needed it to hear. And he would likely need to keep it till his death.

A *descendant*.

Every muscle in my body twitched. Only a descendant of Mr. Ruteledge would have eventually taken possession of that very trumpet. And such a person would have learned all about the treasure from Mr. Ruteledge himself . . . as well as the terrible grudge against the Drake family. But who at Avonthorpe could possibly be related to Mr. Ruteledge?

I imagined the painting I'd seen of the business partners, the narrow face and dimpled chin. I swallowed hard. Mr. Ruteledge did remind me of someone, someone I knew very well. My heart folded inward as I shook my head, the thought too painful to examine.

Mr. Arnold.

But he was a friend, a confidant. Miss Drake's final moments flashed into my mind. She'd pleaded with me to trust him. I never questioned her judgment, but her voice had been fading at the time, every word more difficult to utter. I replayed the scene over and over again.

Had Miss Drake actually been shaking her head when she stumbled through the disjointed words? Had she coughed out something I'd missed? Was it possible she'd actually warned me *not* to trust Arnold?

My breaths came short and fast as memories poured through my mind. Arnold was perfectly situated on the estate to hunt the treasure. He'd gained not only my trust but Miss Drake's as well. He must have known she was terribly close to the end when he made the decision to end her life. He couldn't let her find it before him. And the cottage? He'd been using it for years. The Drakes had destroyed his family, and revenge was a powerful motivator.

I'd trusted him, confided in him. The room swirled before me and I gripped a nearby pew.

He had learned about Miss Drake selling the Sèvres vase the night she was killed—from me! And later, he'd acted so strange when he found me in Miss Drake's bedroom with her jewelry. So coy he'd been, telling me only what I already knew. And the crossbow! He would have known it was at the cottage because he would have handled the storage of Miss Drake's things.

And the sickness of Graham's dog. It was Arnold who had handed me the picnic basket. He would have had ample opportunity to add the tainted milk, and he knew exactly how close I was to uncovering the treasure. He would have wanted me out of the way for a few days.

My gaze shot to the church door. What about Graham? What about my father and Mr. Montague? They had no idea Arnold was involved, what he'd done for greed. Arnold had told me he planned to investigate the Fageans, who were at the cove. Everyone I loved could be walking into a nightmare.

I paced forward, then back. Graham had ordered me to stay put, but wasn't that just what I'd done when Jean Cloutier escaped Middlecrest and I regretted it? I paced the long aisle between the pews. I had to warn them all. It was possible that Graham might not cross paths with Arnold, but I had to be sure. I had to find him.

I stopped to pat the bulge in my pelisse where I stored the small pistol Mr. Montague had given me. I had but one shot—how I prayed I wouldn't have to use it.

Twenty-Nine

THE WIND SLAPPED ME BACKWARD THE SECOND I STEPPED around the chapel wall, then ripped my bonnet from my head. I watched it tumble into the darkness, my fear mounting for what might transpire over the night.

I plowed forward, my hands clenching the folds of my pelisse before I broke into a run across the church grounds and down the path to the split, where I stopped to catch my breath. Graham had no doubt already begun his descent of the treacherous stairs, and he was in far better shape than I was.

A sharp pain stabbed at my side, forcing me to walk. Though I'd traversed the narrow steps with little trepidation in daylight hours, the perilous cliff that opened up before me in the darkness made my head swim. I pressed my hand against the cliff edge and took my first step into the chasm. A transient fog had gathered along the white cliffs and left the steps slick with moisture. I felt the ground beneath my heels give a bit.

I heard shouts from down below, men at work. Lanterns bobbed as shadows moved across the beach. I squinted into the gloom but saw no signs of my father or Mr. Montague or, more importantly, Arnold. What if they were all still at the house or watching from far away?

I staggered down another few stairs before rounding the first curve, now able to make out the small rowboat returning to the shore. It would take a few loads to transport all the people to the schooner anchored out in the cove.

Some of the sailors held lanterns, but none that would reach up the hillside. Carefully I made my descent, my back pressed to the cold stones of the cliff, the persistent wind threatening to topple me. The air tasted bitter, the shouts from below a constant reminder of the danger.

I neared the last turn still calculating what I must do when I took an errant glance to my right. I doubt I would have even seen the figure in the cleft of the large rock if not for the merest shift in the shadows. I halted midstep, my heartbeat echoing in my ears. I had no real means of escape; the stairs were too treacherous and the beach swarmed with Mr. Fagean's men. Whoever watched me from his perch behind the rock had complete advantage over me. I was caught and in the worst way.

I shrank as best I could into the shadows of the cliff, my muscles taut. Then the figure shifted, his shadow elongating. He was coming my way.

My hand slithered into the pocket of my pelisse and wrapped around the pistol.

"Phoebe."

My mouth gaped open, and I covered it with my hand. It was my father.

"Hurry, all eyes are on the cliffs."

I followed him into the large crevice where I was surprised to see not only Mr. Montague but Graham, who grasped my arm. "I told you to wait at the church."

"I came to warn you all. There's more going on than you're aware of at present." For a second of charged silence, everyone simply stared at one another and a cold feeling settled in my stomach. "Is there something *I* should know?"

Graham was the one to answer me. "Apparently your father's had the Fageans under watch for months. He believes there's more going on here than simple smuggling—more like treasonous activity."

I slumped back against the jagged rocks, trying to process the ever-changing events. "Miss Chant . . . ?"

My father nodded slowly. "Like I told you earlier, she's my informant, and I'm afraid she's been quite busy of late."

"Then you already knew about the treasure?"

He peered over at the men on the beach, his hand rising to keep my voice low. "A little, but I've no time for a wild-goose chase such as that. I've been after something far bigger, something far more important to Britain."

Another shout drew our attention. We watched the rowboat coast from the dark waters onto the beach.

Mr. Montague crept forward. "I'm afraid we've little time for discussion. Graham and I have every intention of reclaiming what is his."

My father pressed his hand to the rock, blocking Mr. Montague's exit. "My mission is paramount. Patience, my good man." Then he turned to me. "Here's what's going to happen. You, my dear, are to stay hidden right here while Montague, Burke, and I find our way onto the last rowboat. Then you'll go for help."

I shook my head. "I cannot leave, not alone. It's not safe. Arnold could be anywhere around here."

Graham jerked back. "Arnold?"

"I have so much to tell you. He's not who you think he is—"

My father jerked forward. "It's time, and we have to be extremely careful. No shots, understand? The men cannot be permitted to alert the ship to our presence. Surprise is our only hope."

"Agreed." Graham hesitated. "We'll talk more later. Don't leave this hiding spot." He slid past me to the opening, his hand brushing gently against my shoulder. I couldn't say whether it was intentional, but it felt that way. I glanced up in time to catch a lingering look as he removed his pistol from his jacket.

My body numb, I settled down in the corner of the crevice as the men left one by one. How terribly foreign the beach felt in that moment, the sand a sickly gray, the jutting rocks hostile, the wind hauntingly cold. I tucked my legs against my chest as the two most important men in my life headed straight into danger. I thought waiting in the church intolerable, but watching might be even worse.

There were but four men left on the shoreline as my father's group slunk along in the shadows behind them. I saw the flicker of movement as Graham lifted his arm, the handle of his pistol firm in the palm of his hand.

The sailor edged a step around the bow of the boat and glanced up. "What the—"

Without a pause, Graham's fist careened into the sailor's cheek, and the man staggered back a pace.

A blessed moment of confusion passed as the three other sailors came to grips with what had occurred, then pandemonium broke loose. Shouting was met with wild fists and fury. My father leaped forward like a young man, ripping a shotgun from one of the sailor's hands and flinging it into the turbulent waves.

Mr. Montague had his own man in check, but it was four against three. They had to be quick.

The sailor Graham had initially assaulted recovered all too quickly and came to his companion's aid, a newfound rage to his step. Graham, however, met him head-on, striking first one then the other, but they were too much. One man caught Graham's arm on a misplaced strike and twisted it behind his back, all while the other sailor fished something from his pocket. A large horse pistol emerged and Graham's eyes widened. "Montague!"

Mr. Montague had just flattened his own assailant and glanced up with only a second to intercept. Unbidden I crept closer to the action, desperate to help in some way. Thankfully, the instant the pistol was leveled at Graham's chest, Montague thrust the man's arm up and dislodged his finger from the trigger. He quickly gained possession of the firearm.

Once the pistol was in hand, Graham struck hard across the sailor's face, knocking him to the sand, then turned to meet his other attacker. The man held up his hand as he crept backward, but I saw the gleam of silver tucked into the back of his trousers and the insidious quest of his eager fingers. He meant to fire.

Graham had slowed his approach, assuming the last remaining sailor would not be difficult to manage. How wrong he was.

I knew I couldn't fire my own pistol, so I raked the darkened area for another sort of weapon, but the shadows were too dense. Everything looked black. I darted forward, my pelisse banging against my leg, but it wasn't simply the pistol I felt in the fold of my pocket. The shell Graham had given me on our ride was still tucked in the inner folds.

As fast as I possibly could, I wriggled the shell into the night air and dropped it on a jagged stone. My half boot came down hard, splintering the precious limpet into two sharp pieces. There was little time to examine the damage as I grasped the small piece between my fingers and raced into the fray. All I needed was something that felt sharp.

The sailor jerked his hand free of Graham's the second I arrived, and extended the weapon. I plunged the shell as hard as I could into his back, hoping the man would believe I possessed a knife. "Drop the pistol or I thrust this blade the rest of the way in."

I felt his shudder of indecision, then the pistol fell to the ground.

Graham's eyes were hard on me as he took the man into his power. Belatedly a smile crept into view. "A knife?"

I held up the broken seashell and shrugged. "It was the best I could do on such short notice."

He cocked an eyebrow. "And quite effective, I must say. Pity it had to be the white one."

"We'll find another . . . together."

My father dragged the lifeless man he'd overcome past the two of us and plopped him onto the sand like a sack of potatoes. "The caves will have to do for a prison for now. That ship isn't going to wait for us long." He motioned to the rowboat with his chin. "Help me gather the rest of the rope and tie these men as best we can." Then to me: "And you are going straight back to the crevice."

I nodded.

The entire operation to tie up the sailors and place them in the cave took but a few minutes, then the rowboat was adrift, my father, Mr. Montague, and Graham on their way to the schooner—where there would be many more men to overcome.

I squinted into the dark night and carefully made my way back to the stairs, trailing the sight of the rowboat as long as I could. Yards from the stairwell, I heard a rustle behind me. My heart climbed into my throat, and I whirled about to see Daniel emerging from the far rocks, the very spot I'd seen him traverse so long ago.

I shrank against the cliff side, the cold, damp moss pressed to the nape of my neck. He didn't see me at first, which gave me a precious few seconds to think. Why was Daniel at the coast . . . the very night the Fageans were loading their ship?

Then it hit me, a painful lump thick in my throat. My dearest friend was involved in some way, but how? Daniel wasn't in need of money or anything of that nature . . . but as easily as I dismissed certain ideas, others flooded my mind. Had I jumped to the conclusion about Arnold too quickly, or was everyone at the house involved in some way?

Mrs. Fagean had lured Daniel to the Equinox Festival, and it was then that everything changed. He'd admitted to kissing her, yes, but that didn't explain his presence on the beach now. Had something else occurred that night? Something Daniel still hadn't told me about? Could he have gotten in over his head?

My muscles stiffened as the truth found its way to my mind—blackmail! Mrs. Fagean was always using someone for something. It was what she did best. I pushed away from the wall and walked over to meet him.

Once he was firmly in view I couldn't miss the way he smashed his hand into his hair, how hard his gaze lay on the water. And when he saw me, everything shifted. His nostrils flared and sweat dripped down the side of his face.

His movements were jerky and he darted a glance behind him. "What the devil are you doing here?"

I propped my hand on my hip. "I could ask you the same thing."

"Dashitall." He clenched his fists and shook his head. "Oh, Phoebe. I did everything to keep him away from you. Why now? Why here?" The energy left his voice. "I suppose all my dealings were for nothing."

A cold feeling blossomed in the middle of my chest and spread out like tiny spiders on an icy web. "*Him?*"

Daniel closed his eyes. "I tried so hard, but you would be so impulsive, so trusting. I half thought you might run away with him. I swear I could beat you right now."

My shoulders folded inward as a piece of the puzzle I hadn't even realized I'd been missing locked into place. I'd been so distracted. All this time Daniel was trying to protect me from my past. "You've had a visit from Jean Cloutier?"

"Not a visit, Phoebe!" He planted his legs wide. "Mrs. Fagean means to smuggle him onto her husband's ship . . . tonight! Don't you see, that's why she's been stealing all those items from the house. It's not cheap to pay off a whole complement of sailors on her husband's schooner, particularly when her husband is unaware. She's working with Mr. Haskett."

So that was the treasonous activity my father was after. And Mr. Haskett—so they were together! My attention jerked to the dark horizon, imagining what Graham would find when he reached the ship. Mrs. Fagean was Jean's ticket out of here—of course she was. She was lonely and desperate. Jean had been busy indeed. No wonder she had been drizzling . . . and the thievery! Mr. Haskett's clothes came to mind, the outdated style, the thinning fabric. He must not have had the money to pay off the sailors, at least not this time.

Daniel inched closer. "You've got to get out of here. There—"

Without warning, his eyes went blank, his face motionless as he tipped forward into me, then slumped lifeless onto the sandy ground.

I gasped, the utter shock of what was happening numbing any sort of a response. I remember gaping down at Daniel's strange form slumped over on the sand, then I stared up, straight ahead into the dark eyes of Jean Cloutier. He still gripped the rock in his hand.

He tried a boyish smile, his French accent roaring to the surface. "I did not wish to do that, particularly after your friend has been so accommodating. I could not have made it these past few days in the cave around the corner without his help."

I tested my voice, but it came out as if far away. "You've been here . . . on the coast . . . all this time." No wonder Daniel had been at sixes and sevens over the past few days. He'd been bringing Jean food—to keep him away from me!

"Awaiting transport, yes. I told you—I wish to leave this place as soon as possible. Mrs. Fagean and Mr. Haskett have helped several of my comrades."

Slowly, carefully, I slid my hand into my pelisse pocket, all kinds of suppositions racing through my mind. So this was why my father had been watching Avonthorpe for months. He was after the people smuggling French spies from the Napoleonic Wars out of Britain—Mr. Haskett and Mrs. Fagean of all people. Was that why Miss Chant couldn't leave with Vincent to America when he wanted her to? Did it have nothing to do with money? Had she suspected Mrs. Fagean and her fiancé's employer all along? I adjusted my pistol into position and slid my fingers around the handle.

Jean Cloutier was clearly ignorant of my little friend in my pocket as his smile only deepened. "I'm to be smuggled aboard the last rowboat bound for Fagean's schooner. It won't be long now."

He still thought everything was on schedule. Daniel must have been checking on what was taking so long. "Have you not noticed the beach is empty, the men all gone?"

For the first time since he'd sauntered forward, his face lost a bit of its charm. "They will be back for me. Mrs. Fagean has already paid for my passage. It's a matter of honor now."

"How you use people with such finesse, then toss them away as if they mean nothing to you." I positioned my finger on the trigger of the pistol, ready to draw it at any moment.

He angled his chin, his dark eyes so keen in the starlight. There was still a small part of me that yearned for some sort of closure with him, that part of me that wanted to believe the best about people, to hang on to the hope that some facet of our connection was real.

But I was no longer a fool.

He took a long breath, his eyes piercing in the starlight. "You know, you could come with me."

My heart stuttered. Come with him?

"Yes, come with me, Phoebe . . . to France. We can have everything we spoke of before. We can finally be together." Then I saw it, that imperceptible slant of his gaze—a concealed glance—checking my pocket. He knew I had a weapon.

I brandished the pistol and took immediate aim straight at his heart. "No more lies, Jean. I'm not so easily manipulated as I was before. I've given my heart to a man ten times your character. He would never poison a man to escape."

"A pity." He inched forward, testing my resolve. "Surely you cannot have given up all your passions, Phoebe. We were special—you and I. And I don't believe you have it in you to shoot me now."

"Kill you?" I shrugged. "Probably not, but I'm Lord Torrington's daughter. I could certainly hit your leg from across the beach. Care to try me?"

"There it is. That is the woman I love." He shot me a wink. "Seems we are at an impasse then. What do you propose, *mon amour*? You'll not be able to force me up those stairs with such a little pistol. And if you shoot, we'll simply be here until the sailors on the boat come back for me."

"We shall wait right here for the rowboat to return. I—"

Footsteps stilled my words as a familiar voice slid over my shoulder, the muscles freezing in my arm. "I see you've caught yourself a very large fish," Mr. Arnold said as he wrangled the pistol from my hand.

The beach shifted beneath my feet as a strange look of satisfaction crossed Arnold's face. He took a better aim at Jean. "You, sir, are an enemy of Britain. And I have to confess, it does give me a twinge of delight to be the one to end you." He fired, straight at Jean Cloutier's heart.

I screamed, my mind awash with confusion.

Jean writhed on the ground, clutching his right shoulder. He had missed certain death by inches. Blood, however, was pouring from the wound. It wouldn't be long before he became desperate.

I fell onto my knees beside Jean as I wrestled a piece of fabric from my muslin slip and tied a makeshift bandage, still an unwitting passenger on the ship of utter bewilderment.

How could Arnold simply shoot Jean without questioning him or anything? Without any shred of remorse, without . . . ? I had been right in the church. My head spun.

I took one last scared look up and I knew for certain. Mr. Arnold, esteemed butler at Avonthorpe, could be none other than Miss Drake's murderer.

Thirty

It seemed like a lifetime before Arnold finally turned to face me, a horrible few seconds of heart-twisting unreality that I shall never forget. His smile was even worse.

He knew—he knew I'd figured it out.

He gave me an icy shrug, then tossed the pistol onto the sand, useless now, and I backed away from him.

"It's been *you* all this time, racing me to the treasure, making me believe that Mr. Fagean was the real culprit."

"I certainly never thought Miss Drake would share the clue with you, or I wouldn't have snuck away when you appeared so decidedly at the wrong moment." He almost laughed to himself. "I would have reloaded the crossbow." He dipped his hand into his pocket and fished out a new pistol, his crooked teeth gleaming in the moonlight. "Oh yes, I've one of my own with me as well, a flintlock. And I promise you, my dear, I shan't miss again."

My gaze slanted down to Jean hunched over on the sand. Though he'd been rendered lifeless, my makeshift bandage seemed to have staunched some of the blood. He lifted his head an inch, casting a knowing look at me. Could he move? Could he help me in some way?

I angled my subtle retreat carefully to the left, removing Jean as best I could from Arnold's line of sight. Only a miracle could get me out of this horrid fix. If only Jean could recover enough . . . to what? I swallowed the difficult thought as quickly as it came. I could no more trust him than I could Arnold. I was trapped and in the worst way.

Arnold cast a look over his shoulder at the caves, then at the rocky cliff that jutted out to the waves.

The crossbow! My mouth fell open. "You had plans for these caves, didn't you? It's where you meant to stash the treasure. You must have been terribly surprised to find a person living within them. That's the only reason you could have had for hiding the crossbow on the cliff's edge."

A devious smile. "You seem to have it all worked out." He motioned to the stairs with the end of the flintlock. "I had no intention of ending your life, Phoebe. But you had to find that dratted ear trumpet, linking me to my ancestors, forcing my hand."

"The treasure is already on the Fageans' boat. You've no way to recover it now."

"Rather clever of Mr. Haskett to put it in the sarcophagus. An idea I should have thought of myself."

"Then you knew? You're working with them?"

"Don't be absurd. Who do you think alerted Lt. Burke to their movements tonight? No, that lot couldn't have found the treasure without Miss Chant whispering in their ears. And you had to be so foolish as to share everything with her. Did you not even stop to think about the desperation she felt, how her fiancé needed the money more than any of us?"

But my father had said she was working for him. A furrow crossed my brow. "I know you're a direct descendant of Christopher Drake's business partner. Half of the treasure is yours. Why didn't you simply reveal your true identity to Miss Drake from the beginning?"

"I was right not to. You see, we were friends initially, coconspirators, but after she stumbled upon the second clue, she began to search in secret. Those blasted Drakes—they care for no one but themselves. I discovered her treachery and was forced to blackmail her to maintain my position at Avonthorpe. The treasure belongs to the Crown. One word from me and the Drakes would be cut out entirely. Thus, it became a race to see who could find the treasure first. I had no idea it would take years, but I owed it to my family name."

I opened my mouth, but no words would come.

"I had hoped for the entire treasure; however, I only need a small lot to set me up for life. When they return to the beach I'll require something of a distraction to steal a small portion, and your sudden death will do nicely for that."

Arnold was indeed mad. "How do you possibly think you can get away with my death?" I motioned around us. "With all of this?"

"An accident, of course. I really couldn't say. I was distracted by everything that went down tonight—the faithful butler just doing his best." He repositioned the pistol in his hand. "Shall we walk a bit closer to the waves?"

Arnold took a step backward, and it was just the opportunity Jean Cloutier needed. His hand shot out and wrapped Arnold's ankle, jerking him off balance. I plunged forward and crashed headfirst into Arnold, centering all my force on the arm with the gun. A shake or two and his grip failed, the pistol flinging into the shadows of the rocks and the sand.

We both stared around desperately, searching the wet ground where the weapon had fallen, but Arnold was ahead of me, wasting little time before whirling back to face me. He was a foot taller, broad shouldered and strong, but he was in his dotage and the earlier fall had stunned him.

His arm shot out, but his wild grasp missed its target, and I bolted for the stairs. Gravelly footsteps pounded behind me, accelerating with every second, echoing the frantic beat of my heart. I nearly cried out in frustration.

Just when my half boot slammed onto the bottom step, my head was jerked back by my hair and I was thrust onto the ground. A rock shocked the bones in my spine, and the world dipped into a spin.

Arnold's face drifted into my dreamlike view, a dark, brooding silhouette. "There's no escape, Miss Radcliff. I wish there were. I simply cannot keep you alive and get any part of the treasure that's mine by destiny. My ancestors lost everything for this wretched family, and I'll not allow you to keep it from me now." He swiped something from the sand, fisting it in his clenched fingers. "And without my pistol, this shall be decidedly more messy."

He raised the jagged rock over his head and I closed my eyes. Strange how quickly Graham's face appeared in my mind's eye, then my father and sister. How precious life was . . . and so terribly fleeting. I'd had so many dreams and plans for this world. I only hoped Juliana could recover from another death in her life.

A shot rent the night air. A savage grunt and my eyes burst open. Arnold staggered to the left of my vision, then across to the right before toppling onto the ground. I jerked my head to the side as a red stain poured from the hole in the center of his chest.

Jean tucked the sandy pistol into his trousers as he staggered by me, heading for the stone steps. He paused only for a second to leer over his shoulder. "Consider us even, *ma cherie*. A life for a life."

All I could do was lay there in utter silence as I watched Jean trudge up the narrow stairwell and out of my life. I knew quite well that my father would never stop hunting him. Two years prior, when Jean had been ripped away from me and hauled away in chains, somehow I knew I'd see him again. This time, however, was different. I would never set eyes on the notorious Frenchman again, and I never desired to.

A part of me wanted to believe he'd told the truth about Giles Harris's murder—that he didn't know what was planned, that he was a patriot to France—but I doubted it. All I knew for certain was today, on this beach, he'd saved my life.

The minutes that passed felt more like hours. Daniel revived somewhat from his head wound and Graham's rowboat full of men slid onto the beach. I'd sat there in careful silence, holding my friend, praying for the lives of so many of my loved ones, completely helpless until a familiar form came rushing toward me.

"Phoebe!" Graham's face was filled with quiet dread, his eyes darting about the beach. "What happened?"

Recounting all that had transpired in his absence was more difficult than I imagined, but I did my best to cover every last detail of Arnold's murder and my strange rescue. My head pounded and my vision remained unsteady due to my own battering.

Graham touched my cheek. "That's enough for now. Take a breath. I've a few things to arrange and I'll be right back."

Graham's military tone emerged as he barked orders in all directions. I couldn't help but smile to myself. Underneath all that authority was a kind, deep thinker, the very best sort of gentleman, a man filled with compassion and the propensity to love. And loyalty—something I'd never given much thought to, even after all my dealings with Jean. Graham Burke would never give me cause to worry or question his attachment. How terribly attractive that was now. My chest warmed as I imagined the future before us. How could I possibly be so lucky?

Footsteps pounded around me as Mr. Montague was tasked with assisting Daniel up the stairs and the other men headed for the prisoners in the cave.

What had started out as a gloomy night had opened up to a brilliant tapestry of stars, which in turn glistened off the water in sparkling surges. I was told my father remained aboard the schooner to question the sailors.

Gentle hands caressed my head as Graham leaned down to my ear. "It's all over now. The treasure is recovered. Are you badly injured? Can you stand?"

"Perhaps in a moment. My back was hit hard, but it's not broken."

I could hear the men's cagey voices discussing the procedure for dealing with Arnold's body.

"You'll be much more comfortable back at the house." He tucked his arm under my knees as if to carry me, but I stilled him.

"What happened with Mr. Fagean?"

A momentary pause and Graham settled down at my side. "I was right. He was woefully ignorant of his wife's plotting. Our surprise visit was not opposed. According to his men, Mrs. Fagean has been using his ship to smuggle French nationals out of Britain for some time, she and Mr. Haskett of course. Thankfully, Mr. Fagean turned on his partner at once. Mr. Fagean, for all his faults, is not a traitor to Britain, nor is he the least bit mawkish . . . We in turn exposed the truth that Mrs. Fagean and Mr. Haskett's relationship is more than simply friendly and has been for some time. Mr. Fagean was not amused, to say the least."

"And the treasure?"

A quick smile. "Was in the sarcophagus, just like we thought. It's right over there." There was a second of palpable silence before tears filled his eyes, and he clutched me against his chest. "Why did I ever leave you alone?"

"You had no idea what all lurked in the shadows of the beach." A wan smile tugged at my lips as my arms circled his back. "Besides, you had to see to your adventure."

Slowly, gently, he shifted me away from him just enough to bring my face into view. His kiss was so beautifully tentative, which he followed with a long, careful look that stirred my heart. "From now on, Phoebe Radcliff, I plan to share all my adventures with you and you alone, and they shall be of only the mildly dangerous variety . . . agreed?"

I nodded, which prompted a cough.

Graham assisted me into a better position before guiding me against his shoulder to rest, leaning back against a nearby rock.

We sat in relative quiet for a long moment, the waves gently rocking against the shore. His hand found mine, and at first I thought he meant merely to hold it, but his fingers slid down until they circled my fourth finger. "I never did have a chance to tell you why I wrote to your father, why I wanted him to come to Avonthorpe so badly."

I smiled to myself. "No, you didn't."

"It was regarding my upcoming proposal of marriage. I was so dashed anxious to declare myself."

Warmth filled my cheeks as a newfound energy filled my chest. "You'd already decided . . . days ago?"

He pulled me tighter against him and took a long breath of my hair. "Oh, Phoebe." He rested his chin on my head. "You're like my own personal artist. You've painted over my entire world."

His arms slid so comfortably around my waist. "You've opened my eyes to the future, and from where I stand, it looks glorious. Mr. Montague has been saying it all along—you bring out the best in me. And I can't exactly explain how or why that is, because you can be terribly maddening at times."

A small laugh. "All I know is that I yearn for you whenever we're apart. I can feel what you're thinking, what you're feeling. Who would have guessed we'd fit so perfectly together, so naturally I—" I could hear the hitch in his voice, feel the subtle tightening of his arms. "All right. I'll stop my lecturing. Words are not really needed. They never have been between us. All I'm saying is that I love you and I want you to be my wife."

For the first time I knew without a doubt Graham was seeing me, all of me, my imperfections, my mistakes, my inner joy, and most importantly my heart—and he wanted me as badly as I wanted him. I relaxed every muscle in my body, reveling in the feeling of peace and security I only ever experienced with Graham. My heart was completely safe in his hands.

But there was one thing I needed to know.

I sat up to face him. "Are you certain you want to marry the first passable lady who crossed your path?"

Graham blinked and his mouth popped open before his lips twisted into a smirk. "I knew you were in the stables that day."

"Or is it my paltry dowry that's attracted you so?"

"I daresay life with you shall never be boring. Truly, you must know I had to say those things." He licked his lips and laced his fingers around mine. "I couldn't let Mr. Montague take an interest . . ."

I leaned forward and pressed my lips against his. "I will marry you then . . . ten times over . . . if you but agree to one condition." I laid my hand on his chest. "Don't ever change, Graham Burke, not in essentials, at any rate. I love you just the way you are."

A wide grin stole across his face and he looked behind him. "Are you well enough to see what we've been searching for?"

"The treasure?"

He helped me to my feet and wrapped his arm around my back to keep me steady.

"I don't know if I'm ready."

"It's extraordinary."

The sarcophagus was still in the rowboat and Graham had to use a bit of strength to slide the heavy stone lid to the side. My gaze fell immediately onto two gold crosses glinting in the starlight, then below to hordes of cups and goblets, dishes and flagons, a candelabrum studded with precious stones, then finally to the royal regalia and coronation robes.

I ran my fingers across the faded fabric. "Weren't these usually held by the Templars and the Hospitallers so long ago?"

"In general, yes, but they were with King John that day." Graham sounded incredulous. "Look at these golden vessels ornamented with pearls. Rumor says they were from the pope. There are clasps, rings and pendants, swords and scepters." He held up an intricately gilded crown. "This one was from Germany." Then he unearthed a second regalia. "Just look at these belts."

The first was black leather with roses and bars of gold. The second was made of padded leather with red sandal and great stones set in a chase. This lay atop a collar dripping with diamonds and rubies.

In awe, he carefully laid the items down. "There's also a case with nine great necklaces made with precious stones, more crowns and crosses. It's beyond what we ever imagined."

I was speechless, overcome. All I could do was stare at the man before me, then back at the glorious items. We'd done it. With everything standing in our way, we'd done it.

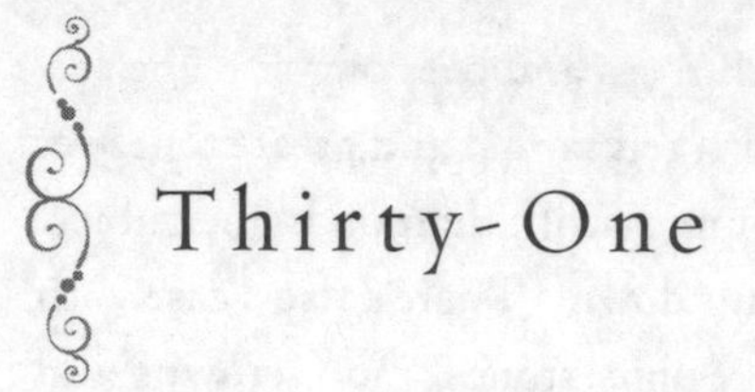

Thirty-One

I HAD JUST TAKEN A SEAT IN THE DRAWING ROOM BESIDE a large fire when Miss Chant entered like a mouse. Her fingers were busy at her waist, her eyes heavy. She was still in her pelisse, the mist from the ocean wet in her hair.

It took me a moment to process the whole of what stood before me. "You were on Mr. Fagean's schooner, weren't you?"

She nodded slowly at first, then with more determination. "But it's not entirely what you think. I told him everything—last night."

I narrowed my eyes. "Told who?"

She advanced across the rug and took a tentative seat at my side. "Your father, of course. It was part of his plan for Vincent and me to be there tonight."

I lifted my head, my shoulders heavy. "I don't know what to believe about you. It's all a jumble in my mind."

"Believe our friendship first and foremost." Her mouth twisted into a frown. "But I will admit I have not been entirely truthful."

"So you did tell Vincent about the clues to the treasure? Even the one about the fifteenth stair?"

I suppose guilt has its way with people, changing the light in their eyes, tearing them apart little by little. Even Miss Chant's mannerisms seemed affected. "I started out working as an agent for your father. My mission was twofold: to root out the person smuggling Frenchmen across the channel, and to keep you safe. My intentions were honorable at first, but the hope of even part of the treasure was too great. You had promised to help me with my passage to America, of course, but Mr. Haskett was guaranteeing us far more. It would have changed Vincent's life, and mine. And I meant for you to marry Lt. Burke. It was how I made peace with my deception. I figured you'd be taken care of. I'm still so sorry for that argument we had. Vincent took me to task for angering you."

My expression must have displayed my annoyance. Her hand shot out. "Please . . . I beg you not to think quite so ill of him. The plan to steal some of the treasure for ourselves never sat right with him. He was the one who begged me to tell your father in the end. He couldn't do it. He just couldn't do it."

I could feel the tears welling in my eyes. "And what is to happen now?"

"Your father has arranged for the two of us to leave for America at once. It was all part of the deal I made last night." She scooted closer to me. "Oh, Phoebe, Vincent and I didn't know how it would all play out. We had hoped . . . well, never mind. It's all just a shame now."

I stared at her a long moment, hurt brimming in my eyes as well as an unexpected wave of sadness. "I'm going to miss you."

She clutched my hand. "I'm so sorry . . . for everything."

Years ago I would have handled her revelation quite differently, but life had taken its toll. God had used my own mistakes, as well as Graham, to soften me. I looked up and said confidently, "I forgive you."

There was a moment of disbelief, then she pulled me into a tight embrace. "You're an extraordinary young woman, Phoebe Radcliff. I hope you write to me, because I shall long to hear of how you make your mark on this world."

A shuffle sounded outside the drawing room and we sprang to our feet. Mr. Montague had brought Mrs. Fagean from her room and was directing her to the front door. She too had seen little sleep this evening. I could only imagine the scene in her room when she was confronted with her treachery.

I heard the front entry swing open, and I rushed to the drawing room doorway. I could not let Mrs. Fagean leave without facing her one last time. But I must admit, the state of her dress brought me to a halt. Her hair lay in stringy clumps, her clothes disheveled, her face powder streaked down her cheeks from crying.

She wrinkled her nose. "Come to gloat, Phoebe?"

"No." My voice was weak. "I simply came to ask why."

She huffed, then gave me a lazy smile. "You think I haven't a layer of depth to me, that I could sit here in this insipid house day after day being ignored by my husband and do nothing. Mr. Haskett loved me and I loved him. We had plans . . . so many plans. His mother was French, you know, and he was always loyal to her and her country. When the time was right and we'd rescued the last stranded Frenchman, we were never going to come back." Her eyes narrowed. "What a coincidence that you and Mr. Cloutier shared a history and ended up here as well."

Then she shrugged. "Of anyone, I thought you would understand my plight. Cloutier told me of your past romance. You and I are not so very different, hmm?" She gave her head a little shake.

"No, Mrs. Fagean, that's where you are wrong. I was a fool when I allowed Jean Cloutier a piece of my heart . . . But even amid all my mistakes, I continue to strive to find the good in people. You have only looked for the worst. You set out to discover all of our weaknesses and then used them against us—your husband, Daniel, Miss Drake."

Something about the way she looked at me, the dramatic tilt to her head, her pensive gaze, took me back to the moment she'd rushed off to gather the money I'd obtained from her drizzling. My heart sank. "You were the one who took the clues from my jewelry box. No wonder you knew just where I kept my money. You'd already been rifling through my private things earlier in the week."

Her bright eyes narrowed dangerously as further revelations seeped into my consciousness.

Graham had been entirely correct. "It wasn't Mr. Fagean who opened the sluice gate at all, was it? He was probably just checking out what had already happened. It was you . . . and Mr. Haskett all along."

A slow smile crossed her face, but she said nothing further.

Mr. Montague stepped forward. "I'm sorry, but we must be off." Then angled his head. "Miss Chant?"

She squeezed my arm. "I'm to travel with them to the constable to discuss everything I know." She pressed her lips together. "I won't be coming back to Avonthorpe."

Mr. Montague motioned her to the door, then turned back to me at the last moment. "Your father asked me to inform you that in all likelihood he won't be back tonight."

"I understand."

He nodded a moment, then a sly little smile snuck out of the side of his mouth. "He wants me to travel with him back to Middlecrest Abbey. He thinks I can be of use with some of his, eh, intelligence work there. And I believe I should like to dip my toes into a bit of espionage myself."

I had a feeling my father's sudden interest in Mr. Montague was more than just an idle idea, and I grinned to myself. "My family will be pleased to meet you. And there is nobody better to work with than my father."

Mr. Montague bowed and ushered the group out the front door but didn't close it, as Graham popped back through the opening.

He narrowed the space between us with his wide strides, dignified but not proud, determined, almost eager. I thought he meant to address me, but his hands were at my chin, his body pressed to mine, the wall hard at my back. I could feel his heart hammering against my chest. One look and his lips were on mine.

This was a kiss unlike any I'd experienced. He was assured,

bold even, and I gave a little gasp as his hand found the small of my back and tugged me closer. Glorious dizziness followed before he inched away.

His hair looked windswept and wild, his cheeks red from the cold. "I rode back all this way from the constable's, as I don't intend to make any further decisions in regard to the treasure until I hear your thoughts." He seemed almost flighty.

"What do you mean? This discovery will soon be public knowledge. We have no choice but to turn over the treasure to the Crown."

"Yes, but the course we take needs your input as much as mine."

"But I'm not a Drake."

"Not yet at least . . . well, sort of . . . You'll be a Burke soon enough, which is vastly superior in my mind."

I searched his eyes for the meaning behind his sudden jaunt to the house. What was he getting at?

I sorted through all he'd said over the past few weeks until the answer came to me quite clearly. "The treasure does belong to the Crown; however, you want to barter with it to ensure it will be shared with everyone."

I can only describe the smile that emerged on Graham's face as brilliant, because it was. His hand settled on my arm. "Precisely. It might get a bit sticky, but I have plans." Then he lowered his gaze. "Avonthorpe will still have to be leased."

My fingers contracted. "Surely you know by now that I only want to be with you. I understand your home is Brooksheed Manor. How I long to see it. What possible use have I for the gilded halls of Avonthorpe?"

A shuffle sounded at my back, then I caught a flurry of movement. I turned just in time to see Creature plow through the open door and straight for us. His tongue was exceptionally pink, his eyes round. He darted a look down the long gallery but whirled his ramshackle approach directly at me. A split second and his humongous paws were on my chest. I certainly would have toppled to the ground if Graham hadn't supported me.

"Down at once, you cursed mongrel. How on earth did you get out of your pen?" Graham took a sheepish look back at me. "Whatever shall we do with him?"

"Love him, of course."

Graham turned to Creature. "You hear that? I've found the only lady in Britain who can tolerate you."

Then in his pretend dog voice: *"Do you mean she's coming home with us?"*

"That's right, Creature . . . home . . . with us . . . though we don't deserve her." He closed his eyes for a long second. "Oh, Phoebe, when I set out to follow those clues, I had no idea that the real treasure was already right in front of me."

I smiled. "Nor I."

"Then let us have the banns read as soon as possible, for I cannot wait for the day you'll be my wife and I can finally take you home."

I squeezed him tight, then pulled back, unable to hide a smirk. "I don't need King John's stuffy jewels, but I will need some paint and a few more canvases . . . or I suppose I can set to work on your walls."

He stole a sideways glance in the direction of the ballroom. "Honestly, I wish you would. After appraising the job you've completed here, I've come to the difficult conclusion there's not a painter in London who can rival your talent."

I knew Graham's opinion could hardly be objective, but I leaned forward with a wide smile and shot him a wink. "I'm just glad to finally hear you admit it."

Acknowledgments

TRAVIS, I COULD NOT WRITE ONE WORD OF MY STORIES without your constant love and support. Thank you for brainstorming with me nearly every night and listening to my endless "what-ifs." I wouldn't want to share a minute of this crazy life with anyone else.

Megan Besing, thank you for your endless ideas, your wise critique, and your heartfelt encouragement. I hope you realize just how needed you are. #iheartyou

Mom, you've been such a huge part of not only my writing journey but my very sanity. Thank you for being the one person who always, always wants nothing but the best for me.

Audrey, so much of Phoebe's characteristics came from your adventurous spirit and your passion for life. Thank you for inspiring me every day. There's no one in the world like you. Just keep shining that light.

Luke, you're the calm in the storm when I need it the most. Thank you for your steady presence and your caring heart.

Bess and Angi, thank you for sharing my joy.

Nicole Resciniti, my awesome agent, you've been such a fantastic support to me this year.

My editors, Becky Monds and Erin Healy, you both elevated and transformed this story in so many wonderful ways. I'm blessed beyond belief to have you guys working alongside me and sculpting my words. And to the entire team at Thomas Nelson: Kerri Potts, Jodi Hughes,

Nekasha Pratt, Margaret Kercher, you guys have given me such phenomenal support. I am thankful every day I get to work with such a brilliant group of people.

And to my Lord and Savior, Jesus Christ. To you alone be the glory.

Discussion Questions

1. Phoebe spends a great deal of the book avoiding facing a prior mistake. Have you ever found yourself running away from something in your past?
2. Phoebe imagines the relationship with her father is fractured beyond repair; however, this turns out not to be the case. Have you misread a situation with relatives or friends that caused distance that proved not to be true?
3. Phoebe is caught between duty to her country and compassion for Cloutier. Would you have made the same decision she did in regards to keeping his whereabouts secret?
4. Do you think the Napoleonic Wars or the betrayal from Graham's friend affected him more?
5. In what ways did Phoebe and Graham grow during the course of the book? And how did they help each other along the way?
6. Where do you think the real jewels lost by King John ended up in reality? Why weren't they ever found?
7. If any character besides Graham could actually keep the treasure, who would you entrust it to and why?
8. Do you agree with Graham's assertion: Do antiquities have any place in private collections?
9. Moreover, should nations today keep artifacts they recovered long ago from other countries?

From the Publisher

Help other readers find this one:

- Post a review at your favorite online bookseller
- Post a picture on a social media account and share why you enjoyed it
- Send a note to a friend who would also love it—or better yet, give them a copy

Thanks for reading!

About the Author

Author photo by P. Gardner

ABIGAIL WILSON COMBINES HER PASSION for Regency England with intrigue and adventure to pen historical mysteries with heart. A registered nurse, chai addict, and mother of two crazy kids, Abigail fills her spare time hiking the national parks, attending her daughter's diving meets, and curling up with a great book. Abigail was a 2020 HOLT Medallion Merit finalist, a 2017 Fab Five contest winner, and a Daphne du Maurier Award for Excellence finalist. She is a cum laude graduate of the University of Texas at Austin and currently lives in Dripping Springs, Texas, with her husband and children.

acwilsonbooks.com
Instagram: @acwilsonbooks
Facebook: @ACWilsonbooks
Twitter: @acwilsonbooks